From Up River and for One Night Only

From Up River and for One Night Only

A Novel

Brett Josef Grubisic

NON CANADA

Publisher's note: This book is a work of fiction. Names, characters, places and incidents are either the product of the author's imagination or are used fictitiously, and any resemblance to actual persons living or dead is entirely coincidental.

Library and Archives Canada Cataloguing in Publication

Grubisic, Brett Josef, author

From up river and for one night only / Brett Josef Grubisic.

ISBN 978-1-988098-07-4 (pbk.)

I. Title.

PS8613.R82F75 2016 C813'.6 C2015-908439-3

Printed and bound in Canada on 100% recycled paper.

Now Or Never Publishing

#313, 1255 Seymour Street
Vancouver, British Columbia
Canada V6B 0H1

nonpublishing.com

Fighting Words.

We gratefully acknowledge the support of the Canada Council for the Arts and the British Columbia Arts Council for our publishing program.

For M (1966–2014), deeply and daily missed.
And for B and D with love . . .
apologies too for making a hash of source material.

They may have arrived at an appearance that bears no relationship to them. . . . . They may have picked an ideal appearance based on some childish whim, or momentary impulse. . . . Some may have gotten half-way there, and then changed their minds.

—Talking Heads, "Seen and Not Seen" (1980)

Contents

III

END MATTERS

I

Happy Days / August

Before you play a note, your band begins as a series of decisions: Which bands inspire us? Who do we want to sound like? What are we going to call ourselves? These early triangulations often lead to everything else falling into place: bass lines, vocal affectations, guitar tones, production, album-art style. They say a lot about the band you intend to become.

—Jayson Greene

"The Gor gons."

A jubilant tone of 100% approval burst from the punctuated syllables of Gordyn's voice. And he counted out the impact of that phrase of perfect beats with left hand miming—a fist bud that blossomed into triumphant, fully spread pink-fleshed petals, *Godspell*-style, repeat—in case we somehow misheard the poetic arrangement's golden pitch.

After a final stage-honed pause Gordyn sped through the six words on the remaining recipe cards with the bloodless, hasty indifference of "CraigM.DaveMcC.CraigW." From eighth grade on that trio of all-thumbs, Shaggy-haired dweebs—a towering stick-legged beanpole but only math-smart; a husky waddling crybaby with toxic BO and droopy creased gym trunks; the school's legendary case of pathological shyness, eye-magnifying glasses, and Sasquatch feet encased in tripping-prone size 13 North Stars—had been chosen dead last for every team activity.

"TheSubsonics.TheBeehives.TheBel-Airs." Gordyn placed these nominees face down and edge-to-edge across the table. His index finger tapped one card, "The Gorgons" in green ballpoint.

Subliminal suggestion, I suspected, having chosen the subject for a disgusted Socials report the previous year and distributed Exhibits A and B, scissored-out magazine ads for Gordon's Gin (a sketchy outline of a lady's naked torso sprawled over ice cubes) and Charlie ("S E X" spelled out, more or less, in the perfume bottle's shadowy recesses).

"Okay, I can connect the dots—"

"No, Gordy." Dee made a crossing guard's Stop motion. "Band name votes are supposed to be secret."

"What's the diff? I recognize everyone's writing."

"That's not the point."

"Okay, okay. So, it looks like we all agree 'The' is decent. That's just terrific." Alongside sarcasm, eye rolls had threatened to become an epidemic for us over the summer. "And it's Gordyn, *s'il vous plait*, alright Deeeannnnnna? We can get back to the name later." He slid the cards into a neat pile. "How about our sound or look?"

Em, hunched at the table, craved a smoke. Peering at hot pitiless glare outside, she curled her lip. "This oughta be good." She slumped further, uncomfortable but savouring the middle finger to oldster wisdom about sitting up straight or risking, in years to come, the ugly curled posture of a canned shrimp and a back brace costing an arm and a leg. Brow cocked, she drew Dee's eye and relayed a shared thought: *Why not just call us The Gordyns? You're already halfway there. God.*

When her gaze shifted before reaching mine I guessed she felt steamrolled, pushed into the little sister's junior secretary role. As usual.

"Two order egg roll." Mrs. Kwong slammed down the oval platter. With shell game speed she whisked a dislodged parsley sprig from the table's mottled grey surface.

Obsidian-eyed Mrs. Kwong: a one-woman assault on the ideas about Orientals townies had absorbed from watching nine hours of *Shogun*, stooped, kindly, and shuffling but otherwise mute Mr. Wing, who'd been selling heaped burlap sacks of onions, potatoes, and carrots from a weatherbeaten olden days barn across the river in blink-and-it's-gone Flatsqui since WWII, and beautiful—powdered, perfumed, black candy floss coif, unchanging hibiscus lipstick—but owlishly dour Mrs. Kim, patrolling for shoplifters while doling out pop, Sour Chews in five-cent sandwich bags, and bundled cigarettes from her stool perch at Cherry Rd Store.

Prawn Gardens' public face, Mrs. Kwong never shied away from banshee-bellowing toward the kitchen, swabbing rivulets on her forehead with wadded paper napkins, and, at summer's fiery height, untying daily-polished white nurse's shoes to wriggle stocking-wrapped toes while dawdling at the unloved table next to the saloon doors three steps from the hallway toilet.

Were we to catch her tossing dice or circling expertly before joining a fistfight in the back alley, surprise wouldn't be our first reaction. Still, we imagined the likelier scene to unfold as the budget-minding restauranteur crouching—hatchet poised, chicken's doomed neck on a wooden block—in preparation for the looming dinner rush of chow mein and egg drop soup.

Weighted down by a history of drudgery, Mrs. Kwong also possessed an old soul, we'd decided. The notion came from Gordyn and Dee's mom, a worldweary lapsed Catholic born in Quebec who drank sweet No-Name instant decaf all day long and peered lengthily, and without apology, into everyone's eyes to suss out that very quality. The wisdom of new souls couldn't fill a thimble, Mrs. Edmund Wallace, aka Delphine, would remark in a dismissive voice, so why even bother with them. Old souls knew things, for better or worse.

"Careful, so hot to eat." The restauranteur smelled edible, as though composed of sesame snaps browned in a deep fryer.

Mrs. Kwong—whose first name remained a steadfast but alluring and extraterrestrial-like unknown, and who harboured solid permafrost beneath the friendly-enough veneer for customers that squelched ordinary probing questions, such as "Where were you born?" and "What do you like doing when you're not at work?"—answered calls and greeted every customer, the family's mover and shaker.

A gruff baritone replying with barks or sonorous, furiously-unleashed assaults of words belonged to Mr. Kwong. Deep within the galley kitchen, he might be, for all anyone ever saw, chained to the stove, or a poltergeist manhandling woks and raising fusses upon each of his better half's rapid fire orders or unknown commands spoken in Chinese. (His wife pitched whole paragraphs kitchenward when ours was the only table seated and no one had yet telephoned in an order. At those times she could have been all business, declaring, "Remember, dear, to order more jasmine rice before the weekend." Then again, who could say. With "You devil, your existence makes each and every shift a living hell," her words might be a counter-attack, railing against the clamour of a daily nemesis on the other side of the order window. We didn't understand one syllable of their private language. And whatever dark aura flourished just beneath her restaurant-owner's chipper facade—no thicker than the shell of a robin's egg—prevented our asking. As we took in Mrs. Kwong's rapidity and storminess, she struck us as the very opposite of the type who'd encourage customers to learn tourist phrases like "Good day, my name is ____" and "Pardon me, where is the embassy?" just for fun.)

Compared to the well-oiled machine of The Jade Palace—a gracious, unstained hostess on gliding legs ensconced by a soft shimmering column of golden or ruby satin; steaming platters delivered with a magician's stealth to the table's Lazy Susan centre by a choreographed troupe of young waitresses in black and white who emerged from a muted, never delayed, and barely glimpsed kitchen of gleaming steel; a décor of Buddha and dragon statuary worth the fifteen minute drive past the bridge—the Kwongs appeared unsuited to the core for the servile niceties of restaurant success. On weekends the host-owners of Dino's and Athena's greeted townie regulars with hearty chiding ("Joey, long time no see!"), flattering recall ("A double Manhattan, right, three cherries?"), and personalized recommendations of authentic lasagna or rack of lamb with mint jelly. Ever matter-of-fact, Mrs. Kwong spat out "Sit, sit!" or "You take out!?" and "Ready order?" Seconds later she'd jet into the back or grab for the ringing wall phone's green receiver.

Contracted to a marriage that might be a wreck and chained to a restaurant placing a distant third season after season, the Kwongs had every reason to batter crockery and shake bitter fists at the sky. For River Bend, we'd concluded, that fate made sense.

Prawn Gardens wasn't the only Chinese restaurant lining the main drag.

Directly across two car lanes sat a long-empty lot choked with shooting fireweed and enclosed by galvanized chain link fencing—the former location of a pawn shop destroyed, rumour declared, by its owner, a failed but stubborn businessman and arsonist. Following godfatherly orders, his family refused to rebuild or sell until the firebug's release from one of the barred cells of spooky, cross-shaped Oakalla prison.

That fat open rectangle presented the Kwongs with a partial view of evergreen pastures and spindly cottonwoods along the spongy river flats. On days when mill bosses scheduled no sawdust burning the panorama pleased the eye. Right next to this weed-clotted emptiness, the Golden Valley Cafe persisted at the corner year after year. A cavernous and empty box six days of seven, its Sunday buffet brunch of All You Can Eat Chinese, Western, Hamburger paid the bills, to the rolling boil chagrin of Mrs. Kwong. Had she possessed Charlie 'Firestarter' McGee's gift of pyrokinesis—an enviable superpower with zero drawbacks in Em's estimation—Mrs. Kwong would have peered out the window between orders and charred that rival into cindered ribs. "Without a second thought," Em claimed as well.

With nine tube-legged tables, side walls coated in a Pepto-Bismol shade adjacent to the hypnotic pale mint that hospitals rely on to keep patients in line, a zigzag face of tan and rust bricks, and a rickety air conditioning unit that rattled and dripped, Prawn Gardens fell to us, we'd decided, to claim.

Mrs. Kwong didn't mind if we ordered ice water and eggs rolls and loitered for an hour. But the very minute the phone began to trill, aromatic tea refills in stout white barrel cups dried up and she began glowering or toe-tapping rapid notes of impatience. Business was business. While one table of mopey teenagers did help fill Mrs. Kwong's drawer of white work nylons, take-out dinner combos for two, four, or six paid dual mortgages.

The forlorn, deserted feel of the place after school readily informed us that—thankfully—no one else considered Prawn Gardens worth a second glance. Decorated with paper fans, airbrushed wooden slat calendars, and a black cat wall clock with a sinuous tick-tocking tail, its diamond in the rough status appealed to us. We appreciated the find. Especially since the luck of a stranger on the TV news who buys a Van Gogh at a rummage sale for a dollar struck us all as Pluto remote.

When she remembered, Mrs. Kwong jammed in one of three cassettes of orchestral music. Featuring Chinese ladies warbling above sour fiddle and flute notes, the tunes sounded tragic and miserable and slow, a dirge a marching band might play when leading the funeral procession of a beloved child who'd died in a terrible, easily prevented accident.

From *Happy Days* we'd learned one certifiable truth: because school and family represented huge clumps of obligation that nobody but runaways and dropouts could skirt, a secondary place—a hangout—became essential. Tough kids on the verge of flunking out who stood chain-smoking, showily not giving a shit, and glaring at traffic just half a pace outside of school property during even the worst weather capitalized on that insight while handily cementing their cool rebel stature.

Like a kinder version of the island in *Lord of the Flies*, the first purpose of a hangout was to let kids naturally fine tune their roles from school. Or else, to bypass the solid lines or packs that the school's garrison mentality—the concept lifted from Mr. Smyth's English class and supposedly about staying alive in the middle of nowhere during pioneer days, but useful when applied to classrooms, family events, and hallways of staked and defended territorial claims—summoned into existence. Sparsely and indifferently patrolled, a haunt offered danger and freedom at the same time, because who knew what could happen. Thanks to hormones every teenager-only society rested on a foundation with built-in pockets of nitroglycerin volatility.

To us, that potential disaster looked better than wall-to-wall fossilization.

River Bend City and the cheerful Milwaukee of the Cunningham family stood a universe apart, though. And even if the need for after-school hangouts had pulsed through every teen Bendite brain, one instant problem would have materialized: suitable venues stood few and far between. Practically-minded or plain stingy, the town's founding entrepreneurs hadn't set aside a thought about catering to a ballooning leisure class of kids. Also, when teenagers way back in the war years had managed to stay in school until Grade 8, they must have barreled home seconds after the final class bell's ringing, the unending chores of barns and fields the beckoning fate propelling their feet. To them, loafing about for an hour must have looked unaffordable, a luxury for others.

Prawn Gardens didn't look too bad, then, especially in light of other candidates.

Marooned by a highway car dealership on the riverside highway toward Ruskin and, eventually, the Pacific Ocean, the A & W drive-in run by the Chisholms made sense only with a car. On top of that, the purveyor of root beer in frozen mugs served directly to the driver's side window—the primary reason anyone bothered—made a showy production of its ineligibility. The owners insisted their waitresses hassle customers the very minute they lifted trays of leftovers and balled napkins: "Anything else? Here's your change. Use the exit road behind the kitchen, okay?" Time meant money, and they'd call the cops if they saw any of the *commotion* and *nonsense*—those widely mock-quoted words from the pursed mouth of Home Ec's frazzled Miss Hanson and Geography's hot-or-cold Mr. Steuben—that routinely broke out with Fonzie at Arnold's. Besides, the Greek side of the Chisholm family was "respectable and not in the business of handouts," according to their calculator-toting daughter Melanie (aka Melon-y, aka Cantaloupes), who'd lately been swanning around school property letting no one miss the news of her already booked plan for an eight-city bus tour through Europe right after driving across the entire country in a new silver Trans Am over the summer of graduation. "Spreading my wings," she'd say with flapping arms, never sticking around for the crude jokes that followed. When tired of embroidering on her Cinderella graduation extravaganza, she'd remind anyone who didn't walk away about the family's expansion plans, as though owning three burger joints gave Papa Chisholm a leg up on Emperor Trajan.

A braggart to the core, Melon-y had long worn out her welcome. Even her twin brother Nardo, who was Leonardo to his mother and Lardo behind his back at school, made fun of Greek facial hair (wisps of moustache and sideburns, hers, an open secret) and called his own sister Cans, true if not that witty.

Three blocks away at the east end of the main drag and convenient, the Dairy Queen's management pasted No Loitering signs inside restrooms—a needless precaution: who'd loiter in a dinky grey room with two repulsive toilets and one sluggish fan?—and on every table. The onion rings and soft-serve attracted doddering war vets as well as surly pairs of losers with piled-on eyeliner, rabbit fur bomber jackets, strollers, and death ray glares. Those girls had dropped out of school to become moms afflicted by the deadliest of boredoms: unrelieved drifts of spare time and jack squat for money.

Any hangout ought to be fun, cheerful, and lively, we'd agreed, not a depressing cave perfumed by seared beef patties and lit with the prison severity of a Siberian bus station. Dingy? A giant step in the wrong direction.

Butted against the DQ and worse: the crummy—along with "downmarket," "shithole" and "seedy" were terms as yet undiscovered; and "trash" then brought to mind only the chrome-topped canister beneath the kitchen sink—Dineteria stuck in the Bargain Basement of Field's, the town's low budget department store. Hotdogs, its glistening top seller rotating on spikes inside a glass display, gave every clothing purchase, from socks to pajamas, a fatty hickory odour. Windowless with a low ceiling tracked with bare fluorescent tubes, the Dineteria performed the demi-miracle of turning the hospital cafeteria's refrigerated rainbow jello cube parfaits and aluminum coffee urns into seductive beacons of fine dining.

The last options: totally barrel scrapings.

Everyone's elders called Eddie's, an outskirts diner a mile from the A & W on the highway, rowdy, a Hell's Angels clubhouse, and a standing invitation to Trouble.

We couldn't get by the front doors of the Legion or the Belle-Vue Hotel Cafe and Pub, and even if we did we'd run into tattletale friends of our parents.

Discounting hitchhiking, Suicide Creek required a car and thirty extra minutes—and, besides, along with the gravel pit, kids drove there for partying after sunset, making out, or turning donuts, and not to idly shoot the breeze. And when the weather turned, Suicide looked morose, a speckled stone graveyard with icy rushing water.

River Bend City, a monument to getting by that had long ago made its life calling the handing out of lessons about compromise and relativity—somewhere in the world, the town's air currents and alleyways presumed to whisper paternally, you'll find places far less interesting and accommodating—couldn't resist wagging a finger about hangouts, either: accept the pittance offered and say thank you very much.

Physically standing, not unfriendly, and within walking distance, Prawn Gardens proved good enough.

That might be just as well, we figured.

Had Big Al's drive-in jumped from TV and sprung up overnight pennant-festooned and neon lit and Pied Piper magnetic to kids, a never-diminishing social hub and an ongoing invitation to River Bend High's entire population, our lowish status there would be questionable on a good day, and nothing but Piggy-terrible on the flip side. The letter jackets of belonging and solved-in-an-episode quarrels of *Happy Days* implied a benign, accepting world, one with near limitless opportunity and easily jumped hurdles. Discouraging, runty, better-than-nothing River Bend City dropped hints that felt far from optimistic. We'd all watched *Little House on the Prairie* and *Grease* too; Walnut Grove and Rydell High seemed truer to local life: losers and winners, outsiders and insiders, fat chance for mobility.

Cool kids represented the dart board's bullseye: fifty points and the zone every player yearned for. Considering the size of the entire board and the shirt button island at the centre, successful players prayed for a good eye, steady aim, and dumb luck. Odds were, though, they'd wind up in the outer rings.

Any hangout less of a hike than Prawn Gardens likewise called attention to an out of the question impossibility. Built in the lumber-booming 1950s and situated thousands of steps from the main drag, the Bend's high school stood back from and high above the town centre—an effect, depending on point of view, akin to a British aristocrat's country manor. Or Alcatraz.

Lanes and subdivisions now faced each side of the rectangular grounds, but during construction all the windows of the two-story U must have gazed at a rolling eternity of cow pasture interspersed here and there with plantings of corn and strawberries that in winter rotted into nothing other than spiky furrows of mud and pooled downpour. For students coming from farms, that panorama could have served only to remind them of the past, present, and future. And for others expecting to be hired on at a lumber mill, the trek down to log booms and rusty teepee burners at the weedy river flats would have taken half an hour at least.

As for why, the official account involved collective municipal wisdom about keeping student bodies safely away from main street traffic and river banks that overflowed in five-year or so cycles. And, we'd heard, these devoted visionaries had predicted an era when the Bend—rich from thriving industry—burst at the seams with citizens whose litters of children required ample space for track meets, parking, football games, and, of course, classes.

Our suspicions landed at bribery within the town hall. A back-up theory of juvenile delinquency stood close by too. The school's site had been agreed upon when that term first began to spring from the fretful mouths of parents, teachers, cops, and upstanding members of the town council. In line with Devil's Island, their plan sought to secure upstanding civilians while punishing spitting, smoking, and engine-revving delinquents with flipped collars who stood for nothing other than a rebellious but lazy criminal class in the making. While the lack of evidence meant this speculation couldn't be confirmed, the guesswork sounded as worthy as gospel truth.

Other than the public library, then, killing time indoors was impossible between school property and downtown. Still, after exiting right at the bell and through the school's southeast doors, any determined strider could stand in front of Prawn Gardens within fourteen minutes.

We didn't know the original use of the building, as old as the Depression-era post office a few blocks away and made from the same bricks, but Prawn Gardens had been serving egg rolls on main street, which was technically 1st Avenue, before any of us had even heard of the Bend.

No locals claimed the three or so blocks comprising main street offered a feast for the eyes. Or that they ever had. In sad contrast to rosy earlier forecasts, the town, following lumber industry setbacks thanks to building slumps and tariff skirmishes with Americans, currently wheezed "its last gasp." That's what everyone reported as a headline fact.

And yet no different from those comatose patients on *General Hospital*, limbo had become a way of life. Even with a terminal diagnosis the patient appeared no better or worse than six months before. Based on the evidence, the place could bankrupt and shutter tomorrow or just as easily hang on until a ripe old age.

If the Grim Reaper hadn't yet shown up with his hourglass and scythe, town elders still clucked about portents and expected the worse, a ghost town maybe, or a cemented reputation as the kind of cursed place any self-respecting up-and-comer looked forward to glimpsing in the rearview mirror. When the Eaton's outpost closed and a shopping mall with chain stores expanded across the river in Abbotsford and, later, a brand new one with a spectacular pitched roof and stained glass opened downriver, main street suffered daily insults of newspapered windows, fly-by-night and money pit businesses, and snowballing notoriety as third-rate to the very last street lamp, a stop handy only because on that afternoon driving out of town demanded too many extra minutes.

Run-down, past its prime, or fading by the inch but not quite expired, the single consolation was the situation could be worse. Further east in the valley or a minute across the bridge nowhere hiccups languished, ringed by puddles, cow and chicken pen stink, and green-then-funereal swaths of corn, strawberries, and Brussels sprouts. Locals insulted them by nicknames alone—Agony, Flatsqui, Hatshit—and defined the armpit appeal of their next eras of dimming existence.

One minute from the blocky Legion at the downtown's westernmost edge, Prawn Gardens split a building with a bakery.

On that block's outside corner: the River Bend Cinema, dark and locked since *Every Which Way But Loose.* To any passerby who bothered to look up and notice, the defunct business left parting wisdom. On the unlit marquee plastic letters spelled "ThxsAlot," a reminder to stake a claim somewhere with a higher likelihood of silver or gold.

Front pages of the *Valley Observer* reported that revitalization and city council raced ahead joined at the hip. We'd never seen the city's supposed glory days and thought its condition in six months or a decade didn't matter much. Our earning years and remaining there could never exist in the same universe.

Instead, we pictured and fully expected important, magazine-worthy artistic careers far beyond the pitiful reach of River Bend City. And not in any nearby big city, either, but on stage in London, reclined in Concordes soaring toward Paris catwalks, and shooting commercials for jeans—our own brand, sold at Sak's Fifth Avenue—in New York City.

Though we scrubbed away and drew in fresh details—who'd be where and when exactly and breaking through into what style-conscious business—the "general picture," as our guidance counsellors termed it, envisioned a decisive arrow. It shot along a graceful and undisturbed arc from a nowhere on whose every sidewalk we'd trod to that somewhere of somewheres with unknown addresses surely awaiting our arrival. At minimum, we'd be spotted in European cars with gull-wing doors, or noteworthy as reservations in exquisite restaurants we couldn't name but sketched as haute and so exclusive their whispered names appeared in no phone book.

We predicted bronzed faces emerging from cavernous limousines and, better yet, dropped pearls (jawbreaker big) of news—". . . jet lag . . . ," "Calvin said . . . ," "Rive Gauche"—casually scattered during high school reunion conversations as former classmates, now terminal Bendites, as sallow and paunchy and sausage-curled as their respective parents, countered with ". . . babysitter . . . ," "mill shift . . . ," and "Reno, maybe, one of these damned days."

We etched back up plans for our back up plan, and talking them all over felt as thrilling as flipping tarot cards: good, bad, or ambiguous, clues about a destination fated to unfold past main street, pastures, and river banks were, while entertaining, also completely serious. Memorized from TV, jutting distant skylines indicated how a hand's-on real life we'd shape like wet clay began.

As for the span between then and now? Negligible. Sand grains. An obstacle erected by an ant.

Meanwhile, we tolerated River Bend as a meagre nest. Made of pokey scrounged twigs, cedar mulch, and scraps of debris stuck together with instinct and spit, once abandoned it could become someone else's temporary necessity, or else crumble into dust and scatter into forgotten nothingness.

We spared our three parents these feverish projections, knowing and fearing that they'd detect in them an opportunity to trot out another the-facts-of-the-matter lecture about realistic prospects.

Edmund and Delphine, whose rabbity chromosome for caution, Gordyn and Dee claimed, had skipped a generation, murmured about security and a sensible fall-back plan with the devotion of a nightly prayer, just in case a dream didn't pan out: "It wouldn't hurt to have an Accounting diploma, you never know" and "Dental hygiene, now there's a blue chip stock."

Whenever he stepped away from the mirror, Joey, our dad, thought that although understandable, dreaming big equalled falling hard for an out of reach beauty queen, a bad idea not least because of the results: a broken heart and humiliation as impossible to remove as grass stains. Practical businesses stood immune to economic hard times, he'd mention with the subtlety of a hammer, unlike designer jeans and photo shoots. He'd nod slowly as though burdened with the Wisdom of the Ages: "People always need new roofs and eavestrough cleaning." For Em's benefit he'd add, "Dental hygienists too." (And on other, less nurturing days: "C'mon, Jesus H. Christ, give your frigging heads a shake.")

The logic presented no challenge. The trouble was, if served on the menu at the school cafeteria, Five Decades of Climbing

Ladders and Scooping Out Rotten Leaves would make our stomachs heave. We thought we'd rather starve.

A destiny of peering downward and scraping off plaque tooth by tooth fell to someone else. As punishment.

Mrs. Kwong returned with a teapot and reclaimed the oil-streaked egg roll platter. She hovered, a late afternoon on Tuesday apparently a lull stretch for orders. Or else she expected one of us to grab for the orange slice.

We didn't mind. The topics of our discussion had hit ominous but we hoped not deadly snags. Besides, between collective goat stubbornness and Gordyn's pending shift at Brownie's Chicken we had no choice except to take a break.

After another bout of rejected names, Blitzkrieg and The Demerits stood out as the only suggestions that none of us hated to death. And we'd tried two rounds of bands to cover, with the progress of a boxed turtle. Gordyn had sped through the shuffled nominee cards. Round one: " 'Devo.' 'Gary Numan.' 'Martha and the Muffins.' 'I couldn't decide on just one. Maybe Blondie?' " With a weary sigh, he mouthed the final lot: " 'How about Voulez-Vous?' 'Whoever sings Pop Muzik.' 'The B-52's.' 'Something creepy like Lucifer by Alan Parsons Project.' " And we'd all squinted, trying to discern the necessary common thread.

And we'd already pushed another question—distant but weightily important, the elephant-in-the-room one—past the horizon: "What will the crowd want to hear?" (And hiding dangerously beneath that and accompanied by projections about beer bottle missiles and flaming Molotov cocktails: "What will they reject and what will they *do* if they hate us?") The troweled-on makeup Kiss wore turned them into local gods: " 'Detroit Rock City,' man, rock on!" The pale ruffles, wispy frosted hair, and glossy lipstick of pretty boy clotheshorses like David Bowie and Roxy Music? Brent T regularly spat an assessment—"Buncha fuckin' cornholers"—that summed up the prevailing valley attitude.

Biding time until we arrived in our fated metropolis sounded reasonable, especially because the opposite—an undertaking we hoped and feared would put us under actual spotlights—spelled risk and with it related possibilities, head to toe embarrassment the least of them. Then again, a trial run, an actual rehearsal that took us away from blowing hot air about occupational dreams, made sense too.

"That school project?" Mrs. Kwong pointed to the stacked recipe cards Dee had lifted from Home Ec and distributed before our meeting.

"After-school project, Mrs. Kwong. We're starting a band."

"Like school marching band, play Citizen Day?"

"Not exactly," Gordyn said.

"Rock and roll." Dee made guitar solo motions and tossed late summer's honey-blonde streaks.

"Oh, you originals." Mrs. Kwong wagged a finger. "You try talent show."

Held every December on the purple-curtained fir plank stage of the Legion and a leg of the Downtown Revitalization Project, its assemblage of grandparents, dads, moms, siblings, and cousins offered neither the sort of spotlight nor the audience we'd tentatively decided we craved.

For a handful of ambitious graduates the Hope Slide, almost a two-hour drive away, stood heads above all others as the ideal location for a proud announcement. The giant, flat-faced boulders that settled there in 1965 (after crushing occupants in cars still trapped beneath the vast rubble field) had long been serving as tombstones and also the reverse—"RBCSS Grad 78!!!" in green and white spray paint visible from the highway, immortality celebrated until painted over by "MS + GH Tru Luv 4ever" or graduates of the following years. For those on foot, nearby bridges and businesses with exposed side walls sufficed, as did the party to beat all parties before full-time adulthood began with the following Monday's lingering hangover.

We pictured the band as a similar but better gesture, practical too.

If we put our minds to the project and willed it into public existence—a momentary reality, built from the wispiest of ideas but solid, documented, and historical—then what else could the band be but a brilliant omen? A complete, if small scale, success created from thought alone, our band would be a billboard sign of permission and, we predicted, a go-ahead for future accomplishments on an international stage. That big time success, we understood, wouldn't be instantaneous. Other kids might possess such naivete. Not us. But after the years of elbow grease—two, three at most—we'd *arrive*.

Dee concluded the air guitar solo with a flourish. "Yeah, I guess. We'll see."

"Kylie can, ah, be with you? She need . . . better friend."

"Oh, she's probably too busy." When he tried, Gordyn could be the voice of diplomacy.

Social climbing as automatically as regular people breathe, Mrs. Kwong's daughter wouldn't bother with the useless reputations attached to our names. Through her crimped bangs, she watched for ways up, not down.

Between questions, Mrs. Kwong fanned her face. In summer, spying her squatted on haunches in the back alley, cigarette and tumbler of jasmine tea in one hand, wasn't unusual. "So hot," she'd say to anyone taking the shortcut that passed by the restaurant's aluminum screen rear door. She'd open an azalea pink fan—snap!—like a switchblade.

With the exception of August, Mrs. Kwong set aside no words for the weather. At the onslaught of mirage-level heat, she obsessed about finding shade and the sticky discomforts of work.

Our barely-formed picture of China, Korea, and Japan included bonsai trees, kimonos, pagodas, chop sticks, pearl divers, and the fantastical landscapes of matchstick wall calendars—misty narrow waterfalls tumbling down sheer unclimbable mountains toward tiny fairy tale bridges. And *M.A.S.H.* showed Oriental weather that was, unexpectedly, more extreme than our northwestern corner of the continent: cedar sauna temperatures that all the fans in the world could never blow away, cold that rendered the bulkiest of parkas suddenly flimsy.

We guessed that August's skyrocketing temperatures reminded Mrs. Kwong of a terrible place she longed to forget, where she'd slaved in soggy rice fields or under the thumbs of cruel, magisterial parents, who'd foreseen her eventual fire-sale marriage to an ugly but crafty merchant as their one and only ticket to a comfortable retirement. Along with her first name, Mrs. Kwong's history before these week-long shifts of drudgery at Prawn Gardens shimmered as a mystery that inspired crazy speculation.

The phone's ringing set Mrs. Kwong in motion. "Okay, okay. Number 6 combo, extra egg roll, twenty minute, you pick up." She clipped the paper to the order wheel and swatted the bell.

"Crap," Gordyn said, "I've got the get to work." He'd climbed a rung to Assistant Manager at Brownie's, a half block opposite. "Harjinder and Fiona will be goofing off already. Losers."

"Assignments!" Dee cleared her throat as we piled up coins and joked about "Count your blessings," four identical fortune cookie messages.

Before Dee "quit" Pioneer Girls for a smoking scandal, she'd been a Trailblazer and tackled assigned clerical duties. At Frontier Girls (briefly, earlier) and Camp Luther (later), any task related to organization and counting belonged to her. "ID, money, instruments, costumes, songs, a place to rehearse." She adored lists. "Oh yeah, and someone that'll hire us. Plus, a van. And a photo shoot so the band looks professional. Oh yeah, a portfolio . . . but we can totally make that up. Money's the biggest thing, though."

"Jeez, anything else?" Em said. "I thought this was supposed to be fun."

"It will be. Eventually, anyway. We'll come up with who-does-what on Friday or so."

Leaving the money and a tip on the table, we left pocketing paper fortune strips to tape on dull-grey locker doors we'd open the following week.

We figured Mrs. Kwong was sneaking a few puffs in the back alley, enjoying freedom until her other half completed the pick-up order that she'd bag with plum sauce packets, napkins, and soya sauce. She'd probably count those extras carefully as her brain conjured a pleasing vision of bills piling high in a bank vault. And escape routes.

II

Realization / September - February

When I was younger, I lied all the time, because once you understand the power of lying, it's really like magic because you transform reality for people.

—Louis C.K.

Venture: 9-5 / September

Still volleying the who and what of myriad assigned tasks, the gang split.

They'd swap new and revised ideas during the herded stampeding between classes. With luck, notes secreted into passing pockets and lightning debates over a few lunch breaks would pin names to responsibilities. The world would hardly stop spinning if they didn't decide about A or B by the next meeting. A clock's ticking? They could barely hear it.

Eying the traffic lull, Gordyn decided the hassle of the crosswalk was worth the effort. Cops ticketed jaywalking erratically, which meant his perfectly understandable urge toward efficiency—the steely backbone of the Industrial Revolution, according to Mr. S in Western Civ—needed to be measured against the fact of fickle law enforcement.

Gordyn turned to watch his sister, who gesticulated plans and commandeered the lead while marching backwards. Waiting to catch the eye of the family's self-defined go-getter before the group disappeared around the corner confirmed Gordyn's sense that she'd be magnetic on stage. A natural.

Dee stopped. "Hey, Gord!" She shook her arms as though pleading for a driver to help. The bellowing startled a trio of elderly shoppers in cardigans, who craned their necks before returning to an intimate conversation of slow nods and clasped wrists. "How about 'The Original Eggrolls'?"

Gordyn waved goodbye, pretending he hadn't heard. He seethed with a spike of anger that felt fitting and necessary. "Typical Dee," he sighed, "drum roll, please." That idea? Vacuous, a total joke. No one needed to tell him otherwise, though his mother would sweep away this "overreaction" to Dee's lack of standards as age-related, a ridiculous phase. Teachers too. They always tsk tsked, sighed, and pressed their lips, chiming in wisely with exhaling lungs and seen-it-all resignation about the volatile cauldron of hormones known as the teenage body. A social problem, apparently, lashing out and hotheaded since the Cro-Magnon era. Right down to the resigned tone, his burdened parents used those same exact lines. Maybe an adults-only meeting had hatched all-purpose clichés designed to aggravate their target. What did they know.

The Anne Fucking Murrays, he thought, that sounded way cooler. Or The Bends, which drew to mind hasty divers in pained, unnatural mannequin poses.

He'd grab a ballpoint at work. Maybe on the next round the gang would finally see the light. He thought of the War Measures Act and wished he could just *impose* a band name. The group's democracy needed a helping hand.

At the passageway to Brownie's he rearranged the rolled cuffs of beloved jeans—the only pair his mother hadn't hemmed—that helped disguise bony spider legs. To win the Battle of Hemming and unpredictable skirmishes over ironing he'd used guilt trips that blamed the Cause A of her constant interference for the Effect B of his constant unpopularity.

Smelling Brownie's newly vinegar'd windows Gordyn pictured the wool-heavy, loose fitting but tight-necked spun nylon work uniform, at a glance vaguely reminiscent of a chicken. God knew where the lot came from. He could sew a better uniform with his eyes closed. Orange peel bright with four saggy yellow pockets at chest and belly levels, his had been worn by countless rank teenagers: already warm and ripe with leftover BO in winter and pure reeking torture in summer.

He prayed that for the next five hours no one from school would order a family bucket for pick-up. Dreams of any oasis free of insinuating and taunting male voices captivated him. And a girl turned into mouthy Ms. Hyde only when hooked on her boyfriend's arm.

Brownie's specialized in take-out by the tub, and Mr. Swanson, who owned five franchises throughout the valley, had economized by leasing a postage stamp of uninviting commercial square footage tucked in an easy-to-miss corridor between competing real estate agencies with street-front entrances on 1st. The food wasn't that cheap. And the bare-bones décor—an islet of bandage-pink Arborite counter for napkins and condiments; a variegated spider plant hanging in beaded jute macrame (courtesy of Mrs. Swanson); three bunched stools, just in case—offered nothing to admire and clear reasons to vacate. Still, with no other poultry franchise in town Mr. Swanson trumpeted, and not seldom, that Brownie's gave him a license to print money. Modesty didn't appear to exist in the man's vocabulary. "In a war or other contest, the winner gets the booty," he'd announce when counting bills, quoting an unknown authority.

Right off, the tycoon installed a wall with an inset order window to keep the deep fryers, prep area, garbage pails, and storage racks out of sight, correct in assuming that the less customers saw, the better. During peak hours or shift changes working back there felt like organizing a broom closet with the door shut.

The whole operation gave off the typical main street aura of living hand to mouth, appearance in this case distinct from reality. Mrs. Swanson, never without knife-crease Gloria Vanderbilt jeans and spike heels when on occasion she dropped off bills for the float, drove a two-tone Cadillac Seville, custom ordered in Burgundy and Candy Apple Red. Furs on hangers at home, everyone bet, and no wonder her husband needed an empire built on coleslaw and crispy drumsticks.

Gauging by the crammed closet of identical black nylon pants—Mr. Swanson called them slacks—and short-sleeved shirts he appeared to own (all of powdery hues: blue, yellow, and, just once, rose), her husband couldn't care less about fashion. But Mr. Swanson switched between the Econoline van on weekdays and a prized 1978 Corvette for Saturday appearances, an Indy 500 pace car replica ("Look-a, but-a don't-a touch-a," he'd enthuse, with fake Italian passion he thought hilarious). A rare gem, one of only 6,500 ever manufactured, and also money in the bank, the waxed and polished trophy appeared to be one sight that made Mr. Swanson's heart skip beats.

Mr. Swanson fondly reminded his bantam River Bend franchise team of these important automobile statistics, for which he expected slapped on smiles of appreciation.

"She's a beaut alright," Gordyn replied whenever the proud owner raised the topic, feeling no different than a speaking doll with a pull-cord dangling from its back. "Yeah, that's a lot of horses. Wowee." He drew the line at whistling and running his hand lovingly along the buffed haunches, seeing plainly why anyone would hope to become their own boss.

No one disputed the man's nose for business. From the boss himself Gordyn had heard "Between the two of us, kid ..."—his jumping off point with all staff—that the coaching of the Brown Broilers, Brownie's team on the Valley softball league, likewise attained similarly top-notch results thanks to foolproof mind over matter techniques. Gordyn had never bothered to attend a game; even if he could warm to the sport, he believed two after-school shifts each week and intermittent weekend fill-ins gave him plenty of exposure to Mr. Swanson's backslapping and surefire tips for success.

"I should write a book," the man exclaimed at the till, prep station, or cubby-hole office, as though a wonderstruck witness to his own, ever-escalating brilliance. He refused to call his franchise rival Mr. Chisholm by name. "That half-assed turkey out on the highway," he'd remark in the back, and launch into a dismissive story that normally ended with "blind luck" and "can't tell his ass from a hole in the ground." He reserved crudeness for guys alone. His wife refused to tolerate a potty-mouthed word at home: "She wouldn't say 'shit' if her mouth was full of it."
Until realizing that his boss believed "familiarity breeds contempt" didn't apply to phrases pouring from his own mouth, Gordyn had loved that one for a couple of shifts.

To anyone asking, Gordyn said philosophically the job had plusses and minuses.

All that protein from the officially free meal each shift would help fill out his bony frame; and the assistant manager position did pay forty cents above minimum. He'd hear about shrinkage, spoilage, and till discrepancies from Mr. Swanson, though, and be told to refute each comment from the locked suggestion box ("On May 12, your counter girl was so rude"; "The young hooligan you hired shortchanged me and then said No Refund"), even when no one would mistake their prank status. ("I seen that fat chick picking her ass," Mr. Swanson would read with the chilly seriousness of Judge Hathorne in *The Crucible* and wait for Gordyn's rebuttal, his pursed face set at a time-is-money expression. To testify that "There is no fat chick, Mr. Swanson. And no one picks anything" without a trace of sarcasm required bit-lip concentration.)

As for the minuses with substance, grease took the prize.

Gordyn dreaded every pimple outbreak, though his parents cooed hormones, hormones, hormones—as he knew they must, just as they cautiously murmured "lean" and "aerodynamic" when he detected only spindly and gaunt and POW camp refugee in the bathroom mirror—and that four years into the future the indignity of acne would be a faded distant memory, like bed-wetting or a mixing bowl haircut. Gordyn appreciated the effort but heard white lies just the same.

The smell of chicken fat clung to his clothes too, right down to underwear and sock level, gummed up his lungs probably too. And the pasty flour-and-herb top secret dredging mixture always crept deep beneath his nails. Now and then he'd catch the stink of garlic powder residue wafting from his fingertips.

Still, when he caught sight of guys at school who grabbed night shifts chicken-catching and bragged about close calls, livid scratches, and chucking uncooperative asshole birds into whirling ventilation fans—where, reportedly, the hens exploded into a pungent white cloud of bloodied feathers—he counted his blessings. Feather plucking, the back-up choice, gave his current job a golden sheen.

Telephone orders, timed deep fryers whose beeps shrieked angrily, counting cash, and hair nets—all a means to an end, a used car, foremost. Gordyn knew that if he expected to pay for university with Brownie's money he'd have needed to accept shifts while in kindergarten.

★

Gordyn pulled open the glass door. Except for the distant sizzling of deep fryer oil Brownie's ran quietly. A man of lists and inflexible rules, Mr. Swanson frowned at the intrusion of radio waves, convinced that laziness and blaring songs went hand in hand. The almost imperceptible haze of chicken-scented oil informed Gordyn that a busy shift meant the back room would still present him with a flour-caked disaster area.

As expected, Mr. Swanson had stopped by his newest operation in the morning. There were bigger hens to fry, he'd yuk, and the 1st Avenue franchise—by turns his baby and the runt of the litter—caused none of the heartache its willful, misbehaving beauty contestant siblings, the real breadwinners, took pride in meting out.

Mr. Swanson enjoyed surprise inspections. "Count on 'em," he impressed on all new hirees. That meant temptation—the Brownie's uniform slumped on a chair for the shift, net-free hair left falling properly in a matching pair of curtain-like hanks, bones from gorged meals heaped on the prep table—remained out of the question. He granted second chances to little kids, the boss explained. Anyone who could drive ought to know better.

Gordyn checked with Harjinder, who'd been there since late morning. The fourth-in-command remained gruff and monosyllabic, and had been so since Gordyn's surprise promotion. Six years older, punctual, and an employee for a year longer than Gordyn, he divided his fury between hacking apart chicken carcasses with a special cleaver brought from home in a leather envelope and giving Gordyn the silent treatment.

Though he'd witnessed nothing in person, Gordyn guessed Harjinder regularly horked in the coleslaw, his convenient variation on "revenge is a dish best served cold."

"It's plain as the nose on your face," Harjinder had said, suspecting that only prejudice blocked his rise up the ladder of franchise success.

On the day of Gordyn's promotion Mr. Swanson had confided that he'd caught his morning man—more or less—skimming from the till. Harj couldn't be trusted, "not then, not now, not ever." As for the truth, Gordyn suspected each side of tailoring.

Gordyn realized that he didn't need even elementary school arithmetic to calculate his savings for the next twelve months; fingers alone sufficed. At four and a quarter dollars an hour he'd be able to vote by the time he could afford just one instrument for the band, never mind a whole car. A black Gary Numan synthesizer on chrome legs? That was as faraway a dream as the cliffside Hawaiian vacation home he'd designed, drawn, and tacked above his headboard.

Begging Mr. Swanson for a few extra hours each week looked merely logical when Gordyn had to stumble on a miracle. Where were the gold nuggets lining a creek bed, or the canvas bags tossed in a ditch and stuffed with bills stolen from a bank?

Sluggish and uneventful the shift slipped by.

Harjinder touched up his meticulous side-part in plain view and stalked out without a goodbye ten minutes before six, as though daring Gordyn to record the defiances. As in school, finking ranked lower than brown-nosing with correct answers and after-class volunteerism. Gordyn didn't care about the small potatoes skirmishing; the two men could work out their differences without him taking any side.

Skipping, twirling, and belting out lyrics between the till and prep, newly hired part-timer Fiona never stopped chattering. School gossip—students lipping off and spectacular teacher outbursts, rumours about the worst transgressions at last weekend's parties (sex, fistfights, vomiting; better still, a combination of all three), who'd broken up and why and who'd already begun secretly going out with someone new—competed with always updating announcements about what she deemed her Fate: to get noticed by Brian K ("So cute, oh my goodness, I cannot stand it!") while she gushed at one of the basket/volley/football games where his flaxen hair shone and bounced; winning the lead role in the school production of *Our Town*; snapping the wickedest, artiest photos for the school annual; trying out for Maria von Trapp at summer camp.

A bubbly Jesus Freak with a love of singing that never plateaued, Fiona held on to her faith and the boundless, untroubled conviction of God's foresight and goodness despite her fatherless family's widely ridiculed secondhand store poverty, greasy hair that the world's best shampoo failed to strip clean (and a fondness for hats and braids that fooled no one), and twin reputations as a sucky know-it-all and a complete raging slut—one deserved, the other a total fabrication—that chased her year after year.

The deep fryers sizzled and the till beeped and clicked during the ninety-minute dinner rush. When Gordyn answered the phone he'd say "Good evening, Brownie's, how can we serve you?" as instructed. For Fiona's entertainment, he'd stick a finger in his mouth and mime gagging.

By 8:00, Gordyn asked Fiona to start ticking off the boxes of Mr. Swanson's end-of-shift list. The clock turned slowly on Mondays; barring a surprise visit from the big cheese, they might even close up before nine.

VENTURE: *L'Orange* / SEPTEMBER

On the framed map of the municipality hanging opposite the Principal's office, Cedar Hill Road appeared perfectly straight, as though drawn with a newly sharpened pencil, the professional metal ruler required for Physics, and a confident hand. Hurtling up the road's length on foot (a feat demanding a full hour at an energetic clip) revealed instead two skinny dirt paths along a steady climb of a slope rumbling with logging trucks, a flat section of fenced pastures after a new church and Mrs. Kim's corner store, a sudden dip, and a final steep pitch on oiled gravel that terminated matter-of-factly with an uninviting dense U of damp salal, ferns, and salmonberry bushes hemmed in by the typical salad mixture of conifers. Although that last rise had been logged to stubble during the town's pioneer frenzy with Swedish saws, the pungent vegetal air and cool elongated shadows lent it a permanent and vaguely ominous air of mystery—the step off the gravel simultaneously a step into the wild remote past.

Normally, and at least five days of seven during school, Em and Jay turned left just before the summit of the first hill's gradual slope. Direct along Best Rd or wandering the circuitous routes of the half-finished four-stage subdivision development below it, homeward marches gave them ample chances to stay caught up: to swap news about teachers, students, and events (directly witnessed and heard second- or third-hand) while looking at the familiar houses, yards, and cars they'd pass judgement on. Or admire.

Bored with the scenery they'd joke around, wagering an extra turn washing dishes: at home when Em called the Wallaces would Dee be flipping through *Vogue* while sprawled on the chesterfield, the bedroom carpet, or the bed? And they couldn't overlook her posing practices that relied on ads and magazine photo spreads for inspiration.

When advisable, Jay picked up rocks and sticks and hurled them in the direction of ditch weeds, fence posts, buttercup clumps in cow pastures, and the occasional talkative crow.

Though starting at main street, the afternoon's trek ran otherwise no differently except for the unfolding planned for the early evening, the predicted ordeal prompting a change in topic for the winding conversation.

There'd already been a few sneaky drop bys taking place later at night and behind closed doors, but Joey had announced his "new lady friend" would show up around 6:00 for the official first visit. For the momentous occasion his lieutenants would prepare a cookbook dinner.

Interpreting the signs—from his increased whistling and chore assignments ("This place needs to looks spick-and-span") to slackening minor rule enforcement—they'd convinced themselves that the countdown had begun for Stepmom #2, who'd also be Wife #3 and Fake Mom #2, a total stranger they'd be encouraged, and later instructed, to call Mom. If asked, they'd vote No for any wedding in the future—near or distant. And No to the installation of a shacking up trial mom in the meantime. Yet they knew better than to expect any grown up, least of all their father, to bother with such questions.

"Nature abhors a vacuum," Joey spouted by way of explanation for otherwise unexplained excursions and sudden after-dinner outings in jean and sweatshirt combos or grey dress pants with knife creases (Em's chore) and a shiny white shirt open wide as curtains at the neck. Alone together later, Jay and Em worked on snappy replies that orbited around "abhorrent" and "whore."

They'd seen the whole crazy process once before. The spare room formerly reserved for Stepmom #1's Ultrabronz Riviera machine for tan maintenance between October and the May long weekend now sat empty save for a creaky metal ironing board she'd used like a fiend in pursuit of a daily philosophy of pressed, Kodak-ready appearances. When she'd first shown up in the driveway, she'd been introduced to them as "your new mom," the unannounced marriage at city hall earlier in the week another surprise, that one formalizing the deal.

Passing by yards showcasing Japanese maples and pruned junipers, they joked weakly about sprinkling rat poison over the looming mother's food, serving Drano as a cocktail, or severing brake cables on the sly, fully aware of their complete powerlessness before what news anchors always called the march of time.

Come hell or high water, their dad promised, he'd get marriage right. "As if," Em usually sighed when out of hearing range. She loudly echoed her brother's resolve to avoid even one trip down the aisle. Who needed the hassle?

This month Joey drove to a power line stretch an hour downriver, paid for boring storm damage repair tasks that drew his complaints. He yearned for another big project up province. Tonight he'd arrive in grubby clothes just before the mystery guest drove over from Clearbrook, where she worked at a travel agency. As he showered and got gussied up, she'd sit in the living room, or maybe at the breakfast table as they peeled and diced. They'd entertain.

Having met other examples of their father's foxy ladies, they knew the diplomatic angel routine: "Smile, ask some questions, make her feel welcome." With a ready-made family Joey had a lumpy old package of intimidating size to sell, so the less lip the better. Following the test evening, she'd either show up again or disappear entirely, a single line on the already turning page of a history book.

When they'd glimpsed the latest candidate for the first time, pulling into the driveway in her red convertible with the muscle car muffler, they'd noticed the jean shorts and a Coors sweatshirt with red lettering that failed entirely to disguise the globular pair of attractions that must have made their father's blood rev when he'd first spotted her—whenever and wherever that had been.

At the muffled front door knocking Em ran to the stereo and dropped the needle. The start of two discs of twangy Patsy Cline running through the devastating aftermath of romance—heartache, abandonment, triangles, craziness—charged the air.

Jay lurked in the kitchen, carving the thawed broiler hen into parts.

Both played at being cheerful and efficient servants, like the hostess and chef of an expensive restaurant.

At the landing and ascending the staircase Em skipped through the light patter for company: "Please come in," "It's so nice to meet you," "Oh, feel free to keep your shoes on," "You must be tired from the drive," "Make yourself comfortable in the living room, Dad won't be long," "Oh, thank you. We're quite proud of the place," "We'll have to give you the grand tour later," "Can I get you a drink?"

"Oh my." She, referred to as Nicky by their father but having chosen to introduce herself as Nicolette, patted the one flat area right below her neck, as though overwhelmed by the choices, or to imply that she'd just vacated the nunnery on a day pass and could barely formulate the phrase "Gin and tonic, tall, extra lime," never mind drink such a worldly beverage over the course of a single evening. "Well, well, well, and what do you have?"

Their father loved to proclaim the lie of his perpetual honesty, that he "called a spade a spade"; mousy characters, then, and shrinking violets lacking definite opinions and passions had no deep effect on him. He'd never choose such a specimen for his better half. Nicky's elaborately polite—and false—performance, they saw, matched their own.

"Everything and then some. Our dad says a fully-stocked bar is any gentleman's first commandment."

"Can you make . . . a daiquiri?"

"Sure, with my eyes closed. Lime or strawberry?"

"Well, since you're offering . . . Strawberry sounds, well, as sweet as you."

"Coming right up. I'll be right back in two shakes." Adept at the insincerity, Em passed her brother a smirk while cutting a diagonal through the kitchen—she'd handed the responsibility for entertaining to him.

Jay dried his hands, feeling pangs of dread as he slid in socks along the linoleum and stepped into the living room. "Hi. Those are—." He bit his tongue on "way cute earrings." He'd say that when shopping with Em, along with "That colour really goes with your complexion" and, depending on the outfit, "No way in hell" or "That's *trés* rad."

"That's—." Complimenting the cut or fabric of her outfit, or the choice of perfume, sounded just as bad. Ditto for other competing lines: "Our dead mother's hair was styled like yours," "You're chunkier than the last one," "If you leave right now, we won't mind," and "I'll bet being a travel agent is quite exciting." With his father he'd watched *Swedish Fly Girls* late night on a TV station from the city (lying on the floor to squash his boner), and now believed that any career involving planes ended with spectacular crash scenarios or flirtation with blonde stewardesses that led to full-on sex.

As for the bubbling questions—"Have you also been married before?" "You are how many years younger than our father, exactly?" "Where did you two meet?" "Do you know what you're getting into?" "What can you possibly see in him?—they represented easy to resist temptations. If Joey's brief last marriage had felt unwelcome and useless and, later, deeply unsettling, as bad as standing in a wobbly row boat buffeted by the heaving ocean, the divorce had been educational in the sense of revealing that between arguments, accusations, and R-rated confessions during adult driver-kid passenger car rides, plain answers to all these questions would eventually leak out.

"I hope you're hungry."

She smiled and crossed her legs. Jay caught a glint of chain around the left ankle. "That's from your dad. For our anniversary. One magical month!"

Wiry as a pipe cleaner thanks to diets with ingredients such as grapefruit, cayenne, and boiling water with lemon juice, Stepmom #1 had favoured giant silver hoops, chandelier earrings tiered with stamped fake coins, bronze slave bracelets set with amethyst or topaz, and cage-like arm bands of entwined metals. When she joked that she was reincarnated Egyptian royalty, Joey snapped that she sure knew how to spend his gold.

"Nice. It looks nice." Every idea popping into his head sounded retarded or pervy.

She'd crammed herself into a cranberry velour skirt, with a matching blazer and vest. A creamy satin blouse that tied with a droopy bow at the neck and grey suede heels finished the look. "D-cups—at least," Em had whispered in the kitchen, cheeks ballooned and eyes bulged comically. Their Dad called himself "a leg man," but they both knew he'd be more truthful if he said "a tit man."

Nicky must have driven directly from work; the weather felt way too hot for the outfit. Beneath the thick layers, her body must be baking.

The formal dinner had been Joey's idea. He'd nixed barbecued steaks and potato salad for reasons spoken only to himself, though making a sterling impression would have been a safe bet.

"Here it is!" Em's voice boomed from the stairwell. Jay reached for a coaster. "So, travel! Tell me all about it! I'll bet you get free trips to all kinds of tropical places!"

"Well, if we're going to eat before midnight, I should get back to the kitchen."

"Yeah, good plan. I'll keep the guest of honour company until Dad's ready."

Jay slipped by the record holder next to the stereo. With "Walkin' After Midnight" plane wrecked Patsy Cline explored another deranged facet of love: desperate searching and not finding, and continuing the quest despite the constant bleating of common-sense.

Joey, who'd opted for silver cufflinks and bone-white patent leather slip ons, pulled out the chair at the table's lately vacant mother position and made a fuss about tucking the cloth napkin into Nicky's blouse. "You might have to undo a button or three," he said with giggling innuendo, and she muttered something about re-tying the knot—at which point Em rapped on the cupboard below the sink, storage zone for household poisons.

With Joey's appearance, Nicky's comfort grew, spreading through the main floor with the ease of an oil slick. Her gaze fastened on décor and furniture, as though deciding their soon-to-change destinies while erasing the recent past: rearrange, exile to another room, banish altogether. With satisfied hands on satisfied hips she'd mutter, "A woman's touch," and survey her accomplished nesting.

She matched Joey's double Manhattan in the living room, and whispered "Chin chin, baby" as he topped up her glass of Mateus while leaning in with "Clink clink, my dear." Only Patsy Cline, falling to pieces through the speakers, warned that romance could be something other than a lovely and eternally fragrant bouquet.

Jay crouched to peer in the oven while Em tossed the salad. "Chicken *l'Orange* with Duchess potatoes? Sound fancy," Nicky declared. The words themselves sounded pleasantly neutral, a description of a meal a few notches above beef stew or tomato soup with grilled cheese sandwiches. Minutes earlier she'd stepped into the kitchen as Jay cut oranges for the glaze. "An apron, eh? That's pretty fancy."

Applied to him, "fancy"—with a stretched out 'f' and a hissed 'c'—added undertones that practically spoke a warning, a criticism, as had "You're the perfect little gentleman," another strike, as he announced dinner.

The compliment shone, an ocean's calm surface that hid a Great White inches below. The coded, doubled words stood in the vicinity of "That's . . . different" and "Where'd you pick up . . . *that*?"

with a smidgen of "light in his loafers." "A bit out there" never stood for an unorthodox but admired character trait, just as placement in Special Ed informed the world of a perpetual limitation—that this supposed distinction defined and confined, severing the stricken victim from the general population as surely as a lame arm or a missing leg must.

"Yeah, we learned it in Home Ec."

"Home Ec, eh? Lots of girls to keep you company there, I'll bet."

"I guess."

"Is that a Yes or a No, Acey?"

"Yeah, Acey, tell us." Em switched sides on whim.

"It's a Yes."

"Yes what?"

"Um, yes sir?"

"Salad is served!" Em banged the salad forks. "We'd better eat it quickly before the bacon wilts the spinach into mush."

Joey had never said anything about how well his dream woman should handle her booze, but Nicky's liver clearly couldn't keep up with his. She slumped, loosened and kicked off her shoes, rested both elbows on the chair's carved arms. Fanning her face she toyed with her food. Instigated by her, conversation took detours, turned to the nice weather, the nice mountain view from the dining room, the nice back yard.

"Cish and fips and pasghetti," Nicky abruptly announced to the man—her man—six feet distant at the head of the table, "dat's what little Nickets likes." She crossed her knife and fork over a perfectly browned cone of potato purée that she'd flattened.

With tremendous boobs fighting for release from their velour prison, now a third unbuttoned, the sunken and meandering expression, and the outburst of sexy baby talk, Nicky struck Em and Jay as slow, a dimwit with a temper, or as the bizarre and fully grown version of the prematurely sprouting girls in junior high attracting the insistent animal notice of greasers, jocks, and almost-men who'd already repeated a grade or two. Shame-faced those girls shuffled hurriedly with crossed arms before mysteriously disappearing when everyone else made the jump to Senior; from then on they existed as wisps of rumour—as preggers, runaways, drop outs, welfare moms, cashiers at gas stations, or teens working on their parents' farm until the unknown father fessed up and made the honourable gesture once he found a full time job.

Joey stood, dropped his napkin on the chair. "Kids, we can clean this mess up later." He held his hand aloft as he approached the opposite side of the table. "Why don't you head upstairs to your rooms. I'm going to head to the bar and build some Spanish Coffees for me and this vision of loveliness."

"Well, that was Baby Nickets . . . " Em flopped on the carpet of Jay's bedroom and stared at the ceiling, "God, do you think I'm going to have to babysit our new mom? I tell you, I am *not* cut out to be a nurse."

"Probably. I know, that was *the worst*. God. I vote for heading outside for a bit. Things need discussing. And I want to check out the coop . . . I have an idea. We can leave these 'adults' to their own devices." Jay used finger quotations just once. The gang had been ragging on him for their constancy. "It's affected," etc, etc. Gordyn had even said, "Everything in moderation." What a joke.

VENTURE: 9–5 / SEPTEMBER

Beetling along as snugly as possible to the fronts of unlit businesses, Gordyn reminded himself to keep conscious of swinging arms or swift nervous steps. They might attract bellowed jeers—or worse—from quickly unrolled car windows.

Cunning jocks and stoners in revving beaters managed, with bloodhound instincts, to cruise along main street at the precise wrong moment. Far from the curb, though, he might escape notice.

At a scurrying pace he tamped down familiar accusations. His pores did not give off a queer scent that cut through deep-fried chicken and Clearasil. He didn't beg for trouble. Like everyone else he strode with one foot followed by the next. A two-legged version of toxic Love Canal was not his crown to claim. No, fault originated with them. Well, their bigot parents too. And practically the whole of history.

With main street a graveyard he sighs a thank you.

Gordyn counted. He'd reach Acapulco's Waterbed Emporium, Gifts & three minutes after signing Mr. Swanson's checklist and locking Brownie's front door. He'd left the lights blazing per the list: in contrast to other merchants on main Mr. Swanson believed that the break-in prevention compensated for those dollars of added electrical expense each month.

In Gordyn's view, thieves would be completely grossed out by the only item worth stealing: plastic tubs of refrigerated chicken they'd still have to dredge and deep fry.

He kept the exact rough-stuccoed destination in mind—two and a third blocks—and shut his thoughts to outside realities like intimidating guys on the hunt for fun at the target's expense. Or classmate accuracy with knife-point insults, pop bottles, and phlegmy spitballs that would give missile engineers green-faced envy.

Though 99.9% sure that Acapulco's had closed hours before, Gordyn decided in favour of a few minutes of wasted time. Windows of opportunity didn't open frequently. His parents' outsized worry led to a delicate living room question period if he arrived home after nine, his father hopeful that his eldest had run into a burgeoning group of friends that included a hefty portion of available girls, and his mother predicting mischief and harm as though the family's misfortunes also included residing in Dresden in the final months of World War II.

Two men sat on stools inside the emporium and appeared engrossed by a card game. They leaned over the display case, right next to the brass cash register. Laying down cards with the slow deliberation of hard-luck gamblers placing children in the pot, both smoked, swirled highball glasses, and bantered.

Gordyn recognized Merv, the grizzled owner, whose shadowy reputation as a booted, leather-vested biker, a rifle aficionado, and a two-time veteran of the gated, top secret drying-out program run by the Salvation Army in Miracle Valley made sense considering the waterbed store's equally bad stature as downtown's eyesore of eyesores and a "den of vice," whatever that meant. Kids just called it a head shop.

When in the vicinity Gordyn mostly thought to recommend a fixed sign. *Gifts & what??* Merv's sloppy, couldn't-care-less attitude made his eyes ache.

Gordyn figured that if he stood in front of the post office and asked one question—"Excuse me, Ma'am, what's the number one symptom of River Bend's City's decline?"—the clear majority of the clucking taxpayer replies would not be the Belle-Vue Hotel, where drunk guys settled beefs with fists between the trucks angle-parked out front, nor the bowling alley, magnetic to slumped anemic men (and their home-permed dates) who looked like they'd already been smoking a pack a day while in the womb, nor the Legion, a part-time home to wobbly war veterans nursing their decades-old sorrow until closing time. Instead, right off, they'd answer "Acapulco's," the place and its owner viewed as a worrisome black hole that sucked up every effort at goodness and respectability made by the upstanding rest of the Better Business Bureau's membership.

Merv's guest surprised Gordyn, and not only because, if anything, he expected another Merv-ish guy in an unbuttoned vest and faded black T-shirt.

An equally storied figure, though from the days before the Bend's latest slump, and widely viewed as harmless loony bin material, Chester provoked giggles and whispered comments, though nobody deigned to converse with him. If passing by Chester on the street, Bendites nodded, remained silent, or said, "How's it going, Chester?" briskly, as if to imply the man's notorious but somehow leprous celebrity meant every local knew him on a first name basis and that since the surprise run-in coincided with a moment of supreme busyness, no one really possessed a spare heartbeat to catch his moon-faced answer.

As spectacular and unconfirmed as Merv's, entwined stories circulated with a life of their own and filled in for Chester himself, solid and categorical as fact. They grew bells and whistles, Gordyn thought; maybe the plain truth could hold no one's attention.

Apparently, he'd lived with and been cared for by a dotty mother until her death; Chester believed he still breathed the air of 1955; he was mad as a hatter; the shock of the car accident that accounted for his mangled, rubbery left arm also explained his contentment with blithely tiptoeing through the same day in the past; the sky blue Thunderbird, now a pristine restoration, sat polished in the carport of the _____ family home (if Chester possessed a last name, no one could certify it); and, he'd refused to bury his mother, whose preserved body, eternally dressed in a teal Sunday morning outfit, now lay enshrined like Nefertiti, but in a museum-style diorama that had, decades before, served as the master bedroom.

The surplus of far-fetched history grew in part from Chester's silence and the strange habit of spending whole days in a constant half-smile and far-off gaze as he strode up and down the town's main streets. More so, his appearance: lustrous hair dyed Count Dracula black that, with gobs of Brylcreem, he combed into a high, unmoving pompadour, a style so different from the usual feathered look sweeping down from a centre part that he may as well have been Louis XIV in *talons rouges* and silk stockings.

Chester wore a battered leather motorcycle jacket with a fully buttoned white dress shirt on cold days and switched to an aqua blazer with skinny lapels and too-short sleeves when the thermometer lifted. Upon close inspection his ageless face possessed the artificiality of a mask; grapevine mutterings pegged him as wearing mortician's makeup. To sighing parents, the local legend was "a real character" (good mood) or "that crazy old greaser" who ought to be locked up in Riverview asylum and put to work at its Colony Farm (bad). But for those born after the Age of the Greaser, Chester fit into no known category, except maybe *nuts*: in high school, someone displaying that excess of eccentricity wouldn't last a fraction of a semester.

A shocking revelation, the fact that Merv and the loon were evidently capable of an normal extended conversation and laughter over a game of cards reinforced what Gordyn already comprehended about the gap between empirical fact and the fanciful words that erupted from people's throats. Merely drawing near a thought—*What stories circulate about me?*—made Gordyn's stomach lurch.

Gordyn tapped a knuckle on the glass.

Startled, the men looked up from their game. As Chester's gaze resumed the depthless facade known to every local spotting him on main street, Merv, visibly annoyed, displayed a watch on an arm that ended in a fist. He added a thumbing gesture: get lost.

Face heating with apology, Gordyn retreated.

NOTEBOOKS / SEPTEMBER

What about The Incubators???
Seriously!!

VENTURE: RUSH / SEPTEMBER - OCTOBER

Intimidating—gruff of voice and appearance, rampaging grizzly bear demeanour—Merv brought to mind the bloody skirmishes of *Jack the Giant Killer.* The trouble was, Gordyn's plans included neither slaying nor outsmarting this husky, laser-eyed leviathan. Instead, the goal fell under the heading of Diplomacy: he needed to reach Merv's pocket of good and ingratiate himself with a solid force of nature, a booted motorcyclist with beefy hands who butted teeming cigarettes into a green coffee can at the till as he raced tight-lipped through round after round of Solitaire and waited for brazen customers to approach him with questions or, preferably, merchandise for which he drove as far south as Guadalajara twice a year. To befriend him, in short.

Gordyn foresaw scenes of failure—his secret goal nakedly transparent in one, nerves frayed and tongue tripping in another, skulking right past Acapulco's without slowing in yet another—and thought that substituting Dee might be the wiser idea. She'd appreciate the feat of seducing a worthy foe with an arsenal of titters, tossed hair, batted lashes, and her favourite, a snug fuchsia T-shirt with cap sleeves and a sparkly iron-on red rose.

Besides success at the till, though, she'd grasp one of Gordyn's secrets. And knowing his sister, Gordyn predicted blackmail: "You know what, Gordy, I'm feeling a bit under the weather today. How about you clean the main bathroom this time?" Dee relished *or else* in the way romantics dreamed of candlelit dinners of chateaubriand for two.

The first task, the easiest of the pair, demanded the vulnerability of exposure: letting a potentially hostile stranger peer into your eyes as your mouth revealed how he alone possessed the object of your lust.

Gordyn wanted Rush, a risky venture. Only Acapulco's sold these brown bottles with yellow labels affixed with a scarlet lightning bolt. They sat under the glass display beneath the till with a cardboard sign Merv must have written: "Room De-oderizer."

Gordyn had puzzled over this deodorizing claim. Though the liquid—heady and chemical, like concentrated gasoline or model airplane glue—could snuff out just about any household smell, who'd want their carpets to reek worse than the solvent bath at a mechanic's garage? The placard was a false front, he decided, an advertisement for a discerning few, misdirection for the rest.

As for why, the only answer pushed Rush into a unique category, a species of wolf packaged in sheep's clothing.

A few lunch hours each week Gordyn sped home to Kite St., watchful but, as ever, stamping down cold sweat scenarios of riled up and jeering guys trailing behind him, as dangerous as a mob of torch-wielding villagers. That crew waited instead, conscious that he'd eventually return to their territory at an intersection near the gym. He'd heard of *keep your enemies closer*. In his view, advice couldn't get any dumber.

With her daytime companion of easy listening music seeping from the radio at a comforting volume, Delphine served him a can of tomato soup and two grilled cheese sandwiches on a wooden tray. He'd carry the meal upstair to his desk, slip on headphones, and listen to cuts of Heart and Pat Benatar.

Two or three songs later, he'd stretch out on the checkered bedspread, weigh the pros and cons of a snuck cigarette exhaled as he leaned outside the window, and opt against the risk. His mother's reformed smoker's nose detected a match strike from a hundred paces. She'd be up the stairs before the first smoke ring.

At Doug M's house twenty minutes away Gordyn had tried model plane glue drizzled into a paper bag and one of his mom's Valiums. The fumes gave him a pounding headache that later inspired thoughts of melted lungs, death by asphyxiation, and embarrassing police questions for his bewildered family. "We didn't know," they'd say, ashamed and hurt for eternity.

While he turned down Doug's ongoing bids to get totally wrecked at lunch, last summer's temptation from five provinces over proved altogether difficult to resist. When Gabrielle, the eldest of his mom's handful of sisters, had visited from Quebec with moody J-P, her lanky, bandana-wearing son who'd dropped out of college ("to find 'imself," Gabrielle explained with a mother's kindness), J-P surveyed the living room dismissively and quickly addressed Gordyn: "Let's 'ang howt."

Back pressed against the mahogany panelling and particle board wall of the basement's almost-finished guest bedroom, J-P pulled out Pointed Sticks and Dead Kennedys records from his suitcase. Song after short song, Gordyn—who still harboured moments of deep fondness for the sappy grandeur of Barry Manilow's "I Write the Songs" and "Mandy"—heard nothing but assaulting cacophony and homicidal anger. J-P rocked his head to "California Über Alles" as though suffering from epilepsy.

"Try dis." J-P displayed a dwarf glass container, gripped with vise strength.

Gordyn copied his long-haired cousin's deep inhalation through a single nostril, and then sat back stupefied and grinning. Beneath the discord and instant headache, he caught faint notes of pleasurable melody from the speakers. Rush, it turned out, had been well-named.

Gordyn thrilled at finding a sandwich bag containing a skinny joint and a bottle, nearly a quarter-full, nestled in his sock drawer after waving goodbye to J-P and Aunt Gabrielle at the city-bound bus stop. He extended the gift's usefulness with miserly, single-lungful bouts. Still, the supply—already teensy to begin with—had dried up two weeks later.

The purchase of a few joints or even a quarter ounce took no more effort than saying Hi to the stoners on either side of his school locker. But until catching sight of the stubby sample bottle of this room deodorizer between the thick glass pipes with psychedelic striations and the boxy incense burners of Mexican clay in Acapulco's display case, Rush had hovered completely out of reach.

After all, he could hardly ask his mother to pick up a few bottles on next summer's visit with Gabrielle, Sandrine, Marie, and Beatrice, who'd settled within spitting distance of each other in Pointe-Saint-Charles. And even if she didn't see right through his scheme and agreed to actually ask J-P for directions to the disreputable shop that must peddle Rush, Gordyn could predict the likelier scenario: she'd say with a slightly impatient, matter-of-fact tone—one of her Francophone specialties, spoken as if yellowed fingers clamped that morning's twentieth Export "A"—"Gordy, if you don't like the smell of your room, there's an easy solution. It's a handy machine; we mothers call it a vacuum cleaner. You might have seen it? Inside the entryway closet? Hoses and attachments? And beneath the kitchen sink there's a bottle of Nilodor, that's handy too. Just put it on the vacuum filter. No more than a couple of drops, otherwise you'll suffocate the lot of us. And while you're at it, pew-ew, maybe keep those gym sneakers outside."

And then he'd have to go through the motions, hauling the Hoover upstairs and letting the motor run for ten minutes.

Gordyn guessed he'd solve the problem with a letter to J-P. Then again, his cousin seemed the type who'd salute for "Seize the day" instead of "Brother, can you spare a dime?"

To obtain Rush required Merv's mere reach beneath the counter. He'd barely need to bend. Troubling, though, any buyer first needed to ask him to do so.

Gordyn's hunch: a casual approach —"Merv, a bottle of your finest," or "Some Rush, please" spoken inconsequentially, as though choosing between Combo #2 and #3 at Prawn Gardens. That tactic presented good odds. He'd appear both worldly and up front, and his usage a reflection of a mature outlook and a veteran ability to handle the bottle's contents. Cashiers didn't give his father a second glance when he bought a gala-keg of Hochtaler and made cracks about his mother-in-law's impending visit. Gordyn thought to aim for that same seamless kind of banter.

Rehearsing scenarios in his bedroom or during the occasional solitary trip home from school, Gordyn foresaw that moment of recognition as having a brutal, one-way exchange of energy, as when, on TV, a man caught between a rock and a hard place slinks toward the gloating, impatient loan shark sizing him up behind an imposing desk carved from oak. Shortly after a humiliating exchange he accepts a bundle of cash for which he pays retaliatory interest. And all the while the poor guy's selling off a hefty portion of his self-worth.

In real life—not yet a year ago—Gordyn had yearned for a pair of tobacco suede Adidas, and his dad, capitalizing on the admitted fact, agreed to purchase ("splurge on," his words) the costly item instead of the usual white and blue North Stars *if, if, if*: if Gordyn gave his mom a break by offering to wash the dishes every now and then, thought about the common good once in a while, and, if it wasn't not too much to ask, kept his room tidier, knocked the mud off his shoes before he stepped inside the front door, and remembered that the lawn didn't cut itself—and neither, for that matter, did the toilet scrub its own bowl.

Gordyn scrubbed and mowed and washed and kept his shirts in neat piles and, before all that, nodded vigorously at the hazy notion of this desirable common good. Yet whenever he looked down at the soft tobacco suede he'd sense two sets of feelings at once: sweet (the pleasurable knowledge of strutting ownership of the finest shoes of an entirely cool brand whose gym bags alone lent even him glimmers of credibility in hallways between classrooms and lockers), but also sour (the creases appearing on his father's face when he handed the credit card to the cashier—a lopsided smile that meant "You're welcome" directly and easily, and something else too, not so admirable perhaps and certainly less clear, that Gordyn interpreted as "Now you owe me" and "You have a hunger for something that I do not share but can provide and that gives me power over you"). Scrutinizing that expression, Gordyn gave his father the benefit of the doubt. He'd pinched a lower back nerve earlier that week; the pained smile may have been nothing other than a wince caused by the exertion of turning to hand over the shoebox.

Indebtedness, he'd decided, created new problems bigger than the one it solved.

As a stranger with unknown and possibly—probably—impure motivations, Merv stood closer to the loan shark scenario. That imbalance worried Gordyn. He'd discovered that in approaching people, each could be measured like a dog. From a distance, generally, anyone with half a brain could tell which would growl and lunge, wag its tail, or else let off a hysterical frenzy of barks before rolling playfully onto its back. With four-inch blue anchors tattooed on two forearms, a perpetual vest over a series of baggy Led Zeppelin T-shirts in faded black, and a propensity for belly laugh eruptions, Merv fell into a limbo, the exception to the normal rule—the affable mutt on the opposite side of the fence that might just transform into a Nazi guard dog without a blink of warning.

Other than the milk of human kindness Merv had no personal reasons to be nice or accommodating. Business-wise, and in contrast to Prawn Gardens, Gordyn's appearance at Acapulco's wouldn't be automatically welcomed because his very presence drew in curious new customers from the sidewalk.

Making a sale might not matter, either. For all Gordyn could tell, the bulk of the money in Merv's bank account didn't come from cocoanut shell mobiles, tie-dyed halter and tube tops, bongo drums, waterbed sales, or replacement bulbs for walls lined with black flocked posters from which peeked fluorescent green dragons and orange Bruce Lees.

Though likely not the criminal mastermind said to be singlehandedly demolishing the town's reputation, Merv might do hefty business on the side.

Humdrum shops that fronted gambling, drinking, and ladies of the night in basements or behind trick walls seemed common enough on crime shows. They had to be more than figments of writers' imaginations.

NOTEBOOKS / SEPTEMBER

Déviation: PRACTICAL ADVICE

A boxed cluster of mottled and irregular pieces incomplete on their own until fitted together to reveal one familiar sight (the Matterhorn, kittens and yarn balls, an olden days mill with a water wheel), the basic definition of a puzzle normally applied to people too.

Joey liked to call himself an exception to the rule, and Jay sometimes believed him. While a head doctor could type a thick report about the parental unit's individual bits, once assembled and presented to the world the finished project depicted serial

Joeys, each different from the next and none any more real than the other.

Em and Jay had witnessed him as the dutiful son who'd link arms with his mother on the way to Midnight Mass, the grinning bright light of the party, the charming lady's man, the incorrigible diner flirt, the murderous driver, the grocery aisle crooner, and the host with the most who mixed "the stiffest Tequila Sunrise north of Tijuana." Private at-home-only traits likewise varied, with the main addition of the scab-picking brooder with a rolling minefield of black, ornery moods, the majority as sudden and hard as the springs of a rat trap.

Jay saw too that his only-son status opened a passageway to further pieces that his father decided against showing Em. As with any secret club, Jay intuited that a crucial rule for membership hinged on *keep it to yourself.*

How the man operated when on his own—for electrical transmission tower projects that stretched on for months near muddy trailer camps—and which selves he permitted the guys to glimpse there, Jay could only guess. But an early father-and-son-nearing-adolescence moment dropped a hint. The conversation, on the way to the municipal dump in the truck, had taken the form of advice for the pending future: how to respond like a gentleman when winding up with a hooker suspected of being dirty. Dirty mouths, cops, and hookers fell into separate piles, Jay had learned. His dad's story involved VD. While Joey offered no background on what cleanliness looked like or the specifics of detecting its absence, he explained the necessary corrective steps with an anecdote.

"God, this one time—," he recalled, in tale-spinner mode. "I had a weekend in Calgary, I was feeling lonely and, well, you know." He looked away from the curvy road, asking for acknowledgement. Jay nodded. "I knew of this cathouse."

The episode concluded with the bequeathing of valuable wisdom gained from lived experience: "Go to the john, okay, right after you're done—just tell her you need to take a leak—and piss into your cupped hand over the sink. Wash your riggin with it. Good as new. Do it anyway, can't hurt."

Though the story's remote setting (a "perfumed cathouse," a "money-grubbing Polack madam," a "dirty hooer" named Marlene) might be pondered later, the immediate revelation lowered Joey's status still further: the job north of Calgary, practically prehistory in his father's telling, aligned with the middle of his first marriage. His dad's wandering eye, then, was no recent development, its cause stemming in no way from Stepmom #1's bedroom shortcomings.

VENTURE: COOP / SEPTEMBER –

18th Ave, which was technically also Best Rd for historical reasons that got no one worked up enough to investigate, ran high above but roughly parallel to the river. At the extreme western point, a bulbous dead end about ten minutes on foot from Em and Jay's address and well after crumbly and pungent oiled gravel faded to puddly or cracked dirt marked with tire tread, any passerby wound up at the property of the Wales, two generations of tree farmers.

Wales Sr, a widower, occupied the original family house, gabled whitewashed stucco and surrounded on three sides by weedy rows of trimmed pine, hemlock, and fir. His son had stayed put until his wife's first child and later built a modern log house on a precipice at the far edge of the property. Below the kitchen prospect, seasonally overgrown trails furrowed between nettles, ferns, salmonberry bushes, and the occasional Devil's club tree. Moss blanketed everything.

Eventually these winding paths converged at Silver Creek, an oasis of rushing currents, where cool green pockets held quicksilver trout fry and sunken beer bottles. Flat slippery boulders speckled with cigarette packs, and, occasionally, condoms or rain-bloated tampons, stood close enough together that frog-leaping from one shore of the creek to the other wasn't impossible. Regular hikers knew to prepare for missed targets and soaked feet.

Decreed off limits by parental finger wags, a woeful property sprawled out across the road from the Wales farm. Reputedly owned by Old Man Thesen, the hermit had let thorny brambles and fireweed conquer the former yard and pasture. Sprouting new forest, in the form of fledgling alders towering over blackberry clumps, dotted the property and contributed to its long-gone-to-seed aspect.

Since the land teemed with greenery, rodents, and fleet-footed deer, but not one human, the folksy picture the farm's name inspired came to stand for a cheat, a deception. Old Man Thesen persisted as a rumour only—bald and shrunken maybe, or hairier than Grizzly Adams, no one could say—and remained invisible as a body with needs and wants. The man's cabin-sized house, covered with brick-effect tar paper but featuring no rocking chair, hanging planters, or beckoning porch light, sent out a resolute message, a defensive back turned to the world of onlookers. Naturally, the property's emptiness invited snooping.

As for the when and why of this determined retreat, those presented further mystery. The area's dozen households suspected the usual reasons: he'd gone crazy; paranoid misanthropy had taken deep root; his wife had died or left him, and lacking the courage to commit suicide or rejoin society he waited patiently inside the hovel for a massive heart attack, a stroke, or time to finish the job. "Each to his own," neighbours agreed. No one dropped by with a casserole or offers to mow the former lawn.

In all their years of wandering by and through the land on the way to Silver Creek—and on the rare occasions the weather allowed it, to a mosquito-breeding slough that briefly hardened into a private skating sanctuary at winter's zenith—Em and Jay had never seen any indication that Old Man Thesen could solidify into anything more than idle talk. Nothing, not even smoke from the brick chimney or fresh car tracks in the muddy driveway, hinted at activity, a daily routine, or the use of supplies. Spectral, the man had equally ghostly requirements.

Em and Jay supposed that the Thesen offspring, if real, resided in a far off city and sat on the land, hoping for the day subdivision developers (or better: Mr. Wales) took notice of the wasted expanse. In the meantime these calculating relatives relied on gossip to keep vandals and hobos from settling in. Either that, or Old Man Thesen had bit the dust inside, a mummified or putrid corpse, poised to be discovered in the near future when a city official visited him for failing to pay property taxes. They entertained the possibility that the cabin represented a trick, like the farmhouse entrance in *The Andromeda Strain*, four boring sides and a roof that hid a trap-door entrance to the sterile labs of the Wildfire Complex. They gave up that fantasy: the truth hardly ever turned out so exciting.

As a ghost or a permanently warm item for speculation, Old Man Thesen possessed the kind of power normally hitched to mysteriousness, a local one, true, but otherwise a distant relative of the Bermuda Triangle or those spaceship landing strips in Peru.

And while the house itself seemed slightly dangerous because of who—or what—resided inside it, nearby buildings, unused as well as unlocked, practically opened themselves as gifts set in a field. Trespassing and exploring the cobwebbed passageways? A foregone conclusion.

A stable and a long building that, they believed, must have once been a chick hatchery stretched out—planks faded, cedar shake roof spongy with moss—a minute's stride behind the homestead through waist high grass crisscrossed with deer trails.

Inside, the stable's rough whitewashed and mud-splattered planks felt forlorn, as though their only purpose for decades had been to provide surfaces for dust to land and mice to nest. Other than a pitchfork and an aluminum snow shovel, the interior was sparse, preserved but unused, like a museum's Pioneer Days display.

The second building, squatter, rickety, and roughly U-shaped, resisted definition.

Single story and made of cramped walkways, it did not match the usual notion of any barn. And unlike the stable, the structure contained no individual stalls for horses or cows. Instead, chicken wire and wood cubbyholes lined long walls, each level one foot above the next. This skyscraper of enclosures reached close to the pitched rafters. Whatever purposes the building had once served—egg production or chickens for grocery stores the best guess—the shelves now teemed with cardboard boxes, as though half a dozen

Dust Bowl families had abandoned possessions there years before and never managed to return.

Em and Jay had snuck in on several afternoons and torn through the boxes. The trove included clothing, the contents of several kitchens, empty canning jars, LPs, tools, books, and bundled pornographic magazines.

Along twenty feet of one shelf alone, they'd pored over photographs in a magazine called *Oui* after riffling through old dresses, fur stoles, gravy boats, and an entire crate of wood planers. If the boxes mostly belonged to the world of a grandmother's basement, *Oui* matched the stack of "reading material" their father kept in plain sight downstairs. One featured powdered Lady Jane, in Marie Antoinette finery and a wig, being seduced by Rodingo, a servant in white satin breeches who eventually served his erect penis on a silver oval platter surrounded by pink roses.

As for articles, they perused those too, their father's joke being that the rumpus room's magazine pile served as a library keeping him informed about current events.

Drawn to the title, Jay read "The 3 Most Important Things in Life," but along with the X-Rated pictorial it spoke of a world so foreign it may as well have been the Cradle of Civilization: "Muh-fugguh! Gahdamn muh-fugn stupid piece'a shit. Dumb sunbish cah-suckin' piece'a shit garbage . . . *Leroy*!" Puzzled, he didn't finish. Clearly, no newspaper would ever hire that writer to replace Ann Landers.

With so many boxes to pore over, they skimmed the top layers just below the dusty flaps. Whole days might easily be passed unpacking all the contents—toasters with rust-flecked swing doors, china plates with floral borders, dirt-caked garden tools, sofa pillows, nails and screws in jam jars, entire boxes stuffed with tea towels. They'd stop and look up, spooked by a noise that hinted at the dramatic appearance of Old Man Thesen, and stab a finger toward a safe exit.

The coop broadened at one foot of the U. A gently sloped rough concrete floor, a sturdy table, and a row of old-fashioned windows with square panes gave the special room there a comfortable airy feel. Minus the debris of hay, dried mud, and cobwebs, they decided it would serve well enough as a rehearsal place.

Gordyn's asthma might act up, Em remembered, and that made their first move a revisiting with him and Dee in tow. With that success, a bigger challenge: electricity and actually knocking on the hermit's front door to beg for permission.

They braced themselves for the chance that no one would answer. Or that they'd nudge open the door and find him—dead, rigid, leathery—reclined, a corpse in an armchair. The other expectation came from farm trespassers they'd seen on TV: a front door slowly swinging inward and a rifle's snout emerging from the darkness to force a panicked retreat.

Before the knock they decided on and embroidered the details of the best story and who should tell it. The unreeled explanation needed a salesman's force—to create the highest likelihood of softening the old man's armoured heart and convincing him that letting four wholesome kids (as pleasant as daisies) practice within earshot would (a) not really affect his monastic routine and (b) represented a moral good, at least a downpayment on a ticket to heaven.

If the geezer's heart still beat, of course.

If they knocked, didn't receive any answer, found the door locked, peered through the kitchen window and caught sight of the stiff (their father's word), they'd also encounter a forked path: tell their parent and call the police, or take his death as a Welcome mat from the universe that proved they were meant to practice there. His vacated body, in that case, stood for approval from beyond the grave. A cadaver could scarcely signal otherwise.

Déviation: Show Home

Joey hadn't needed to sell the advantages of the place. They were, after all, moving from a single-wide Knight trailer parked on an island in the flat middle of nowhere to a classy house with three levels, five bedrooms, two and a half bathrooms, and only a twenty-minute march to the nearest school. He led them though floor after floor of perks nevertheless, harping on previous ownership by the architect, who'd designed it from scratch and knew a thing or two about high-end fixtures and customized details. "Swimmin' pools, movie stars," Joey drawled. He christened them Elly May and Jethro for an afternoon.

"We sure could use a fresh start," he announced, with a sharp turn down the steep driveway and into the empty carport.

And who'd dare turn down a home with a hillcrest view of the Valley and room for them to grow? One without wheels, a hitch, and sky blue siding. And free of any history involving them. A new address would help erase memories of the two-track dirt road where they'd played catch, badminton, and Meteor!, an elaborate made-up game requiring rocks and dinosaur models. There, Em and Jay had raced—unknowing witnesses of a portentous accident—toward their mother, who collapsed on a sunny long weekend morning in May. She never spoke again or opened her eyes. Comatose after a brain aneurysm, she died under hospital blankets a week later. "Bridge Over Troubled Water" played at the funeral, their father said afterwards, having decided against their attendance.

Below the roof's irregular cedar shakes, Tudor style prevailed in smooth white stucco interrupted with cow patty-shaped lumps, rough one-by-six fir washed with chocolate stain, and a bank of aluminum window frames painted brown, the panes themselves appliquéd with thin heavy tape to create the shape of playing card diamonds. "Elizabethan," the real estate agent had told Joey, who passed on the detail.

The standard entry next to the garage was convenient, and from it up one set of carpeted stairs stood a landing covered with the rust stone-effect linoleum also used in the kitchen. Any approaching stranger would assume the extra-wide double doors there could only be the main entrance, just as a drawbridge is for a castle. Everyone else eventually heard about the creaks and stony heaviness of that fussy custom-ordered entrance and knocked on the plain side door.

At the landing a three-foot plaster Spanish conquistador statue kept guard with pewter armour and a bladed lance. Joey stroked the figure's helmet and named him Don Quixote.

The living room: for guest visits only and made hazy from never divided sheer blinds behind the chesterfield. The stereo cabinet butted against a wall of smoky mirror tiles shot with gold veining. Stepmom #1 had picked out carved and notched Mediterranean furniture upholstered in lime green velvet that echoed the shag's dominant hue. Joey's chore list for company meant Em tackling the area; she swiftly locked into memory raking in one direction. "Don't bother otherwise," she'd been warned.

A scrolling railing in wrought iron matched the crystal and metal table lamps. Their gauzy shades echoed the drapes. Seated, company faced another conversation piece, a mottled brick wall with a corner planter for a serpentine philodendron, a medieval-style fireplace of roughly cut black-painted iron, a coat of arms with steel swords crossing a red velvet heart, and a large portrait, painted on black velvet by Joey over the course of two November weeks. In it, a matador flourishing a cape braced for a desperate bull already stuck with darts as big as stakes.

Arranged in a L, the chesterfield and twin armchairs peered at the formal dining room, whose feature wall the architect had opted to cover in cedar shingles washed a sage green. Right in the middle: a display for decanters and crystal glassware, inset and made of mirror.

From the oval dining table capped in white marble-print melamine guests could watch the host at the stove (chestnut, a built-in: special ordered). He'd stand on the paving stone flooring and occasionally let loose about a one-of-a-kind medieval ventilation hood, of varnished iron scored with hammered half-moons. Every family member had yelped and checked for blood when delicate scalp flesh met its sharp, unyielding corners.

Venture: Rush / September – October

Gordyn left home early on a Saturday and told his mom that Mr. Swanson had called a staff meeting a half hour before

Gordyn began job task number one: double-checking the float in the till.

"Alright. Make sure that man pays you for your time. You know—."

"Thanks, Mom, see you later." Gordyn thought his mother's views about a roving population of rip-off artists verged on the paranoid. What could she know; she barely left the house.

Nearing downtown Gordyn passed by the hydrangeas and white pickets of 2nd Avenue yards. If Mr. Swanson caught sight of him before the shift, Gordyn predicted that he'd corral him in with that saying about early birds and worms, brought up at least once each shift and sure to appear in the first chapter of the tips-for-success masterpiece he crowed about writing.

Gordyn inhaled at the top of Welton Street, and mapped out the footsteps to come: downhill past Overwaitea, turn left, breathe steadily while pulling open the door, survey the room, make eye contact and smile, and veer directly but leisurely for Merv at the counter; not too different from racing from the fir-plank wings to glossy black centre stage, the situation didn't faze him. Launching forward, he imagined this new winning streak as bright and burning, with a comet's awesome tail.

Smoggy with burning sandalwood incense and cigarette smoke, Acapulco's could easily pass as a den of vice, Gordyn thought, a tropical one thanks to a mystery container leaking sweet cocoanut oil.

He'd already decided against dawdling: no phony checking out waterbed frames or strolling along the bank of numbered posters. As planned, he barreled starboard—straight for the till and Merv behind it, elbows on glass.

"I'd like a black light, please."

"25 watt or 40?"

"Hmm, I guess 25." He pretended to admire the objects in the display case. Were Acapulco's his shop, Gordyn would arrange the pipes for maximum impact, in a half-circle, like rays shooting from the sun. Merv's placement felt artless, as though he'd dumped a wheelbarrow of merchandise and paved it flat with an indifferent hand.

"Nice, eh? Blue swirly ones there are Meh-ican." The case rattled at Merv's knuckle rap. "Guy up by Brackendale makes the rest."

Gordyn's movie of this glass-blowing hermit near the minimum security prison featured the guy as a mousy ex-con uncomfortable anywhere except close by his cellmates, a classic case of Stockholm syndrome. "The incense burners are pretty nice too. I bet my sister'd like one of those."

"I'll throw in a box of cones or a pack of sticks—your choice, *muchacho*—if you pick one up."

"Thanks, I'll keep that in mind." Gordyn paused, excited but nervous about the conversational flow, and eager to match Merv's miserly use of words. "Birthday's coming up pretty soon." Sentry still, two bottles of Rush stood between the pipes and the clutter of pyramidal and cubic baked clay burners perforated with sets of holes. "Get paid next week. You won't sell out by then, right?"

Merv shrugged.

Gordyn left then. The pocket of free time meant he'd arrive early at Brownie's unless he loitered in the dull aisles of Field's. Thought aligned almost perfectly with action and result, he concluded, at least sometimes.

NOTEBOOKS / SEPTEMBER

What about <u>The Incubators</u>???
Seriously!!

<u>No way</u>! Too farm-y, like we should play banjos and wear overalls.

Déviation: DISCOGRAPHY

On the return trip from the Thesen ex-farm, they heard their father's yodeling—enthused and aloft in the breeze but peacock squawky.

Neck craned Em spotted him straddling the peak of the roof in costume (work boots, utility belt) checking the TV antenna, whose support braces demanded close-up investigation after the previous week's house-rattling thunderstorm. Peering down he warbled jokily, yet hungry for applause. Following tradition they listened for a respectable interval before waving and cutting for the side door. Until an audience made an appearance he worked diligently and in silence, they knew, surveying the vicinity now and again for any approaching pair of ears.

Today's lyrics ranked high on his list of ATFs: "I'm a lineman for the country," the single line bellowed loud enough so that nervous cows in distant fields cocked their ears.

They regarded Glen Campbell as Dad Music that doubled as a tool not radically different from those barometer clocks old folks displayed, where a blue bird emerging signalled high pressure and clear skies while its pink sibling indicated clouds or rain. "Wichita Lineman": when he publicly celebrated but also lamented his status as a dutiful, earthbound hero whose lonely, demanding occupation takes him far, far from the comforts of home. "By the time I get to Phoenix" for maudlin Joey, who'd had a couple of pre-dinner drinks followed by a Spanish coffee or two, and feeling twinges of guilt for leaving a note that says "I'm leaving you for good" (while simultaneously covering his tail by having told the dumped lady that he'd already told her so because he couldn't be tied down). "Galveston, oh Galveston" when he was rallying the troops for a car trip. "Rhinestone Cowboy" possessed a trickier message, either a regret that life hadn't delivered the fame and prosperity it had once promised, or else a rueful confession that even those closest to him, who'd spent years in his company, could only ever guess at the true soul behind the dazzling performer. Burdens and disappointments, the dark themes of a ballad never played by any radio station: "The Life and Times of Joey G."

Outside of the house and car, the warm and jovial public persona held sway. Waylon Jennings in the produce aisle. "Luckenbach, Texas" or "Mommas Don't Let Your Babies Grow Up to be Cowboys" for the benefit of shoppers in the check-out line. Serenading "Do you want to make love, or do you just want to fool around?" to harried waitresses, whose tolerant, ready smiles and lack of embarrassment or annoyance hinted that customers of his stripe were hardly exceptions to the rule, just a reality filed under Things I Do for a Tip. In diners, that boastful question alternated with "When You're in Love With a Beautiful Woman"; at home the same song's rhyming accusation—"You watch her eyes . . . You look for lies," usually coupled with "Lying Eyes," felt like a bear's growl that led to one of two expected outcomes: the wounded man-beast stalking off in a snit (to the rumpus room bar) or, far more likely, the subtle flexing and dilating eyes that hinted at a lecture, a living room meeting, or worse.

With some ATFs—"Don't piss down my back and tell me it's raining," "You can't kid a kidder," "Don't shit me," "He can't tell shit from chewed dates," "As phony as a three dollar bill"—Joey advertised a penetrating wisdom, worldliness that saw through mirages and made short work of facades that tripped up gullible lesser men.

The king of them all, though, "Bullshit baffles brains," had origins they'd been able to piece together from fragments. They'd heard the saying for years and never given it much thought, assuming the phrase, with the others, shot from parental mouths everywhere. When they occasionally met a schoolmate's dad, they heard maybe one cuss to their father's dozen, or else swear words in new combinations like "Shit or get off the pot" for "Get it in gear," "Dipshit" for "Idiot" and, once, "Fucktard," which meant stupid too.

On story-spinner bouts of unpredictable frequency before, during, and after Stepmom #1, Joey returned to one over and again, as though in the retelling he'd eventually figure out its essential truth. No bullshit, he claimed, it involved a man, an acquaintance back when he was in his early twenties, "foot loose and fancy free," and enthralled with *The Dean Martin Show*, Joey Heatherton (a bombshell and va-va-voom, reportedly), and all things Las Vegas. This friend was variously an inventor, a mechanical genius on par with Leonardo Da Vinci, and far too intelligent for joe jobs and a normal routine but, regrettably, incapable of fitting in with the guys and knocking back a couple of brews after a shift. Outsider status aside, the actual trouble with this wide load of intelligence was that it made him unstable, erratic, and impulsive, his ideas so wildly impractical—a plumbed La-Z-Boy recliner so he could pour himself water without getting up; pest-free cherry and plum trees webbed with exposed wires that he could plug into a socket—that a jail term for manslaughter seemed inevitable.

After years of dreaming up and sketching designs on graph paper, this guy, "half a bubble off," decided on realizing his magnum opus: a circular residence that would rotate as a result of massive clockwork gears and a motor located in the basement. The story presented key ideas: there was no practical purpose for the rotation (the ability to make it happen reason enough) and the man went stark raving and had to be institutionalized right after completing the project. As for where this house and this crazy engineer existed, those practical matters stood beyond the tale's scaffolding.

Brains alone, then, were categorically different from and lesser than savviness; street smarts took braininess too but cut it with useful practicality. A street smart guy could not manufacture a perfectly cubic two-car garage of glass that floated inches above the ground, no, but nor would he want to: whoop-dee-do, big fucking deal, why bother? Not only were brains suspicious for their ability to dream up useless nonsense, but a super-abundance represented folly and a one-way ticket for the nuthouse.

Wary of pure intelligence, Joey felt guarded about chiselers too, craftily intelligent, yes, but with a corrupt core. Their upstanding kin, though, he regarded as entirely worthwhile. Outsmarting, undercutting, bluffing, snowing, laying it on thick for strategic goals: all these he gauged as acceptable, even admirable.

He'd quit high school to help his dad's floundering delivery truck business, he reminded them, and had come to learn of the advantages handed over to those with education. But Joey dug his heels. Diplomas did not reflect natural intelligence or ability. No, they gave their holders avenues shut to drop outs. In the face of prejudiced beliefs and fundamental unfairness, he created a mythology of the hero who can read situations and other men in ways that those who merely read books could never conceive. For individuals of that rare disposition (those self-made Franks and Deans and Sammys), the world was an open book and his oyster—whatever that meant.

Interpreting and translating his points of view later, when free of ears that connected to lecture-prone adult mouths, Em bet that the lessons related to the importance of not standing heads and shoulders above anyone and being wary of everyone's evil motivations.

Although Jay agreed, he added that when it came to paying for tuition, they'd better look elsewhere.

Origin Story: II

Gordon and Jay had not fallen into a shared orbit because one had spied the other from across a mobbed school foyer and sensed fireworks, magnetic commonalities, or crucial reasons to strike up an immediate friendship. "Like a rich jewel in an Ethiop's ear" rightfully belonged in a play, they'd have said if asked. No one inquired, of course.

Give or take, the boys had begun conversing for the sake of utility.

Gordon dreaded the table saw's mechanical whir with its deadly toothed blade and screeches, a requirement for Woodworking assignments; and secants and tangents fogged Jay's mind while chalkboard phrases—"Law of Syllogism" and "Equivalent Statement"—seemed exactly the same, even though his test scores proved otherwise.

Looking over Jay's slumped shoulders at C- and D in red felt pen and crumpled evidence of tanking Geometry 10 grades, Gordon nudged the quiet boy's shoulder with a mallet fist and leaned forward: "Hey, I got a deal for you." He muttered the words in a rumbling monotone, suppressing inflections and any implied hiss or exclamation point, and completely scrubbed out correct grammar and "Have I got!!" as options. He'd already absorbed the fact that along with the single finger shoulder tap, extensive whispered exchanges, crossed-leg sitting, and hands resting at hip-level, note-passing, his first impulse, landed dead centre in the forbidden, visit-and-pay-the-price territory of expressive girlishness. As with tough cops on TV just before they broke down a door, he'd pound. The kid's shoulder could take it.

The boy who sat in front of him looked safe, a quiet loner. And Gordon felt bored and miles ahead of the pack, anyway; he could teach the material better than Mr. R, who paced the length of the blackboard while droning and made zero effort to disguise habitual wristwatch-checking every two minutes.

At the thudding nudge, Jay half-turned. He kept an eye cocked for Mr. R too. Everyone swore the man got high from upholding rules, Silent Until Asked way up on the list.

After Mr. L gathered the all-boy class of twenty-two around to gawk and run thumbs along a cut of wood made by Gordon in order to touch splintering and imperfect lines and to illustrate the many, many good reasons to use the circular, jig, or hack saw—even teeth: "Hell, my dentures could do a better job"—Jay also noticed Gordon's affinity for frenzied sandpapering when a belt sander would do the work in a twentieth of the time. Ditto for the hand planer and drill. He returned Gordon's favour from Geometry.

Making cuts for someone else's double-decker spice rack, tripod stool, or Parsons table demolished the grades of both rule-breakers, so Jay snuck pieces of Gordon's projects into his stacks of cedar, mahogany, and pine. After Jay finished, Gordon would drop by the work bench and pretend to offer sage advice about angle cuts, nodding and shaking his head and stepping back for longer-range examination of the problem for the benefit of Mr. L, their potential audience. With put-on absentmindedness he'd retrieve the wood, cut to exact specifications. All the while the boys struggled to keep straight faces.

Despite claims to see everything, Mr. L didn't catch the underhanded operation. If another boy picked up on the ruse, he kept it to himself. No one could stand a rat.

Better still, Mr. L slowed his visitations upon discovering no further ready-made lesson-giving opportunities. He'd wander outside and quickly suck in smoke through a hand-carved pipe. On the return tour of duty he'd regale the class with incidents of severed fingers and lost eyes with a barnacled sea captain's windy enthusiasm, as though he'd never trotted out the tales of recklessness by the dozens since the alleged accidents in the heyday of Vietnam.

By Grade 10 and his second semester in Bend High, Gordyn, still introducing himself and spelling his name as Gordon, had already passed the inkling stage about his impending school status: from neutral-as-Switzerland to skid row to leper colony, his present and future amounted to a graph chart of a doomed business. Or, an economy lurching from inflation to recession before sinking into ruinous long-term depression.

He'd never been a top ten pick for any gym class sport and resented (with bitterness or resignation, depending on the day's events) whatever Physical Education instructor had dreamed up the us-and-them method of sorting; the guy must have been trained in the army. In about thirty seconds Gordon could replace the current regime with another whose fairness smiled on nobody in particular. Names from a hat, anyone? At the same time he felt quite sure that he'd never choose his double if expecting a team win.

Gordon stood huffing about the usual unpopularity contest one January morning when Mr. W chose Dave R as the yellow team's captain. For a long minute the vying captains followed the eternal ritual—two apples of the coach's eye ticktocking choices with name-for-name predictability. Popularizer and possible inventor of the attack-word *scungebag* and renowned as the smart ass of smart asses (as well as gross and crude, a disruptive agent regularly shuffling from the Principal's office to the waiting room of Mr. S, the boy's counselor), Dave R whined loudly as the selection dwindled to the dregs.

"C'mon, Coach, how about we just bench the rest, especially that frog cornholer?" He pointed at Gordon, and Gordon watched his fellow pariahs lean or half-step away, creating an effect like a pinpoint spotlight for his sad carcass alone. "I don't want him near my balls."

"Just pick someone. And get the lead out." Whenever fights broke out Mr. W said that students needed to learn how to cope with petty squabbles. He alleged that the practice paid off after graduation, just as teamwork helped prepare students for the workforce.

Operating on automatic, Gordon's brain manifested a Roman Candle display of singeing retorts, all of which would make the situation worse: "I wouldn't want to be near your balls" could be turned around to suggest he'd be fine up close to those of someone else, while the effect of "I bet you want to get near mine" would involve Dave's R's beating him up outside and in front of a thrilled rabid circle after school, saving face his rationale but pure sadistic joy at destroying a weakling before jeering admirers the core motivation. Huffing and puffing and "I will end you." Another hometown hero: to see the outcome, Gordon barely needed to think.

In the first few months at the new school, Gordon hadn't imagined himself wholly invisible but he supposed he'd attained blended-in status, a vulnerable chameleon passing as lichen-speckled granite. He made sure his clothes, hairstyle, shoes, gym bag, glasses, and shuffling walk approximated the normal without mimicking it exactly (Thou Shalt Not Copy another hallway commandment kids accepted as an enforced law just below Thou Shalt Not Stand Out in order of importance). But for some reason—Quebec, maybe, or new kid status, or who knew what triggered anyone—Dave R had taken notice of a trait and decided on a public venue for the humiliating punishment that helped maintain his reputation.

Gordon had pictured a gavel slamming down with guillotine blade finality and sentencing him to two years of maximum insecurities.

By the end of the terrible, epochal day Gordon had been called a queer, a homo, a cornholer, and a filthy fucking faggot a dozen times; and meaty shoulders checked him in hallways, stairwells, and anywhere near his locker. He lost count of fingers pointing and girls leaning together to whisper about that kid from out of town and the newly discovered and damning fact about him. Guys spread word as though communicating with ESP. By that Friday, a passage of forty-eight measly hours, his notoriety hung in the hallways, just words but as set and touchable as the plaques along the Hollywood Walk of Fame. A pariah, just like that. He'd barely opened his mouth.

Panicked, he imagined losing hair trying to figure out *undoing*. He'd need magic or science to time travel backwards to that class and to stifle Dave R's throat before he piped up. Better, he could go back even further and arrive in the Bend with a gym bag of trophies, a Firebird, and a hickey chain—double, triple—circling his neck. He'd demand blow jobs from popular girls; revving, dunking, kicking, slamming, and spiking would be second nature.

Other than physical facts—being taller and skinnier than average, but not freakishly so—Gordon sensed cosmetic similarities with the rest of the students: hair neither significantly longer nor shorter, glasses thicker than normal by a fraction, jeans and shirts of accepted brands and from the same stores. He'd thought a regulation appearance would be enough. Striving, he squelched friendliness; and in striking items from his list of characteristics—talkative, demonstrative, theatrical—backed himself into the loner corner.

Dwelling on but not putting to paper a documentary exposé of a poem, he'd pictured a metaphor: his own vital juices squeezed out, he existed as a dry sponge that would return to its saturated and useful state once exposed to the waters of New York City. Before and after that one promising idea, though, he couldn't figure out where the poem should go.

Gordon had abandoned the project. Writing and poetry would probably only curse him further, he figured.

Within the inaugural month of a new school and atmosphere, Jay found himself drifting toward the welcoming "Hey, man"'s of confident boys on teams. Without pining or having asked, he felt embraced by virtue of his stride, body language, width of shoulder, name, voice, colour of eye—who could guess: the funk of change rooms made him wonder if guys, basically dogs walking upright, recognized others as friend or foe based entirely on smell.

Out of the blue, members of the volleyball team asked him which school he'd transferred from and what sports he'd played while there. Able to answer truthfully with "Soccer and volleyball," he confirmed the white magic of partial revelation. Just like that. Say "Mellon" and—poof!—the door flung open. The words were white lies too. He'd tried out for soccer and played one game on the home field and another at Central Elementary (an imposing grey institution with columns that looked like overgrown jail cell bars, and rumoured to be a terminal for all the bad apples—juvies, Remedials, and miscreants already kicked out from other schools for smoking, fighting, or lipping off—from outlying schools). During that second match he decided that the constant running bored him and that he'd rather wander around after school looking for valuable discards in ditches, feed lunch apples to horses, and hang the No Trespassing sign on his bedroom door and re-read *The Fellowship of the Ring* until his dad bellowed upstairs for help with dinner.

As with a desired pair of shoes whose combination of details spelled cool but whose fit did not match all feet, he quickly noticed the problem with the boys' invitation.

The guys roved in small tight packs ideally, tolerating pairs and trios when necessary, as though trained. They talked about upcoming games and girls and cars at the expense of anything else. Ever in motion—mouths readying spit, knees jackhammering, hands reaching for a ball to twirl, bounce, or toss, hawk eyes perpetually on the look-out for mousy targets—and eager with plans that always began with "Let's," they seemed propelled by might-is-right instinct to glue themselves to the group nucleus.

Three hours alone in exile on planet Terminus or with the Bene Gesserit nuns, Jay supposed, would drive them crazy. Moving in a herd gave him hives.

Group-brained, the boys took irrational but undisguised pleasure in singling out the rabbit—goofs, dweebs, brains, faggots, sluts—to their sharp-toothed and relentless wolf that didn't think of the cruelty or malice for the simple reason that the concept existed beyond its scope. In never managing to stay out of the way, the picked-on practically asked for the trouble that found them. As with bugs that fried under a magnifying glass, these losers played a crucial—if undesired—role.

Swept up in the same irresistible current, the girls that Jay had spent his free time with over the past two years mouthed Hi in hallways, stairs, or foyers. Before and after school, though, and during lunch and the morning break, their cliques stood or sat fortress-like, exclusive.

With the shift in routine Jay watched his former project-, recess-, and class whisper-mates Bonnie S and Cindy R look around the cafeteria or rear foyer where the bakery sold glazed and maple donuts. They laughed, leaned in to express a choice set of judging words, and glanced around the room with knowing expressions, as though every single person existed there to be weighed for value on a scale—accepted, exposed, or ridiculed. Or, in the case of Brian K and Ward C, projected into near and distant futures that began with "Can I walk you home?" and crested at an engagement ring, promises of eternal love, and clinked glasses as the honeymooning couple soaked up a glorious Honolulu sunset.

For their part, the group welcoming him followed a similar route. In place of creating a map of future togetherness with Miss Right, though, they evaluated the girls according to physical and reputational worth: plusses ("I'd poke that"; "Nice jugs"), minuses ("She did it with a German Shepherd"; "No tits"; "I heard she blows older guys for car rides"), and neutral ("She's a total virgin"; "She won't even let you finger her"). The guys equated minus girls to hamburger: cheap, quick, and easy, and they made guys appreciate the steak when it was finally served. They spoke in matter of fact tones, as though discussing the weather, but Jay felt sure everyone lied and not a soul challenged the total BS in order to keep the peace.

The guys never mentioned nor appeared to notice the rotations of outfits and accessories the girls—"chicks," suddenly—tried out, Jay noticed. Their eyes sought past the clothes, hunting for outlines of nipples, cleavage, glimpses of pubes, bra straps, camel toe, and the bow-legged waddle thought to indicate recent sexual history. For them, outfits existed as obstacles, the fewer of them the better.

The guys did not, he'd divined, design and sew ensembles for their sisters, nor photograph the modelling of the Important Dinner and Friday Night at the Disco outfits with a Polaroid. And wouldn't ever. When they happened to flip through *Vogue*, they were alone in their room with their pants pulled down.

If Em ever wanted to kill his reputation, passing out a single cassette with a recording of their wonderful afternoons pretending to be *Vogue* reporters assigned to describe New York City fashion shows would do it. Instantly. His awareness and admiration of Mary McFadden's famous pleated fabric couldn't be explained away or justified. Not ever.

Behind a shut door in Dee's room in the final month of Grade 11 Gordyn admitted—in the strictest of confidence and under the threat of massive retaliation of unknown design but capable of destroying life as she'd experienced it so far—that he was bisexual. He announced the category as though a projection, hypothetical, an abstraction, as though he'd received a sketchy transmission from the distant future. To the false admission of having made out with a girl (unnamed) in a darkened, unchaperoned corner at a gym dance and pawed beneath Fiona's bra because the Bible prohibited nothing of the sort, he also omitted evidence of their cousin and of department store bathroom stalls.

Updates occasionally charted changing percentages, from 90% into girls to 80%.

Dee, a veritable Blue Chip stock, remained at 99.9% into guys.

In her mind the number stood firm at 100%, but just as she'd thought smoking was a disgusting habit until taking test drags from Em's cigarettes, actual try outs could make all the speculation in the world as pointless as clogs—she'd received a pair at Christmas 1979 and had clomped around for an afternoon before deciding they deserved to be yard shoes, as in what a Dutch farmwife slipped on between the back door and the cow shed, and they'd sat ignored on the front door mat since then. The accompanying note had claimed they were "all the rage" in Montreal. Dee supposed that her mother's sister must have studied her fellow ward nurses, because without spike heels clogs looked as good as dead to girls her age.

Déviation: REMEDIAL/ADVANCED

Ridiculed but feared, Rose la Touche Elementary's Remedial program operated out of a clammy beige classroom, a portable severed from the school's main body by six feet of gravel. Difficult to open, its windowless door always slammed shut. Kids avoided hanging out anywhere near the entrance.

Em, "in need of a challenge" according to her latest report card, faced the opposite destiny of being potentially saddled with Advanced standing. Bobbing comfortably in the exact middle was the position she wished for.

In the opening week of Grade 5 Mr. M rewarded her—along with Cindy T, Carol, and Cindy Z—with a spare. "To develop your talents," he said, which sounded like a lie. Instead of the gift of an empty orphaned room, the girls had to sit in a front corner next to his desk, exposed as zoo animals. Finger circling, Mr. M motioned for them to slide their desks into a square with the front corner edges touching. Em scrambled to slide hers so that the normals saw only the back of her head.

The magnified visibility, a strange punishment dressed up as a reward, discouraged their first inclinations—fervent whispered conversations and testing out proposals for plays they'd write and perform.

Either lazy or overburdened by the demands of his other students, Mr. M informed the girls during their single after-school meeting that one of these days he'd get to the Advanced Curriculum. In the meantime, he advised in singsong, they could pick themselves up and get back in the race.

By ignoring "What race," the question in Cindy Z's raised hand, he'd opened—they concluded immediately afterward—the way to unchaperoned freedom. But no supervision along with front-of-classroom placement resulted in a quandary: they could do whatever they wanted for Advanced Period so long as they remained perfectly silent and virtually non-existent.

Mr. M had a regular class to teach; he expected them to monitor themselves. "You're smart," he instructed, "don't make a fuss." As if one cancelled out the other. Ever-impatient, the stooped redhead who wore a tweed jacket in toffee with a yellow shirt every day replaced Mrs. D's kindly class-wide inducements the previous year to "Put on your thinking caps" with "It's not the Apollo mission, for the love of God."

Em had run into a similar situation before: two grades earlier and in another school, she and two other girls had been assigned Creativity Class by a Miss L, a recent graduate and much given to removing a guitar from its case for "I like New York in June" and "I really don't know clouds at all" for Language Arts classes. For Arithmetic she strummed the multiplication table in singsong.

In a free classroom by themselves for an hour three times each week, the trio sat cross-legged on chilly blue vinyl gym mats and gushed about events (from summer, the classroom, holidays) and used toothed Spirograph discs for card creations they presented to favoured grown ups. Bored of those, they began writing plays and pasting together fragile costumes using construction paper, excited at the thought of performing before the rapt class.

Their masterpiece—about an evil, girl-sized chicken's heart terrorizing two best friends on a camping trip—didn't make it past a dress rehearsal for Miss L, whose forecast for her girls had envisioned a blossoming of a peace-loving and altogether angelic creativity with clear goals of an Important Lesson (if not world harmony). The heart costume decorated with paper chains and a face painted murderous and red with watercolours appalled her. Instead, she recommended an inspirational play based around "I'd Like to Teach the World to Sing."

Comprehending the inevitable victor in a battle of wills, the group volunteered Em to ask if they could rejoin the regular class.

★

Mr. M, who pitched blackboard erasers at any student who muttered rude remarks or spoke out of turn, possessed none of Miss L's youthful ideals. Naivete, Em knew Mr. M would call it. His all-purpose saying, "You say potato, I say vodka," highlighted the man's towering indifference to debate. His eyes gazed into a calm future—the afternoon he'd submit a letter of resignation.

Em guessed that the Advanced Class represented another administrative duty imposed on him by the Principal, who also taught gym and organized colleagues and children with a whistle-blowing militance. After Mr. M made the girls arrange their desks, he dismissed them with "Okay, the world's your oyster" and returned to his grading book. Em had frowned. Oysters came tightly packed in metal cans that required a key to open. Mottled grey with ruffled black edges and oily, they appeared as edible as rancid brains.

"Why don't you read," he suggested, eyes peering over reading glasses. "Or something." As for what, he didn't dictate a single title to spark their Advanced brains, nor did he point them toward the library. He left them with "Nature abhors a vacuum."

They began with magazines. Carol, the sneakiest of the four, who'd learned to stroll with a lit cigarette tucked into her palm without burning the skin, brought copies she'd borrowed from a rack in her parents' corner store. Hiding the gory covers inside atlases, they pored over the stories from crime and detective magazines, thrilled to read and puzzle over a case about a woman raped by an old-fashioned potato masher (what made it *old-fashioned*?). Others described crazed ladies seeking complicated and gruesome revenge against rapists who wandered the streets with old-fashioned potato mashers hidden in coat pockets.

Exhausting magazines, they turned to a skinny secondhand paperback by Anonymous, which Carol tore into wafers and distributed. Piecing together the unordered story added to the thrill—glass needles of heroin, rapists everywhere, and screaming trips to the loony bin. Another, with a hard cover, they shared chapter by chapter. Among the lessons: being blonde and possessing *eyes like the sunset* (orange? fading? still hot, but not as scorching as noon?) paved the way to Bel Air and the Best Dressed List. That specialness also tended to turn into a two-pronged path. Being rich and famous (but running into trials, heartache, betrayal, or accidents before eventual happiness) or else possessing *haunting beauty* turned ladies into targets for demented cult leaders and nice-acting men who pursued them when they supposed their vaults dripped with jewels but then took off the moment they discovered non-aristocratic origins and dime store rhinestones. Or else raped them.

Oddly, the road to success also doubled as the way to ruin. At every pit-stop, men and women posing as best friends lingered with every kind of cruel, sabotaging plan.

When they whispered too much, Mr. M coughed and squinted over glasses at their reading material, occasionally muttering about a quiz or a progress report if they didn't pipe down.

Em believed a filament as wispy as a single strand of Christmas tree angel hair connected Bel Air and Benedict Canyon with her own world of roads, pastures, and fences. Sure that a Rolls Royce hadn't ever whizzed by her trailer court, she bet that jet-set glamour required supports (mink coats, diamond chokers, spa treatments, silk peignoirs, boutiques) that existed nowhere in the Valley. "The road to ruin is paved with good intentions," she'd heard from adults, but from *The Fan Club* and other alarming tales lifted from Carol's store the lessons darkened: ambition is a double-edged sword; beware of the motivations of others; trying to predict the future is as useful as settling on the weather next June 15 at 9 am.

Venture: Coop / September –

Jay decided they'd spring the good news on Gordyn and Dee, who'd currently taken lead in the easy rivalry springing up over the band's huge, distressing to-do list. Gordyn's claims of "something in the works" and Dee's efficient secretary act riled them to secure the rehearsal room. And since the alternative—a basement, a carport—had no appeal and the wish for an empty home with electricity still switched on and neighbours who wouldn't bother to cross the front lawn to investigate seemed as probable as snow in August, the coop's antechamber (Em's word) stood out as the only reliable contender.

On a Saturday after lunch Dee and Gordyn climbed up to Best Rd. As arranged, the gang met on the road just past the western edge of the Gee's yard. "It's just easier that way," Em said when Dee asked about this preference to meet out of sight.

Cutting across a field minutes later Dee complained about distance (and, once inside, the dirt), but admitted that a frenzy of sweeping, or, better yet, a few gallons sprayed from a hose, would calm her down. Her brother experimented by inhaling in different areas; breathing freely after ten minutes he gauged the coop 90% safe and good enough.

For the dreaded return trip Em and Jay lingered at the entrance to Thesen's driveway. Each lie they'd thought up set them back, the problem's solution a mirage.

The vista appeared unchanged: quiet, empty, fringed in green. Still, their feet hesitated. On *M.A.S.H.* they'd learned that the effectiveness of mine fields resulted in part from the innocent setting.

"Well, let's give it a try." Em swept newly blonder hair behind her ears.

"Okay. What's the worse that can happen?"

"He comes out with a shotgun?"

"Yeah, or else he's rat food."

"Gross. If he's mummified, okay, but if he's maggoty I'm going to spew."

"Right after me." Other than roadkill in the distance, a pet cat that had frozen outside in winter, and the stuffed porcupine their father had brought home from a garage sale and placed next to the avocado plant, their exposure to corpses was minute.

"Who should talk?"

"Let's both. We can figure out which one of us he responds to and go from there."

Em's knock on the aluminum screen door rattled. *Who comes a'knocking*, she thought, placing herself in the old man's shoes. Other than friends, neighbours, and family, only Jehovah's Witnesses (like clockwork, once a month) and children seeking cookie sales or sponsors for walk-a-thons dropped by their house. If Mr. Thesen heard the knock, he'd probably assume it belonged to money grubbers or doomsday-predicting soul savers. He'd be smart to let them knock until their knuckles split.

Em pressed the handle's cool button and yanked open the screen door. This time the knocks resounded.

Jay crossed to a living room window and peered inside. Weak light coming in from the kitchen window opposite revealed an empty but neat living room and no movement. Frowning, he flipped his palms upward.

Bellowing preceded thundering toward the front door. "I'm coming, hold on a damned minute." A thud, as though a *Webster*'s dictionary had slipped off a table. "What's this racket all about? There's a sign, says No Trespassing, can't you read?"

A mole-like shrunken character in a ratty cardigan who spent whole days on the lookout for the Grim Reaper did not swing open the door. Nearly as tall as the door frame and wide-shouldered, a man offset a bald head with a polar beard that must have taken patient years. Mr. Thesen, if that's who he was, looked like he'd escaped from Russia at the time of Rasputin; his horn rims, heavy and black, featured one thick lens. The other, opaque glass, hid a blind eye or an empty socket.

"Aha, junior sales agents come to my doorstep. Okay, sprouts, whatcha selling?"

"Hi Mr. Thesen." Em held the screen door half-open. "We're not selling anything. I'm—."

"Oh, I see, so you say." Standing a foot below the door sill forced them to crane their necks. Jay wondered if Mr. Thesen had arranged that on purpose. "Everyone everywhere's selling something."

"We're wondering if—." Intimidated by the man's booming words and force of will, Jay sputtered. "We need—."

"We're buying something, Mr. Thesen."

"Is that a fact?" The old man's face relaxed. "Junior executives, then, are you?"

Em opted for honesty, between smiles and pauses explaining their band, the need for a private rehearsal place, and the coop's antechamber. The old man seemed too wary for on-the-spot half-truths.

"Antechamber, eh? That's pretty fancy. How do you know about the slaughter room?"

"We peeked in the window one day."

"And you're flat broke? What's in it for me? Scratch my back and I might scratch yours."

"We can help around the place?"

"What makes you think I need help?"

"I guess everyone does?"

"You guess, hey?"

"I can do yard work." Jay recalled his grandmother reminiscing about men in the Depression who'd wandered from house to house and taken odd jobs for a meal or spare pennies. "I worked on a construction site." Jay borrowed the lie from Gordyn's joked-about summer job that lasted eight hours and extended its range. He'd helped out with his father' interminable yard projects—weeded rock walls, swept driveway, trimmed juniper shrubs, raked cottonwood catkins and leaves—and that counted as résumé-worthy. He could unscrew an oil pan and check for spark plug corrosion with his eyes shut.

"And I could—." Sensing a dingy kitchen stacked with rancid dishes, cobwebs and dust piles in corners everywhere, and a bathroom on par with an outhouse, Em's felt her goodwill retract. "Read. I could read something to you." His one good eye had to be strained.

"Bartering, eh? I suppose you can haggle too. Those old shacks are on their last legs, so don't blame me if they cave in while you're making all that caterwauling. I had a Zane Grey on the go, but—." He peered down. "*Riders of the Purple Sage*. Can you read that?"

Em watched the man's face, wondering when whippersnapper would makes it appearance. The grumpy-old-man movements seemed like a routine, a mask he put on, even though the smile in his magnified eye seemed to announce its ridiculousness. "Okay. We need a plug in too. So, maybe I can read to you and do all the voices?" *Riders of the Purple Sage* meant nothing to Em; it sounded like science fiction. She liked accents, though, and counted them as one of her definite talents.

"I can—." Basic upkeep, never mind keeping up with the Jones' was alien to Mr. Thesen. Jay guessed he could offer to paint the house and rototill the garden and attract only a Pope's head shake—nearly imperceptible but absolute—from the man.

"I'll think of something, young stuff, you can count on that."

Rehearsal: Prep / September

With the ideal band name as elusive as Bigfoot they relied on lame, punchline temporaries—The Question Marks and Big Blank—interchangeably, budding with faith that while striking at intervals both sporadic and random, inspiration does inevitably show up. It just had to.

On a summery September afternoon when Gordyn deep-fried bucket after bucket of drumsticks, Em, Dee, and Jay skirted past the shack's tarpaper exterior and swept the rehearsal room in an excited frenzy. They swiped at cobwebs and rubbed their eyes, quipping that Gordyn would have wheezed to death. Either that, or they'd have expired from his hypochondriacal complaints.

While searching waist-high grass for an outdoor tap, Jay located a squeaking old-fashioned pump. They lugged a black rubber bucket and ice cream pails of water, sluicing the windows and whitewashed planks until straw filaments, fly bodies, and decades worth of dust ran outside in a mini-flash flood of sludgy waves. The dripping room looked refurbished enough. Better, the air smelled clean and promising, rinsed free of history.

For the trek Dee had opted to leave her famously pocketed sack of a purse at home. Lifting a knapsack from a peg, she extracted brushes and pucks of childhood watercolour paints, basement finds, with a game show flourish. Before her bandmates could object she pointed out that Mr. Thesen had no cause for booting them out: just as they'd revived the room with a few splashes, they could strip off all their handiwork with the same.

Canvas shoes drenched and jean cuffs rolled high, they decorated, guided by a rule of no rules. The wall of windows, the crumbly sloping concrete floor, and the low ceiling of rafters and planks they left for Gordyn.

Within an hour the remaining walls boasted loud patterns in caramel, buttercup, and cherry plaid, huge billowy poppies of scarlet, tangerine, and lime, and snakes, gravestones, and crosses in oily daubs of black. Here and there pockets of moisture made the colours run, as with a portrait made with melting crayons.

They knew Gordyn would easily guess who'd done what, just as they felt certain he'd shake a can, aim the nozzle, and spray out fuzzy gold lines—triangular figures with exaggerated shoulders, cinched waists, and aggressive bristling hair. These nighttime creatures he envisioned as regular sights on Berlin streets and inside London nightclubs. Each figure smoked, wielding a cigarette holder like a saber.

In the spirit of creative partnership, they switched canvases. Snakes invaded plaid; flowery garlands adorned grim black crosses; weft lines ran through flowers and ended halfway through the cemetery.

"The Happy Mansons," Em exclaimed, surveying the artistic statement.

Dee retrieved a spiral notebook from her pack. "We'll add it to the pile."

"Yes, ma'am." For a self-defined free spirit, Dee often parroted the Principal's secretary, Mrs. Have You Made an Appointment? Too much babysitting, Em thought. Children could turn anyone into a nag.

Rehearsal: A Cappella / September-October

Before the first authentic rehearsal Dee printed copies of the lyrics of "Eat to the Beat" and "Heart of Glass" on sheets of lined notebook paper during English class free-writing. The activity drew favourable attention from elfin Miss L. The teacher sang praise—"You're on fire, Deanna. That's terrific!"—from the island of Do Not Disturb, which was also her sharp-edged fortress of an oak desk.

Aggravated that some bands refused to print lyrics on the record sleeve, Dee'd listened to "Eat to the Beat" about a million times and still felt pretty sure she misunderstood a few of the run-together words. Anyone would. Miss Deborah Harry herself probably faked them from time to time.

Fudged, then, met their needs. Close enough.

After ten minutes Miss L chirped, "Time's up, switch with your neighbour." Dee rubbed ink off the pulpy outer edge of her palm, PO'd about the southpaw's curse and at scientists, who'd managed to invent x-ray machines and launch satellites into outer space but hadn't gotten around to ink that dried instantly.

Dee gave Tamie G a rocker chick's squinty and pursed get-your-mitts-off-my-boyfriend scowl and leaned directly in front of the pale nobody. Ever since Tamie G had snapped "God, get with the program!" at Dee in earshot of Miss L, Dee had settled on a reign of terror that kept the suckhole jumpy. The prim gold-star keener wore sock-length nylons and chirped *ad nauseum* about invaded personal space. She actually recorded her stream-of-consciousness drivel per Miss L's calorie-waster of an exercise, instead of engraving pages with red ink doodles—preferably "666" in a clover leaf shape, arrow-pierced hearts that dripped blood, or a tragic lady's face with a long trailing teardrop—or line after line of "Fuck Fuck Fuck."

In tormenting slow-motion, she bent across Tamie's desk to mime an exchange of material with Em, one row over. "Lez," Dee hissed when Tamie's gaze met the scalloped edge of her scoop neck. As the class scribbled on, Dee smirked at Tamie's prissy gasp.

A Blondie song might not make the final cut, but Dee figured the band needed common material to read from. Group memorization? Not a chance.

Overcast and threatening rain, the Sunday afternoon they'd agreed on arrived. Delays—a suddenly hands-on parent, bad moods, Brownie's—had allowed worries to lapse, and now they understood the day would test the resolve of their ambition.

Dee and Gordyn walked up the hill in a blur of talk and knocked fifteen minutes early. Em and Jay, yelling "It's for us!," rushed to the front door. Outside in socks seconds later, they stuffed their feet into running shoes, heels crumpling the backs as they'd been warned against doing a hundred times at least. Since the government made money from paper, they'd joked privately in reply, it did grow on trees.

Noticing how quickly they beetled down the road—noisily too: exhortations, questions, chiding, laughter, and rebuttals overlapping—the gang projected themselves nervously into a probable near future, picturing wobbly Shaggy legs and sickly faces (blood-drained despite thumping hearts) as they squinted through stage light glare toward a shuffling audience that was definitely not wall-to-wall parents and miscellaneous relatives squirming on wooden folding chairs as they waited to catch the offspring's annual turn on the stage and raise an Instamatic with a flash cube to their eye. Instead: strangers with major expectations.

Add Gravol to the band's shopping list, they decided.

They acclimated inside the abandoned coop, the still grotty place Gordyn insisted on christening The Killing Cell and Chicken Treblinka. He dropped these names strategically, promoting one or the other as the band's name-to-come with a frustrating lack of success. Hearing "God, Gordyn, give it up" and similar from Jay and Dee, and "Close but no cigar" from Em, who currently felt drawn to Overdose or The Legionnaires as a snappy band ID that fit them, he vowed to slyly introduce a naming contest he'd rig.

Admiring the janitorial handiwork and the gold, red, and black wall graffiti, they faced the panorama of tall whiskered grass with a fluttering alder border—enticing and uncritical through clean but streaky and old-fashioned warped glass squares.

Despite age and relic status, the poultry processing room did not revert to the expected chaos of spiderwebs, mouse pellets, and dust-clotted surfaces. And as much as Em and Gordyn wished for visible evidence, the pitted concrete floor and plank table with a chiseled drainage culvert hinted in no way at a ghastly history of cleavers, squawks, spastic corpses, and trickling blood, and assembly line decapitation. (Em and Gordyn weighed The Spastic

Corpses momentarily before deciding that name didn't suit them, not quite.)

Volleying plans and inspirations they grinned at the cavernous wooden hollow that soaked up their decibels. Such useful acoustics could only be a positive sign.

Rehearsal #1 made them see that a band without instruments amounted to pea-brains on a stage looking rudderless, on par with a cartoon of a foolish vacation-bound family strapped into a car with no engine, tires, or doors.

Head shots, the band's name and look, and fake ID turned suddenly trivial, mere specks of detail.

Within minutes, they realized that an a cappella substitute meant complete hopelessness too. Gordyn's leadership efforts, lifted from barbershop rehearsals in a rotation of basement rumpus rooms and jamboree weekends, incited rebellion, questions, resistance, and what Gordyn named "hysterics"—"Who said you're the boss?" and "Why should we do it that way?" and "No, let's just start and see how it goes." And Gordyn's forceful sighs, eye rolls, and dismissive teacherly references to U.N. small-minded pettiness helped in no way.

Practical obstacles aside, shyness of varying degrees gradually suffused the room and led to talk of postponement—plan-making for rehearsals if and when keys to depress and guitars to strum arrived.

Despite almost daily interactions as duos, trios, and a quartet and at least twice-daily phone conversations, singing aloud in plain sight—being looked at, listened to, evaluated—inside the enclosure generated bulky knots of awkward feelings, of being guarded and self-conscious and thin-skinned and vulnerable.

A weak or quavering or pitchy or tone deaf voice, bad timing, flubbed lyrics, and sincere emotions transported through mellifluous intonation: each felt on par with a giant pimple, a bullseye visible from the other side of the room and a perfect target that practically begged for everyone's attempts at ribbing that sparked notes of merriment—the derisive laughter at someone's expense so familiar from school—and, for the target, an overwhelming desire to skulk and huff inside a locked darkened room until the year 2000, or, better yet, to not bother ever appearing in public at all.

Anticipated at every spot where two or more human beings stood together and a condition to be avoided at any cost, embarrassment and humiliation—the nightmarish duo might as well be capitalized and riding horses, alongside War and Famine—tracked the gang's scent with wolfish ingenuity. Effort felt futile. Pointless.

Dee recommended taking turns and finding their groove.

Before starting to fret about the eventual audience—Valley guys and girls indifferent and talking, or drunk and obnoxious, or there for a good time and not finding it because they expected to rock out to "Cheap Sunglasses" and "Highway to Hell" and not puzzle over pretentious weirdos cloaked in black—they needed to step onstage and up to mics with casual expertise, total professionalism. The goal: to send the message that the stage and location represented only the latest date on their impressive, continent-spanning history of calendar pages. Also: knowing every angle, every note as well as the colour of their eyes, at least in appearance.

Dee expected the gang to fall into place, bending to a natural expertise—hers—that had been honed by *seasoned experts*. In the opening minutes of introductory classes, Dee had witnessed three times, modeling instructors in it for quick money warned roomfuls of naive—and obviously way too short or wide—girls that "fashion is hard work." One worth his salt, though, skipped by the obvious and revealed that every model should become best friends with Disguising Flaws While Highlighting Strengths, a foolproof technique and industry secret. In the same vicinity as close-set eyes or a too-abundant forehead, the band's fumbling and nerves and inexperience required fixes, she intuited, insider tactics to draw an audience's eyes toward charismatic, trophy-winning plusses.

As for what to avoid altogether, no problem. Over a decade of experiences—seated at desks watching uncomfortable and occasionally know-it-all pupils reading (in fact: stumbling over or speeding through lines of blocky printing on foolscap) about family histories, summertime activities, dad occupations, the most admirable character of *The Chrysalids* and why (followed a year later by the significance of the Blasphemies and why), the importance of agriculture in Mesopotamia, the impact of the Red River Uprising, and then standing next to a teacher's desk and reciting much the same—had illustrated how stupefying dullness spread with the speed of Spanish flu after WWI, a topic that both Jay and Dee had spoken about in strangled voices inside classrooms in different school districts.

Clutching a rake handle mic and careful to stay clear of its painful, tetanus-shot causing iron teeth, Dee stood two steps from the central pillar where she'd tacked a totem of song title cards. Adjusting her face into "haughty," which she'd perfected the previous summer, she gazed toward the silent audience of dappled late afternoon light across the meadow. She pictured Deborah Harry's enigmatic but cool expression on the *Eat to the Beat* album.

Turning to glower, she requested generosity: "Don't laugh, okay?!"

She closed her eyes and imagined the opening bars of the song, seeking to settle into its chanting but jerky rhythms and 100-yard dash speed in a way that reminded her of joining in, years ago, at rope skipping.

One, two, three, and she was there: "You gotta jump up, a-to the beat-a / S-s-stand up, wo-on your feet-a."

Minus the loud backing of instruments and the all-for-one company, she heard only a thin, dry voice evaporate inside old planks. Flashing to a three-minute agony of shame on stage, her day-lit sense of nakedness felt real enough for goosebumps. Panic clamped her throat, frightened lyrics from memory.

"Toes are tippy tippy tippy tapping." Em had no intention to sing while grasping a rake. Nor at a mic. And that meant encouraging the others to stand in her place.

"Oh, right. I totally drew a blank. God, that's not good, is it?" With the thought of choking—"Um, er, oh, God"—at a raised setting in front of a pool of upturned faces showing desires they'd paid to have fulfilled, Dee sensed the gut-deep contraction and snaking hot pulse that instructed a body to seek a toilet *pronto*.

"Um, you're standing in a chicken coop and singing into a rake while three people are gawking at you. You're doing better than I would." Em shot a look the boys, who nodded their agreement.

"Thanks, Em. Um, did you guys see a, oh, I dunno, an outhouse on the property?"

Positioning Em behind and slightly to Dee's left, Gordyn almost within reaching distance, and Jay near the right edge of the stage, they realized—Gordyn starting with "There's no way . . . " and the rest mouthing the stratospheric levels of embarrassment—how ridiculous they'd appear with Gordyn seated at the Tex and Edna Boil's Emporium organ bench, currently unloved and tucked in a corner of the Spencer's living room.

They'd be received with jeers. Idiotic and the very opposite of cool: no better than a spiritual caravan of bible-thumping do-gooders in colour-coordinated turtlenecks and cuffed polyester slacks with built-in creases bringing God's Groovy Word to a Sunday School clutch of uncommitted young sinners-in-the-making while burning through an irresistible roster of modern hits—"Put Your Hand in the Hand," "Rivers of Babylon," and that nun's discofied version of "The Lord's Prayer." Smiling, radiant as saints in the clouds, and faithful that their radiant enthusiasm would coax onlookers to clap along when they sensed the holy spirit lighting up the room and their own evil-tinged hearts, in truth they'd probably face annoyed drunk hecklers or a beer bottle rocket sailing through the air. The gang's parents owned the same old record of The New Christy Minstrels on whose cover ten joyous believers—bliss-drunk, as though stuffed by a holy taxidermist—dangled from a boxcar. Anyone that happy in 1980 could only belong to one of two categories: Moonie or Stepford Wife. Or else, freshly dosed and newly released from the looney bin.

"There's no way around that." Dee reached for her purse. "Let's put that in the Top Five of our get-it-done list."

"Woo hoo." Em tossed a pen to the lead singer.

Notebooks / September

Not to sound all sucky ect, but just think about the <u>hidden meaning</u> of "Count your blessings."

I think we're in this together, so that's definitely a blessing . . . (Ok, God, that was pretty sucky!!)

Rehearsal: A Cappella / September-October

Better than nothing, fake a cappella would have to do in the meantime.

Grey plastic and crammed with D-cells, Joey's ghetto blaster was portable but heavy. They'd use it for background, playing each recorded song at a roaring volume to drown self-doubt and singing along with it until they'd memorized the idiosyncratic phrasing and abrupt poetic shifts.

As Gordyn and Jay flipped the slaughter table and dragged it into what had been the actual coop where chickens clucked and laid eggs before having their necks slit, the girls lugged water in buckets from the squeaky well pump. Fearing discarded and shrunken heads with missing eyes or a pile of mummified claws underneath, they found only scattered feathers and a gauzy quilt of dust.

They guessed Mr. Thesen crept out of his house in their absence to check on the damage his tenants—"those damned kids," they bet he named them—had caused. Dee folded a note in a crack between two planks to explain they'd right the table and move it back later. She signed it, "Yours sincerely, The Band."

Crunching gravel and soccer-kicking stones on a return of slumped, deflating-balloon moods, their conversation swung between bursts of rallying, c'mon-we-can-do-this affirmation they sometimes heard in gym class and doomsday negatives related to a staggering amount of wasted time, perilous long odds, utter pointlessness, and bailing before anyone felt sharper or deeper pangs of disappointment.

★

Of the two that loomed, the instrument-less band problem incited greater laughter than grimaces. Scrounging up equipment meant creative thinking, true, but so would the starting-from-scratch era sure to follow right after getting off a bus in New York City. In that metropolis, no doubt, a torrent of career-minded young people arrived every single hour with identical faith in a park-view apartment (almost immediately) and the city's movers and shakers eagerly embracing their unique and yet necessary talents and, eventually, celebrating their dazzling, history-altering achievements (two years later, three tops).

Far simpler at a glance, a matter as basic as *singing* had caught them off guard like a stomach punch, which also made them feel stupid, as clueless as children.

Gordyn had crooned with his father in public and alongside other students in Drama class productions. But at the coop and in front of his own band of friends, he paused and stammered—unexpectedly shy and tongue-tied. The unsureness spelled trouble. With an eventual audience of worker drones, bastard guys with nasty tongues especially, who probably would have relished tormenting him were they a few years younger? Nothing but four sitting ducks. Easy targets.

Singing meant revelation of a peculiar and uncomfortable sort, one with physical symptoms prickling right beneath the skin. To their logical minds singing was no big deal. But their hearts raced and their faces flushed as though their mouths shared deeply personal information to a whispering assembly of students and grown ups—a D test score; pointing out this week's crush; how deep a belly ached after the newest, loudest public humiliation thanks to the caustic jock wit of Brent C or Glen R; or confiding to panicked thoughts that bubbled up out of nowhere about a future of staying in the Bend and a step-for-step copying of parents' timid accomplishment of sleepwalking through life.

Instead of delight, this public singing unleashed emotions closer to intentionally letting someone observe every private detail of your morning bathroom routine or watch you burst a zit on your back with the help of the mirror. To freely exhibit the best or worst or most interior, private part of yourself on a stage: who would choose such a thing and why?

The usual—bellowing the national anthem and "God Save the Queen" in a packed crowd at school assemblies and once in a while before hockey or district championship games with mandatory attendance—reduced that revelation to zilch since the group setting provided safety in numbers, for one, the bonus opportunity to mumble or mouth the words or insert joke lyrics to score points instead.

As a disembodied idea, the solitary act of standing before onlookers and letting "Once I fell in love and it was a gas" spill out appeared no different from speaking the same words in an ordinary conversation. The listener might say "Oh, really?" or "Me too" before the exchange moved forward.

In practice, though, the easy switch from speech to song—an inconsequential matter: of minutely rearranged muscles, air flow, and intent—and from everyday chat to special performance, attached singing to a squirm-inducing and vaguely shameful intimacy that (along with masturbating or sitting on the toilet or nose picking or care for skin prone to volcanic eruptions) registered at gut level as naturally and fundamentally private and personal, best reserved for a locked-door room in an empty house rather than a bare stage, a rowdy bunch of gaping spectators, and no protection whatsoever from spotlights.

If they, a band composed of four individuals, stood on a stage and performed in a way that knocked them and their onlookers back to all the dull book reports and stuttered haiku readings and cheesy historical skits foisted on them by teachers and performed with the bare minimum of enthusiasm because "Remember, this counts as part of your grade," then they wouldn't be wasting time (their own and everyone else's) exactly, but neither would or should anybody clap for half-assed mediocrity. As a boding of an adult future, that failure struck them as worse than ominous.

When Em and Jay's dad warbled snatches of lines from Glen Campbell and Waylon Jennings and that one-hit wonder who'd written an entire song but everyone and their dog from Atlanta to Alberta had memorized just two lines, "Do you want to make love / Or do you just want to fool around?"—what did that question even mean?—he brayed and bellowed and yodeled with a wink, all of which advertised the man's supposedly lovable, larger-than-life personality.

For an audience he'd drawl "Kaw-liga" and "Yer Cheatin' Heart" at full volume, but never continue with the rest of the lyrics. The performance fell into the same category with the Osmonds, Dean Martin, The Irish Rovers, and The Mormon Tabernacle Choir: whatever the truths might be, once the performer hit the stage, like an animated mannequin, he never varied because, whether toothily wholesome or a wobbly boozer who's seen it all, he was playing a character people expected (and traveled and paid good money) to see.

Though Dee and Gordyn's dad's sonorousness tried for greater tunefulness, the performance looked . . . not false exactly, but self-conscious, with one winking eye in the mirror and the other at an audience trained by experience—white mice in a laboratory maze—to anticipate a standard path.

To witness either man in a living room with an acoustic guitar and singing "Killing Me Softly" with misty eyes while recollecting the tragedy of a bitterly regretted withered romance and the living pain of a broken heart would give them a performance to emulate. Based on experience, though, that much revealing plaintiveness had a snowball's chance.

Sincerity, authenticity, the wonder of intent coinciding perfectly with outcome: anything less than that heightened state—the giddy, skating-too-fast sense of being 100% alive—would strike onlookers, they decided, as underwhelming, a let down, and not exactly useless but within that general dead-end zone: going through the motions.

If not time itself, then the perception of it could be transformed with the right performance, they counted on that. What a heartless ticking clock defined as four minutes and eleven seconds exactly could be experienced magically, expansively though song, as both deeper than 4:11 and broader and more infinitely rich. Instead of the simple—unremarkable, insubstantial—line (0:01 ——— 4:11) anyone might sense while pacing at a bus stop or bleacher-seated during a dull assembly in which the Principal spoke at droning length of an important matter that had just been brought to his attention, another, better possibility transported the listener (body alongside consciousness) somewhere nearer to eternity. They'd all swooned over that before, with eyes closed, earphones on, and the volume jacked up high. The gang wanted and needed that.

The point, or the crucial point amongst others of lesser importance, was not just dreaming up the idea, or saying "Let's start a band" aloud, or putting in the time to figure out how to play an instrument or a few songs adequately enough, or scouring newspapers and billboards for a suitable amateur night and fighting nerves while summoning the courage to lift rubbery legs onto a stamp-sized raised platform of a stage in a crowded room and turning to a wall of faces (expectant, bored, sloshed, etc) before muttering, "We're The _____s, and tonight we're going to start off with a little number by Blondie."

No, anyone with half a brain could accomplish those with enough spare time and effort. Anyone.

The first principle, then, couldn't also be the bare minimum or Satisfactory, that flat, piddling word from old report cards. People reserved "It'll knock your socks off" for truly meaty, face-flushing gossip, or a newly concocted barbecue sauce/salad dressing/ combination of liquor and mix that represented the very peak of their inspiration at that moment. For lack of a finer poetic phrase, knocking socks off seemed reasonable as a motto, the collective's raison d'être.

Rehearsal: A Cappella / December

Dee imagined Deborah Harry—everyday listeners called her Debbie but true fans knew the name the blonde artiste preferred—and Chris Stein in a dingy, multi-lock New York City apartment, a puzzle locale she'd pieced together from cop shows,

Rhoda, and *Saturday Night Fever*. They jammed deep into the night. Years before Fame had reached out and blessed them, the aspiring idols worked three jobs each and wore clothes thrift stores sold by the pound and stuffed into brown paper grocery bags.

The next afternoon the feline blonde unfolded a scribbled sheet of paper in the teensy recording room of a budget studio made of wood panelling and glass that they'd scrimped to rent for exactly sixty minutes. An engineer watched from a control room.

Eyes closed and body clenched Ms. Harry unleashed into the microphone: heavenly.

By the tenth try, she'd grown frustrated and tired, frowning at a closing window of opportunity and her dwindling bank account. Fretfully checking the clock, she listened for technical problems with the know-how of a mechanic before a coughing engine.

Appearing on mirrored disco stages all over the world years later, she'd perform mechanically, the act always seeking to replicate three historical moments: the epiphany of realizing that proneness to love normally meant vulnerability to a broken heart; the one-of-a-kind purity of the song's very first complete performance in the crappy budget studio; and fidelity to the pressed vinyl single eventually shipped by the thousand and played on the radio everywhere, from Anchorage to Adelaide. These perfect moments were irretrievable, stuck in the past; all Ms. Harry could do was approximate, pretend she'd clasped what in fact stood forever out of reach.

To Joey's magmatic chagrin, his son stretched out on his variegated green bedroom carpet and listened to *Cross Country Checkup* for hours on lazy Sundays and *Saturday Afternoon at the Opera* when sheets of downpour gave other Bend families bouts of cabin fever.

Jay had found the opera program by fluke—a "happy accident," his grandmother would say—and found the distant world absurd and fussy and monkish and fascinating, especially the Opera Quiz, with questions as complicated as Algebra to a preteen and answers he'd never guess, or unearth after long stretches inside the Bend's public library: "The first aria in Act 2 of Henry

Purcell's *Dido and Aeneas*, 'The queen of Carthage, whom we hate'"— "Of course, simply divine," "Yes, superb," "Too lovely," the men's voices enthused, suggesting that in their unimaginable high society such obscure detail formed the basis for mundane but opinionated supper conversations—"was excised from"—a pause for gasps of outrage all around: who dared to commit such a sacrilege?—"the Plaza Hotel's production on February 10th, 1923 that was performed by the girls of the Rosemary School, but revived by the Society of Friends of Music rendition that took place on January 13th, 1924 at the New York City Town Hall. Now then, gentlemen, who edited the book for that later, and shall we call truly legitimate, production?" The men tittered, sputtering lines, "Oh, please" and "Slap me awake when there's a challenging question," and correctly named "Artur Bodanzky" a split second later as though they'd been asked, "What are the Big Three automakers?"

When formerly reserved Joey at last designated public radio "for snobs" and opera "nonsense" and "squawking," and the quiz master and contestants "fruity," Jay heard the usual divisions of us/them and safe/sorry as well as a strong undercurrent of worry and fear connected to another unwanted sign that in spite of a lifetime of fatherly efforts—"I picked you up a toy truck/hockey stick/baseball mitt," "Give me a hand with the wrench/pliers/screwdriver," "Take a look at that wiggle/those gajungas/legs up to there"—his son would almost certainly bypass a car show filled with sexy women in half-zippered jumpsuits who sprawled across gleaming hoods in order to read a book alone for an entire afternoon; and instead of wanting to help file lawnmower blades or oil the chainsaw, he preferred to listen to fruits gush about the women they secretly wished to be.

Jay conjectured that parents worldwide used the local equivalent of "I'm disappointed" or the sighs and frowns and sad eyes that signified as much in order to keep their kids on The Right Path, or at least their notion of the straight and narrow. In his case, that path meant Joey Jr., a man he did not sense inside himself whatsoever and, besides, had no wish to embody. He understood the predicament. Were Joey his son and hellbent on striding in Fonzie's and Frank Sinatra's footsteps, Jay guessed all the smiles in the world wouldn't mask his disappointment at the betrayal.

Opera's exoticism intrigued Jay in itself. Better, as challenges to his father's unwavering parenting beliefs, careers plans, and expectation of girlfriend after girlfriend, Puccini's tragically expiring Japanese butterflies and French bohemians looked the same as potent ammunition.

In part because the name conjured a Transylvanian aristocrat in a stone castle built atop dank catacombs of bones, Jay chose Frederica von Stade as the singer he'd follow. Listening to the Opera Quiz he'd learned aficionados collected rare pressings of their favourite singers and that they never grew tired of proposing this or that soprano as *a voice for the ages*, one who stood infinitely higher—since purer, clearer, and more effortlessly powerful—than some other supposedly ordinary woman who "couldn't hold a high F above a high C for all the beluga in the Caspian."

The glamorous name aside, he couldn't argue with the mezzo-soprano's vehicle, which announcers labelled with words that required his door-stopper *Webster's*: sublime, ecstatic, ethereal. Von Stade possessed magnificent diction, apparently. He listened for these qualities and couldn't discern magnificent diction from merely "competent," that kiss of death. What he admired, though, was how via pulsating and penetrating waves the voice commanded attention, far more than the opera's flat characters and idiotic Benny Hill plots warranted.

If the band could reach that level of glorious radiance for even a few lines of lyrics, he'd feel contented.

Drawn to and appreciating the startling impact of hair dye in unnatural hues, masks of geared-to-late-night makeup, and outlandish clothing (Devo and Gary Numan's future-oriented uniforms; the thrift store get-ups and bygone wigs of The B-52's; Siouxsie Sioux and Visage's vampirish cloaks and black-on-black shadow dweller ensembles) and atmospherics (unlit brick alleyways, neon signs that buzzed, dead houseplants slumped in pots, cigarettes flicked at puddled water whose oily surface showed distorted reflections of the fearsome city; the technological horror/ fascination captured in grainy black and white photographs by Cabaret Voltaire and The Normal), Gordyn and Em envisioned a performance that gave people an unforgettable eyeful. Vocal intensity was good too, but visual punch really mattered.

That's what audiences talked about after the fact, remembering Davie Bowie and Sid Vicious's costumed postures, not their honeyed, one-in-a-million larynxes.

Venture: ID / September – October

Striding through a misty rain shower toward his shift Gordyn smiled at the chess-like opening move of his improved Schlieffen Plan. He'd screw the lightbulb into the bedside mushroom lamp, and return next week for an incense burner, the cube-shaped model definitely, which he'd wrap when Dee's birthday rolled around in late spring. The two purchases would transform him in Merv's eyes: a return customer spelled loyalty and continuing business, not pretend-browsing teenaged hooligan on the lookout for shoplifting opportunities. Gordyn expected that new status to open doors.

Merv might not see him as Chester, someone he'd invite in at night to share drinks while playing cards, but he'd not likely gauge Gordyn as a problem—a narc, a time waster, or a thief. "Trust is something you earn," his father hammered home during dinner table lectures. The same law applied to scammed trust. Just dodging "Beat it, kid" implied progress.

Now that Rush had practically tumbled into his reach, he could ready the other prong of the attack, the challenging eastern front, a problem from Dee's to-do list for the band. The situation required a different strategy: since both buyer and seller risked exposure, proving that neither party smelled a rat became goal number one. Gordyn predicted the ritual circling of pro-wrestlers at the start of a match: two contestants bracing for looming body slams while figuring out the opponent's Achilles weakness.

When the band came together—or if: instruments and rehearsal spot secured, songs decided on, talent discovered and honed, and a name chosen: the catalogue of ifs nerve wracking and close to overwhelming—the next step would entail performing for a live audience instead of each other or for neighbourhood kids in a basement. Long-hair rock bands called The Ooligans and Spiral Staircase came to school now and then for sock hops, Christmas pageants, and graduation, and in that case no one demanded a specific age requirement. And for the Fall Fair talent show, contestants needed only to be enrolled students for donated prize eligibility. Past the auditorium, though, any place a band could perform (besides churches, birthday parties, and inside the bandstand on Citizen's Day) served drinks, and that meant whipping out credible ID—x4—to law-abiding managers.

For that fix, the gang needed Merv's handiwork.

School rumour certified that Merv's hydra-headed criminality extended beyond motorcycle gang membership. Gordyn felt unclear about what major criminal acts a gang could actually do locally, other than taking pride in ratty hair and obnoxious, ear-splitting exhaust pipes. Still, the grapevine placed Merv's fingers in many small potato pies. Kids said he bought fish illegally from Indians, lent money with loan shark rates and hammer-to-knee repercussions, and visited hippies with dope patches in California and Mexico.

And supposedly one other finger snaked its way into River Bend Senior. There, John D hung out near the cafeteria at breaks and at the auto shop after school, puffed up with pride: his name always came up if you sought fake ID capable of fooling authorities with jaded, suspicious eyes.

Living for joke set ups in Remedial and Industrial Ed classes, John D's talents didn't seem to reach much beyond rolling under cars to unscrew oil plugs, bellowing declarations ("Blow me") in the form of elongated burps, going on about the itchy discomforts of chronic crotch rot ("Worse than crabs!") and, his greatest claim to fame, slobbering and spitting profusely after he fake-masturbated—using his flabby neck as foreskin—as though on a quest to obtain the world record for grossing out girls.

Like rich kids with Trans Ams, John's importance resulted accidentally, by virtue of blood. Word was, kids approached him in cloak and dagger tones; he'd snap a few pictures and take their cash. After pocketing a cut he delivered the material and remaining money to his cousin Rene, a drop-out from years back, who happened to ride with Merv. The trail of gossip faded there. Either the two men had friends in common or else they collaborated—perhaps in Acapulco's rear office—to supply ID cards, museum-quality forgeries every time.

Gordyn understood that he could poke around school, but wanted to sidestep the school's scuzziest level. For a price—money, yes, but also the lasting humiliation of needing to ask and being tormented for mouthing the question in public, and having every last person's nose eventually in your business—some kid's older brother always made time to pick up bottles from a liquor store. And toughs at the smoke pit would sell the very cigarette out of their mouths for ready cash.

But asking around entailed further questions and personal information being passed from mouth to mouth, like mono. Worse, following the path to the smoke pit or the gravel lot behind the Industrial Ed shop meant forking over five and tens for the privilege of merchandise specially overpriced for him and a volley of insults bellowed across the room for the benefit of all listeners, save one—"Hey, Bobby, faggoty stick boy here wants to score some dope so he can get wasted with his bum buddy." Exiting, he'd drag his feet, blanketed by another strangling layer of reputation: the total head who totally gave head.

Merv hadn't been in school for decades and, Gordyn figured, he didn't give a crap about anybody's personal lives. His spirit felt entrepreneurial. He'd serve Hitler and Ted Bundy if they handed over the right bills. On par with everyone else, he might badmouth you when you were out of sight. But at least that condemnation didn't take place within spitting distance in school corridors. Better still, Gordyn's parents would never catch wind of how their eldest spent the pay cheques Mr. Swanson left under the cash drawer. Gordy predicted another benefit too: alongside the furniture warehouses on TV that slashed prices because they'd cut out the middleman, Merv's asking price for ID would likely be a relative bargain—it had to be, Gordyn calculated—because of John D's complete lack of involvement.

Two obstacles made him sweat. He'd have to work up the nerve to ask. And posing the question, he believed, turned a few simple words into a Conspiracy to Commit a Criminal Act.

And before that step into the dark side, he needed to ascertain the truth: just as the rumoured resting place of Chester's mummified mother floated far nearer to fantasy than fact, Merv's reputation as a source for ID may have stemmed from the coincidence of running a store whose stock looked hardcore (waterbeds, sheepskin rugs) and illicit (black lights, pipes, Rush): guilt by association.

Without Merv, though, they'd have to fork over money to a rocker at school with a gossipy mouth. In that case, Gordyn would rather give up altogether.

Déviation: Harmony

Even though once upon a time he'd caved to pressure and agreed to make an effort, Gordyn could admit that his opinions about the Barbershop Harmony Society had lurched drunkenly from the get-go. The weekend gatherings organized under the Society's firm if benevolent rules (which under certain light looked fascist, Gordyn thought, a benevolent dictatorship) felt constricting enough already. Worse, the endless quest for "Let's track down that darned overtone, gentlemen. From the top, 1 and 2 and 3—," that holiest of grails, edged him nearer to insanity.

He reported these facts to Dee. Her dull parallel experiences with their mother meandered from a placid stream of easy listening radio tunes before and after torturous *Canadian* TV to pulverizing crackers with a rolling pin for next week's casseroles #1 and #2 while listening to reminiscences about girlhood crushes and huge family picnics in Quebec. Moping, Dee stared out from shut windows and wished for a pet—something high-strung and requiring long walks, preferably.

Intellectually, Gordyn saw the sound reasoning of events reserved for fathers and sons. He admitted too, the choice could have been worse. Like Jay's dad, his might assume thrilled, bellowing attendance at the rank air—BO, popcorn, and snuck booze, reportedly—of pro-wrestling matches. Or, debate-worthy and fierce dedication to idiotic ring heroes named Mr. X and André the Giant. Or, Edmund could similarly expect eternal low-wattage bouts spent in grimy striped coveralls while stuck beneath a car on jacks in an unheated garage. And see his face register signs of deep caring about the manly arts of eyeballing spark plug corrosion and oil viscosity.

Selling the surefire barbershop quartet idea, Edmund had tousled Gordyn's hair (prompting corrective mirror time shortly after). He lured him with the inevitability of trips to fancy hotel banquet rooms in historic Philadelphia and sun-dappled Sacramento. He'd repeated "We'll have a blast, just you wait and see" with an air crash prayer's desperation. That last promise proved exactly halfway correct. The former anchor baritone of an army barracks quartet, Edmund returned to the stage with unabashed gusto, eating up the attention, Gordyn's mother commented, like an elephant with peanuts.

Two years and seven months later, the upcoming events—definite anti-blasts now—loomed greyly, ominous as mushroom clouds. Blind to his son's heels-dug body language, or simply ignoring it, Edmund charged headlong into literally harmonious crowds, visibly eager for trial runs of fresh jokes he'd scooped up at the office and revved to propose catchier arrangements for standards.

They'd made it as far away as a plum-curtained stage in a high school gymnasium on the outskirts of exotic Spokane, Washington, Gordyn noted sourly, the Versailles of eastern Washington.

Earlier, Gordyn had predicted that Edmund's enthusiasm would turn out to be a phase. Over and again, he felt annoyed by that paltry, flawed intuition. Instead of a showdown he continued to go along, never not straggling. Sooner or later his father would grow weary of his captive son's clearly signalled acts of going through the motions and giving not one breath more.

Permanent authentic smiles cemented on, gleeful Evergreen District fathers, visiting from as south as Oregon, strutted and yukked in escalation, saying "Right as rain," "Smooth as silk," and "Fine as frog's hair" as they adjusted velvet bow or string ties and twisting waxed moustaches (real and mimed varieties). They threw in "23 skidoo" alongside hearty backslaps whenever possible, as though they breathed in the Edenic air that had circulated before the invention of mustard gas and trench warfare, when everyone exclaimed, "Golly gee whiz, what a humdinger!" whenever one of those bicycles with an enormous spoked wheel wobbled by.

Surveying the rooms coldly, Gordyn thought that bygone became bygone for a reason. Each and every one of them took strides away from the past each and every day, so why pretend otherwise? "Knucklehead," he'd hear, sure that none of the men used that one at home. "'Rapscallion'?" he'd hiss. "Yeah, right, dipshits." He yearned to spray "Wake Up, You Fuckers" on walls using black paint.

The sons, meanwhile—of two unequal-sized camps: dutiful but sullen and watchful for cigarette-sneaking opportunities, or chirpy chips off the ol' block—milled around perimeters until instructions boomed from one of the handful of regional bigwigs. The Big Cheese would whip out a brass kazoo and declare they ought to all clear their throats and warm up with "Wait 'til the Sun Shines, Nellie" before the actual competitive harmonizing hummed into buzzing life. "Gentlemen, start your engines," and another round of yuks echoed.

Alone on washroom breaks, Gordyn would sense his father's need for a renewed display of mooing enthusiasm. He'd stub out the hour's one pleasure and blow smoke out any window he could crack open. "Fiddlesticks," he'd mutter, on a roll, and dawdle a few extra minutes. "I'll skedaddle a while, crocodile." Activity in rooms with toilets was sacrosanct to Edmund. He'd never ask.

Even ad libitum, the true love of barbershopping that had once sparked Gordyn's sense of wonder, gradually tarnished due to continued exposure. Returning on Saturday nights, and sometimes Sundays, he'd crumple the Delphine-sewn green and white striped vest at the bottom of his closet. But like a magical fairy tale object its reconstituted form—laundered, ironed, folded into a perfect square—appeared in a T-shirt drawer at the dawn of every barbershop weekend.

His mother made no secret that she appreciated the father-son hobby slot. More to the point, Gordyn suspected, she relished the serene, joke-free household of their occasional days away.

Everyone grumbled about The Chords of Damocles, a weak, nonsensical pun of a quartet name, but since a previous generation had voted it in an abrupt change seemed tantamount to an insult, a back rudely turned on glorious history. And if nothing else, barbershoppers bowed deeply at tradition, or one wholesome strand of it at least.

On nights before the other classic warm-up number, "Hello, My Baby," launched in wolfish croons that bounced around the hall, the painfully distended "rag time doll" of an otherwise unremembered dream woke Gordyn before sunrise. At the twice-yearly meet-and-greets with perfumed clusters of Sweet Adelines in billowy translucent pastels and churchy white stockings, childhood complaints about a sudden fever or catching a bug sprouted on Gordyn's tongue.

Oblivious, his father pushed him toward girls, pointing right at one or another he'd deem "a beaut." And as Gordyn got older Edmund added "Old enough to bleed, old enough to butcher" in a husky, hopeful whisper.

Gordyn always said "Cute outfit" in a clipped voice that implied the spite-full opposite. "Did your grandmother sew that at home?" He absorbed details with Mr. Blackwell precision—constellations of white cotton eyelet, a bubble bath froth of lace trim, satin ribboning from the More is More School. He regretted the girls' dismay, but couldn't resist; any shame evaporated quickly.

By mid-Grade 11 Gordyn felt certain that if he spotted one more copy of the Norman Rockwell poster of men harmonizing with sharply parted oil slick hair and comically high-waisted pants, he'd heave. He embraced the dramatic scenario of going postal or transforming into a mad, crashing china shop bull, foreseeing his father's embarrassed expression and beet-cheeked vows to never return. As an idea, raving lunacy had its uses.

Edmund, now on the Evergreen executive, hoped to leave his mark and bring the group's name up to date. West Coast Express, he offered (with sincere if tentative alternates: Vest, Left, Best), but everyone thought it reminded them of a passenger train.

Beyond tuned Society ears, Gordyn recommended The Dapper Hams, and said as much whenever the topic arose. His father wondered aloud how someone so young could get so cynical. The hurt expression guilted Gordyn into screwing on a smile and tilting his neck and aligning with the lonesome, moon-worshipping wails of the rest.

Déviation: Last Words

"Do you know what a hard on is?"

Em studied her white tube socks, which sagged and belonged to Jay technically.

Jay stared through the living room's sheers—drawn shut, as dictated by the Law of Décor. Cold rain splattered on the glass.

Stepmom #1's question sounded tricky, with every possible answer too revealing. How much biology should a girl going into Grade 8 have under her belt? How much experience? What would "Well, duh" for an answer imply about a boy eleven months her senior?

Besides, Stepmom #1's tone clearly indicated a starting point. Tanned and fully made up even now, the woman didn't have a dreamy bone in her body. No philosopher, she'd never ask a spacey, open-ended query along the lines of "Do you think we're alone in the universe?" Her occasional questions to them always led to somewhere concrete.

The woman had never spoken to them so personally. Mostly, she seemed indifferent to their presence altogether: she had her rooms, they had theirs, and when their bodies happened to intersect at meals they exchanged polite sentences. Breaking composure for another woman's moody kids? Not likely. Based on the evidence, she reserved her strongest passion for combining dresses (never jeans), jewelry, and makeup for showstopper looks.

While Joey had gone on a drive—a habit he'd grown addicted to in the past month—Stepmom #1 had called upstairs and told them to park themselves by the stereo and wait till she showed up. Nervous with anticipation they'd chosen the paired crushed velvet arm chairs at a right angle from the matching chesterfield. Normally reserved for guests, the living room glowed in vivid shades of green.

Stepmom #1 chose against sitting. She paced in heels instead, sharply dressed and in gleaming marine eye makeup, black-dyed hair an expertly backcombed dome, as though completely ready at two in the afternoon for a fancy dinner out.

With rubbed hands and mumbled phrases, Stepmom #1 crept up to her topic: "my two cents," "lying bastard," "two sides to every story."

Their dad had warned Jay and Em of the end of the woman's reign at Best Rd. With the divorce she'd vanish as simply as she'd appeared four years earlier, a situation of plusses and minuses.

After all the arguments and silences and gunned engines and slammed doors and loud whispering and trips to the downstairs bar for refills, there'd be the comfort of quiet. They'd have to pick up the slack, though, and who knew *what* he'd drag home next. Or how soon. His talent lay with selecting cantaloupes, not stepmothers.

Back and forth for a minute before stopping to study their faces with her ringed hands resting, model-like, on a proud wasp waist, Stepmom #1 related a straightforward account to them, "a typical episode," she sighed, set just two months earlier.

After the embarrassing question, she watched their evasive faces for a moment before a cocked brow and, "Hmm, well, I'll bet that you have an inkling."

The question mattered because her tale of an ordinary evening out with company soured at an unwelcome surprise—freshened drinks in hand, she'd approached the rec room and caught her soon-to-be ex-husband with Lorraine, his best friend's wife. Without a care in the world and in her own home Lorraine ran her hand—a ringed left hand, Stepmom #1 made sure to underline the fact, as though that gold and diamond band had broken her resilient but ultimately fallible camel's back—up his thigh, tugged down his zipper, and fished around inside. "Going at it like a pair of complete fiends," she reported in a calm voice. "Well, anyone could see how much he appreciated the attention. He always does."

"Oh." Jay and Em could think of no other words. How did she expect them the react? "Thank you" made no sense. Ditto for "Go on, please." And pleading for her to give the overgrown adolescent the benefit of a doubt and a second chance meant only a recipe for a wider disaster area.

"Anyhow. What's done is done. Before leaving I just wanted to explain things from my perspective. You deserve the truth. In years to come, it might come in handy."

Jay couldn't grasp the story ever holding value. "Okay, thanks." He pushed himself from the chair, escape the only goal. "I have to finish a Socials report." He made a c'mere gesture to his seated sister. "If you want to colour the title page, Em, you can."

She smiled, knowing he'd already finished the writing and drawn a title page using a scarlet pencil crayon. "Okay."

Now that the information had been let loose, the real concern formed around where to file it. At the moment, "Nowhere" appeared to be the single answer—a note crumpled and tossed in the garbage can. But dissecting the gruesome details in secret in his room felt urgent and wise. They'd sat on that very couch while Stepmom #1 and Lorraine played pool.

When their father got home he yelled "Pizza?" up the stairs.

At Dino's twenty minutes later, he grinned and leaned close to the hostess at the reservation stand. "Just the three of us from now on, my dear."

Jay and Em couldn't tell if the chipper tone meant victorious or fake-victorious.

NOTEBOOKS / OCTOBER

I found an instruction manual at the Ladies Aux. Coles Bongo Drum Course. (5¢!!)

Want it? If not, here's the message:
"Remember:
Study this book
Listen to Records
Practice
and you will find hours of fun as a bongo drummer."

Déviation: Routine

He worked as though that's what he'd been born for. He kidded around, pinning a "beast of burden" label on himself or making a cracked whip sound while complaining with "slavedriver" even though he appeared to delight in every undertaking, motionless for a sliver of a minute before flipping the lawn mower to file its blades sharp, adjust clips holding wheels in place. Self-appointed, *sprucing up* became an eternal full time job. In an earlier, bloodthirsty era he'd have schemed for an empire that spread with the ease of oil in a hot frying pan.

And without what added up to a dawn to dusk schedule of chores he paced, seeming to lose solidity with each passing hour. Between bread and butter repair jobs in the city and three-month contracts in the sticks, he wandered "the acreage," surveilling its contours for invaders—dandelions, mole hills, saplings—and dreaming up projects. A rock wall extension. A gazebo. A cord of fireplace wood re-stacked tightly. Gunning it to the property's far edge at the recently stained and erected back fence, he'd stare back at the house as if willing paint to buckle or fade, eaves to clog with leaves, or cedar shakes to age, split, and tumble to the ground. With trees dropping leaves in October, Em and Jay quipped, he practically slept with a rake and wheelbarrow.

Stability and order prevailing, snap inspections fired him up: had debris clogged the driveway drain, an exposed house foundation begun to erode; could the front walkway use a sweep or the car a wax, and what about that weed situation in the ditch across the road? For him, a dose of Alaska Fish Fertilizer sprayed over gardens and shrubs presented a weekly temptation, as though he'd been orphaned at a salmon cannery and longed for the rank pungency of home.

Come a dreary wet winter, when snow dustings or slush meant not only no pesky weeds but no driveway or walkways or roof to shovel, he nested for hours in his recliner chair in the rumpus room and turned television-watching into a spectator sport, bellowing out answers or numbers and insulting contestants—"Give your head a shake, you stunned sack of shit"—during *The Price is Right* and *Let's Make a Deal.* And when no wrestling or *Donahue* or *The Edge of Night* with Monticello's vendettas, amnesiacs on the run, poisoned makeup, and loan sharks to grab his attention, he pulled out the thick world atlas, a pad, ruler, and pencils and drafted future handiwork that would top realized ideas already in his field of vision (past the swooping branches of the hated avocado tree—that had begun as Stepmom #1's toothpick-stabbed pit in a glass at the kitchen window ledge—and the stuffed porcupine, a yard sale find): a high-gloss, glass-topped coffee table made from a salvaged oak mill wheel, patio planters of inverted triple-groove porcelain insulators, and halved barrels stained the same brown as the house trim and made from scrounged then sawn barrels into which he'd earlier poured boiling water to extract amber display whiskey. With a backward neck twist he'd glimpse the pride and joy creation every visitor came to know inside out, a dry bar on wheels clad with panels of walnut pattern melamine and padded orange vinyl, all reflected in gold-veined mirror tiles that carried over from the upstairs hallway.

Outside, nature's perpetual bounty meant vigilance and taming: grass to mow, bedding plants to cull and weed, lawn edges and branches to clip. A rotation of chores inside included reviving trampled shag carpet and buffing bathroom fixtures till the chrome gleamed. That's how troops pay for room and board, he'd say in jokey seriousness.

Vacuuming countless yards of carpet too.

The architect had covered the master bedroom in inch-high with the jungle hues of a snake plant. The contrasting wallpapers in iridescent pink shot with metallic striations and white with black flocking had been the inspiration of Stepmom #1. "My first kick at the can," she'd exclaimed when taping a clothesline's worth of bright, loud, or bright and loud samples to formerly eggshell walls. Hanging from an antique gold large-link chain in the corner where pink met black: a swag lamp conversation piece in which armless Venus painted bronze stood amongst fronds of plastic greenery, caged by filaments of thick fishing line, along which ran slow thick beads of mineral oil.

Joey called changing the special bottom pad on the waterbed purchased at a head shop a two-man operation. While he struggled to lift a corner of the thick plastic bladder of warm water, the agile accomplice needed to tuck a floppy U of elastic around the amoebic form, like a game of *Twister* and putting underwear on a blubbery passed out drunk at once.

Jay didn't mind the chore so much as the unchanging banter that went with it.

After his father smoothed the quilted cover, he swatted the white polyester expanse blotted with yellow stains and boasted "Pecker tracks!" A mysterious invitation, perhaps, or a boast of conquests, the words lingered in the air.

Normally, Jay snorted and grinned to indicate that he got the joke and thought it funny. He'd look around the room with a "What's next on the to-do list?" expression meant to steer activity away from the conversation. He couldn't grasp what his father wanted. If meant as pure bragging, what was the best way to sidestep it? Or to stop the routine altogether—the same "Pecker tracks!" once a week for just one year would send him over the edge. And the invitation, if that's how Joey meant the exclamation, confused him further. Did his father really want friendly competition with a story of the same vein ("Ha, that's nothing, you should see my sheets"), in the way that guys in the locker room or hallways entertained their groups about exploits with girls that inspired bigger responses from the next guy (". . . and then her sister showed up!")?

Brisk purposeful movement, Jay hoped, would let his father register the lack of genuine enthusiasm without offending him.

Instead, he could throw it on the growing pile of interests they didn't hold in common.

Though tucked on a corner of the main floor and naturally bright because of filmy white drapes hanging across a sliding patio door, the room oozed subterranean mysteriousness, like a catacomb, Em thought, or an Egyptian burial chamber. And its contents and atmosphere seemed inseparable from the man who slept there.

Visiting it—and snooping through closets and drawers of stuff—felt natural, vital, necessary. Inevitable. Solving any mystery required hands-on investigating, after all. The room's hints at the shape of the grown up future they might eventually possess if making lousy choices and giving into every impulse proved likewise irresistible.

Inside one drawer on his side of the waterbed, Joey kept Kama Sutra powder in a squat, slightly oily canister that smelled of honey and sandalwood. Inside, a soft brush. Mesh-front and nylon-back gonch in powder blue and black and a bulbous bong with a lower compartment filled a quarter way with murky water lay atop a letter of rejection from *Playgirl* magazine.

Years before in the frontmost drawer on the opposite side, which had lately stored undershirts, they'd discovered a manila envelope of photographs stamped with "Alameda Studios, Los Angeles."

All of the shiny black and white studio portraits studied one woman, whose long hair had been pinned high in festooning coils. Legs crossed, she sat upright and serious on a striped armchair, or reclined, head tilted, on what looked to be a pile of grey pin-striped mattresses three feet high. She wore a parted waist-length veil that appeared to originate from an ornately pronged accessory stuck into the hairdo's backcombed pinnacle. The black lace tumbled over her bare shoulders and fell across her front, but opened enough so that the woman's almost-exposed boobs—B-cup, Em determined—became the first detail to catch the eye. She wore no brassiere. In the reclining photos, the woman showed off the sides of her leg (in thigh-high nylons in two pictures, with high heels in the others; she was never barefooted).

After studying the photographs they realized that the woman had to be Stepmom #1, although unknown years in the past. The six images raised questions rather than answering them.

Em decided that detective skills would uncover the truth. With harmless small talk that sounded natural and new-daughterly, not snoopy, she began in the spare room that stored the ironing board and tanning machine: "Did you ever want to be a model?" and "Have you ever lived in another country?"

"No" and "Yes," the case-closed replies, didn't encourage additional inquiries or supply juicy details they hoped for: "Yes, I took a chance and moved to southern California for two years and during that time I tried out for roles in movies and supported myself with part-time modeling and a job slinging coffee at a 24-hour place right next to the LaBrae Tar Pits."

Studying the photos' backgrounds for clues (and finding nothing worthwhile) and staring into the dark eyes that stared outward toward a camera and photographer (ditto), Em yearned to ask, "Modeling for what?" She couldn't think of any way to raise the question without sounding judgemental. *Dying of curiosity* captured her exact state of mind.

Until the unfolding of the letter, the 8 x 10s of what they called the Spanish Lady held their attention with bear strength. Unremarkable in a normal business envelope, the letter began, also usually, with Dear Mr. ______: and the date.

Short and typed, the reply thanked their father for the photographs and explained that while they contained merit, the sheer number of foxy guys sending in photographs from all over the world made the selecting process a true feat, because from the hundreds of submissions only a handful could even hope to become finalists.

They giggled and passed the page back and forth, re-reading its words hungrily. "Foxy" would not be on the top twenty list they'd use for a police sketch artist were their father to go missing.

The polite rejection made sense. Unless *Playgirl* wanted to champion a man with a beer gut, home-permed hair, and a moustache with the orange patches of a calico cat. Plus, he could be the actual dad of some of the tanned models posing inside the magazine.

As with Stepmom #1's ups and downs after Agony—a hometown without promise—and before Best Rd, the what ifs mystified them. A father who wanted to show off naked to the entirety of North America was embarrassing enough, just a notch less than someone flipping through the magazine in a drugstore and saying, "Well, well, well, take a gander at this" and passing the information. Eventually news of the magazine would reach their children, who would no doubt shoplift a copy, bring it to school, and tape up the evidence somewhere visible and requiring a ladder to take down.

A notorious parent meant bad news, unless falling into the "His dad owns the mill" category. Girls spoke of getting their period while in school and wearing white jeans as the worst possible nightmare, but having every kid see snapshot proof of a father chasing notoriety as a sex symbol by posing totally naked? Unspeakable. They wondered who'd taken the photos he'd slid into the envelope. And where and when. *Playgirl*'s office hadn't returned the snapshots, thank God. Nor had he tucked them far from prying eyes: they'd searched every drawer and shoe box, reluctant but avid.

Snooping and uncovering strange items that required explanation or interpreting conjured an image, one similar to a TV movie character: *Joey G: Portrait of a Middle-Aged Sex Fiend*. They'd divined that switching bodies with Dee and Gordyn would sink them into another kind of generation gap. Even so, unless Mr. Wallace had a shadowy personality that he cautiously locked away in the basement, they considered him—a father who made purposefully bad jokes and maybe tried a bit too hard to be closer to a kid than an adult earning barely enough money for a second-hand car—alright. He caused Gordyn embarrassment of the "Oh, Daaad, stop it!" variety, while Joey, who didn't fit into any known categories of Dad-ness, presented a forking series of challenges.

For a Halloween party midway through marriage #2 he'd worn a red and black negligee of filmy translucent nylon. He stole the spotlight from Stepmom #1, who'd picked navy trousers and kept her short hair combed boyishly flat. She mentioned *Cabaret.*

He didn't say where he'd found the outfit—the fit looked snug but roomy enough to not have come from his wife's closet—and that mystery gave them the least discomfort. Beneath that swirling sheath of bedroom fabric he'd opted for panties. Skimpy lace ones. He'd modeled the costume in the living room, their eyes taking in the tangerine lipstick and rouge. A promise: "The wig comes later." The chandelier earrings stood out as well, especially since they competed with longish sideburns and a bandit-style moustache (he'd begun the change to winter-length hair that month). Visible depending on his movement and the cast of light, the coiled snail bulge of his privates stuffed inside too little fabric threatened to burst free; and as he pirouetted in a mince they saw the rear of the panties had been swallowed inside the crack.

He'd stuck with his own dress shoes, of white patent leather.

Em's thoughts had skipped to Deb S that night. Three doors down, Em knew she fumed in her bedroom (she called to keep Em up to date about every *outrage* visited on her by devout parents), waiting for a father-dictated ride to the basement of the Kingdom Hall for a special service. Not for the first time, she'd asked her father for permission to dress up only to be told that Halloween was a pagan feast passing itself off, devilishly, as harmless fun. With the annual affront to the one true God and the sanctity of the family's untainted beliefs, their burden and only duty was to turn righteous backs on the unholiness and accept cleaning up egg shells and streaks of dried yolk the next morning as proof of the sinful world in their very midst. And their exalted place within it. With the resignation of martyrs.

From experience Em expected to hear her friend bawl with frustration and anger at the total unfairness (her ATF accusation by far) on the path to school on Monday, resolving by the school grounds that on the very day she turned 18, she planned to get pregnant with the nearest rocker, shack up with a lez, smoke, drink, and gamble without a break for four months straight, have an abortion, and then pitch the blue-grey foetus at her father's front door on October 31.

Em had imagined listening and laughing, adding poetic twists to Deb's complicated revenge scheme. Much of her attentiveness would be designed to keep Deb from probing closely into her own Halloween night. With a psychic's talent Deb could tell when Em told half-truths and outright lies. If Em said, "Nothing much," it'd be two minutes at most before she was describing her father's anatomy beneath the nearly see-through nightie.

Jay had learned from TV and from other kids that education behind closed doors about anatomy and babies was considered an important if awkward component of parenting. Even their JW neighbours, whose parents gave their daughters notes to excuse them from the Family Health classes, must have offered their daughters a glimpse: say unto, lay with, beget, fruitful, multiply.

Jay had listened intently to Em after she'd been invited to sit with Stepmom #1 as she baked poolside while swabbed in cocoanut oil. The closed-eyed lecture—Stepmom #1 dedicated to her tan in the serious way that Gordyn and Dee's mom followed the news—mentioned love in a snorted sigh, like an incomprehensibly mystical gravitational pull that began and ended everything. But she'd dwelled at such length on unplanned pregnancy, VD, and a destroyed and never-resurrected-again reputation that love began to resemble a trap, the kind in the forest that was a deep hole filled with carved spike-ended stakes and covered over so that it struck prey as both harmless and inviting. But the very moment the unsuspecting creature tumbled in turned out to be a rip-off, the last it drew breath.

To illustrate an already clear point, Em had theatrically relayed "the upshot" at the window overlooking the driveway where a Venus Flytrap grew on the sill. She grabbed a fly by its wing and pressed the buzzing creature into the fringed trap. (The plant died, from too much handling Stepmother #1 claimed in the kitchen before throwing its slumped form into the garbage: no one could resist touching and feeding it.) As with the small town girl getting off at the bus station in downtown Los Angeles and being met by a man in a fancy plumed hat and a fur coat, the trick—apparently—was to be wary: know that nobody offers you something in exchange for nothing and that a man's promise of care, guidance, and protection comes with a heart-stopping price. So with love. When the boy says, "You know I love you," the wise girl must ask "What is the nature of the trap?" or "If I step into it, what next?"

As an instruction, "Be careful!" presented no obstacle; anyone could understand it.

And while Jay's education contained elements of caution, he discovered other layers, pieces he couldn't put together. From his father he'd learned that that women could be frigid, as well as disease-carrying prostitutes, a kind of black market situation that men felt drawn to while knowing that the same principles from regular commerce didn't apply. No policy for returning broken or damaged goods existed, no writing a letter to the Better Business Bureau to complain of shoddy service.

He learned that men talked incessantly about—and were *supposed to* talk about—women's gajungas, the bigger the better, and to read, as a math wiz might, the degrees of women's wiggles and the corresponding significance, from frigid and proper to willing and trampy. Jay had followed his father's gaze as he braked, eyes agog and appreciative, in a parking lot or right on main street, and made the proper throaty noises and hubba-hubba eyebrow movements when his dad pointed, elbowed, or whistled, and enthused "Take a look at that pair!"

He understood initiation rites from movies and TV shows about frat houses and teams, and saw, dimly to start, that his father was undertaking three performances at once. The first showed him being himself as he must be with other men. The next served as education: just as raccoons and bears taught their young how to climb a tree and sniff out a meal, his father was showing him how to behave, passing the torch, the wisdom of the ages. Lastly, in addition to setting himself up as a role model, he offered an invitation. This last part confused Jay, because it hinted at Jay "wetting his wick," as his dad liked to say, in a cathouse as the end point, with him in one room and Joey next door (or, possibly, on the same bed). Replying with "Thanks for the invitation" and

"I'm honoured to accept" seemed both easy and obvious. But what if he didn't accept? Consequences abounded. When striding away from the frat house or the team of yahoos, the hero faced a mazy path of opportunities: a different frat, sharing a ramshackle house with misfits, a bachelor apartment; badminton, long-distance running, curling, or no sport at all.

And if he played along? There must be a word for joining a group in which you didn't belong. What kind a person did so, and why?

VENTURE: THRIFT / SEPTEMBER – OCTOBER

Cityward busses with a stop at Bottlesburg lurched away from the Bend on a bewildering schedule. Departures changed from day to day but always appeared convenient to dawn-rising retirees and the unemployed with nothing to do on mid-afternoons. Worse, each dusty steel rig made roadside and unincorporated village pitstops so often that bicycling seemed as fast.

From experience Dee and Em knew the cavernous rear of the bus—with the iffy folding door and chemical toilet fumes—attracted losers in faded jean jackets shingled with rock band patches. They sprawled beneath green-tinted windows, sneaking smokes and either messing around with their drop-out girlfriends or offering to share the row with phony smiling eyes and generosity, upturned hand resting lazily on the adjacent seat, cobra dangerous.

The front third looked as bright and wholesome as a church picnic. But surface benevolence disguised Old Testament wrath: in the first eight steps along the narrow aisle, hatted old vultures understood eye contact as an invitation to seethe about high prices and loose morals, and the fact that, once upon a time, the country hadn't been going straight to hell in a hand basket. And young people had remembered manners.

If you dared mention slavery or resorting to boot soup in brutal winters or the Final Solution, they'd conjure a witchy stare and invite the daring so-and-so to view herself as yet another symbol of modern degeneracy.

Sometimes, the biddies smiled, said "Hello, dear," slipped you a *Watchtower*, and asked if you'd prepared your soul for the Kingdom of Heaven's arrival, predicted by unknown calculations to occur any day soon. They required no peep of an answer because their eyes could fathom the only possible honest answer with the least glance: No.

Even middle ground, the emptiest rows between the two tribes, didn't guarantee the safety of isolated anonymity. On the bus weirdos ruled.

The guys in driver's seats—gruff and heavyset or as bug-eyed and reedy as Mr. Furley—acted like prison guards who'd witnessed too much over a career of shifts and lost faith that anyone possessed goodwill, innocence, or a friendliness free of ulterior motives. Expressing general contempt for their fares, they appeared to rank passenger safety and comfort several notches below collecting pay cheques and adding to roadkill. The drivers managed to keep arrivals and departures on time, at least.

By process of elimination, hitchhiking, strictly forbidden and an open invitation to harm (from kindly souls whose good samaritan offers masked Charles Manson lunacy, or, if discovered, from distraught but apoplectic parents), raced forward as the next best option.

After a tragic scouring of the Bend's Hospital Auxiliary shop—souvenir day dresses with Hawaiian prints, sock monkeys, mismatched dinner plates, and, in the display case, a thick white illustrated bible wedged between tiered china serving dishes—Dee and Em talked over potential sources for the band's statement look. Other than garage sales and their parents' closets, rummaging through the remaining used goods shops in town, the Lost and Found box by the school counsellor's office, and Field's had revealed only tackiness and possibilities even too lame for Halloween.

From back seats during family outings Em and Dee had both noticed a Salvation Army and a St. Vincent de Paul in Bottlesburg. Less than an hour downriver, the town could be sneakily visited in an afternoon.

Paired together on the road, they envisioned a united front as a double luck charm, assuring them of rides and protection from drivers with evil motives.

They'd pretend to be sisters.

The first driver—a middle-aged housewife in a two-toned Thunderbird—took them as far as Whonnock, a blip scarcely ten minutes east. Voice tightening and volume mounting, the mother of two posed a genial question—"Where are you two gals heading on such a fine day?"—before ragging on them about "flirting with disaster," "paying the piper," and "breaking your mother's heart." Although zooming down a narrow two-lane highway rumbling with logging trucks, the woman turned around frequently, firm in the conviction that laser eye contact prevented any listener from forgetting her wisdom, or, heaven forbid, spacing out.

Em explained they were visiting their ailing grandmother, and when that news didn't shut down the woman's lecturing about sickos, foolishness, and danger—as though orcs waited as they trudged across the Plateau of Gorgoroth—Dee requested, sternly, an immediate drop off. In the middle of nowhere—smelling burnt wood and cedar chips and seeing only trucks and hillsides where morning glory snaked through heaving blackberry vines still abuzz with bees—they scrapped the rest of the trip. Bottlesburg and band ensembles could wait.

Wary of an impending return-trip lecture, they single-filed on a dusty rut along the highway. Em kicked at annoying loose stones and the ugly resilience of plantain weed.

Life taught valuable lessons, supposedly, and from this episode they pieced together that friendliness could be a ploy and women drivers picking up hitchhikers had an axe to grind, most likely.

They didn't learn that grown ups can never resist a lecture; any child easily comprehended that keeper by the second grade.

For the next week, they vowed, key changes would include looking older, worldlier, and Marine Corps capable for fending off any and all threats. Sunglasses too; they'd help. With peals of laughter they discarded Em's suggestion for stuffed bras.

Since taller and outgoing Dee should, they thought, take charge. Seasons of clerical duties had educated Dee: "I know how to handle them, trust me."

They bought gum in Whonnock's only corner store. And an elderly man braked mere seconds after retracted thumbs shyly reached out. When they climbed onto the truck's bench, he said, "Make yourselves comfortable" and "I'm going as far as Agony." No lecture, no questions, and no sudden detour down a sinister dirt road where fishermen would later find their rat- and coyote-gnawed bodies dumped in a culvert. Happy for company he hummed, wrestling with and cursing a tricky stick shift whose torn rubber cover gave passengers a view of the blacktop.

They chimed "Thanks, mister" at the Legion.

"What comes around goes around, right?" he replied, glad for a fateful encounter on the horizon, tables turned and them in the driver's seat.

Origin Story: 1

Although Gordyn and Jay could thank Mr. G for the officially recognized account of their meeting, neither spoke any word to the man except answers (that drew grudging approval with "Correct" or dismissive ire with "Anyone else?") and "Thank you, sir," the phrase demanded for returned quizzes—all the while remembering the man's stern caveat, "And that's all."

Inattentiveness, sarcasm, lippiness, indifference, ignorance, assumptions, attitude, muttered criticisms, and thoughtless gibberish from students earned them a wrath that never subsided from an alleged math whiz with elephantine recall. "'In your case an 'educated guess,'" he'd mimic in a disdainful tone, "is a contradiction in terms."

After classes, naturally, and beyond the door frame borders of the POW camp in room 204, the mood changed for every kid. Recipients of teacher publicized C- grades or worse, visible-from-space red felt pen question mark/exclamation point combos, and his withering blackhearted attention, then, and only then, dared to posture and lash out—"balding Hitler," "Aryan asshole," "midget tyrant," and the like—in the surging crowds of bodies stampeding from one class to the next, grateful for the safety cushion of hiding in plain sight.

Giving guff in the form of outspoken disagreement, insolence, or backstabbing by reporting their teacher's militance to the boys or girls counselor meant promises of instant transference to a dead-end remedial class or a classroom existence of "living hell," which typically translated into a fusillade of uncomfortable questions that sabotaged the foe's rise—"What do *you* think?" "Are you *sure*?" "What makes you say *that*?" "Might this 'feeling' have any basis in, say, a formula the rest of the class has managed to learn through discipline and hard work?"

Mr. G was not, he announced at predictable intervals, interested in their "so-called personal lives," or there to "win a popularity contest," or paid to illustrate the usefulness of geometry in daily life, which had lately become a fashion. He aimed for students to master principles in the abstract. And right on schedule.

In the first days of class, he'd repeated, "I'm from the 'my house, my rules' school of thought" and "I stick to my guns." Unsurprisingly, the man kept his word.

If it hadn't been for the geometry teacher's surly impatience with the epidemic of whispering, and the snuck conversations of girls in particular, Sharon K and Tracy F would not have faced the embarrassment of realizing that instruction had ceased altogether for their benefit and the entire class encouraged by teacher dagger-vision to pay scientific attention to the cross-aisle faint words the girls had imagined as beneath notice.

Pulling back from an exchange about weekend plans, Sharon K and Tracy F stopped to find everyone staring at them, expressions set at Rabid Mirth (practically everyone) or Infinite Annoyance (keeners in the front row; Mr. G).

Following five seconds of high-voltage silence, Mr. G—who sat stiffly behind his desk, hands clasped in prayer formation, still as a missile—sighed. The teacher refused to raise his voice: "After those last test scores, young ladies, I imagine your parents will be anything but pleased with a note—yet another—outlining this continued reluctance to apply yourselves."To underscore the adult disappointment, he lifted his left hand high and then dropped it, index finger first, the dive bombing an animated chart of their perilous decline and an ominous indicator of twin futures as townie morons barely able to count coins.

Raising himself with dramatic parental weariness, Mr. G frowned with irritation, swung his head slowly, and surveyed the room with the acute eyes of a vulture. "You there," he pointed at Gordon's seat midway along the window row, "switch."

"That corner desk there"—behind Jay's—"that looks about right for you, wouldn't you say?"

Perceiving the question as rhetorical, Gordon closed his notebook and moved.

As flush-cheeked Sharon K and Tracy F grabbed their books and purse straps, the entire class soaked up the unfolding episode, wondering if one of the up and coming girls to be reckoned with had the nerve to snub or cross the fearsome dictator. But no: they'd save the public performance of outrage and badmouthing for their friends later, followed by promises and threats about an egged house or a rock through a windshield, criminal acts they'd encourage their boyfriends to commit in exchange for a flash of bra or front seat groping.

At the bell the boys hurried for the exit and exchanged words: "Good show" from Jay; from Gordon an uncompleted witticism, "If Tracy were any more stupid she'd—."

They both admired Sharon for showily applying lipstick and using her powder compact's mirror and pointedly not paying attention when Mr. G returned to the favourite pet topic number two, axiomatic method (the impossible advances of the ancient pyramid builders, which left him flabbergasted, claimed the prime spot).

The ongoing silent quarrel entertained the entire class, and later, the rest of the school.

Her *my natural beauty and perky charisma will take me places your circles and triangles and equations can't imagine* easily vanquished *Missy, you'll go nowhere fast*, the teacher's unswerving prophecy.

VENTURE: STASH / OCTOBER

Jay didn't have to search far before locating a stash.

As per usual, he thought, the mall's money men had bought a big green chunk of rolling cow pasture at the edge of a subdivision and hired a crew to scrape it flat with machines. The new mall's builders had focussed on a lure to snap up shoppers who'd otherwise drive to their old favourite. While a gargantuan expanse of paint-striped parking lot and brand name shops might do the trick, the long airy passageway with stained glass panels and a pitched cedar plank ceiling—instantly familiar to anyone who'd ever looked up while choosing a pew—spelled awed captivation. And with that splendour just a few paces from four quadrants of convenient asphalt, the planners could afford to neglect the property's edges. Soon enough they'd plant shrubs and sprinkle gravel there.

For the plan to succeed Jay needed the stash. Wandering through department stores with a gym bag or its cousin had to be a dead giveaway. If it wasn't, it should be. He knew about store detectives; everyone did. His dad called them "house dicks." Their fearsome power came from anonymous invisibility and sudden visibility and also from the fact that they'd been trained (another mystery: in X ways by X experts in X locations) to pick out lowlife shoplifters from the crowd of upstanding browsers and loyal customers.

Jay, who wouldn't mind that job, pictured himself following lurkers, the trench-coated, tight packs of whispering teens, sunglass wearers, the shifty-eyed, and regulars who haunted aisles but never bought a thing. But aside from obvious suspects, what facial tics or clothing choices tipped off these sly employees? What cast of eye? Surely any shoplifter with half a brain would clue in to the trouble nervous perspiration and a huge shopping bag caused and correct those flaws. With luck his disguise—in a white T-shirt straight from a drawer and a tobacco cord jacket with STP and STOP patches instead of his soft faded Lee—as a Clean Cut Youth who made actual purchases would throw them off his dirty scent.

He carried a floppy old army backpack on his first trip and found a dusty neglected area of juniper shrubs nearer to the mall than the bus depot. He'd store stolen items there; the sage green fabric blended in perfectly.

Later, once he'd stuffed a pocket, sock, or an underwear gap with whatever he swiped, he'd evacuate the premises, walking in casual zigzags and fake-browsing while keeping eyes peeled for any figures swooping in. A few steps past the exit? Home free. In school he'd heard that a law prevented store detectives from grabbing any suspect who'd made it ten feet outside the premises. At 10.1 feet, the law ruled that these agents reconverted to ordinary powerless citizens. For any worst case situation he counted on that as a true fact.

Crossing the lot, he wished for a pen. He'd try to remember his latest band name inspiration, The Statistics, and promote its prize-taking coolness before the gang's next meeting.

For trip #1 Jay strolled around thinking *reconnaissance* and *you're only as guilty as you seem*. With put on absentmindedness he peered behind glass cases for lockless access; he noted areas where clerks congregated. Instead of sweaters, shirts, and knick knacks, he required goods that he could easily unload. A watch. Jewelry. Swiss pens. Figurines. He'd picked up this idea from cop shows.

Unguarded contents of cash register drawers: that would really be something. But the complicated how-to scams—fire alarm, mannequin display sabotage, a tipped wheelchair-bound granny requiring medical help—and the potential for complete disaster kept that hope earthbound. He'd have better luck turning cartwheels on a lake.

Déviation: Shed

In the rumbling, tremor-prone weeks that followed the afternoon departure of Stepmom #1 and her bronze four-door, Joey moped in the city after work.

If talkative once home he'd say, "I stopped for a few." He'd ask about dinner and hint that sitting at the dining room table while he ate would be a wise gesture toward the man who kept clothes on their backs.

Slamming the convertible's door on other evenings, he'd kick off boots and woolen socks outside, and not bother to ask about or look for the covered plate in the oven. After changing into Blue, a ratty pet sweatshirt Jay and Em had rechristened Bad Mood, he mixed a Manhattan, parked on the recliner, and stonily clicked through channels. Now and then he'd drag his slippered feet from the rec room bar to the couch upstairs and listen to the Freddy Fender record with weepy songs about wasted days and teardrops falling while studying his matador painting. Handling these grizzly routines meant tiptoeing, stealthy transparency until called upon.

Jay had to agree with Em's impatient assessment: "It's not like he got dumped at the altar." Some self-pity just looked pathetic, a toddler's tantrum over its own mess.

On the Saturday morning that Em and then Jay peered down from the kitchen as a quarrel of hand gestures with the new neighbour about the man's baffling unwillingness to mow the lawn as far as the common property line escalated into mutual shoving and two stunning punches to the slouch's defeated and shocked face, Joey requested Jay's help with assembling the garden shed. The boxed aluminum parts of the catalogue purchase currently waited at the foot of the driveway.

"The less said about that incident, the better," he warned. "You can't solve every problem with $2 words, Berm." Joey's little joke: book and worm squashed together into a nickname.

Still tearing open the cardboard they'd dragged into the back yard, Joey grumbled that the trouble had really started with *her*—Stepmom #1's actual name stricken from the history books, *verboten*—D and C way back when. "A Dusting and Cleaning procedure, right," he added for clarification while making a vague circular gesture in the crotch area. Jay uselessly searched his memories for a major blow up during a chore weekend. "I met that frozen bitch in Agony. What else is there to say?"

Jay guessed that whatever his opinions on the subject might be, Joey didn't care for them. The conversation flowed one way only. Jay widened his eyes to convey deep interest. That trick worked equally well for teacher finger-shaking lectures and grey-hair reminiscences.

Joey's official line, "It was time to move on, kids," contained a second part, for Jay's benefit only, that hinged on guy-to-guy universal truths—"frigid as a nun" and "a man has needs"—that rendered a fuller explanation pointless and the question of duty or vows or responsibility closed. He let it slip as well that wife #2 had moved to Los Angeles with a short-lived dream of becoming an actress, only to wind up "being an escort that called herself a model." He'd known about this wrong turn when he married her, and felt, as a result, that she should have cut him some slack with Lorraine, she of the married-but-willing wandering hand and foolish husband who thought a gold and half-carat trinket could tame the vixen's wild side.

At "Fucking settlement got rid of her for good, let's hope," Jay wondered about the eventual target for the pent-up rabidity. Other than the obvious, maybe he'd punch a tree trunk, break rocks with a sledge hammer.

Bored and listening to "You hold 'er, I'll screw 'er" for the umteenth time as he positioned a dismal fraction of the shed's exhausting supply of bolts, nuts, and screws in front of his father's tool-clasping hand, Jay couldn't wait to tell Em the LA business. When Joey brightened and moved on to a survey of better news—that the shitbox Volaré of Stepmom #1 no longer dripped oil all over the driveway and her ridiculous hairspray bills had come to an end—Jay scarcely listened.

Calculating the hours needed for the shed's assembly felt harder than those baffling Arithmetic questions about same-track trains and varying speeds and looming collisions. He could bring a practical example to class—

Father A is badmouthing Ex-Wife 1 at a rate of 3 insults per minute.

Shed X contains 42 sharp-edged, pressed aluminum panels that require 252 screws and 24 nuts and bolts to assemble.

Each panel requires 6 screws that take Father A 7 minutes to properly insert.

How many insults will Son B hear before he is free to tell Sister C about Ex-Wife 1's former occupation?

NOTEBOOKS / NOVEMBER

Deviation: DELINQUENCY

With the blunt factuality of a bank robber dangling from a scaffold noose, or a thief in forced retirement begging at a Third World marketplace with a hand severed neatly at the wrist, Bend High students understood the potential cost of sticky fingers. Even with details sketchy or cut altogether and replaced with a realistic fiction, a legendary Grade 8 incident in what would be Gordyn and Jay's graduating class passed from mouth to ear to mouth with feverish rapidity, the underlying lesson missed by no one.

In Science, a weaselly straight Cs kid, a practical joker (student view) and troublemaker (in teachers' books) hadn't listened so much as watched. Enraptured.

Intoning "Stay back, please" and squeezing tongs with a surgical caution, goggled Mr. Mc had extracted a volatile cube of glistening material—lithium, sodium, or potassium, the identity changed with each telling—stored high on a metal shelf inside a lidded glass jar of *Paraffinum subliquidum*, a term introduced for no reason except quizzes. Metallic with cheddar-like density, the substance could also be sliced, coming away with cold butter's fractured curl. And it ignited with a toxic flare—nature's own dynamite stick fuse—once the viscous coating slipped away.

Not yet a school-wide scandal, the boy could see nothing except an invitation, a chance for an excellent, reputation-cementing prank. During the hubbub at the bell (or sneaking back during lunch hour, or during a gym assembly possibly: specifics didn't matter since the result always turned out the same), he reached into the glass and lodged a chunk in the front pocket of his jeans. Striding the hallway in victory a minute later, the story went, the cotton fabric began to smoulder. White-hot flames—supposed eye witnesses reported—erupted. The boy screamed, ran, and stumbled, puddling into an agonized curl.

The student didn't return to classes after a lengthy hospital stay in the city. Even with skin grafts and plastic surgery his eventual crotch area, rumours swirled, looked bald and damaged, a pink Ken doll's with nothing to reveal but seared and permanent evidence of his mistake.

The boy's planned joke based on the stolen goods remained an unsolved mystery.

Hardly a rarity, shoplifting began as a dare or whim and sometimes grew.

The first time she'd gotten caught, Em told the gang when her turn rolled around, Mrs. Kim hadn't followed the steps Em had learned to expect.

At the gang's customary table, Em looked around for Mrs. Kwong, who might, she guessed, play cards with the Kims or show up for lunch with them after church service.

Everyone in elementary school had the built-in cautionary tale memorized by heart because a friend or a sister or a cousin had related the first- or secondhand experience, a horror story: the store owner clutches the sinful wrist with vise strength, hustles the exposed criminal to a back office or storeroom while spitting out every cuss word in the land, and makes the culprit sweat there as he calls the police; disgusted and sad, the men in uniform extend the process of punishment and rehabilitation by parading the thief, now the Guilty Party and a natural target for any and all scorn, through the mall or along the sidewalk to their car as merciless onlookers comment about the decline of civilization or teaching a lesson the scum won't soon forget, and, eternal minutes later, dial the loser's mom from the station as the living joke—propped in an uncomfortable wooden chair, perhaps, or sequestered zoo-like in a barred cell—weathers the uniforms' glares and slow, disappointed head shakes and deep, what-is-this-world-coming-to? sighs. The public humiliation picks up speed once two parents, united by demonic fury, show up either ballistic with anger ("Let 'em rot there as far as I'm concerned, that's no child of mine"), or suffering quietly from tearful guilt by association and unspoken accusations of bad parenting skills or, tsk tsk, trouble at home. From the bedroom to the kitchen and at all points between, the apprehended fool—the offender, the criminal, the reprobate, the awful blemish on the pristine-until-now family name—receives any number of punishments, from a wallop or three and stunning absolute silences accompanied by shaming disgusted glances, to such mandatory acts of restitution as a formal apology to the store owner in front of a glowering throng of parents, management, and, preferably, holier-than-thou shoppers, profoundly unfair grounding ("'*For how long*'?!? Don't you dare ask, you no longer have that privilege!"), chores so plentiful that Hercules would complain, close monitoring, and "What the hell is wrong with you, what will your grandparents think when they hear about this, I suppose I have to lock up the valuables at home now, do I, check my wallet every single minute of every goddamned hour of the day?"; and the final punishment of death by a thousand cuts—nearly constant sarcasm, assumptions of future and escalating guilt ("Do you really think I can trust you enough to pick up a carton of milk for me without breaking the law?"), and biblical laments aimed at the sky in the what-did-I-do-to-deserve-such-a-child? tradition—merely fated, a matter of course.

Instead, Mrs. Kim said, "And ten cents extra for the candy in your pocket."

Em heard no accusation, but didn't protest. Denial struck her as impossible. As did doe eyes and "Pardon me??," the strategy of innocence. She slid a dime toward the coins already on the counter.

Inescapable, Mrs. Kim spoke with an absoluteness about the crime she'd witnessed. And with weary semi-benevolence: she'd charged Em double for the nickel candy.

Em, on her way home on a June afternoon near the end of grade 7, heard the implied threat: *Young lady, in a heartbeat I can make a scene and a call that will dynamite life as you know it.* After that, Em steered clear of danger zones in corner stores and abstained, even when friends in pressuring clusters dared her to take five-finger discounts. With every "C'mon Em, it's safe," she'd say, "Then you do it!"

The actual first incident, during that previous August, accompanied by Stepmom #1, and unreported to the gang, served as a lesson of a murkier sort.

She'd taken candy from the supermarket's plastic bin—a one-cent cube of cocoanut caramel wrapped in crinkly cellophane—and held it so tightly in her fist that she felt the shape losing its sharp edges. In this exact supermarket she'd watched her father take "free samples" from the same row of clear bins, pop grapes and berries into his mouth, and eat an entire chocolate bar while piling the cart with packages and cans and afterwards shove the wrapper in his pocket. From these incidents she learned that while doing so was technically wrong, the division of wrongness it belonged to practically didn't count because everyone agreed so. The situation fell into a special category like the driving above the speed limit or without a safety belt: no big deal, not really, until an uptight so-and-so on a vendetta decided to draw the line and make a federal case of it.

What Em hadn't anticipated was Stepmom #1 reaching for her hand in the glaring sunlight of the busy parking lot. She'd never done so before.

For once, "I'm not a baby, you know," a usually foolproof statement of reluctance and independence, worked against Em. Stepmom #1 insisted. Em dropped the candy, full of desperate conviction that it would fall unnoticed.

Within a minute, fuming Stepmom #1 stood arms akimbo and white purse resting on a counter as she waited to ask a cashier to point out the manager's office, Em understanding all the while that a candy worth one cent meant exactly nothing to them both; at any given location they could spot a lost penny and would never bother with the crouch required to retrieve its nothingness from the filthy ground.

Instead, the emphatic adult performance—"This *is* serious" and "I *can't* imagine what got into her. She's certainly been taught the difference between right and wrong" and "How would you feel, young lady, if Mr., er, Denkins here snuck into your room and took *your* belongings?" and hers in reply ("I'm sorry, I'll never do it again" and handing over the entire contents of her coin purse after Stepmom #1 spoke the words "make amends")—related to teaching and learning values and glueing down principles.

And to having the slippery slope revealed, too: one day you're stealing a penny candy and before long you're rushing into a bank while waving a rifle. A nipped bud meant that poisonous flower would never bloom.

Dee and Gordyn said they'd been tempted of course, but sobering worry about capture and consequences stopped them altogether. Worse, before literally expiring of embarrassment their mother would throttle them.

Jay claimed that since his crime spree remained undetected, he had no story to tell. "Getting caught is for girls," he teased. "Right, Em?"

VENTURE: LYRICS / OCTOBER

"'Cracked mirror'—"

"Hmm, 'crystal clear'?"

"'Listen to the crowd jeer.'" Em expected inspiration to strike with a bracing slap. The forked lightning suddenness—searing arc-welder bolts that tore open the ordinary night sky—meant *eureka*. She'd felt the sensation before and thought the mysterious experience and process amounted to a taken-for-granted miracle: who could explain how such rich material originated?

Holding a pencil-thin volume at arm's distance, her English teacher—middle-aged and still favouring block heel sandals, loopy crochet shawls, three-tier earth tone hippy chick skirts, frizzy black hair imprisoned by plastic barrettes and a severe middle part, and not even lip gloss for makeup—periodically chose to usher in class with a brisk round of claps, the warning signal for a "patented warm-up exercise."

In a sing-song voice she'd read lines of poetry already chalked across the board. The challenge: to update the settings to the here and now. Compared to "Man vs. man, man vs. the environment, or man vs. himself?," the exercise invented by the district school board in the Dark Ages, this one drew excited chatter.

Em had aced "No man is an Island, intire of it selfe; every man / is a peece of the Continent, a part of the maine," with a jokey version that depicted an incontinent man in pain on Hatzic Island. Along with everyone else, she'd flailed with "So dawn goes down to day. / Nothing gold can stay." and "My mirror is clouding over— / A few more breaths, and it will reflect nothing at all," which drew silence, confounded expressions, and mutters of "heavy" and "morbid."

Sensing resistance, Miss T, who'd just then taken another public step toward Crazyville with the assignment, swiped the felt brush along the words in a disappointed pique. Moving on to by-the-book (themes in "The Short Happy Life of Francis Maccomber") and a hovering threat ("Pay attention. Never discount the possibility of a quiz"), she drifted back into normalcy

"How about 'several years'?"

"'A veil of tears.'" Em scanned road, ditch, and sky for inspiration. "'A shadow nears'?"

"'A burp of beer'? 'Oh dear, oh dear'? How's 'big fat rear'?" Dee sighed, rolled her eyes. Em couldn't resist flickering candle melodrama. In a past life she'd have stuck beeswax dolls with hat pins and prayed backwards, or chanted an incantation to a cobra goddess while spinning like a dervish in a haze of incense and charred animal bones. As for "I dunno, it's a bit much," Dee swallowed that back. Her mother, Mrs. Better Safe Than Sorry, whipped out that exact phrase for every third idea Dee spoke aloud and every second ensemble she proposed for school and catwalked in the kitchen. If it wasn't a bit much, then what was the point? Chipmunks blended in, mice too, and look how much security that earned them.

"'The moon draws near.'" Whatever the image turned into, Em felt convinced that *atmospheric* needed to be front and centre.

"'Something, something queer'? So, what's this song about anyway?"

Watching the occasional car cruise by and enjoying the gift of a rare cloudless sky, Em and Dee reclined, elbows crooked, on a sloping patch of brittle dry grass flattened, they suspected, by families of overnighting deer. Warm October sun had given them the go-ahead to kick off canvas sneakers; they'd retrieved them from the ditch below earlier and picked burrs off the laces.

Behind their perch: a pair of scratched yellow backhoes with scoops half-raised, burdened with loads of gravel, and still as if frozen in mid-battle—a little visual gag from workmen who'd left for the weekend. On either side the field had been scraped down to newly exposed blackberry roots and a crust of powdery dirt. Further back, raw wood pickets and garlands of pink fluorescent tape outlined the curving lanes to come and, a few months after that, the six models of houses with neat rectangular parcels of rolled-out turf that would line them. Streets named after trees and historical locals had already been used up by developers. Joking that Slug Street and Mosquito Way reflected the vicinity, they decided on a dollar bet. Em made a claim for Pheasant Place.

Dee stood firm that a workman would eventually erect a sign for Raccoon Lane: "How adorable would that be!"

Now and then guys in cars slowed down to gawk, at the digging machines perched on the bluff and the land's rapid evolution from horse pasture to subdivision maybe, or else the girl's equipment. Mounds and holes of all kinds seemed to fascinate men. Meanwhile, they'd pass right by babies in strollers that halted cooing women in their tracks.

This hangout that steadily disappeared week after week appealed to them because they'd fooled around there, as brats they now thought not quite two years after the fact, on intermittent evenings soon after they'd met. Then, their games involved daring, with "I dare you to lie on the side of the road when a car passes by" or "Pretend you were in a hit-and-run and see if someone stops for you." Shadowy nights of eerie fat moons worked best, though they'd opted for twilight when necessary. Other takes on the dare demanded greater commitment: zig-zagging on the side of the never-busy road, to all eyes concussion dazed, or stretching out flat on the middle yellow line and timing chickening out's arrival.

Wary drivers did rubberneck or slow and a few braked in alarm, at which point the tragic roadkill or supposed escapee from the Emergency Room bolted up the bank and disappeared into the leafy dark, where the other crouched, choking with laughter and ears burning as the guys yelled out threats that began or ended with "one of these days!" or "damned fools!" Tires screeching, they'd leave.

Eventually branding the fun as immature and a bore, as the kind of crude prank childish boys found hilarious, they stopped, just as they had with "twerp" and "nimrod"—an idea tightly, lovingly embraced, used and used until threadbare, and suddenly necessary to discard. The girls understood that getting older meant shedding layers in the same way they outgrew clothes and categories (although—and despite physiology—"little girl," which barreled from fatherly throats in an assortment of grating tones, had annoying staying power).

Years before their first meeting, they'd lived and breathed for linked-arm chants in similar schoolyards of gravel and patchy green. Then, prank calls elicited the constant squeals of mirthful daring. "Wanna gum? Chew my rubber bum!" and "Half past a monkey's ass and quarter to his balls" had sounded outrageous and infinitely clever too. But a new self required fresh expressions: "What a dork," "Piss up a rope, you wedge," "Drop dead," "God, she's *so* exhausting,""Don't be so paranoid / such a complete bitch / a pain in my crack!"They sneered,"Just check your watch, loser" if someone their age tried out immature "monkey's ass" when asked for the time. "What's the diff?" and "Get lost, dag" while shooting lasers of scorn matched their current stature, tough and hard a better shell than mere smart aleck. Under the law of sting or be stung—"Say it, don't spray it," "Smooth move, Ex-Lax"—only timing mattered.

(When a good mood managed to surface, Em and Jay's dad would reach out with a joke he'd taught them years before: "What time does the Chinaman go to the dentist?" They answered "Tooth hurty" immediately and with Instamatic smiles, understanding that honesty—an eye roll or "3:15" or "Geez, Dad, that's so corny"—would open the way for a few Manhattans and a mandatory lecture that surveyed mortgage-payer disappointments of a Niagara Falls volume.)

During basement drumming practice with Dee, Em had confided that she wanted to write a song for the gang to perform. She'd try something relatively normal, fairly certain that weird music no one had ever heard before could ruin the mood, soaked napkin wads or beer bottles arcing across the room soon after. Familiarity did have its uses: before a game, even the crappy student band honking out "Refugee" with clarinets, French horns, and a tuba could attract a scattering of woohoos from a gymnasium crowd that wouldn't hesitate to hurl volleyballs or insults with the first bar of "The Entertainer" or anything remotely Beethoven-y.

"It should be about something important, I guess." Leery of sounding pretentious, Em didn't fill in the blanks.

With Jay she'd passed countless hours during weekend afternoons of rain or snow listening to records and cassettes. They'd whisper-sing along while reading lyrics and stare at the mysterious intricacies of album covers, or else record from radio stations and stop/rewind the tape to figure out and jot down lyrics. Although Em recognized hundreds and hundreds of songs within seconds of their opening notes—she'd be a whiz on *Name That Tune*—her heart's racing told her that the elusive and profound were the most worthy by far of interpreting and locking into memory. "God of Thunder," "Nights in White Satin," "Fool's Overture," "You Lie Down with Dogs," "Kashmir," "Calling Occupants of Interstellar Craft": deep lyrics with epic gongs turned her crank, she'd say, even if her dad labelled such tunes stoner music. What could she expect from him, a man who bet that any jury would find "Mammas Don't Let Your Babies Grow Up to Be Cowboys" at the very apex of the song-writing heap.

Anyone could write "Heart of Glass" or "Da Ya Think I'm Sexy," Em believed. Lyrics that inspired cosmic wonder, that practically demanded that listeners slide on earphones, close their eyes, and listen over and again thrilled her in the same way that lines of poetry appeared to throw Miss T. into a tremor of bliss when, adored book in hand, she acted out "Experience—and no matter what they say / In books—is good enough authority / For me to speak of trouble in marriage" at the blackboard and along desk aisles. The teacher persisted, pacing and theatrical and enthused, all the while fully aware that bored, indifferent, or snide faces imitated and ridiculed the performance in hallways minutes later. With her song, Em hoped to scale at least part way to those Himalayan heights.

"Okay, 'important.'" Dee held up index finger quotes. "As in nuclear bombs, or more in the neighbourhood of getting dumped?"

"I heard you should write what you know." Em had listened to a succession of "draw what you know"s in junior high, her newbie art teacher—perky Miss Something or other with a glossy blonde Dorothy Hamill—repeating that line to everyone as she wandered from table to table because every single student whined "What should I doooo?" at each fresh assignment she dreamed up. Gradually she'd replaced that motto of total freedom with precise instructions: Mt. Baker in 8 x 10 watercolour; a 5x life-size dandelion in oil pastels; a cardboard 2B pencil sketch of one grandparent based on a photograph brought to class. She'd also substituted "Good effort" and "Nice, I can really see what you were aiming for" with Draconian ("Look it up") penalties for incomplete or misinterpreted assignments. From that semester's class Em had also picked up "Procrustean," but found few opportunities to apply it.

"That's helpful. I *know* that the moon orbits the earth and that 15 x 15 is 225—"

"Sure, give that a shot, Dee. 'Cracked mirror, and Pluto is nowhere near.' That's great. C'mon, try to be serious." Em's glance caught the enviable curve of her friend's cheekbone, which Dee matter-of-factly described to practically anyone looking her way as custom-made for the catwalk.

That's doubtful until braces fix the crooked front teeth, Em thought now and again, ashamed at flickers of satisfaction with the surefire knowledge. Mostly, though, she felt protective. When she'd overheard girls making fun of Dee's future in modeling horse bridles and bits, she warned her friend that cooling it about publicizing far-flung career plans might be a wise idea. No one liked a snob, she explained, and, besides, jealousy makes catty people spew out the cruelest hisses of pure acid.

"Okay, what *do* we know?" Staring intently at the peaceful blue sky, Dee sensed only moisture beginning to seep into her sweater. "I'm being serious, alright, as in what do we know that would make for a good song? And, by the way, what does a broken mirror have to do with your life? Do you have a deep dark secret to share?"

"No. It's cracked, not broken. Actually, I got the idea from a movie"—secondhand: Jay had stolen five whole minutes from her day to describe a grisly murder scene. "It seemed like a cool way to start, a concrete image." Miss T. of the frizzed hair and white girl's barrettes shaped like bow ties lusted after concrete images, "solid bedrock for any good poem."

"So you're not taking your own advice?"

"I am now. I wasn't before, not quite, okay?

"Okay. How about a mixture of both. We can start with what we know, or end with it, one or the other, and then chuck in your cracked mirror when it makes sense."

Right off, they eliminated songs about sailing, cars, gamblers, and riding like the wind as beating a dead horse.

With never knew love like this before, victim of love, lost in love, radar love, all out of love, falling in love with a dreamer, never loving this way again, better love next time, a crazy little thing called love, looking for hot love, love stinks, love hurts, a bad case of loving you, I was made for loving you, and a love hangover instantly at their tongue tips, they struck matters of the heart off the list: what else could possibly be added? Besides, they were both aware the other had merely ridden the kiddies' roller coaster—crushes only, and from a safe distance—since elementary school; getting lost in love or sinking body and soul into the pool of love with anyone, let alone a dreamer, remained a titillating dream.

They agreed to reject nuclear war too, only because, unlike Gordyn, fretting about nightly world news but not changing a thing amounted to nothing more than an *exercise in futility*, a newly discovered phrase with abundant targets.

Breathing and being conscious, which they could talk about first hand, struck them as a bit vague and pointless, as did getting by in a small town. Living at home? Either boring or too personal, and, besides, what crowd of adults would want to see the pouts or hear the pitiful moans of teenagers not very different from the ones they'd left in bed at home?

As for their money-making scheme with needy men in waxed and polished cars, they thought of "Bad Girls" and imagined—. No, they might as well strut around naked and totally spotlit; and anyway, they couldn't figure out how to tie in a broken mirror.

School, the remaining option and a topic whose atmosphere of BO, spritzed perfume, chalk dust, caf food, and janitor's bleach they'd literally breathed in for years, held promise. And other than that song about learning at seventeen that the game is unfair for the world's ugly duckling girls, they didn't remember any radio hits about hallways and teachers and cliques. But what song-worthy perspectives did they own about high school? Zilch. Popular enough and pretty enough and good enough grades didn't add up to "Fool's Overture." Or a Top Ten hit. Or anyone giving a shit.

But songs didn't come with a Ten Commandments, they decided; the band's needed to be catchy, not a word for word life story. Bending the truth, who said that couldn't be done? Did Deborah Harry actually have a heart of glass? Probably not. She struck them as tougher than nails.

After reciting the best school scandals, the anguish of which resulted from the shame of being caught and comprehending how the news had leaked dangerously and to all four corners like A-bomb radiation, they remembered Cheryl M.

Last spring this smiling, friends-to-all honour student who'd planned to become a missionary in Africa had died just like that on a family vacation. Right by the Carousel of Progress in Disney World. Reportedly, inside a public washroom her heart sped up and then stopped—right as her mom, dad, and brother stood before a huge map and listened to a theme song about the best time of your life while brainstorming about when and where to eat lunch. Afterwards, everyone shared the exact same opinion that a life cut short was not only an injustice but the greatest tragedy and that the universe had a perverted and malicious sense of humour.

After all, it should have happened to Melon-y Chisholm. Kids didn't even bother to *whisper* that.

Dee pelted the empty road with the handful of pebbles she'd plucked from the dirt and watched them scatter and ping. The tragic song had potential, but Em's obsession with the cracked mirror meant their tank remained empty. "How about we borrow from the basic story, but change the details?" She stared ahead, imagining the sky as an expanse of Tahitian sea she'd someday visit, otherworldly coral and fluid rainbows of neon fish within reach. "So, she's looking at her own eyes in the mirror, alone, maybe there's something wrong like . . . she's late. Or already preggers. Or wants to run away from home. Her family's outside, happy and totally oblivious—."

"Yeah, that's excellent." From her purse Em shyly withdrew a pocket-sized notebook with a bright yellow cover and a pencil attached with matching string. She wrote, then read out "'Sad face in a cracked mirror / she cries but outside they can't hear.'"

"That's not half bad."

"Hmm, wait. I think 'cannot hear' sounds better. 'Empty face'? 'Sad eyes'?" Em had written haikus and sonnets as class assignments in junior high and continued on for months afterward. She'd spent the next summer toting around a diary covered in turquoise Chinese silk, not so much because her mind needed an outlet for constant metaphors and private confessions as she believed that diary entries signalled the mark of artistry, just as shifty eyes predicted a secretive criminal in the making and insistent tuneless whistling signified lifelong idiocy.

Em added a follow-up line and changed her mind. Just in case, she didn't erase it. A neat line through let her retrieve the material if she reconsidered: ~~"Cursed to be born"~~. Garbage should be thrown out; but until deciding belongings—school notebooks, a faded pair of jeans, inspired words—could never be useful, she hoarded everything. She printed "Mechanical heart?" and added a faint "Robotic" right after, fairly sure one would eventually fit. "Remote control??" she jotted before snapping the cover shut.

"Neat, that's a start at least." Dee sat up and rocked on her tailbone. "Hey, I gotta go. In her own way, Mom blows a fuse—'I'm on my last nerve, young lady'—if I'm not there to help with dinner. God, according to that she should have no nerves left! Like cutting meatloaf needs four hands. I swear Gordyn and my dad don't even look at the food. They're so wrapped up in the news on TV. I can just picture them at the war training centre, or whatever it's called. Dad cracking jokes and Gord searching for a plug-in for his blowdryer. God."

"Say Hi from me. And that chart's due for Bio tomorrow. Don't forget." Em had noticed what Dee had apparently not: her all time favourite excuse "Oops, I forgot" had lost the last remnant of its credibility long ago.

"Oh, right. Crud. Well, there goes the evening."

Rehearsal: Talent / October

Em fretted, gnawing index nails down to sore nubs.

The blind leading the blind? That looked alright to her. But as dead weight in a lifeboat situation, the weak one standing out with the giant L stuck on her forehead? No way. Based on her calculations, though, moving to Loserville all by herself seemed the likeliest outcome. A foregone conclusion, as clairvoyant teachers decreed when they glimpsed the thudding futures of unmotivated students.

She feared embarrassing herself and forcing the gang to kick her out (Dee their representative: "Um, Em, we have no choice but . . . Sorry. *You understand.*"), or, worse still, them pretending—with smiles frozen at kindly-but-condescending—that her problems could be solved with encouraging comments and extra bouts of practice. Remedial lessons with friends. Just picturing the scene, her brain throbbed.

Although she knew better than to do so, Em sometimes dwelled on basic facts. Unavoidable ones. That, for instance, half of the band came from a musical family.

Dee had been blessed with a voice like a choir of cherubs—so promised Mrs. Wallace, who'd been raised attending Mass; the living testimony had yet to come—and on top of that one-in-a-million gift, Dee cultivated what she called stage presence, the angular art of being posed photographer-ready, an essential for a career in modeling and ideal for attracting the right kinds of attention.

Gordyn meanwhile packed years of professional experience under his belt, with barbershop quartet performances with his dad and school musicals stretching back to kindergarten. "The dregs" and "total amateur hour" according to him, but still.

And Gordyn could—and did—list membership in bands (trumpet, clarinet) that performed behind haggard uniformed men during Remembrance Day assemblies and at centre stage as part of what every principal on the planet announced as *A Cavalcade of Talent* year after year at Christmas concerts. When he'd lived closer to the city, his school's band entered provincial competitions, one time taking a yellow ribbon.

Em adored listening to the radio and believed she had excellent taste, but her limelight moment—uselessly blowing air through holes in a chocolate brown plastic recorder that had probably been slobbered on by generations of students who'd gazed at the same sheet music—amounted to three frustrated weeks in elementary school. During those hours of unmusical squawks and "Okay everyone, once more from the top," she learned about a puzzling and set inability to follow/guess/fake the notes of "Frère Jacques." She'd also confirmed a suspected mile-wide impatient streak.

The same might be true of Jay. He could shatter a mug or scrape metal chair legs across a concrete floor and, she guessed, label the painful results remarkable: improvised, untraditional, or free form jazz, whatever that was. Missed notes or falling out of synch or a total lack of skill he'd classify as no accident and *avant garde*—unique vision that small minds wouldn't comprehend, or special insight they could never attain. "Call a spade a spade," one of her dad's expressions that she actually liked and spoke aloud, didn't apply to Jay. For him, truth and the words used to describe it had the volatile, on again/off again relationship of movie stars. She pictured him as excellent in politics.

At other fret-free hours Em mentally teleported herself into the ex-gross chamber of Old Man T.'s coop. Instead of finding herself the miserable picture of aloneness (pathetic, a hyperventilating deer cornered by wolves) and the other three pointing at her from the closed safety of a winning team's huddle whose boundaries did not and would never embrace her complete void of talent, she saw only all around snarling and blame—four souls lost in the woods, stripped of faith and hope, trusting that the other three had no ability whatsoever to secure their rescue, "Fuck you, you, and you" the only blaming words left to say. Though saddening as death, this petty fantasy of a disaster afflicting everyone equally did console her with its democratic vote equality.

She much preferred four cases of talentlessness to just one. Who wouldn't?

As a band, she wished for them all to share a common grade point average: everyone satisfactory at least, a B- or a

B, no hand-raising keener at the front of class and no back desk dweller counting the miserable seconds 'til the bell and the hustled stride across the lawn to grab a quick smoke.

And even with an impossible outcome on the first try—an expertly coached relay team's admirable, graceful coordination transposed instantly to them—and excluding the fact of their distinct personalities and the butted heads (subtle through to blatant) that occurred with calculable variations (Gordyn versus Dee, Dee versus Em, Em and Dee versus Jay, and so on), she felt convinced that the thing itself—"Ladies and gentlemen, it's The Blanks"—entered into the world with the dooming fragility of a porcelain doll's hand and consequently with, as her father fondly predicted of myriad efforts, a snowball's chance in Hell. Well, almost.

As with trying to force slithery loose-weave polyester through the sewing machine's feed dogs, snags and knots and frustration and "I give up!" were built into the very fabric, ditto for an eventual grave in a garbage can. That's life, she thought: trying and trying and just maybe succeeding.

She pictured a salmon and envied its automated determination: never once sulking "Why bother?" and instead fighting strong currents and serious obstacles in order to reach a singular goal. To have such an iron will and no awareness of doubt!

Outside of Gordyn, Em said Hi to a couple of kids in Band; as for a rock band, she'd never met a soul, amateur or professional. Even so, she could, like every kid, recite the meteoric arc of bands. Its Big Bang began with explosive and temperamental personalities joining together uneasily with a mess of ideas and plans—in own their case, a five-legged race with each person blindfolded—and normally ended with bitter, marriage-crumbling accusations and spiking resentment that lasted for decades after the band had drifted away into dust.

Bands squabbled because each member had an ego the size of Jupiter and expected to grab a fair share of the spotlight. Naturally the definition of "fair" changed radically from person to person. Or else: they fought because a make up, then break up romance finally curdled, or one member slept with the other's girl and couldn't share the stage with a backstabbing supposed friend. And besides piggish appetites for needles and liquor, creative differences angled in too. The drummer, a guitarist, and the lead singer might violently disagree about which direction the band should go, so maybe different directions alone worked best for everyone involved. From the look of it, the gravitational forces shattering a band into useless bits far overpowered the simpler bonds holding everything together.

For a band with a built-in expiry date like theirs, though, these scenes might never take place. There was little at stake. She pictured The Blanks sliding further from disaster-in-the-making territory.

Rehearsal: Talent / November

In part because nobody brought up the fact or thought it worth mentioning in conversation, not ever, Em wondered why locals instinctively fell into lemming herds when it came to driving the main street circuit on Friday nights or milling at and kidding around in the parking lot behind the track field after school, but never if the topic of building rafts for the river or playing badminton in Centennial Park arose. Or starting a band.

Legs dangling in the hanging bamboo chair near a matching white rattan bed frame from a Daddy's-little-angel phase now four grades out of date, Em balanced the disk easily on her middle finger, unlike clumsy boys who tried the same with basketballs. The accidental bird-flip to the day made her smile.

Rain still ruined the afternoon in dismal sheets, she saw, and two floors below and in the carport, Jay sighed and fidgeted before and after handing sockets and grubby rags to their dad. Within an hour he'd be complaining in her room. In the future she and Jay would drop off cars and instruct the mechanic—their own father, perhaps—that they'd like to pick them up by closing time.

She spun the disk, watching the music label's bleeding colours and forms—cloudless winter sky and Tahitian blue, an i in outline in front of a bright green palm tree and a yellow and orange ball representing a tropical sun. On a whim she'd bought the album at Phantasmagoria. Also, she'd wanted to investigate: the sneery, rude daring of The Slits had shocked her for a few moments and sparked a hot flush across her cheeks. She hid the record in her closet, just in case.

The actual music had bugged her initially; and after a few extra listens she stopped trying. As with Kansas and Peaches and Herb, the songs didn't speak to her. The daring album cover, though, made her gawk. She'd studied the photo's background—a dark drainpipe and a few towering rose bushes blooming in front of a creamy stucco wall—and guessed the photographer had chosen the house, or else it belonged to one of the band members in England.

She returned the disk to its sleeve and pencilled in a couple of ideas—"The Drainpipes," "Tower of Roses"—that she'd show to Jay if their coolness survived twelve hours into the future. The homework supposedly commanding her attention and accounting for her closed door sat unloved and unopened on her glass-topped desk, of stark white wicker too, and brilliant against swampy carpet filaments.

For the album cover The Slits wore flimsy loincloths that might have been made from soaked dish towels. With the exception of hacked and messy hair the trio posed slathered and gooey with mud—freshly applied since still glistening. The mood did not imply that they'd risen from a mud bath at a spa nestled by a Swiss mountainside but instead a far less civilized undertaking, as though they'd just wrestled crocodiles or hunted as a pack for eels.

Em thought the women looked defiant and unapologetic, their glances at the camera and to record buyers the beginning of a fight: "What the eff are you effing looking at?" and "You got a problem?"

The three sets of braless boobs registered immediately, of course, but hinted at proud and warrior-like owners, as Amazonian. Tits, Em thought, that word sounded better, harsh and unapologetic, challenges rather than vulnerabilities needing elastic straps and pillowy protection.

In extreme contrast to pretty local girls who posed in the usual smiling ways to prove their standard prettiness and to naked seductresses in *Penthouse* whose purpose amounted to paid enticement—inviting men, every one of them, right inside their paper folds and to spend their money on expensive magazines with tanned fantasy centerfolds—The Slits broke rules and denied expectations. They proclaimed that their contentment relied on nothing but themselves and laws of their own making, which they more or less obeyed.

Em wondered about their troubled parents—ashamed mortified mothers, ashamed riled up fathers—muttering about prying neighbours and urgent transmissions along the grapevine. They'd huff and sigh and plead. The family name dragged through the dirt, and so on.

To instructions for the nth time to cross their legs, sit up straight, and speak in tones befitting a lady, these reform school girls would mouth words that offended authorities of every sort.

In her lyrics notebook, Em wrote: "Reform Skool Girls??"

Rebellion took the form of sentences—"Up yours, Dad," "Back off, Mum," and "Sit on this and rotate, the both of you"—and decisive actions, the most public of which included yelling "Ladies and gentlemen, we're The Slits" from stages all across the homeland and selling thousands of copies of what amounted to a radical photograph visible in record shops over the entire globe until doomsday. Their every action gave a finger, an immense one, to the properly dressed world.

The steps needed to get there perplexed Em. Did their motivation stem from furious resentment? Or from complete indifference to everyone and everything except their own vision?

The collective parents, Em mused, must avert faces red to their very bones. Meeting over dinners of fish and chips, the six would try but fail to console one another. At least when your child robs a bank or murders their spouse, they have the decency to disappear, out of sight in jail or a premature grave and well out of mind. No such luck with these brazen visible daughters.

Thinking of the solitary white stucco side of the Best Rd house that faced a horse pasture, Em pictured Gordyn standing on the sloping lawn with his dad's camera after she and Dee had coated their fronts with a mixture of clay and warm water they'd stirred in a bucket. With weather tolerable, embarrassment vanquished, lies successfully told, and probable obstacles shoved aside (a parent suddenly psychic and curious about what was going on outside, a film development clerk wagging a finger and pointing out the store policy that included the words "have the right to refuse," that busybody clerk calling Mrs. Wallace and using sentences that featured "concerned" and "we thought we should let you know"), she still foresaw misery and disaster: the eternal threat of reform schools or nunneries or grounded forever. Or: "You can count on the fact that you'll never be out of sight, not even when you're in the bathroom" put into practice alongside a sudden Bend High reputation so awful that the daily humiliated low-totem girls—who'd whisper and point and laugh harshly with the others—would also be grateful that someone worse off squatted below them. "Thanks for getting them off my back!" Em supposed one of them might slip her that in a note blending sarcasm, kindness, and relief.

She'd never find such pure rebelliousness, the utter lack of concern for reputation. Or consequences.

Suspended in the gently swinging rattan and watching endless rivulets of rain scroll down the glass, Em saw that force of habit along with tradition's momentum accounted for the shape of the world. For a reason no one could ever fathom, a Cro-Magnon had dropped to his knee and slipped a ring of woven willow twigs over his mate's scabby knuckle and for the next thousand centuries or so the situation hadn't changed much. Moms passed on what they'd absorbed from their moms, and so forth.

And she suspected, even while comprehending the impossibility, that the vicinity's air itself played a part too, so that if someone wandered away from the centre and tried a different path or a brand new activity the absence of oxygen kept people in check: if you didn't stay where the oxygen was, you might perish. As for why, she couldn't work that out. A cause in the vein of *The Stepford Wives* or *The Andromeda Strain*? Too far out of the question.

Whatever the case, parents apparently did not regale their offspring with stories that began with "One time, when I was in this band . . . ." And the local atmosphere made sure that main street and gym bleachers and the gravel pit's back parking lot remained the focus. Until full-time shifts began, that is. Order maintained.

Even the first band she remembered watching carefully (The Irish Rovers, whose foot-stomper she'd attended holding her grandmother's hand, didn't count) had driven to town and left on the same afternoon.

She'd paid casual attention to the names of bands during junior high special events, where no one volunteered to dance and the entire crowd stood in open-mouthed awe—for an instant no different than the scientists in *Close Encounters of the Third Kind*—while watching the guitarist's solos and waiting for a highlight of blinding flashpots. Until, at last, the boy and girl coaches began to corral stragglers at the far corners of the gymnasium with friendly insistence and "cut a rug" and the like, words nobody had run into since their grandparents' pearl anniversary. The coaches would nudge Reluctant Boy 1 toward Shy Girl Chewing Her Hair 1 and suggest ("Give it a whirl") that he ask her to try out some of the dated moves they'd been recently taught in gym class, to foxtrot or waltz. Maybe they'd Do The Hustle.

With flat long hair or sunglasses or both, these bands featured guys nobody recognized or claimed as kin; they showed up in beater van that came from the city or from across the bridge, unloaded, chain-smoked by the van's back doors, played their 45-minute set that started at 1pm, collected a cheque, packed up the equipment with lit cigarettes stuffed between their lips, and took off. The Bend receding in the rear view mirror and "God, what a hole," Em supposed.

She counted the handful of bands in her own record collection and realized that being an American in a real city or a college town helped too—Akron, Los Angeles, Athens, New York City, Detroit. Essentially the same mattered in Canada—Vancouver, Toronto, Winnipeg. Only with numbers shrunken to a tragic handful. River Bend City might as well be Timbuktu.

Normalcy, she thought, shouldn't be brushed aside either.

In 1980 no one wore granny glasses and bell bottoms and wove daisies into their hair—or dressed like Chester—because whatever they crowed and however many times they claimed to be one-of-a-kind and proud possessors of personal style, fitting in with the pack deeply swayed them. And who ever dreamed of being on the receiving end of cruelty, outside of the circle and facing cold stares?

She predicted that if townies could order versions of themselves from a catalogue, overnight they'd all be living virtually identically—like the citizens under the domes in *Logan's Run* whose only concern began and ended with which of the flimsy disco outfits hanging in their automatic closets they'd want to stroll in during the day. Or, they'd pick the same model of body emerging from a decanting bottle; guided by laboratory-injected Beta or Gamma instincts that instructed them exactly, they'd know where to go, who to speak with, and, equally important, what and who to avoid. Harmony, happiness, purpose: as easily held as the dropped envelope at her drag strip job.

In the Bend, she'd noticed, publicly announced dreams already flowed along specific narrow channels. Alongside starting a band, practically nobody mentioned joining the Poor Sisters of St. Clare or painting airy frescoes on ceilings, the apple never falling far from the tree an eternal law.

Instead, dreams seemed either so practical that the word "expectation" made better sense (getting on steady at the mill; a memorable wedding and honeymoon before buying a house and raising a few rugrats), or else they fell into recognizable fantasies that kids at school and her dad's friends unreeled after a few drinks (winning a lottery and moving to the Bahamas; coming into money and building a custom house with a heated garage for two cars and an RV; a miracle inheritance and a schedule of weakly pictured but constant travel).

Em guessed that she could step off a bus in a Manitoba or Wyoming town and face clone-like circumstances, shifts at a ranch or deep inside a mine the only regional variation. Uniformity, as in a prison, but freely chosen.

At the same time she felt hopeful and almost convinced that she could cross an unmarked border—by accident, more or less: one second here, the next second there—and then . . . .

Though the land of milk and honey amounted to a beautiful empty promise, if not outright deception, just like *Penthouse* photo spreads, her faith rested on real locales where rules were known but not so necessarily or strictly followed and enforced. Or where no one thought twice about breaking away from the usual and received no penalty or flack as a result. Where "Give it a shot, try something different" amounted to a community motto. Or: where standing in front of a photographer almost naked and mud-caked was not wishful thinking and something that people tried elsewhere, in a location so remote and hard to reach as to be a mirage. She'd heard of *artists colonies* and guess they offered freedom of that sort. Where these places actually flourished, though, Em had no clue.

Until she decided that a reachable version of Shangri-La existed and possessed a clear conviction about what she hoped to do once there—if she made a list, painting chapel ceilings and dedicating her days to prayer would not be on it—she'd *endure*, one of Miss T's faves, and invested with a heavy sort of gravity that made Em think of inmates pacing cells the size of postage stamps on Death Row.

And hiding within plain sight, she'd watch, notebook always within her grasp. She'd learned about passing in History. The teacher had suggested the tactic—posing as something other than what you are—had been an iffy means to a better end, a necessary evil in a prejudiced society that slammed shut doors of opportunity just because of skin pigment.

In that class the idea had struck her impossibly far off and with no local application—Mrs. Kwong and Mr. Dhaliwal posing as Mrs. Crown or Mr. Dollimore from Olde Englande would elicit laughter and "Crazy old coot." Until she'd thought of Gordyn and Jay and, to a lesser degree, Dee and herself.

On teams or not, popular guys struck grease monkey poses for anything related to gasoline and motors and metal parts and being behind the wheel—off-roading on dirt bikes; weekend pilgrimages to junk yards for parts and the supposedly irresistible perfume of spilled oil and rusting metal; reconstituting abandoned heaps bought for pennies; saving up for chrome bits on muscle cars; painting beaters with dragons or flame-spewing demons for demolition derbies.

Build, wreck, obliterate, restore: she imagined male DNA yelling these instructions like an army sergeant.

Girls didn't mind sitting in passenger seats and appeared to enjoy being driven around (because, Em would bet, the car ride publicly hinted at the inevitable engagement ring to come, the altar stroll with a white train, and the ten-day trip to Honolulu). Given the choice, though, no girl would lift the hood, never mind cut a hole in it so that a chrome air filter could proudly jut out. A car meant a vehicle: getting across the bridge or down the highway to shop for clothes and wander the wide mall passageways filled with planters and stop at the food court to chat about which blouse would give her the most mileage.

At least some of the time she felt the same.

But the extra impulses, the unexpected and perennial surplus of them, troubled her.

Her father looked at dandelions with disgust, as though their very existence in the lawn presented an dire insult that required the immediate response of extermination. Commonplace, that view also defined local common sense.

Comfortable with and even reassured by the firm distinction between weed and flower, he could not see the beauty nor find one reason for a dandelion to persist.

Em could see both. Normally, she sensed good reasons to admire her boundary-crossing interests. Now and then, though, she loathed her inability (unwillingness?) to play by rulebook pages. The sole advantage, self-awareness, gave her a moment to stop before she spoke, and, in essence, to pass as a *Logan's Run* girl.

She divined how proposing a hike of boulder-hopping along a creek bed, or crossing the old railroad bridge and climbing down to the ladder that sank below the river's surface would be met with a blank stare (as though she'd suggested meeting at midnight to watch the sky for UFOs, or for the sake of curiosity, agreed to go on a date with a chimp). Or else: a cold derisive glance that could be translated as "Are you nuts? and "That's not the proper kind of activity for a person of your age and standing."

As a result, she'd long ago given up mouthing sentences that began with "Let's . . . " and ended with a drop from Beta to Gamma (and worse some days). "Watch your step," from her father's teeming stock of warnings directed in a low voice at misbehaving children, his own included, had wider applications than parental control.

She worried that her brother had not learned the same. A boy who shopped in secret for satin and tulle in order to sew nightlife outfits for his younger sister (who was a decade too young and several thousand miles too distant for such nightlife), held a microphone while pretending to be a reporter for *Vogue* magazine, could barely stand to touch grimy spark plugs, and possessed maybe a dozen brain cells drawn to obtaining a driver's license, that first-class ticket to manhood, would also face a world of shrunken choices and whole populations that felt both comfortable and justified in showing him in detail how he did not fit, and did not belong unless as an example, a cautionary tale.

She had to guess too (since daily life offered no examples) that girls forming a band could be teased, or else called lezzes, or else given guarded respect.

While nowhere close to locals, the constancy of Heart and Blondie and Fleetwood Mac on the radio came as an announcement from the outside world that women in bands might be a minority and a novelty but more or less a newly acceptable fact, just as a woman boss or women voting had once been.

For other activities: never. Seeing how girls pinned with reputations as being easy or as sluts were likewise considered natural targets for teasing or baiting or acidic words (and who knows what else after school), Em understood with a 1+1=2 absoluteness that two girls who hitchhiked and received payment for doing sexual things with men their fathers' ages would be viewed as self-made targets for the hatred of other girls, and, for guys, as centerfold women come to life and visited and obliged to sell their wares at deeply discounted price, or else to give them away for free because they were nothing but sluts who had the nerve to charge for it. Begging for troubling, in other words.

VENTURE: ID / SEPTEMBER - OCTOBER

"So, I—"

"Whaddya need?"

"I, um—"

Gordyn anticipated nothing except word-chunks stuck in his throat. Phlegm.

There had to be a language he'd first need to unearth, in the vein of a special handshake or spy passwords. Insinuating, but in-the-know might work: "A little bird told me you might be acquainted with a man in the ID business?" No, coyness sounded ridiculous. Blunt, then: "I need ID. Can you help?" That directness struck him as wrong too, no better than beaming a flashlight in someone's eyes. Gordyn felt stymied.

On TV, hit men surfaced regularly, a dime-a-dozen. And to hire one the client needed only dial a number or order a drink at a shadowy dive bar, and after the minimal exchange of coded small talk slide a photograph along with a bulging envelope of cash in the guy's direction. That secrecy and ease commanded Gordyn's attention. He mulled over yanking Dee into his room and brainstorming but decided the surprise of ID cards spread out in the dazzling manner of a magician—"Hey guys, feast your eyes on what I have here!"—represented an irresistible moment.

When he asked himself, "What's the worse that can happen?" he craved "Nothing much" as the sole answer. Merv and a terse statement: "Nope, you heard wrong" or "'Fraid not, kid, good luck," and then returning to Solitaire as though nothing odd had occurred. A hopeless part of Gordyn's brain refused to let the fantasy assume innocuous form. It generated scenarios—outraged Merv threatening to call his parents and the police, or Merv vindictive and banning him from the shop forever—that Gordyn's calm reason also informed him were next to impossible.

Just that shred of a chance promised public failure and stinging repercussions. His resolve shrank to nothing.

Diary / Rehearsals

I

There's that 'saying' about if monkeys used typewriters and had tons of time or something they'd eventually tap out a Shakespeare play. Ok, maybe, but picture day #1. Clack, clack, clack, clack, banana peels and piles of chimp manure everywhere, and pages and pages of useless junk.

Wdrt5ahpy8z

67f slT93iq YTY

etc etc.

Maybe cluck cluck cluck looks closer b/c we talked a lot (a lot!!). D. acted like finishing touches on our moves were all we needed and regurgitated "expert wisdom" from "modeling school professionals" . . . As. If.

G. told her to shut up for a minute so he could think and she said buzz off and got all crossed-arms and tantrum-y. When they went at it like two cats I went outside for fresh air (ok, and maybe for a few drags). J. took off to dig through boxes back in the coop. We called it quits for the day.

That was it. A set plan, that's what we need. Obviously.

II – III

(Clack, clack, cluck, cluck. No Macbeth yet, not even "Shall I compare thee to a summer's day?" but lots to skuffle (sp?) about. Nothing else to report.

We're 100% doomed.

Better to see that now than finding out on stage, I guess, where my heart would stop from embarrassment. Literally. Also, no sign of Mr. T. or that he wants us off the property. So far, those are the only plusses.

That means there's nowhere to go except up, right?)

Oh, I brought the Purple Sage book home, to read ahead. "I'm sore within and something rankles", which is Western-speak for "I'm PO'd ", is really hard to do in an accent and without laughing.

||||

Everything's harder than you'd expect. You want to snicker every minute or two. Other times, your face gets so hot, like when (for example) you got super-nervous and peed your pants at a kid's birthday party and everyone pointed right at your wet crotch and giggled, even the moms.

I have to concentrate, close my eyes, and shut out the 'noise' b/c as soon as I look sideways at D., or J. makes a funny face . . . Anyways, I think once I'm in the background behind 'the skins' it'll be alright. But when we're all standing there like a pathetic choir with most of its members missing and singing out of order and staring at a field of grass through a window in a deserted old chicken coop that's plunked down on a field in the middle of nowhere . . . who wouldn't laugh?*

The Osmonds might do it b/c they're super-sucky and, besides, they get paid lots of money to look that way. Who knows what they actually do after the 'lights, camera, action' part of the day is over. I bet the von Trapps were the same. In reality (mine anyways), breaking into a fireside singalong on a rainy afternoon just doesn't happen. No "Doe a Deer", not anywhere. Christmas carols at our house, it's like pulling teeth (except for the Xmas ham, who never needs an excuse to belt out a version of "Jingle Bell Rock" from the actual rooftop).

So far, the whole thing's more about trying than about having fun, which isn't what I'd pictured. At all.

(*In all honesty, though, now and then I can detect something kinda good and not just "potential", which is the line you spout to give people hope even though they won't amount to much. I heard that one all the time when I signed up for after-school gymnastics in Gr. 7 and it was pure BS. I didn't have an ounce of potential since I was about as flexible as a pretzel. Ok, "potential" is better than "God, you're the absolute shits, don't waste my time". I guess.

Today G. sang the first minute of "Metal" and then D. did the same. They both shake their shoulders in the exact same way. We wanted to hear which voice fit the mood. It's maybe going to be our first song, and everyone has heard about the Importance of First Impressions. D. tried her natural pitch first, and then tried again in a deeper voice. Lower makes way better sense.

They tried it together and sounded pretty excellent, and even better when they dropped the British accepts. I thought of them changing "I'm" to "we're" throughout, so like it's two 'robots' in the lab speaking about wanting to be fully human instead of just metal, instead of just one. "Our Mallory hearts are sure to fail" etc etc.

J. and I added sounds that filled in for backing vocals and instruments. We all had to agree: not too shabby.)

Venture: ID / September - October

For all the speculation and mental rehearsals, Gordyn improvised naïveté—"Um, what's that?"—on the afternoon he purchased Dee's incense burner cracked open the door.

Merv continued to lay down cards and shoot smoke rings as Gordyn pretended to hem and haw about the right shape for his sister's gift. The proprietor offered no advice and expressed infinite patience, as though Gordyn's choice amounted to a grave matter—the diamond engagement ring sure to set the tone for the rest of the marriage, an inky signature beneath a contract with Satan.

Face clammy and nearing the glass, Gordyn finally opted for the pyramid. As an afterthought he asked about the two bottles sitting in plain view. He ad libbed for an air of authenticity: "Maybe my Mom would like that. She uses Nilodor like it's going out of style."

Merv's chuckle then confirmed the true purpose of Rush related in no way to proud housewives with spick and span living rooms guaranteed to impress judgmental in-laws. "Your Mom should stick to her Nilodor. That stuff, it's different." He held two cards in mid-play. "Shut the door and try it out in your own room first, you'll see."

"Oh . . . okay." Wanting to laugh, Gordyn lowered his face once again to the case. He mapped the situation: Merv saw himself as Lucifer the tempter, the wily crook slyly distributing a forbidden item—as in, years before, Gordyn being allowed to sneak a sip from his father's beer bottle, Dee trying a morning cup of sweet black coffee, and their mom's warning, "Edmund Wallace, don't you dare!," ever-appalled at the live-and-let-live attitude at the man-child she'd agree to marry—while not seeing the truth at all.

"I'll take the cones, strawberry flavour. I guess that's best. And a bottle too." He whispered thanks for a recent pay cheque and a customer pleasing paste-on smile when Merv rang up the costly merchandise. Like Mr. Swanson and his empire of deep-fried chicken Snak-Paks (the real profit-maker, ounce for ounce), the owner of the Rush factory apparently had a license to print money.

With a ready excuse—that he'd changed his fickle mind, and thought instead that he'd purchase sandalwood incense sticks—Gordyn hurried toward Acapulco's. By now he'd begun to worry about too-frequent appearances; the drop in today had to seal the deal, as his dad said, assuming a deal existed to seal, of course.

Gordyn had readied a change of subject from a regular purchase to a criminal one. All he hoped for: opportunity, a topic or a lone word that bridged the two.

No other customers browsed inside; and Merv, slumped next to a cigarette roller, looked no different than on any other shift. Gordyn wondered if he slept in a back room, and rose out of a cot there each morning. Showering, changing clothes, and a blow-dried hair style didn't register as an integral part of the man's routine—daily or weekly.

Gordyn slid the incense out of the paper bag and laid the receipt on the counter. "Can I trade cones for sticks?"

"Yeah, sure. Same price, just grab the ones you want."

Merv's brusque impatience today worried Gordyn. Sniffing the incense packages crammed into the what looked to be a lidless ice bucket, he wished he'd come up with a better excuse to drop by. His plan hinged on Merv's talkative mood, for an abundant clutter of words to point a way for the risky question and mysterious reaction.

He dragged out the appreciation of scents and then smiled, grateful for luck in note form. Once "Spaceship Superstar" wound down, the radio spoke enthusiastically about auto glass replacement and muffler shops across the river in Abbotsford. An announcer's voice took over: "Coming up next, a classic from Elton John."

"Did you ever go to Elton Don's?" Gordyn aimed for an oh-by-the-way tone.

The Bend's one and only disco had shuttered before its first anniversary. Whoever's bright business idea this nightclub had been, the rough colliding with continent-sweeping "Disco Sucks" T-shirts spelled sudden doom. As did the choice of a town where dancing to "I Feel Love" and The Bee Gees in spandex and satin blouses had never replaced plaid shirts and pounding the opening bars of "Smoke on the Water" on the upright piano in the music room. Or, cranking Black Sabbath to full volume when tearing away from school parking areas.

With their neon and mirrors and ladies in slithery dresses beneath fox coats, discos belonged to glamorous, faraway societies—New York City and Paris. But when talk of Spanish-themed Elton Don's (also a mistake in a town where the only Diablo, a rare Spanish name in school, accepted Dial-A-Blow as a nickname) clucked from tongues, cutting tones of disbelief and dismissal sounded: ha ha ha, as fucking if! When the business lurched and, defeated, closed its doors, the failure sparked widespread jokes about idiots with money and no sense. Unlike the creek's bed worth of Pet Rocks that sat on window ledges from Silverdale to Dewdney, no one admitted to having paid good money even once to glimpse what the bad idea's newspaper ad had promised: "A Touch of European Élan in Downtown River Bend!"

"Nah." Merv swatted the crank of the roller machine.

Gordyn waited, expecting a verbal jab—or at least a declaration of preference for real music, such as that recorded by Led Zeppelin in 1971.

Gordyn understood the importance of treading carefully: he guessed that any hint of gushing partisanship would turn Merv against him. He'd talk about the topic, then, as an interesting point in common, making it on par with the building of the new city hall way out in the back forty or the sturgeon caught under the bridge that could be as much as a century old. Local news to shoot the breeze with. As a conversation starter, after all, Elton Don's needed only provide a connection to his true goal.

"We thought it'd look rode hard and put away wet." Gordyn had heard Merv use that expression while on the phone and thought it couldn't hurt to trot it out. "But we never found out. Our parents didn't go—they're way too old—and we couldn't get in. We'd be asked to show ID, for sure." Gordyn made a final inhalation, dramatizing the difficulty of the incense choice—*Women! Can't live with them, can't live without them*—while also hinting that the choice had been made. He grabbed a package called "Hawaiian Jungle," which he thought should be called "Dregs" for the sake of accuracy—vanilla, strawberry, cocoanut, sandalwood.

Gordyn dawdled, sure that Merv was deciding if to pounce—or how and when—as he wrapped up the latest round of Solitaire.

"You look old enough. I'll bet you could go into the Belle-Vue right now and order a beer, no problem."

"Thanks. Maybe, but a back up plan's good. Just in case." Gordyn imagined that he heard the second hand on his watch. Either Merv would make an offer momentarily or else instinct would warn him to clam up. Gordyn paused, listening to the solemn piano of "Someone Saved My Life Tonight."

Merv herded the cards of his losing game into a deck and shuffled. "Ready?"

"Oh, yeah, I've made up my mind. Thanks for the exchange." He reached for the bag and receipt.

"You know, kid, I might be able to help you out with ID. It's kinda busy now, so come back later."

"Really? Wow, that's cool. Thanks." Since Acapulco's still stood empty, he figured Merv wanted to talk with him on the sly after the store had closed. "My shift doesn't end till 7."

"I'll be here, rattle the door if you don't see me. I'll hear that if I'm stuck in the back." He thumbed at a mahogany door by the posters.

The shift at Brownie's picked up after two slow hours of heave-worthy, measured-to-the-ounce coleslaw prep and torturous, shelf-by-shelf cooler inventory. "Details matter": another commandment from Mr. Swanson's doctrine for business success.

Puffed up with excitement and pride, Gordyn listened to Fiona's breathless gossip and bouts of laughter, and, nodding, gave in to requests for evaluation—"100% honest, okay?"—of her new drama and tap class movements. Indulging Mr. Swanson's gags and sermons from noon to 1pm, he agreed heartily to the day's tip for getting ahead as though he could not wait to write it down. He ignored Harjinder's grey cloud silence and chronic bird flipping at Brownie's rules, each printed on laminated yellow paper and clamped inside the thick binder by the till. The shift's final minutes could not arrive soon enough.

At four he called his mom to report that Mr. Swanson had set up training for a new menu item and that he'd be half an hour late or so. "Don't worry, I'll make sure he pays me for that too."

Delphine remarked about his being lippy and getting too big for his britches, which lessened the impact of telling two fibs in one day. His mother acted like a dust bowl farmer sometimes. Who said britches anymore?

Hands and nail beds scrubbed at 7, Gordyn raced for Acapulco's in purpling twilight, relieved that rain had let up in the afternoon. He stood at the front door and rapped on the glass, watching Merv raise a finger and continue to count bills.

He got down to business while unlocking the door. "Okay, you need ID."

"Yup."

"And you know that you're asking for something illegal. You're not a cop, right?"

Gordyn smiled, flattered that he could pass as being old and manly enough to get hired as an officer.

"Yes, I know, and no, I'm not."

"Okay, good."

"Also . . . Um, there's a bit more to the ID situation. I, um, actually need four. Not for myself. I mean we need four, my friend, and our two sisters.

"Shit, man . . . Why didn't you say something before?"

"You said you were too busy." He searched Merv's face for signs of retreat. "So, how much does this all cost?"

"I'll have to get back to you about that. I might find a way to give you a deal. Nothing official, right, gotta keep the taxman off my back."

"Oh, wow, that's excellent!" Nodding, he drove gesture-prone hands into the pockets of his jeans.

"There's a catch, though. No surprise there, right, there's always a hitch. You've been around long enough to realize that too, right? But first things first. The info. Just take a look at your dad's driver's license. And four pictures, the right size too. Check out his license too for that too, and try to copy it exactly. How close up and what the background is. Any bouncer worth the name is going to pay attention to shit like that." Merv's gaze turned to the shop's entrance. "Deal's off if the shots are crap, dig?"

"Okay, for sure."

Gordyn left, excited and deflated at once. Though he'd have to ruin the surprise in order to get the photos correct, he'd almost overcome one of the biggest hurdles by himself. Still, Merv's promise of a discount set off alarms of wariness: in exchange for what?

He passed by Prawn Gardens (a morgue, save for two teacher-aged ladies sipping from water glasses at a window table) and decided on a right at the unlit cinema. Climbing the long hill, one of two routes home, he wondered how his version of the Schlieffen Plan had already gotten hung up on details. Maybe all ambitious two-pronged assaults suffered tragic design flaws and that's why History teachers dwelled on them in the same way everyone still knew about Icarus centuries after the guy's catastrophic plummet.

Flaws can be corrected, Gordyn thought, picturing how the sheen of his nearly shoulder-length hair compensated for a narrow face. He vowed to make a list of potential outcomes. Merv might ask him to put in a few shifts at Acapulco's. That condition? No big deal. Or sweep the stock room and shuffle containers. A breeze.

Passing by the glistening football field, the butt-strewn roadside smoke pit, and the fenced electricity-grid substation, Gordyn's imaginings grew in scope and ridiculousness: blackmail and servitude; replacing John D as the school's new fake ID broker; slaving alongside the ex-con in Brackendale to produce glass pipes in surplus numbers for voracious potheads in big cities. By the turn off at 7th, he'd entered the feverish realm of the fantastic: riding shotgun with Merv, in a van that rolled along a dusty street in the wavering afternoon heat of a Mexican town—dogs with lolling tongues collapsed flat and exhausted on dirt roads, nervous women in floral skirts peeping through white shutters and tracking the sudden appearance of dangerous gringos on a criminal shopping spree. Cocked shotguns and threats of carnage everywhere.

He'd absorbed his mother's fretfulness in the womb, he realized, just as an impressionable kid picks up the wrong habits from a bad influence.

Life does not match an episode of *The Bionic Woman*, he reminded himself. Doomsday weapons, chloroform doses, and marauding fembots in chic black helicopters existed as workaday problems in TV Ojai, but families watching these hair-raising events in warm, carpeted living rooms after dinners of meatloaf, canned peas, mashed potatoes, pudding cups, and the nightly news belonged to the reality in which he'd been born. Nuclear families, yes; defusing nuclear bombs, no.

He snatched the front door key from beneath the potted cedar and let himself in.

Venture: Fence / September – November

Eastbound drivers in no particular hurry could opt for the Bend's Railway Avenue bypass and, depending, be cross or smirking at the Better Business Bureau's graffitied ~~Please~~ Come ~~Again~~ Soon! sign on the other side before their brains had used up the calories needed to form a strong opinion of the place.

Slowing to a sightseer's crawl, though, they'd glimpse Railway Ave's impressive network of weeds and iron railway tracks on one side and assume the rent directly across must tempt entrepreneurs with dreams but no savings. Besides locked-door buildings with absentee owners who no longer tried to entice renters and the occasional address with a curling "Opening Soon" or "Under Renovation" announcement taped to a window, the bypass' low overhead offerings—Pat's Used Furniture . . . and New Too, Mr. Junk's Emporium, The Bottle Depot, and, briefly, Gary's Place, a pool hall—gave passersby little incentive to park.

While River Bend City's main street ran flat and straight from east to west, it perched at the point where flood plain met valley wall. As a result, the shops on the street's north side came with no basements, but all the shops opposite either had stairs to lower levels or came divided into a top floor business with an entrance on Main and cheap rental space below.

Less fledgling businesses like Field's and the chain hardware store maintained entrances on Railway that led straight to bargain areas, their hope being that once inside the customer might wander upstairs. If those walk-ins left with a lawnmower or a 3-pack of Fruit of the Loom, so much the better.

On a prime hilly corner, Belle's operated two cousin businesses linked by a carpeted staircase. Upstairs: collectibles and almost new household goods, from crystal decanters and Royal Doulton tea sets to roll top desks and murky landscape paintings with weighty dark wood frames. A floor beneath: a pawn shop crammed with truck rims, socket sets, chainsaws, and, seemingly, the contents of evacuated houses stacked right to the ceiling. Sellers tacked a cork board by the till with Polaroids of vehicles, campers, horses, double-wide trailers, struggling farms, and fuzzy chicks under heat lamps, all "For Sale by Owner."

With hair that recalled fuzzy grey yarn, Belle had long run the shop partnered with a woman as soft spoken and delicate as Belle was loud and stout. The ladies traded till posts at seemingly random intervals. Belle looked at home downstairs, smoking amidst the tools and recliners while bantering with old guys who dropped by for news, or to barter and leave with less money and what they'd been assured amounted to a great deal.

The other woman, older and infinitely more frail, lived under Belle's shadow to the extent that her name had drifted away altogether. People referred to her as "Belle's sister" and "Belle's friend." Year round, she wore layers of prim nunnish clothing—a starched blouse with lacy collar details beneath a cardigan sweater and a plaid wool skirt with knife pleats, a cloudy hue with hints, bare suggestions really, of lilac and rose. With glasses that hung from her neck on a fine chain of gold links and pearls, she might be the ghost of a librarian, one with a Gibson Girl hairdo matching the faded hue of her skirt. As with Chester, her history possessed a mysterious aura that encouraged speculation—that she was Belle's elder sister and had gone gently nuts after being abandoned by her husband. And popular too: "She's an old lez." Unconfirmed, that rumour transformed Belle into a secret lesbian (or else the sister of one) and painted her establishment with a coat of livid controversy, a taint akin to Acapulco's but different.

Taboos never failed to set Bend lips in motion.

The gang figured that the educational cop, spy, and private eye shows broadcast every week could only benefit them; despite faraway settings in Los Angeles, San Francisco, and New York City, the practical streetwise schooling felt useful in ways that memorizing ancient Mesopotamia's agricultural feats or Henry VIII's rotating door of wives never would. After all, the encyclopedia of murders, thefts, snipped brake lines, blackmail operations, shady cover-ups, and scapegoat dupes, not to mention intimate knowledge of an expansive web that existed just below the smooth skin of everyday routines, reachable, and sometimes even stumbled upon, just by stepping into one particular address, uttering a special sentence, shaking hands with a guy in the know, or dialing a phone number, could be applied to the Bend, more or less.

Over the course of their investigations and car chases, the MacMillans and the Harts, Jamie Summers, Pepper Anderson, and

Barnaby Jones always ran into the concrete fact of this underworld, an invisible pocket of the population that maintained two sets of identities: a respected industrialist, say, but a secret criminal mastermind importing heroin in dolls produced by his factory in the Orient, or a watchful bartender taking in wads of money for a bookie (who, in turn, operated a facade business in plain sight: the sandwich-serving deli in a bustling neighbourhood masked a secure back office with tables of ringing telephones and a blackboard that listed betting odds). The scale of the local equivalents had be smaller—just as no millionaire industrialists chose the Bend, so heroin packets stuffed inside toys existed somewhere else. As did the sheer number of corrupt people hatching deadly plots or under the radar schemes to get filthy rich.

In these shows art galleries, jewelry boutiques, and pawn shops seemed especially prone to criminality. They fronted international forgery rings, laundered money, and fenced stolen gems as though the actual work of selling paintings or convincing engaged couples to splurge on a quarter-carat stone only ever led to an overdrawn bank account.

Basement-less and tangy with sauerkraut, the Bend's sole deli sold Black Forest ham and Swiss cheese kaisers. And Derkson's, already on its last legs because of mall chain stores, displayed birthstone rings and pendants in a terrarium of cactuses and ceramic mushrooms, counting down the days to Christmas and Mother's Day; in the meantime Mr. Derkson relied on clasp and watch repairs to keep afloat.

On TV, one trick of success was keeping noses clean and not suddenly driving a Ferrari and skipping town for month-long trips to Rio de Janeiro. If the deli and jewelry store fronted criminal activity, they kept their profits completely out of sight. Innocence seemed the higher probability.

Judging by her shop, Belle didn't like to say no to the broke and needy. She'd profit from them too. And unlike Pat's, whose inventory of Elvis Presley wall plates and French Provincial coffee tables never sold and instead became less visible with each new car-trailer load of junk Pat couldn't resist, Belle's boomed with the incoming and outgoing.

Jay noticed that new objects in the upper-floor display windows disappeared regularly. *Moving inventory*, criminals said on TV. As far as educated guesses went, Belle's held promise. If anywhere had the potential to fence, Belle's shop was it.

But if Belle decided to ask something along the lines of "Where did this stuff come from" he'd better have a spiffy answer.

He needed cash, not the humiliation of getting kicked out.

Déviation: Reproduction

A brick-shaped room with sliding shower doors of chrome and frosted glass at the far end, the main bath—a realtor's term that had stuck—was a showcase catalogue for bygone Mom #2's decorator's eye. Matching pink guest towels with embroidery daisies rested untouched on twin glossy wrought iron rods, hand variety folded over bath. Imported fish bowl globes in smoky-brown on whose surface pastoral landscapes had been brushed in copper paint hung above double sinks nestled in a French Provincial cabinet with fancy spindle drawer handles. Chains of large antiqued links met at an engraved outlet in the plaster ceiling. A pedestal soap dish in black and an air fern stuck in a white urn of cup height completed Mom #2's décor statement at the upper right of each polished faucet set.

Staring ahead into the door-to-shower mirror (or: sitting on the toilet) revealed the wallpaper—an entire plane of inky illustrations of naked classical ladies applied to a parchment-toned background, as though Marie Antoinette and the Venus de Milo had fled from the halls of stately museums, keeping their upswept hairdos while losing every stitch of clothing but standing in coy profile. Frozen in mid-motion, a collage of perpetual yearning, they reached out for each other's buoyant breasts in panel after panel.

On return from any main bath visit, first-time and repeat company situated with drinks on cork coasters in the living room never failed to comment, sputtering out jokes with punchlines about a lesbo orgy and calling the police, a long absence due to admiring the artwork, or how nice it must be to go through carefree days braless and unaffected by gravity's constant downward pull. *The Mediterranean*, they'd sigh after Joey had made a few runs downstairs to mix a special batch in the bar blender, *the land of grape trellises and ruined temples and constant sunshine. One day, one of these days . . .*

Mom #2 had halted her second stab at a masterpiece at floor level. She'd envisioned an arctic expanse of marble with delicate forking veins. The bother of lifting the lino (russet stone shapes carrying over from the kitchen; highlighted as deluxe—the 'Via Domiziana' pattern—by the realtor) and installing a proper sub-floor required time and organization. Plus, workmen in copious quantities. Yet before all these elements could be finalized, formerly contained accusations and fights had spilled from the master bedroom into the kitchen, balcony, and dining room. Eventually, divorce proceedings that cost Joey a hefty settlement thanks to his wandering eye assured that the gleaming textured vinyl remained permanently cemented in place.

Just as guards inside the Louvre must eventually grow ho-hum about chamber after chamber of headless statues and antique paintings that featured never-suntanned ladies bathing, the illustrated wall and the room's rule of being aspic-set in readiness for guest viewings naturally transformed it from a kingly centrepiece to the standard necessary room.

Joey had labelled the master bedroom's en suite bathroom off limits; and a last resort, the half-bathroom by the rec room downstairs—one of several of his "It's good enough" home-improvement efforts—felt drafty, cramped, and cave-like thanks to a poorly insulated exterior wall, walnut panelling, and a low-wattage fixture. Listed as ivory in the catalogue but actually dull beige, the plastic accordion door required by the odd-sized facility managed to look both flimsy and dingy.

For Jay the main bath suggested a snapshot of his elegant future marred by the fact of a wimpy lock. With a few rattling wrist twists the doorknob's interior cogs popped, and an intruder could appear at any moment while he primped or showered. The earliest version of this B & E had been funny and mutually-loved warfare between brother and sister: a quart canning jar of water heaved overtop during a shower, chilled with ice cubes even better. The shrieks and bellowed promises of retaliation and parental warnings to simmer down had proven endlessly fun, although the game meant standing blind inside the steamy stall with an ear cocked for enemy motion.

After that phase, which died out with the ordinary dimming of a campfire, a second one began. Appearing within moments of the shower taps being tightened, Jay's dad wandered in—with locker room casualness, as though a fully clothed father sharing a narrow bathroom with his naked son represented the most normal occurrence on Earth.

Jay quickly learned to wrap his waist, standing in the tub and reaching around to secure a towel instead of letting toasty vent air dry his feet. "Got hair in your pits yet?" Joey asked with fake-spontaneity. He could as well be checking on the toothpaste supply.

The pattern repeated on an unpredictable schedule, disconcerting clipped sentences that appeared to fish for responses substantially larger than "Daaad!" or "It's called a locked door for a reason":

"Got lead in your pencil yet?"

"You're probably beginning to stink, right?"

"You need to shave yet?"

"Do you know what blue balls are?"

"Balls dropped yet?"

"Growing hair on your riggin yet?"

"Bet you're getting hard ons all the time, right?"

Compared to the Life of the Party, the Diner Crooner, the Supermarket Aisle Troubadour, the Bartender Who Mopes Alone on his Stool While Sucking Back Manhattans from his Favourite Glass, the Yard-Proud Perfectionist, the Playboy Who Wears No Underwear, and the Lesson-Giver Who Uses His Fists When

Necessary, other incarnations of Jay's father, this version behind a closed door eluded a ready-made or simple category.

The audience-eying performer who talked without hesitation and often and not quietly in public about racks and melons and gajungas and "legs up to here" and the origins and forms of frigidity and the clear messages women's sways and sashays sent out, and who took evident pleasure in joking "You hold 'er and I'll screw 'er" every single time Jay helped with any two-man project that required a screwdriver: these stood for the known and typical man, as shameless and odd and dangerous and embarrassing as he might be.

The newly curious father, possessing a mind that overflowed with probing biological questions whose answers he also looked unprepared for, clearly meant *something*. Eyes not averted, lingering and helpful in the evaporating steam, lurking outside the main bath door: what did he really want?

By puberty and junior high every kid knew to expect the mutually awkward follow-up to the elementary school inquiry about the origins of babies assumed to have been temporarily sated by pastel fables of a kindly stork, a sheltering cabbage leaf, or a sudden blanket-swaddled appearance in a maternity ward. Those heart to heart exchanges must have been happening since before dusty Babylonians in goatskin sandals invented language.

As though following a rule book handed out at the maternity ward, parents sat children down and gave them a low-volume speech via science (The Reproductive Facts of Life) or poetry (The Birds / The Bees), or, in the case of the JWs down the road—the girls, JWs now but not for long, had gleefully spread word of their special meeting throughout school corridors—a Kingdom Hall basement lesson gathering all boys and girls of a certain age, who listened to strung-together Bible passages about coveting, fidelity, duty, wantonness, uncleanness, and the marital bed that implied not even a second of fun and a thou-shalt legal contract with ominous penalties attached in the here-and-now and hereafter.

There were other classics too, "You see, when a man loves a woman . . . ," or a medical tome with anatomical cross-sections, colour-coded with black lines connected to clinical-sounding Latin printing: glans, scrotum, vas deferens, semen, ovum, uterus, coitus, foetus.

When the gang had traded details about what they'd heard from other students and what their own parents had doled out, Jay had related gajungas and the man-to-man advice about sanitary peeing after a tussle with a prostitute with questionable hygiene. He kept the troubling main bath part to himself. The strangeness wouldn't cause laughter or gasps of incredulity, just blush-worthy awkwardness and further questions.

As expected Delphine's master bedroom account related by Dee had dwelled on trouble rising on the horizon, from deadly "accidents" and the transparent motives of young men who would ask Dee out for so-called dinner, to a mysterious cruelty on the part of Mother Nature herself that gave men the instinctual urge to "go galavanting" while women, like brood hens, stayed close to the nest, tethered by a strong unbreakable leash.

In the basement toolroom at the exact same hour, Edmund had offered useless words to Gordyn—"signals," "respect," "obligation"—before proceeding to the fruits of his worldly experience: "I'd say missionary's the best all round," "It's not rocket science," and "Remember, it's a two-way street." Lots of "it" and "that," no named body parts, no details, no what ifs: totally unhelpful. And of course nothing about screwing another boy in a condemned chicken shed.

Though she'd never met or heard of Delphine before taking off for good, Mom #2 had patched together a similar pursed-lip account, a vaguely menacing cautionary tale stuffed with insinuation: the basic idea being mistakes (of some sort) could be made that cost dearly (in some way) and took years to pay off (for some reason), and that care (of an unnamed type) needed to be taken always, as though Em was a glass figurine, or had already boarded the bus to the L.A. of street corners and a fleet of cars driven by men she'd be wise, for one reason or another, to mistrust.

Wishing for nothing else but magical words that would cause a father with dogged questions to rematerialize in another room,

Jay managed only "Yes," "Yeah," and "I guess" from a hoarse-sounding throat. With that, his father always nodded and left.

NOTEBOOKS / SEPTEMBER

So, do you think I'm more of a regular catalogue look? Or? Would I fit in this kind of ad?

One's way better than the other.

Look at the diff b/w the two ads (Vogue vs. Eaton's), and let me know.

<u>Be honest!!</u> I can take it.

REHEARSAL: SKINS / OCTOBER - NOVEMBER

Dee babysat all over Ranchero Heights. Hiking to whatever three bed/two bath built within a reasonable distance, she'd already corralled and wiped up after what must count as a village worth of children. The kids learned to respect her reign, which she saw as absolute but way more fun than that of their hassled parents, who treated them as chore-slaves or costly nuisances with terrible, or questionable at best, prime-time picks.

While her wards played, watched TV, or slept (Dee shook her head at tutoring and cooking, Rice Krispies squares excepted), she peered into kitchen cupboards and lifted bedroom mattresses with a voracious curiosity for the details of other people's lives. She felt surprise and relief and annoyance at discovering the smallest of differences between the latest address and her own—an afghan of bright crocheted squares (folded on the back of an armchair or chesterfield), *National Geographic* magazines (stacked or shelved), porcelain figurines (one or two arranged on the dining room table or in a corner nook), cut crystal wine glasses on display (sparkling or dust magnets).

She discovered her parents drank considerably less than average and barely acknowledged the widespread rule about giving brand name liquors—Canadian Club, Tia Maria—pride of place. Nor did they fill used bottles with water and food colouring as festive window sill decorations.

Sneaking chapters of *Fear of Flying*, *The Joy of Sex*, and *The Happy Hooker* stored in bedside table drawers, and at first disgusted by photos in *Hustler* and *Chic*—one gross and tacky, the other's tackiness dressed up with pearls—left in basement workrooms and stuffed in bathroom cabinets, Dee wondered about what Americans, who made and read almost all these, put in their drinking water to make them so sex-obsessed.

She changed her mind slightly once she and Em began their secret career. In the single copy of *Mayfair* Mr. Allard had wedged between the hot water tank and the furnace, she'd studied a mirror scene. The two "Swedish blonde bombshells" of "The Girls Can't Help It" wrestled in order to secure a ride with a dull-looking businessman in tweed and leather gloves who drove a two-seater convertible MG. So entwined did the bombshells—in panties and bras beneath three-quarter length furs—become that the man drive off in a huff, leaving them to their mud-spattered roadside make out session. Projecting herself and Em into the situation, Dee decided that taking off in the car and leaving the guy stranded would be the way to go.

Dee's favourite clients, by a mile, were Ed and Sandra Rusch. Close by and completely trusting, they never quibbled about the cost of overtime. Better, "If you feeling like vacuuming . . . " never sang from Sandra's perfectly glossed lips.

Ed described their lifestyle as spontaneous. That usually meant a call out of the blue and Dee's mother calling upstairs to say the jet setters had decided to galavant into the city or across the border overnight and they required a sitter *tout de suite*.

Dee enjoyed overnighters because of extra pay and staying up late watching TV, unfettered snooping, and grating marbled cheddar on Triscuits and slamming a tray's worth under the broiler. Their black-eyed nine year old Darren—she'd renamed him Damien—barely cried or acted up. When he didn't trail Dee with his mouth hanging open the boy happily pored over *Flash* comics in his bedroom for quiet hours.

With a wink Ed told Dee they considered themselves a mellow couple (she understood the coded word, having located their pipes and a bong boxed high in a master bedroom closet) and didn't mind if she had friend over "to watch TV or whatever." He'd taken her on the grand tour of the house, going as far as the basement, an unfinished area stacked with lumber and panelling and otherwise crammed with boxes—"gravy boats and other crapola from our big day," he explained—and stuffed garbage bags of clothes lumped into a corner heap. To Dee, the heaped collection of equipment—bikes, dumbbells, roller skates, flippers, rackets, hockey sticks—suggested these free spirits also had mysteriously short attention spans.

Over the course of months she'd catalogued their house contents, including Sandra's teeming closet of negligees and baby dolls, and, in the basement, drums with mottled red sides that sparkled like metallic crushed velvet. When Ed pointed the set out, her eyes drifted toward another corner: the star of the show didn't play drums, marooned at the very back of the stage. The audience could barely make him out behind the blocky equipment.

During a lunch break at school Em let Dee in on the fact that she called dibs on drums. And, following her friend's sputters of disbelief (Dee had pictured the two of them harmonizing and colour co-ordinated within reaching distance of the worshipful audience), she confided the partial truth that being hidden away seemed perfect since being gawked at made her blood run cold.

Dee vowed to work on maneuvering her friend forward but in the meantime surprised Em with the basement find. Someone had to drum, after all.

She thought of dropping hints for a huge garage sale and later left Ed a reminder note. With luck the band could buy the drums for next to nothing.

Happily reliant on the never-shrinking wanderlust of Ed and Sandra, the girls practiced without unasked for, we-know-better-than-you-of-course elder brother advice. Gordyn and Jay unleashed it without a moment's pause. The boys seemed drawn to the nosy helpfulness by instinct, even though they bristled with annoyance when their dads weighed in with the same.

To create an inspirational mood the girls filled a Christmas string with red bulbs and pulled a strobe light from the mounds of the Rusch basement's cache of junk.

Em showed up with a cassette player and went straight downstairs, playing Side A and B of anything from her collection. Locked in her bedroom she'd already listened dozens of times to the thundering beats of *Destroyer.* Fingers rapping in time at her desk while wearing headphones with closed eyes, she learned from experience the origins of the word "headbanger." "Homework," she say, if asked. Or "Reading *Vogue*," which gave her dad's eyes a glazed expression.

In the basement she tried to match the drummer's speed and breaks from one pattern to the next while using actual wooden sticks and the bass drum pedal, far trickier to manage than two index fingers and a right foot. As they'd agreed, Dee came down after an hour, and modeled accessories—gold hoops, bangles, a rhinestone brooch—she hoped would catch the light. Every few cycles she'd run upstairs to check on Damien. She'd descend with snacks and pop, reappearing once in a black-and-ivory baby doll. She conceded that Dolls of the Valley would not make for a successful band name.

They soon swapped Em's home-recorded tapes for ones taken from LPs and singles the gang had picked up in the city. After playing one song, they'd rewind the tape and begin again. False starts, "Hold on a sec," giggling, flubbed lyrics, revised choreography, missed cues, telephone rings, "Oh, for God's sake," falling out of synch, weird noises upstairs, and stumbling right off the makeshift stage: before the triumph of their first error-free song, they bet they'd somehow lost an entire year and pounds of sweat.

On a Friday night as Em listened to Dee's complaint eruption—"'Once I fell in love and it was a gas' . . . A gas, who even says that any more? . . . God, it's not like we're in the 1950s . . . Hmm, the instrumental part at the beginning of that song is even longer. I guess it helps create a mood or something, seems kinda pointless . . . 'The mind is slowly failing.' Ra ra ra ra ra ra . . . That chick sings with marbles in her mouth, so how are we supposed to make heads or tails of whatever she's saying? . . . God, how are we supposed to . . ."—her friend's storming ahead bravado struck her as a front.

"It's not like anyone else knows the words either, Dee. We'll just make whatever we end up singing sound, well . . . it'll sound totally convincing."

Instead of a broom handle, Dee brandished a silver wrench as a mic on the Saturday night of their exhilarating victory over the universe, human idiocy, and "Eat to the Beat," inhaling the rare, wondrous air of perfection for exactly two minutes and thirty seconds.

"I need *something*, hold on." Dee grabbed a chrome flashlight from the furnace.

At first they copied, aiming for mechanical, vowel-by-vowel accuracy, intuiting that all the modeling of flashy bangles in the world could never trick an audience into believing that so-so actually meant worthwhile.

Em sat the cassette player next to her on a stool and turned the volume dial high. "Okay, ready? One, two, three." She pressed play and Dee mimicked the singer's jerky pronunciation, slapping on a Queen Elizabeth accent, and danced with the lunatic arms of a robot prepared to march but forced by circumstances to stand nearly still: "Harm ful el e ments in the air air."

On the third try, she stopped. "No way! I'd be standing there like an total idiot until the lyrics began."

"It's not even thirty seconds."

"Yeah, I know, but it feels like eternity. Do *you* want to stand there for that long? Just a sec, I have an idea." She opened box flaps and tried out a tennis racket handle before bolting upstairs. She returned with trial instruments—a wooden spoon, shiny roast fork, pyrex pie plate and metal measuring cup. "I can get a cow bell or a tambourine later. Actually, I know I saw one of those kiddie xylophones on a pull string *somewhere* . . .

Anyways. Right now I just need to make those pinging 'Chop Sticks' sounds."

The basement's scant lighting, sound-dampening surfaces, and the uncritical audience of boxes, ducts, and a grey furnace encouraged them toward the gradual pleasure of unselfconscious abandon, Em hammering *the skins* (a term passed down from Mr. Rusch) and Dee, caring less and less how the eventual breathing and judging crowd would react, growled and whooped and howled, experimenting with minor tonal modifications to make the song her own. Letting loose surprised them. It shouldn't be *that* difficult.

Damp with perspiration they were grinning and giddy by the tenth time Em rewound the tape.

"That was orgasmic. Again? She says 'disorientated,' that's not even a word. Should we change it? Dis orie nnnn ted?"

"I think 'tated' spits out. Even if it's wrong, it's good. Hey, what about . . . Try out Prawn—Pra ah n—instead of Hong Kong Gardens."

"Okay. One more time?"

"Let me—" Dee waved. "I see you there, Demon Child. How come you're out of bed?"

"I heard noises downstairs."

"So you came to investigate? Good boy! I'll come upstairs in a minute, but you go get back into bed, okay?"

A weight lifted, Em's worry eased with the notes that flew from Dee's mouth. However beautiful cherubs might sound, Em heard that mother-love had misled Mrs. Wallace's ears, though not completely. Em's voice didn't grate like fingernails on a blackboard. Lacking a vocabulary for voice descriptions, Em thought Dee's sound nice, especially when compared to her father's comical bellowing in Overwaitea produce aisles and her grandmother's shy, quavering rendition of "(I'll Be With You) In Apple Blossom Time," which she'd perform after a glass of sherry and much coaxing from her sons. Still, Dee's range needed, as men said of old cars, work.

"You sounded pretty good."

"Seriously? Yeah, right. You're just being polite. I'm working on control because sometimes I'm like that noise when you step on a cat's tail. Maybe everyone will be drunk and won't notice anything except these." She made the universal two-hand gesture that meant *boobs for days*.

"That can be one of our backup plans. I'm worried that we don't sound, um, accurate."

"Not yet, give it some time." Dee practiced steps on the taped boundaries of the stage, "Even if the audience knows the song, which isn't bloody likely, they won't expect an imitation."

"Hmm, I think they will."

"What if I say, 'Here's our rendition of a song you might know'?"

"*You* say?"

"Well, somebody says, it doesn't matter who."

"Right." Em felt annoyed but also relieved at her friend's presumption. "Want to go outside before we go back up? We can perfect smoke rings, become total rocker chicks."

"Yeah, let's."

Déviation: APTITUDE

With the exception of absentees—partiers laid up by the 24-hour flu and boys who'd decided that a paper diploma meant less than legit offers for mill shifts—nervous excitement rippled across 176 Grade 11 bodies for two mornings starting on a Monday in mid-October. On the first, the Principal granted boys freedom from classes in order to take a test, a diversion "not mandatory but highly recommended." Girls made their way to one of three assigned rooms on the next. Knock, knock: the future had just dropped by.

In polar opposition to easygoing stretches of nobody pressing much about an adulthood that would assuredly unfold as expected, vague promises that "the world is your oyster" as though that meant something useful, and the occasional practical-minded pointer to stop dreaming and start grabbing a clue, the blue van of city-dwelling representatives of Science and Mathematics arrived to classrooms of fretful whispers to cooly determine students' likeliest slots via exactly one authoritative multiple choice test, the cryptic weapon of their trade.

To teenagers who'd been half-hearing clusters of parental words about grown up responsibility and planning, these fake-friendly arms of the State spoke directly in measured tones about Citizenship, Employment Forecasts, and the Changing Economy. They handed out a glossy illustrated pamphlet with the same name. Their work promised to "direct individuals about to leave the protective bubble of youth with reliable Information," empirical facts categorically distinct from Mom and Dad's hopes and fears, or the wishy-washy, flaky, or jaded commentary shooting from teacher mouths.

Once computed, their tests—a few white pages of pencilled-in ovals, a meaningless pattern to the naked eye—contained powers of clairvoyance any fortune teller would kill for. Pacing up and down aisles the suited men intoned "Don't worry, there are no wrong answers" to a corps of frowns and newly skunky pits.

Assigned to adjacent rooms the year before, Gordyn and Jay had filled in the tiny ovals as instructed (carefully, with the stubby 4B pencil provided). They compared notes right after, their joshing around peppered with dismissive *as ifs*.

When the results arrived three weeks later with a page of small print explanations, the Principal had set aside a spare class to ponder future career choices selected by the machine, which students pictured as blinking and churning as its huge body took up an entire room in one of those futuristic office buildings with mirrored windows at the city's core.

"Aptitude is not destiny," Mr. S had assured his milling wards from the second step of the bleachers, "but it does imply that you'll be far better suited for some sectors than others."

"Like a rabbit is suited to carrots," he added.

Accompanied with theatrical glances toward the gym's high bank of windows, as though the actual future sat right there on the horizon, the earnest speech featured heavy phrases—"a time of important decisions," "careful consideration," and "discuss such matters with your parents."

The man emphasized relative freedom of choice: if the meeting had been taking place in another country, a miserable, drab-uniformed one just a stone's throw from Big Brother—an East Germany, a Soviet Union, a China—all of this would have been decided, iron-clad and no ifs, ands, or buts, by the final year of elementary school. Without a word of juvenile input. By their early years as teenagers luckless kids there were already sorted, no better than chicks at a hatchery. Well before their sweet sixteenth, in other words, their destiny as a specific cog in the machine of the state had been pinpointed; tests and computation mapped it down to the smallest detail. Soldier or plumber, calculations existed to tell them which. Signalling his finale, he hitched "Seriously, now, consider your luck" to a slow, thoughtful nod.

With a no-fuss pageboy that mixed uneasily with hair dyed platinum, perfectly neat and matching skirt and sweater combos in pink, yellow, or white, and year-round beige sandals, the girls' councillor and the Principal's right hand, Mrs. D's frosted pink lips smiled widely with these morsels of news and wisdom. As far as choices went, she summarized, the lives of these unfortunates were as good as over, so count your blessings.

During the period's leftover minutes, Gordyn had fixed on the ridiculous appearance of ditch digger and farm labourer, as though the career list had been compiled in medieval Europe; the only missing options were blacksmith, executioner, and court jester. He also poked holes in the stupid assumptions on the part of the machine's makers (it being nothing but a massive pocket calculator, after all): possessing a strong mechanical aptitude, which his test scores had revealed, did not make the next logical step stopping by a garage or a mill to fill out an application form. Designing a pattern for a shirt and then sewing it, or starring in and directing a home movie made equal demands on someone's mechanical know-how. Arranging a flower bouquet used as much mechanical aptitude as that other popular career recommendation for boys, mortuary technician.

Jay had shoulder-checked Gordyn when he made cracks about "Clerical," miles above Jay's second-place aptitude, "Custodial." Apparently, wrong answers were possible if his earnestness with oval filling had predicted that he'd wind up typing forms for decades or serving his boss coffee. Or humming brainlessly while using the floor polisher, scraping gum from desks, and scrubbing toilet bowls. He felt pangs of envy at Gordyn's the-sky's-the-limit scores, which showed him as possessing aptitude in practically everything. And Gordyn's zingers about hiring Jay as his secretary and Jay's future destiny as a welfare mom hadn't helped either.

"Better a welfare mom than a . . . " Jay raised his voice, "cornholer." Sometimes Gordyn needed a public reminder of the limits of friendship.

Speeding through the door frame Jay slam-dunked the balled paper into the garbage can. The resounding *thunk* had satisfied him, the *up yours, man* noise a warning to anything, print outs included, crowding his path.

The identical process a year later encouraged a brief cascade of tears. Dee's talents, according to her score, pushed her toward the domestic arts: housewife, florist, beautician.

Dry-eyed, Em threw her sheets directly into the trash can, convinced that she knew herself better than any machine ever could. She'd just skip telling her dad, who'd wait about a quarter of a second before the raised eyebrows of "I told you so."

She'd rather slave away in the new fiberglass factory than pass her days poking at patient's decaying teeth and saying "Open wider" from 9 to 5 until eternity.

The machine had practically sent all the girls pastel uniforms, free toothbrushes, and a lifetime supply of bibs. Ditto for sticking needles into arm crooks and taking dictation year after year from suit-and-tie executives in office towers. The girls councillor announced the top slots should be thought of as recommendations. And that being naturally skilled at something didn't mean you'd enjoy doing it. She remarked that fishily the machine had determined that no girl had a natural talent for politics, car repair, or the entire field of law, except for stenography.

"A baby factory. God. I may as well get knocked up this afternoon and lay into a chocolate cake. What's the point!?!"

"Mine has kindergarten teacher, Dee. I swear parents just bribed them. God. Fuck that shit, right?"

After returning the forms and giving a little speech about the importance of following your heart while looking into your heart at the same moment and facing your very real limitations, Mrs. D explained how she had to break the news in two other classrooms. In her absence the girls should take a minute to think over their results.

Dee and Em pored over the lengthy list of careers for which they apparently possessed no aptitude. Em noticed how the dumb machine hadn't bothered to include model, fashion designer, or actress as categories at all, as though they were fantasies that failed to register on the radar because of their ridiculousness or obscurity (along with clown, ballerina, and princess in Monaco). For the no-nonsense girl who dreamed of limelight but comprehended that factory fluorescents were as close as she'd get, the computer offered seamstress, theatre technician, and department store cashier.

Part-time hooker with money to burn? That one appeared nowhere.

Notebooks / October

Maybe we should slip one of the almighty Computer Whizzes a message about overlooked Career Choices?!? I think they've missed a few (haha).

Venture: ID / September – October

Dee and Gordyn memorized their father's driver's license photograph one night as the parental units guffawed at *Bizarre* with popcorn bowls in their laps downstairs.

No fancy background, only ordinary office lighting: an identical picture would require no props, Gordyn understood, imitation instead of artistic flair. As for a plain wall in eggshell white, that could be found inches away—renters who'd moved from province to province until recently, they's had carted around the same shopping mall painting to hang above the couch for years; to save steps Delphine insisted on leaving the paint on all walls untouched.

A grey area, Merv's sketchily drawn and alleged deal worried Gordyn. And when he regaled the gang with his admirable moment of taking the bull by the horns, he dropped the special offer small print of Merv's proposal, "wait and see" his temporary motto.

Gordyn agreed about the few and far between nature of authentic deals. The bakery that sold Long Johns and jelly donuts at recess sold leftovers in the final five minutes at two-for-one prices. The benevolent facade—Mr. Swanson readily explained these tidbits of business tactics at the till—created an impression of generosity while actually getting rid of useless but costly inventory *and* cementing customer loyalty. The same principle applied to discount bins of irregular socks at Field's and, more or less, Dee's "one-time free trial offer" to Ranchero Heights parents giving her babysitting services a test-run.

Gordyn asked to borrow his dad's Pentax. To the offer from Edmund for professional guidance with the lenses and light meter, Gordyn reminded him about school projects and how teachers frowned on parents with helping hands.

"Fair enough. But you-a break it, you-a buy it, you-a catch-a my drift?"

Gordyn wondered whether everyone had practiced being gag-Italians back in the 1950s.

Enjoying the gang's approval, he'd told them the cost was "as yet unknown," a phrase from TV newscasters. No one had the least idea how much ID generally cost, and when Dee and Em asked around the amounts varied crazily. They concluded that nobody else had a clear grasp, either. Kids had far more to say about who dealt in homework assignments for pay. Fake ID was evidently not as widespread a black market as pot and liquor store purchases.

John D's reputation had to rest on illusion, a foundation of supposition. And since he did nothing to dispute it, he enjoyed the heightened stature. With that aha, the gang made a minor revision to the school's pecking order.

At the morning break Gordyn herded the gang into the art classroom (deserted, their ready excuse unuttered) and stood them next to the kiln, the only patch of undecorated wall in the entire place. Em's "Say sleaze" to Gordyn completed the photo shoot. Half-jogging at lunch he returned to school, the film roll deposited at the drug store. Factoring in a curious developer putting two and two together, he'd taken random shots in the classroom to fill up the roll.

On D-Day Gordyn slinked toward Acapulco's, thinking that a word from a French class quiz—*inquiétude*—summarized his gut's lows, highs, and middles. Though by now he'd officially settled on a joe job with Merv such as hauling garbage or taking pointlessly exact inventory, anxious dreamscape images pushed into his vision every so often, landing him in thankless, dangerous roles as Merv cracked the whip without mercy.

For cops on TV, drivers in getaway cars were the easiest to capture and the first to cave in, while ringleaders regarded them as expendable, loose ends. A loser outcome: Gordyn wished—and muttered a prayer to the universe—to sidestep all of them. But he'd accept a window display assignment like a duck to water. Aculpulco's could stand a style-conscious updating.

Merv quickly nodded at Gordyn and returned to teasing the customers at the till. "You can't go wrong with strawberry, ladies . . . Men love the taste of fruit in their mouths."

Gordyn didn't recognize either girl, though they looked youthful enough to belong in his grade. They gushed and giggled and tossed carefully feathered and blocky home-streaked hairdos and told Merv flirtatiously they expected a refund if the promised results didn't pan out. Gordyn held the door open for the blondest, who struggled to balance a paper bag of groceries on the baby stroller's canopy. The air around them wafted sugary lip gloss and spritzed lemon in every direction.

"I kid you not, muchacho, tell chicks it'll improve their love life and they'll buy anything." Merv's voice growled. "Everything primed to go?"

Gordyn unzipped his gym bag and withdrew a manila envelope. He'd paper-clipped photos to four sheets on which Dee had block-printed names, dates, and addresses.

"I'll be damned, looking good." Merv brought a photo close to squinted eyes. "You take to this like a pro. Born criminal, eh?"

"I guess. My mom says I'm just totally organized."

"You can drive, right?"

"Yup."

"My—." The brass bells fixed to the front door sounded as the chatty shopper returned, minus the stroller. "I told my friend I dropped the soother in here." She held it out. "Can you ring up one of these, like yesterday?" She ran an index finger along the middle tier of the wooden platform of natural scent samples. "Um, this one, Tahitian Moon. She's a frigging nightmare for Christmas presents, but I caught her checking that out."

"Good eye." Continuing the smooth talk, Merv crouched at the counter behind the till. "Those are going on sale next week, so I'll give you ten per cent off, let's call it . . . six bucks. I'll put it in an earring box."

"Perfect." The woman slid a white wet-look vinyl purse off her shoulder and retrieved a wallet. She smiled, tapped her wristwatch, and made for the door.

"Okay, where were we?" Merv lit a cigarette. "Oh right, my guy out in Brackendale is, hmm, he's kinda laid up for a bit. The delivery schedule is mucked up."

As Gordyn listened to Merv's "nuts and bolts"—a simple proposal requiring driving but no getaway cold sweats—he calculated gas money and hours swallowed up. He'd have to manufacture excuses (a cinch: filling in for a flu-ridden Harjinder, surprise after-school assignments, extra rehearsals thanks to unnamed cast slacking off, mysterious events with unnamed but date-worthy girls).

Even though the exact amount remained unknown, Gordyn weighed an offer to pay full price for the IDs, which would mean additional shifts and delayed progress for everyone. Plus, he'd feel idiotic for boasting about an excellent harvest when he'd actually only strewn the ground with iffy seeds. He realized too that if he began to back out now, Merv could jack up the price to a crippling level—to teach a memorable lesson about the cruel moodiness of the world. As if, Gordyn thought, I need that lesson again.

"Anyways, Ronnie'll be back on his feet in no time." Merv's waved the envelope.

"Okay." While Gordyn understood that he could refuse—say "Thanks anyway" and leave Acapulco's for good—the option struck him as wimpy. Really, delivering glass pipes to a list of shops in the Valley looked more or less the same as the newspapers he'd once toted around the neighbourhood from two moves ago. True, the range was bigger. A car evened out that. "Oh, my Dad's not big on letting me use his car when he's not in it with me."

"That, my man, is no sweat. I keep the Rust Rocket out back for that very purpose." To Gordyn's unasked question Merv added, "White Chevy van, can't miss it. Piece of shit, but the 350's a reliable beast."

An evergreen grid of roads and pastures, sporadic hobby farms with quaint red barns, and trailer homes plunked in fields and surrounded by derelict vehicle rings, Brackendale began once the northernmost residential streets of the Bend petered out. The area mostly attracted buyers keen to escape inquisitive eyes and the town's hustle and bustle. Gordyn knew its stretch of byways because he'd laid turf there for two weeks over the previous August—at the tail-end of a depressing summer spent trudging downtown to stare at job board cards at a government agency supposedly dedicated to connecting bored students to employment. "Serving Up an Investment in the Future," a sign lied.

Before sweat-drenched days of lugging damp rolls of sod from pallets and unfurling them in neat rows as bored prisoners watched from inside the fence, he'd discovered that men using student workers expected a pound of flesh for the two dollars they paid each hour. A month earlier, Gordyn had been fired and humiliated twice: once by an impatient drywaller who laughed at and complained about his employee over the eight hours Gordyn struggled with gyp-roc sheets and, for the next job, by a man who'd hired him to install insulation ("You swing a hammer like a girl," a businessman with the German accent said at 4:30. "Don't come back tomorrow"). When neither man sent out a cheque, Gordyn stomped down to the agency and filled out a complaint form. His conclusion: if they could get away with it people would still keep slaves.

The grass turf boss—blood from a stone when it came to words, but not a jerk—met with the crew of four as they arrived at Brackendale, telling them at stage-whisper volume (and going so far as to glance over his shoulder) to keep clear of the fence and avoid eye contact when the green rows closed in on the chain link. The crew, he underlined, should not speak *at all* to the prisoners. The boss explained, "They'll ask you to do things," leaving the blank to each teen's imagination. Smuggling seemed the obvious bet, though Gordyn couldn't guess at what they'd want to smuggle out—a letter? If so, why not just send it in the mail? Smuggling *in* made sense, but that would require an exchange of money.

One prisoner did approach Gordyn's area of turf. He asked, "Get me a few packs of smokes? There's good money in it for you." Gordyn ignored him and hurried back to the pallet for another turf roll.

None of the men inside the yard looked mug-shot mean, hardened criminals who'd just as soon stick you with a homemade blade as nod hello. Clean-shaven with short sandy hair, the man requesting cigarettes could easily substitute for the high school's principal or one of the white-coated pharmacists at the drug store.

Merv warned Gordyn twice about the van's tricky shift and joked that Ronnie's personality hadn't ever won him the Miss Congeniality crown. A sash, Gordyn thought, but held his tongue.

Gordyn nodded and strived to appear eager. Still, doubt and bursts of resentment about the effort required for just one item on the band's to-do list swamped his fleeting sense of accomplishment. He'd already asked Fiona to cover his shift when he phoned a doubtful Mr. Swanson with an excuse related to a school play. The importance of maintaining an A average sold him.

The run would fall into two parts, he'd learned: pick up at Ronnie's place and delivery to a string of eight shops in the Valley. Merv had asked—which implied a choice, Gordyn grumbled to himself—for him to drop off the rest on Saturday and thought accomplishing that should take just an afternoon. Gordyn mentioned a drama class meeting; his parents reminded him of their set plans and, feeling guilty or something, left out lunch money for pizza.

A long threading driveway of rutted mud wound through alder clumps and dwindled into tread marks at Ronnie's place. Expecting a doublewide trailer or an A-frame cabin, Gordyn took in a pickup camper on criss-crossed timber posts and, ten paces away, a pop-up trailer with propane canisters piled atop the hitch. Within both, light of desk lamp wattage glowed. Reminding himself about Frank Serpico and going undercover, Gordyn parked closest to the trailer. He'd go into character gradually, improvise, follow Ronnie's lead.

Behind this temporary housing, a frame of weathered two-by-fours and a patchwork skin of buckling plywood sheets spelled out Ronnie's situation: a man of plans if not means or follow-through. At home and across the cul-de-sac, Mr. McKinley's wreckage yard Ranchero under a canvas tarp held down by cinder blocks long since tinged green with slime, and right next door Mr. Toth's brick pile (aka the promised built-in BBQ and a block party "one of these days") showcased dispositions in common.

The pop-up's flimsy aluminum screen door rattled as Gordyn knocked. "Mister—. Um, hello . . . Ronnie? Merv, the guy from Acapulco's, he sent me. To pick up packages."

A low, croaky voice sounded. "That damned latch's stickier than molasses. Just reach through the screen and turn the handle."

Gordyn realized that exploring RV lots with his father had prepared him for mobile vacation home interiors—gleaming, plastic, sanitized. For a backwoods trailer, who knew what to expect: strewn shotguns and dangling grouse carcasses; an entire home's worth of furniture crammed into a tin can; untamed craziness.

Somewhere a window stood open; the trailer smelled of October coolness dank with fallen leaves.

"So, this is the calvary?" The question sounded rhetorical. Gordyn didn't reply. Merv's "laid up" had prompted two images at once—a dad who'd thrown out his back and a soap opera character in a head-to-foot cast—but uninjured Ronnie stretched out on a plaid chesterfield of butterscotch tones, a dark blanket pulled up to his shoulders, feet in white tube socks atop the armrest. No TV or radio blared. Gordyn wondered what he was doing in the murky light. He seemed neither sleepy nor drunk. Ronnie gestured to butcher paper parcels on a pull-down kitchen table and said, "Knock yourself out, kid."

"Okay." Gordyn memorized the man's features, just in case: pipsqueaky—narrow-shouldered, maybe 5' 8"—shaggy strawberry blonde hair, moustache, face not recently shaven and not yet middle-aged that probably grew dreamy at the sight of a passing El Camino.

Gordyn barely needed to move. He counted sixteen shoebox-sized packages on the table, all wrapped in miles of packing tape. Ronnie had written the addresses with black felt marker and underlined each town twice; none of them fell outside an hour's drive.

Gordyn hauled the packages—spongy with plenty of give in the middle, crunchy and hard otherwise—out to the van in four trips. He calculated routes and knew the fastest when he returned to Ronnie's to say goodbye. Ronnie remained watchful but not unfriendly during Gordyn back and forth trots. The silence did not encourage questions.

"Do you need anything?" Gordyn thought the man looked pathetic.

"Nah, not unless you got a couple of gold bricks in your pocket."

"I'd be flying to Caesar's Palace if I had that much gold." Gordyn decided his real answer—"La Rive Gauche," to which he'd fly via Concorde—would set him apart as prissy, a total snob, or worse.

He considered himself an expert at the cost of revealing too much personality. With strangers from any setting, he sniffed the scent and automatically set about mimicking it. He'd seen that invisibility never worked out, even though it looked good on paper. With hiding in plain sight he found better luck. In the adult world, at least. His father tut-tutted about "erring on the side of caution," but as far as strangers were concerned caution looked identical to security. Unless you hung out with the in-crowd, speaking your mind or showing your true face resulted in a penalty of some kind; withholding reflected sensibility, he'd argue, the wisdom of self-defense.

"That'd be living," Ronnie said. "Make sure you re-lock the door the same way as before."

That was easy, Gordyn thought. Ease felt deceptive because it usually meant a cause for worry. A painless exam, jock restraint when he strode by the horde, mirror time showing no new outbreaks: a trick of light, the eye of the storm. He decided to resist slitting open one of Ronnie's bundles, heeding the warnings of dead curious cats and Pandora.

When Gordyn's mother claimed to "see a family resemblance," the communal trait always amounted to a bone-deep flaw in the object of her scorn—foolish with money, wandering eye, lazy as hell, braggart, cheapskate. The men who accepted packages from Gordyn shared an actual familial look, as though they'd all been raised poor and taught not to fret an iota about appearances. With loose and ancient faded jeans, buttoned black leather vests over t-shirts stretched at the neck, hair that hadn't been trimmed recently, and stained smokers' fingers, seeing them carrying coolers of beer toward the annual Canada Day picnic of the Scruffy Family reunion at a lakeshore paved over by water slides and mini-golf courses would not catch him by surprise.

Their shops—of knick knacks (posters, incense, candles, cocoanut shell trinkets, pipes) and furniture (chunky wooden coffee tables, beds, and living room pieces slathered with vanish after being scorched with a blow torch)—shared a family resemblance too, out of the way addresses run by men who felt a deep affinity for Margaritaville and Luckenback, Texas. For them, Acapulco existed as a heavenly state of mind, a Shangri-La, rather than a mere holiday destination on a map.

They greeted his deliveries with agreeable-enough small talk, asking about traffic or joshing about weather on the other side of the river, wondering when Ronnie would get back on his feet. Accepting the packages quickly they slid them beneath the till and out of sight. With no personal questions for the substitute delivery boy, though, they confirmed boundaries: thankful for the packages, yes, but not seeking to make friends—though one sallow man with Brylcreem'd hair in Bottlesburg offered Gordyn a cup of coffee while nudging the cigarette deck in his direction.

A stop took Gordyn under ten minutes from the time he slammed the Rust Rocket's creaking door.

Venture: EPs, Import Singles / September –

Between roadside pit stops and town depots stashed out of the way on back streets, Saturday bus excursions into the city for window shopping and gawking ran a few ticks under two hours. On a good day. For whatever reasons, return trips always made up at least fifteen minutes. Dully familiar, these milk runs tested a body's patience. Yet for the gang they seemed necessary and sensible, pre-requisite baby steps or qualifying runs for the bustling nearby future. The glass, concrete, and white marble skyscrapers testified to the presence of cosmopolitanism in a dense form, like frozen orange juice concentrate, while older, squatter buildings dressed up with hulking grooved columns and carved stone doodads evoked an economy alive and booming when the Bend was only a scattering of plank shacks and a general store hammered together on a stretch of floodplain by dreamy but mud-poor fools.

The central X on an expanding grid, vertical downtown addresses featured entire outlooks remote from those of the Bend. They had to. Banks of light glowed inside these valuable businesses with an international reach that surely helped push the country forward.

And at ground level, the thoroughbred urbanites who clustered impatiently at curb edges for traffic light permissions before they rushed along sidewalks to somewhere important clearly advertised a rat race the gang believed they'd be wise to accept and start training for.

Family-wise, cityward trips had rarely extended as far as the downtown core.

As always, Delphine's "Too pricey" registered with the finality of "Off with their heads!"

Besides, traipsing along the streets like vagabond Okies struck her as pointless, she'd say. Worse, the traffic's noisy lurching—along with the nastily pushy, chaotic, and crowded walkways—left her nervous, prone to snapping and to migraines too, and, once safely returned to the Bend, weary and in need of a dampened facecloth across the forehead, closed eyes, and bedroom seclusion.

Edmund readily agreed to PNE exhibits or boat, home, and garden shows at the Coliseum but waffled about any destination within walking distance of a shopping mall. Right downtown, though? Not bloody likely. They'd get lost or their car stolen, he'd claim with dramatic slow-motion head swinging, and then put his foot down. "No, there's no vote. You're not living in a democracy and I'm the king of this castle," he'd announce, and trigger mirth—unspoken jabs about his long reign on the porcelain throne each and every morning.

If they spoke promises to keep their complaining to a dull roar when around Delphine, he'd eventually compromise and cart them as far as the Spaghetti Factory, whose stained glass windows shone above a cobbled Gastown lane.

With the avidness of ravenous pets seated just below the Thanksgiving turkey platter, Dee and Gordon had locked on to the phrases nestled within Edmund's hazy promises about solo day trips: "mature enough," "old enough," "one day soon."

★

At a Prawn Gardens meeting, Em and Jay had mentioned that Joey reserved downtown's riches for impressing romantic dates at candle-lit steakhouses and cocktail lounges. And who knew where else. Whenever he offered to drive them to the Starboard Jeans Factory, a dreary outlying warehouse stacked to the rafters with rock-bottom prices and counterfeit brands, they said thanks but no thanks to the suddenly thrift-obsessed man.

One visit had been enough. They could buy fashion necessities with their own money.

When the gang traded stories they discovered another commonality, which proved nothing except the fatal globetrotting lameness of parents—no more surprise there than waking to waves of icy rain in November—because these white bread grown ups had already embraced a philosophy of "same old, same old," and on exactly what and where and who they liked and didn't care for, hankering in no way for exotic sights and fresh experiences.

Sliced brownish meatloaf and mashed greyish potatoes followed by an eternally cushiony recliner, a lifelong and punctual subscription to *TV Guide*, clear reception, a foolproof clicker, and "For the love of god, just give me a moment of peace and quiet" would suffice until they arrived at blanketed laps, packaged English biscuits with a pot of Orange Pekoe on a roller tray, and permanent sleep.

Envisioning such an existence led the gang to the only possible decision, they surmised, for a sentient being: "Just shoot me when I'm that settled. God."

Wedged in the broad shadows of a pair of sodden-weather meccas—spacious and air-conditioned rival department stores whose escalator-linked floors of inventory filled two entire city blocks—Phantasmagoria suffered the insult of standing midpoint between A and B.

Gordyn noticed the narrow store's sign while paused before the sleek northern entrance of the futuristic landmark they'd nicknamed the Rotunda. There, a towering cylinder with matching glass doors tinted smoky-brown ushered shoppers onto a serpentine carpeted ramp that wound down to scads of fancy merchandise.

Half a block south, the sign's whorls of trapped neon didn't catch his eye: the electrified gas made the ghostliest impression in daylight. The skinny tubes formed circles atop the grooves of the store's 100% guaranteed lure, a LP of cartoonish proportions, the enormous disk fashioned out of sheet aluminum and painted black.

Otherwise, the usual—a half-inch thick rectangle of plate glass held in place by wood and metal—separated the sidewalk and Granville Street's stampede of foot traffic from the mysteries within.

Having heard from Edmund about the eagerness of money-hungry city cops to issue stiff jaywalking fines, Gordyn raced toward a painted crossway. Seconds later he shouldered the bulky glass door and peeked inside.

Waiting for the pedestrian signal again after a breathtaking eyeful and a speedy circuit around bin after bin of records, he felt thankful for the reliable fact of curiosity and blessed by good luck. He predicted the others would blow fuses at this discovery.

Entering the shop illustrated the idea of a threshold perfectly, Gordyn thought, unlike crossing the border at Blaine, where bedding plants grew identically in each country. At Phantasmagoria's doorway, though, as the rearmost foot remained in official reality the lead had already begun exploring an exotic other, a world just beyond the everyday.

Gordyn felt astonished that practically no one appeared to care. Or to notice.

Season after season, city dwellers who marched along damp, rain-slick, or August-baked sidewalks barely tilted their necks to inspect the awesome map of tower and sky but managed to yank out their forearms every ten seconds to check wristwatches. And along ground level the tall storefront of smoky plate glass and a door with the same translucent solidity faithfully reflected their nearby workaday mornings of business, lunch break errands, and long afternoons of further business.

To all appearances sniffing around was, for rat racers, as pointless as daydreaming.

In order to glimpse inside properly a passerby would only need to momentarily break from routine. Fully halted, he'd draw close (nose almost touching) to the mute surface of the glass and cup his hands. Breathing record shop air two steps later, the noise of traffic and the daily army of pedestrians with 9–5 destinations and worries would disappear as though they'd never existed, rendered out of grasp by the so-called singing—unearthly wails, cooing alien chants, and shrieked or bellowed others belonging to bizarre categories—mixed into gloomy drum machine programming and brutal, piercing synthesizer squawks. Always turned up loud, the vocals sounded affected, fragmented, and artificial, roboticized or mangled somehow after the recording session, as though the standard—pretty and heartfelt or danceably melodious—represented artistic failure and the terminally passé.

During the initial ninety-second tour Gordyn listened to a screeching, possibly drunk-at-the-mic woman bark out and yodel that maudlin Elvis ballad about doing it his way. Her version jumped around from German to English. But instead of exhaling lungfuls of misery incarnate, she seemed pissed off and triumphant. Multiples of the woman, with hair dyed in violent pink, orange, and red chunks, glared out from a display column of jackets whose clear plastic sleeves labelled each disk an Import Single, which apparently also meant Really Expensive. Nina Hagen's raised arm revealed the affront of pit hair in fully grown dirt brown. Her one open eye stared out with unknown but malevolent intentions, moated by thick eyeliner that stretched back as far as her temple, in parallel with paved on rouge.

Immediately after that performance, a rumbling bass voice didn't sing but spat the distorted words "nag nag nag" and other indecipherable lines from the circuit of speakers. It sounded furious but mechanical and demonic, washed over as well by the hissy static of the TV when a station has gone off the air.

Gordyn found no Import Single to match the words. He'd been puzzled and turned off by the ugliness—intentional!—of J-P's furious punker music. He didn't get the rabid-dog singing.

Nor the crude album art. But with the "nag nag nag" group and the German howler with the fiery dye job he appreciated the *style.*

Décor-wise, Gordyn thought, he'd seen better efforts from the old man who sat inside the shack at the Bend's garbage dump.

Motley store staff over the years had tacked up and halfheartedly torn down layer after layer of band, album, and concert posters. For the hell of it, he guessed, they'd also glued chipped records and water-damaged or otherwise warped LP jackets, all at helter-skelter angles. And they'd slopped and sprayed matte black paint on bins, pillars, and the staggered sections of dingy and trampled plywood flooring. The ceiling looked as gross as nicotine fingers but far enough away for whatever management that existed to leave it be, "out of sight, out of mind" its operating principle.

If inspecting the cavernous room, Mr. Swanson would bellow "Pure anarchy!" before slumping over—dead of a heart attack.

Excited with the news, Gordyn catalogued as he raced northward to the Rotunda's main floor. Within seconds he'd known he liked the place. The others would too.

Just as practically anyone could rush through racks and stacks of clothing and decide No No Maybe No Yes in a fraction of a minute, his intuition had confirmed that despite utter strangeness the room and its bizarre occupants spoke a language in common with him. With only a few adjustments, they fit.

As he wound around pedestrians he felt convinced that his eyes hadn't witnessed mere purchases, the dumping of sneakers for combat boots, Jordache slash-pocket jeans for torn stockings and silver suspender clasps dangling at floor level—stuff to spot on a mannequin and wear for two or three years before replacing it with a newer fashion, whatever that might be.

(Intuition worked the opposite way, naturally. And it didn't recede or fade away into forgettable wisps. Distaste crept too, mutating steadily into revulsion, with the alarm of an RPM needle jumping from black to red. The jocks that held court in the same hallway corner in five day sessions from September till June, for instance. If he could dispatch them with ESP rays—to a life raft with no fresh water, chain-ganged at the prison of *Cool Hand Luke*, in a cold eternal purgatory of clammy fog—they'd be long gone, and girls they'd insulted without consequence and guys in his boat that they'd pushed around would view his actions as heroic, as indicating valuable leadership DNA. But, in the words of the song, "If wishes were horses . . . ," and mean-spirited reality let him know that instead of special foe-vanquishing powers, keep-out-of-sight and grin-and-bear-it had to be his daily ritual as he counted down the miserable, tense stretch of days until the last final exam.

Until he'd quit, Gordyn had felt a similar creeping reluctance about barbershop weekends. The sensation grew heavier than platinum as his confidence about the hobby's and alleged art form's infinite lousiness grew into an unshakeable doctrine. The willful blindness about the good old days—slavery barely a generation away—appalled him, as did the head in the sand refusal to see the ill will in every heart on every street of the entire world here and now. Watching the smiling men and their glazed expressions, he seethed with resentment at the idiocy. Why bother fretting about the energy crisis or coast-to-coast nuclear missile silos when you could instead squeeze your eyes shut and transport yourself to an imaginary five and ten cent store, where your gorgeous million dollar baby always waits for you and only you, never aging, never bored, never resentful, never moving on?

Shoulder to shoulder with those nostalgic men and their striped vests, the midnight-clad record store workers with the sullen and moody style appeared honest and unafraid, not cowardly and moony and evasive. Black hearts on sleeves—streaks of angry bitterness and I-don't-give-a-shit indifference—made a world of sense.)

Gordyn regarded the shop as a parallel universe, the glass doorway an astonishing portal disguised as nothing special.

The noisy songs—not exactly hummable, not toe-tapping—boomed from exposed speakers bolted inside plywood boxes (more handiwork with black paint slapped on) and suspended using thick steel chains. And right below, the staff, with faces settled at *ennui*, wore suspenders, shadowy or plaid everything, and leather boots with sandwich-thick soles.

Towering but pointedly non-athletic and slouching, or else rotund and decked out in loud, clashing stripes and accessories in aggressively garish purples and reds, everyone ringed their eyes in tar liner and arranged exquisite dyed hair into sharp angles, asymmetrical swoops, severe parts with bleached bangs, topiary shapes with waxy textures, all of which contradictorily proclaimed Notice Me! and Fuck Right Off!

If some ordinary shopper entered and gazed in confusion at the clever floating cube of records—quilt squares of mental-ward images—and still mewed out a question about BTO tickets or requested an album by Kenny Rogers, they'd show him—so normal as to be contemptible—the door with a quick sweeping gesture and barely a glance. Why waste the calories?

"That was more like it," Gordyn mumbled. He'd bet two pay cheques that New York streets *coursed* with cool people just like them.

He'd meandered through as though he'd already made dozens of visits, had the exact record in mind, and just couldn't locate it. Expressions of shock or amazement were for townie rednecks. Losers. Having heard that word throw at him over and again, he changed his mind. His parents were right to say his own sourness wasn't going to win him any popularity contests. Outsiders, then, would feel shocked. Newbies. Those with one foot in the grave.

When Gordyn had first noticed that he didn't fit in, and later grasped the larger truth that he could never belong—a fact sketched for him with the subtlety of a punch to the face—he also understood and gripped onto another must-be fact: that the Bend, a blemish in the armpit of a nowhere valley, represented a piddling fraction of a so-so country, itself a negligible fraction of the world's immense expanse.

Finding the place he'd at last recognize as home, then, would mean not just one weekend's worth of addresses.

Either that, or—please, no—some internal Stepfordy shift happened. He'd wake up and thanks to a mysterious and stealthy overnight change—a birth of new hormones, a radical rearrangement of brain chemicals—he'd stand more closely aligned with the parental units and the rest of the town. On that same bright morning he'd start putting together a life with the available Lego pieces: job (kitchen helper → working the till → Assistant Manager → Manager → franchise owner), full-on love (lovestruck glances at 36-24-36 forms → asking Tracy S to a movie → going out → going steady → engagement → marriage and honeymoon → two kids and a dog), real estate (etc). Basically identical to *Invasions of the Body Snatchers*, but instead of evil seed pods from space there'd be some natural and evolutionary and irresistible process that allowed the tribe to stick together in a survival-of-the-blandest harmony that assured towns of uncomplicated continuance.

Without much reflection, he locked on to the fact that the Phantasmagoria people—staff mostly, but customers hanging out inside too—with their daring styles, screw-you demeanour, loyalty to a cause that registered as fierce and tribal, and the comfort with all of it, didn't represent a destiny for him.

In a month or three he would not be decked out in a sleeveless black t-shirt that showed off pasty skin and noodle-thin arms. He'd never show up at school glowering with pierced ears and a shaved head. Coach F wouldn't ever feel the need to comment on Gordyn's two tires of eyeliner and fire an index finger in the direction of the change room.

Gordyn appreciated the theatrical sensibility, though. The bold embrace of "all the world's a stage" instead of "all the world's whatever works for everybody else" spoke his language.

Still, that willingness to leap far outside the tried and true he couldn't sense as an authentic facet of himself. Taking a role on a stage for a night or two, or dressing up for Halloween made sense to him. But more than that? No way. Opposite to him and his mandatory uniform at Brownie's, the chubby girl in torn tights, an oversized and belted white t-shirt, and lipstick the colour of dried blood, or the cadaverous guy with the leather vest machine-gunned with pins but shirtless underneath made their way to work in these proud ensembles, no doubt hearing rude comments and facing block after block of glaring judgement. And they took power from the experience.

He regretted that whatever peacock tendencies his dad thought his strange son naturally—and unfortunately—possessed had been tamped down so far as to barely exist at all.

The wide aisle's gleaming speckled floor encouraged a sliding approach, and Gordyn slalomed quickly between the blocky obstacle course of chrome and glass cases, ducking cloying drifts of perfume.

Despite jingles anyone with a TV hummed to, the molecules of scent weren't kinda young, kinda now, or kinda wow as far as he could tell.

Girls at school considered directing the nozzles of their lemon or strawberry body mist at guys as the pinnacle of funny, and his own shirts sometimes reeked of fabric softener when Dee OD'd on it during her turn at laundry chores. Ditto the entire house with lemon whenever she dusted; her model-sized nostrils apparently reacted with less sensitivity than his Gallic honker.

High above, a galaxy of speakers painted to match the ceiling released cascading strings of Muzak—no radio blaring on the counter here—to hypnotize shoppers, or at least lull them into slowing down to touch seductive merchandise.

"Gordo! Gord-oo!" Gordyn sighed, guessing that Gene Simmons still heard his mother call out "Chaim," decades after the fact. And on some days Dee could be so stunned, oblivious as a doll.

He'd tried out a plot starring his mother sneaking around with a grease monkey who signed papers with a crude X. This version of Dee's origin story fizzled out as too improbable: scruples ran through his mother veins in thick clots; she'd sooner rob a bank. He and Dee just emerged from different depths of the family gene pool.

Dee and Em had been sampling eye shadows and rouges in lustrous black cases—all French and pricy, items they'd decided in advance they couldn't afford to shoplift. Especially with those kindly-faced old ladies rumoured as plainclothes cops milling around.

Though the girls had littered the case with tissues streaked with red and black, the counter lady advising them looked on with an expression of infinite patience.

The resident expert, Dee had daubed their faces with foundation that brought to mind the pallid moon surface hue of canned mushrooms. Atop the blank canvas: matte rose shadow on cheeks, eye lids, and lips. She struck a steely pose, karate chop hands frozen at mannequin-stiff angles.

"Ladies and gentlemen, it's The Sex Androids," Em said, the chief android's clone.

"Hmm, what will Jay and I be? Ladies and gentlemen, it's The Sex Androids and their Boring Brothers?"

"That we can figure out later. It's just an idea for now."

"Speaking of ladies and gentlemen, I've just found something you do not want to miss. Where's Jay?"

"He got bored here."

"And?"

"Oh, he said he'd come back in 20."

"And?"

"That means any second now, okay G?"

"Thank you."

"Do you need food or something. You're crankier than usual."

"The answer to my question served fine."

"Meow."

Jay approached in the fall's uniform of moulting caramel cords and a long white t-shirt he'd wear whenever its sleeve cuffs weren't too dingy. The word-bubble above the half-peeled and smiling iron-on banana at chest level said "Mange Moi."

He'd find a favourite and wear it until he lost interest, stained it, or complaints and comments pelted him with the insistence of hail: "Drive Naked. Give the Law a Break," "Support R.U.M.P," with a Royal Ukrainian cop riding a horse backwards, an iron-on of the *Jaws* shark bursting from ocean, "Yup, You're on My List" with a drawing of a seated man reading from an unwound roll of toilet paper, and "You Make My Tetter Totter" which had obvious pervy intentions but no accompanying cartoon.

"We gotta go."

"What?" That code usually meant a newly shoplifted but awkward item, or suspicions about being monitored.

"I just want to show you my discovery before we head back to the bus depot."

"Five minutes? We've got to get the gunk off."

"Now. But don't worry about it, you'll blend right in."

The woman at the makeup counter began sweeping the tissues into a pile.

"Thanks ever so for your help." Dee smiled and turned to catch up with the rest.

"Open sesame!" Gordyn pushed the door and let the gang pass through. He'd anticipated exclamations of "Wicked!" and "Very cool" and basked in success as they wandered into warehouse hugeness, three Ali Babas thrilled to relish astounding heaps of treasure.

With palms protecting his ears, Jay mouthed "Wow." Dee muttered "gross" and sneered at a corner of leaf bits and paper litter. She lifted the cuffs of her jeans and stepped delicately, as if readying herself to cross a swamp.

"God, Dee, don't be a pill. Some days your room's way worse than this." Gordyn watched Em, already entranced and flipping through the bins.

Marching along a rough diagonal for the 4:25 bus, they toted black plastic bags stamped with the store's gold record insignia and felt like audacious criminals—but to all eyes normal citizens—who stowed smuggled goods in plain sight. They'd soaked up atmosphere and leaned against mirrors at headphone stations, eyes wandering compulsively while memorizing record sleeve art, band looks, customer ensembles, and the circus of staff.

For the final decision, they'd based the choice on guesswork, intuition, feel, and colour palette, narrowing the store's bounty of records to an affordable one per person: Throbbing Gristle, Visage, The Normal.

Em made her choice easily upon spotting a sale-priced Import Single. Its jacket featured an eerie black and white photograph of a mysterious woman wearing an overcoat and small round sunglasses. Standing in a stark, wintry setting she held out her pair of long braids like antlers. The singer had arranged to have her name—Lene Lovich—spelled with coils of barbed wire. Whatever "I Think We're Alone Now" was, its singer clearly had a keen nose for style.

They all frowned at Nina Hagen's tough too-muchness.

Street lights clicked on as the gang made hasty strides for the depot. For the next trip, they decided, they'd cut short wandering through department stores and seriously cram, as with tests, at Phantasmagoria.

And, after Jay brought up the idea for the millionth time, yes, they'd probably take up his offer to smuggle a thermos of liquor mixture to make the bus ride less of a drag.

As opposed to dumb rockers who drank and got caught and kicked off the bus in the middle of nowhere by a driver who acted all self-righteous and puritanical despite gin blossoms and smoke stops at practically every intersection, they'd look wholesome and squeaky-clean, churchgoers as far as anyone could tell, and way high on the honour roll. They'd sip and giggle at a low volume so that not even the person sitting across the aisle could recognize the truth.

Venture: Thrift / October

The following Saturday, Em speed-walked to Dee's in a record fourteen minutes.

Head wrapped in Delphine's gauzy old headscarf for a windswept movie star effect, Dee took a hands-on-hips pose at a nearby crossroad, having told her parents the same half-truth—*an alibi*, they'd decided—about meeting up to help a floundering classmate cram for a make-or-break test. Who'd ever question do-gooders?

Laughing, they strode through the subdivision blocks of the Heights and down the hill to the highway, rehearsing reactions like "Get lost!" to probabilities like creepy old men, rockers from school, and middle aged finger-wagger women in two-toned Thunderbirds. Going undercover, they'd gathered, relied on costume changes (as in the case of investigating a prostitution ring) and phony names belonging to fake histories, but nothing too far-fetched (and hence a fraudulence as easily detected as Inspector Clouseau). They stuck with sisters visiting a sick relative; the reasonable pose suited their needs.

At the side of the highway, they stood, faces half-averted, friends of their parents cruising by the very last outcome they wished for. A man in a white van slowed. "No way, Jose," Em said. Serial killers drove those. Or guaranteed pervs.

Passengers in station wagons looked at them with traffic accident curiosity, as though watching the scene of the girl hitchhikers' gruesome close-by fate with a clairvoyant's immediacy. Logging trucks rumbled and pumped brakes but kept going, which was just as well.

A man in a shiny four-door signalled and pulled over. He flashed brake lights in impatient succession. The passenger door window lowered as they approached.

"Hello girls. I'm heading as far as PoCo." The man tucked his chin and lowered sunglasses down his nose. "How far are you ladies going?"

"Just to Bottlesburg." Dee peered inside. No maniac crouched in the back seat.

"Perfect. You can keep me company and I'll get you there. Hop in." He smiled, righted the arm rest. Dee wrestled with the door handle before he said "Oopsie" and popped the lock. She slid into the middle position; Em followed, leaning against the door.

"Snug as a bug in a rug." He accelerated, spitting gravel.

"This car sure is roomy." Dee studied the ruddy sideburns and moustache; the dull shaggy hair, a wet sand hue, inspired thoughts of a hot oil treatment. A style makeover couldn't hurt, either.

"It's a Lincoln, special ordered. Givenchy Midnight Jade." The air around the man smelled sweet. Juicy Fruit gum sat in the ashtray. "You're pretty enough to model Calvin Klein jeans. Your friend isn't quite tall enough, but she's sure pretty too."

"I bet you say that to all the girls."

"Ha ha, only the prettiest of them." He lifted the green aviators and bounced around his brows. "You girls look like you know a thing or two."

"I guess."

"You probably have boyfriends—."

"We sure do. Mine's on the track team and hers works weekends at the mill."

"—and so you know that guys have needs."

"Everybody has needs, mister. Food and water, to name two."

"Ah, so you're a smart aleck." He returned his attention to the road.

"A car like this must cost a pretty penny." Em ran her hand along leather as red as Twizzlers and just as shiny.

"I do okay, least my wife doesn't complain."

"How long ago did you get married? You don't look that old."

The man drove left-handed and gripped the edge of the seat. The girls feigned interest in passing trees.

"I'm pretty full from breakfast. You girls don't mind if undo my top button do you? I think I need the extra room."

Dee turned to Em and offered her a peculiar smile.

"Do you ladies have your driver's license?"

"Not yet."

"I'll bet you want to try steering."

"My Dad lets me do that sometimes." Dee imagined their conversation as flirtatious, a tug-of-war situation. "When I've been really good."

"And what about when you're bad?"

"Grounded. I'm too old to get spanked."

"Ha ha, I'd say that's a matter for debate."

"We need to get part time jobs before we get licenses." Em understood the game being played and decided her role as the no-nonsense girl related to ignoring the man's innuendo, the Velma to Dee's Daphne.

"I could help you out with that. I keep a little of my pay cheques socked away for . . . special occasions. And this has to be one, right?" The man drummed beats on the dash. "Can you open the glove compartment? I keep my travelling companion there."

Amongst the car registration papers, Em saw a leather-covered flask with a fat silver cap.

"Thanks, little lady. Say, why don't I pull over, more comfortable that way, and maybe your friend there can lend a hand."

"No way, Jose." Dee shook her head, leaving no room for debate. "If you stop now, we can report you. You can keep driving and drop off us and give us some shopping money and we won't say a thing. If you want me to rub you while you're driving that's more. And touching you, that's more too. Okay?"

"You little jail bait bitch."

"We didn't ask for any trouble, mister."

While he huffed and muttered curses and accelerated and jerked his head sideways to speak and then changed his mind, Dee leaned into Em and imagined him foaming with rabies. Their sunglasses reflected oncoming traffic.

"You girls are pros, I see, drive a hard bargain." The man's voice sounded flat now, resigned, his business mind taking over. "There's a ten-spot for you."

"For each of us."

"She's not doing a thing, just sitting there."

"My friend has to watch." She nudged Em, who complained on cue: "Yeah."

"Okay, lucky for you sales were off the chart last month. I could afford ten of you for breakfast."

The man spread his thighs, an invitation that had now changed into a contractual obligation. Keeping her eyes trained on the two lanes that cut a line between cottonwoods along the river and blackberry banks, Dee slid her hand across the smooth seat, inhaled, and let her fingers climb to the top of the tan fabric across his thigh, tentatively, as though calming a frightened dog.

Em glanced sideways, astonished at her friend's unflinching nerve.

Dee pictured Aunt Florence's weary face.

When Delphine's elder sister visited from the city, she arrived tense from the drive. After a few rye and gingers "hold the ice" she'd regale them with stories from the hospital floor that starred vain doctors convinced "they're better than Jesus amongst the lepers." In second fiddle positions, heroic but criminally unappreciated nurses stole the show. And, inevitably, saved the day. Clean-up horror stories followed, and turned Cinderella's drudgery on sore knees into vacation activities and chambermaid work into a worthwhile career. Floor to ceiling vomit, pus oozing from ballooning infections, arterial sprays of blood, pungent torrents of urine, and "shit smears for days," she'd report, shaking her head with the recollection. The stench and misery of each episode topped the last. Wails and painful deaths. After the purge she'd clam up again. The minute she left Em's mother would mutter, "Well, I'm glad she got that out of her system."

The gist of Florence's drop by afternoons seemed to be anchored to the necessity of rye and ginger in the face of the toiling life's bottomless trials and humiliations.

Compared to seven-hour shifts of disease-stained clothes, showboating doctors, and angry moaning patients demanding morphine, pillows, and a sympathetic ear, pocketing twenty bucks for grabbing a stranger's wiener for a few clock ticks looked better than a good deal.

"Eeew, yeah, yeah, that's it."

The lump felt soft and hard, similar to packaged uncooked chicken breast with the bone still in. Dee kneaded the mass with a closed fist. Patting the area with the bare minimum of conviction, she wondered if he'd expect attention all the way to Bottlesburg.

"I think he needs some air."

Dee froze her hand. "Air costs extra." Whispering, she thought, works miracles.

The man didn't move, clearly expecting her to lower the zipper and fish out the slave-driver organ. "Men sure have needs," she said, understanding that for this man her reluctance and his being helplessly at the mercy of his own appetite heightened the thrill.

She'd been on movie dates where bulky guys on hockey teams pushed out words of encouragement—mesmerized too before their Napoleonic puppetmaster. An eyewitness to the change from soft to hard, she never match the impressed amazement of its owner.

This man's was pale as a tapeworm, but as large as the turkey necks her mother used for soup stock.

Giddy with alarm Em watched her friend grab ahold and squeeze, Dee's gesture as automatic and professional as a mother of five burping her newborn.

"Oh, yeah, you know it."

She didn't know it, though, and, thinking of treading water, waited for further guttural directions.

"Stroke it some more."

"Faster."

"Oh yeah, that's it."

The man did not lie. He wiped the drooling mess with his sport jacket sleeve and zipped up. Silence filled the rest of the ride.

"Here is good." Dee pointed at a parking lot in front of a pet shop.

"See you around, ladies."

They dawdled mutely at storefronts for a block. The man honk-honked as he pulled away, to all onlookers no different than a dad who'd dropped them off at the mall and would return in one hour sharp.

"That was scuzzy."

"Yeah, I guess. Actually, I almost laughed. It was way better than mopping up chunks of puke."

Em nodded, already familiar with Dee's aunt's shop talk. "Yeah, I guess. More profitable too."

"Should we tell them?"

"No, let's keep this one for ourselves." The situation required perspective, she thought, as when a C+ appeared on a report card page filled with respectable B+ and A- grades: the one an outsider, the rest typical.

Fox stoles with bead eyes, wool coats from World War Two, moo moos in pineapple or hibiscus prints, pill box hats with quail feathers and veils, all cheap and piled in haphazard abundance: St. Vincent's measured up.

For the return trip, a woman in an old flatbed truck who introduced herself as Mrs. Cheema, the wife of a raspberry farmer across the river, offered them a ride. Weary, perhaps, or confident about the girls' survival instincts, she offered no lecture, warning, or religious pamphlet.

Before Mrs. Cheema, Dee and Em had turned away when a few guys slowed. Happily scrounging through racks of donated clothing at the St. Vincent, they'd decided another ride with a single man in a big car would be pushing their luck.

Notebooks / November

For <u>you know what</u>, nothing below you know where . . .
Right?!?

Déviation: Doorway

Relief-flooded and taking in swallows of night's brisk air, Gordyn caught baffled noises from next door—arcs of giggling, start-stop-start drumming, and, distorted by drywall, insulation, and lousy all-treble cassette player speakers, the instrumental build-up of "Metal" in its opening half-minute.

Feeling scrawny, cold, and exposed he hopped from bare foot to bare foot on the concrete pad where his dad stored the hibachi and leaned yard tools against the house's yellow-beige siding. Beyond the fence he heard the creek's faint trickling. Two floors above and across the hallway his parents, he hoped, lay fast asleep.

Gordyn had just discovered a fact he'd had no appetite to know: with the lights out and at 11:30 pm, the distance between the cot in the basement spare semi-bedroom and the doorway to the back yard could be covered in five seconds flat, toe-stubbing obstacles included.

Moderately less clenched and puckered than a few heartbeats earlier, Gordyn's ass stung. The general perimeter smarted too, with the radiating heat of stunned skin after a smack. Pulling his mind away from piercing thoughts of blood and emergency surgery and stitches and rounds of hideously embarrassing questions—"What were you *thinking??*" the least of them—he pictured all those cats into whose tiny bum holes generation after generation of curious, malevolent boys had stuck firecrackers. (So they claimed; the complete absence of maimed tabbies with scorched Wily E. Coyote tails suggested the usual empty bragging instead.) With fresh, hands-on education about the situation of those hapless creatures, he wished their tormentors rounded up and forced to bend over.

He'd had no clue. Either his cousin was a trained pro or built differently—somehow, though wasn't everyone identical *down there*? Or else, Jay really needed to bone up on technique. But Gordyn's experiences of hammering cousin Evan had led him to expect smooth, unresisting ease, a fleshy erect finger steadily poking into 98.6 degree Jell-O. His cousin had never complained with "Ouch" or "Slow down, man." He'd groaned "Yeah, yeah" almost right away, every time, even with the same mouthful amount of spit Jay had used. Gordyn barely needed to warm him up.

And yet. Two minutes before Gordyn had been squatting close to the refrigerated November grass, freaked out (foreseeing rips, getting caught, cleaning up a bloody, stinking mess) and pretty sure he had no idea what to expect next except the dreaded once-in-a-lifetime experience of knocking on his parents' bedroom door and whispering, "Um—."

Unlike a stubbed toe, which caused the throbbing digit's limping owner to automatically sit at any refuge within reach, his first instinct had propelled him right outdoors, convinced that in any nearby quarter-second he'd loosen his bowels with the panicked urgency of a dog trapped inside too long. The alarm's eventual falseness sedated him with drug efficiency.

Not ten minutes earlier Gordyn had been stretched out atop the fold-out next to Jay's. They'd been deep into "My Clone Sleeps Alone" and "We Live for Love," with one headphone cup each, taking turns lifting the needle as the final soaring notes faded. With the help of a flashlight they'd already cycled through the songs four times. The music sounded tacky and mainstream compared to their imported Phantasmagoria finds, they'd decided, but—Oh!—the sheer dramatic force of Pat Benatar's voice! It could shatter glass. And, besides, she'd once slaved as a bank teller in some rinky-dink American town, Jay said. The woman deserved total respect for dragging herself out of that pit.

Sides touching in furnace-warmed darkness had led to elbow jabs and kneeing and playful shoves or kicks, fooling around that—with a mind of its own—became tickling, wrestling, biceps pinned by knees, and wide-set smiling threats about eye sockets overflowing with gob unless Gordyn opened his mouth. From there: Jay's jeans unzipped, Gordyn's sweat pants and underwear pulled down, and Jay's urgent, "Okay, ready?"

Balanced on knees behind Gordyn, Jay had aimed by feel and thrusted in the same ejaculatory way of any blue ribbon long jumper at takeoff.

With discomfort that intensified into alarm in about 0.2 seconds, Gordyn crumpled himself forward. Hunched over wet lawn moments later, he craned his neck to check for upstairs lights. Taking stock, he sensed an equal likelihood of laughter and tears.

Feet lightly slapping on the concrete floor Jay emerged from the basement's cave blackness. He'd wrapped the cot's olive army blanket around his waist and dragged a spare afghan of crocheted squares that Delphine kept on the deep freezer..

"Here." He draped Delphine's handiwork across Gordyn's shoulders. "Are you okay?"

"I dunno, I guess so. The bark was worse than the bite, I think. Maybe."

"I'm sorry. I didn't know, I just thought . . . I guess listening to my first, um, gut instinct wasn't the world's greatest plan."

"It's okay. I've done the exact same thing but with no—. Well, with no 100 yard dash." He told Jay about his cousin's capacities.

"Oh, wow. Well, that's good news. Maybe some guys are better at—. God, well, anyhow, it's better to give than to receive, right? Your cousin?!?"

"True. Yeah."

"And there's always third base, I guess. Or whatever *we're* supposed to call it."

When Jay dropped the blanket, Gordyn swatted the head of his friend's knob. "And there's always 'If at first you don't succeed . . . .'" Stroking and then pulling Jay as if by a leash, Gordyn led his friend back to the cot.

Just in case, he left the door ajar.

Notebooks / October

Venture: Thrift / October – December

Embarking on the new adventure—and why not, they decided after a minute's debate—Dee and Em smuggled notes during class and traded points of view at lunch, measuring themselves in relation to what they'd seen.

River Bend City had no prostitutes that wandered hot summer streets in feather boas, purple spandex tights and high heels as on *The Donna Summer Special*. If these women existed at all, they probably loitered in the shadows and relied on war vets or lonesome mill workers whose wallets looked flush on pay day. Maybe, to keep themselves clothed and fed these ladies hoped for word relayed along a shady tendril of grapevine. Bulletins in men's bathroom stalls might pan out too.

In school everyone, but especially boys, called a pocket of girls both sluts and whores, the terms practically interchangeable, with slut measuring slightly less awful than whore. Wolfish rumours stalked a few girls too. Allegedly, their spectacular Friday nights took them to the gravel pit, where they spent hours on their knees; crazed nymphos, they entertained jostling lineups and whole teams whenever their unseeing parents took off for a weekend. All these stories circulated as gospel truth, even though staying at home and watching TV with the rest of their family likely stood far closer to fact.

Over and again these girls arrived at school on Mondays and their step appeared as unaltered as the look in their eye. Only when the official news of their weekend reached them did their expressions collapse. Ashamed, they darted from locker to desk with crossed arms and sought unpopular corners during breaks. Spitting out counter-accusations, they'd learned, merely confirmed the gravel pit story: ladies protesting too much meant guilt.

The fanciful if cruel stories spread like spores; with the continued dispersal they wormed into lungs and brains as documented events, history. When catching sight of Sonia or Darla, who'd messed with guys of practically any age since junior high according to whispers and finger points, student gazes fixed on the knees of their poor-girl jeans and on their mouths, which they expected to croak gory testimony in the style of that chick from *The Exorcist*.

No one publicly claimed he got blown at the gravel by Darla, or saw Sonia in her bedroom taking on Mike (after Scott, Brent, and Glen), but guys murmured about the girls and elbowed one another and added flourishes along the lines of how the skanks wore knee patches to hide how worn out their jeans had become after so many nights at the gravel pit. People steered clear of Sonia as though she carried a deadly plague.

Dee believed that if these tragic girls' stories possessed the strength of Bible Camp passages, the lessons were simple: stay out of range, don't let yourself become a target, don't make waves.

Otherwise, lessons about girls gone bad could be found anywhere. Dee and Em had thrilled watching a rerun of *Dawn: Portrait of a Teenage Runaway* while Dee's parents played Yahtzee with the McCrays, an older married couple with no kids on the opposite side of the cul-de-sac.

The movie showed that Hollywood, a minefield just by itself, turned evil thanks to pimps, who stole in the guise of protection and who'd make girls pace the streets until they grew exhausted and depressed; and when these guys—users!—found no further purpose for their miserable captives, they slammed the door in their faces.

After that was anyone's guess. But collecting bottles and panhandling for coins looked probable, as did dying of cirrhosis, a knife wound, or a broken heart in a dreary apartment.

All options like waitressing or getting on as a receptionist seemed out of the question when your only job experience was taking rides in cars or checking into motels under assumed names.

There are, the movie took pains to show, worse fates than having a cocktail waitress mother with a thirst for vodka and public outbursts.

When Em, having heard an admonishment about "consorting with criminals" on TV, thought of calling themselves consorts, Dee jotted down the word in her notebook. "Ladies and gentlemen, The Consorts" (not to mention "Ladies and gentlemen, The Scrags"): that would sound excellent and provoking as they made their way to centre stage.

Dee and Em didn't identify with Dawn, a virginal girl running away from a drunken mother who'd shamed her by showing up at prom and calling her a tramp. For one, Dawn was a TV character.

Also, they'd been around and knew the score. They could be businesswomen. "Relief workers," they decided between giggles. The janitor called himself a sanitary engineer or a custodian; likewise, they could skip right past hooker and its bad-address, dead-end reputation.

And if men crossed them or tried to screw them over—"monkey business," a phrase from grandparents, sprang to Dee's lips and caused another outburst of laughter: so clueless—they'd even the score. They talked about carrying Xacto knives or stealing bottled hydrochloric acid from the Chem lab before settling on purse-sized screwdrivers with translucent yellow handles that their fathers would probably never miss.

Survival and the disadvantages of youth plagued the thoughts of solitary TV runaways, who needed legit jobs but lacked the experience necessary to obtain a position in the first place. Neither hungry nor paying rent, Dee and Em saw that their choice was just that: similar to taking a part time job to save money for nice clothes and a trip to Hawaii, this labour looked like an efficient means to a short-range end.

Nobody would know the difference. They'd follow the useful habit of those rebellious girls from Jesus Freak families in school who scrubbed their faces clean of makeup before returning home. Simple. And once they'd raised the funds, they'd quit. Years later they might recall it with the nostalgia they heard in their parent voices when they spoke of rites of passage like dropping out to drive a grocery delivery truck and having runs ins with lonesome housewives (Em's dad) or signing up in the military and throwing up outside a Ratskeller near Berlin (Dee's dad).

If Gordyn's half-promise of convincing his boss to get them shifts at Brownie's panned out they'd have to wear embarrassing uniforms that fit like sacks, hold their noses while chopping glistening tubs of refrigerated poultry carcasses, and arrive home with stringy hair and reeking of deep fried chicken skin. All while making one dollar every fifteen minutes. Adam Smith himself wouln't need to explain the advantage of handling one living turkey neck in a car for five minutes and scoring at least twenty dollars.

And they weren't dumb enough to believe in the goodness of strangers who hung out on street corners. Unlike Dawn. Not for a moment did they delude themselves with the story that anyone could take a bus to Hollywood one day and meet a director at a street corner who wanted to cast them in the next James Bond movie. Nothing ever turned out to be that easy.

What happened to Dawn wasn't her fault, but bumbling naivete sure hadn't helped: she acted as though she'd grown up in a bubble. As she scurried down the street every single person could smell innocence wafting off her—she might as well be spritzed with a perfume called Use Me.

Charting future interactions, Dee and Em aligned themselves with Violet 'I'm a murderess' Newstead, caught up in a man's world but eventually victorious and rich thanks to the help of reliable friends. Dolly Parton's character seemed nicer, but too sweet for the valley.

For them, loss of dignity had no place in the cards.

NOTEBOOKS / NOVEMBER

How about "My Clone Sleeps Alone" (etc.) this Friday??

Dee = next door with a kid and the parental units will be glued to the set.

Let me know.

DIARY / REHEARSALS

卌

Who's going to sing, and who's going to sing which song (and why: I still think all this talk talk talk is just stalling) came up today. Again. Wow, you'd think we're trying to end world hunger or build a spaceship!

What specific four did too, but we agreed to narrow that down later. It's not like there's a shortage of songs to choose from.

Style-wise, G.'s really into 'making a statement'. But when I threw in that anything, even normal clothes makes a statement he gets all evil-faced, like he's got a monopoly on the definition of statement. D.'s right, he's as bossy as the guy in *Nine to Five* sometimes. Aries are like that just naturally, I guess.

J.'s good with not singing, and so am I, but D. and G. thought that was unfair, not to them but to us, as if we're all Communists or something and every citizen must have exactly 3.5 minutes of mic time or civilization will completely break down.

J. shouted out that no band anywhere has four lead vocalists, and that even two was kind of weird. Plus, the idea isn't fairness but winning (or not losing, that would be the worst). And J. made sense when he added that four different singers would confuse the audience, not to mention make coordination harder for us.

In fact, we care about and gawk at Deborah Harry (which is what true fans call her, D. let us all know for the millionth time), not the guy playing keyboards . . . a sketch artist for the cops would get nothing from the audience except, "He had brown hair, I think, and was maybe wearing black jeans".

I agreed that fairness doesn't matter. Talent does. J. added if he sang then everyone watching him would think he was doing it b/c a gun was pointed at his head and not b/c he actually felt like it. Not a pretty picture. That settled it, and they caved.

As for one or two lead singers, we don't quite know yet. We'll settle that later.

When G. said D. had lots of sex appeal and showing that off couldn't hurt, she acted all offended and said, "Ya, right, I could get down on my knees and blow all the judges beforehand and whip my tits out on stage, how's that G.?!?" Whoa, it felt like those two were carrying on an argument from another time, "On the rag," "Don't be ignorant" back and forth faster than a tennis game. Bicker. Bicker. Then mucho sulking, also back and forth. I meant to ask her about it, but we zoomed up to our house together (= no chance). Something to do with him being a control freak, I'll bet. That's the usual. She sees control freaks everywhere.

Ok, but if 'sex appeal' had come from her mouth, she'd strip in a second. I just know it.

Starting a band with family members might be the worst idea ever.

Now I'm even more suspicious about the Osmonds and their perfect Miss America smiles. Creepy robo-family or what? I bet their dad is a complete slave-driver. 'My way or the highway' etc etc. Or like those people in cults. They just obey, as if they're hypnotized.

卌 |

Ok, the news is we voted to try one song at a time. Doing the whole 'set' was just a complete disaster area. We can stitch them together like a quilt or something. Eventually.

Right now, we'd get booed off the stage and then laughed at and there'd be legit reasons for both. God, <u>I'd</u> boo us, huck a few tomatoes too. Splat! That way, we can get one down pat from beginning to end and work in the choreography that D. keeps bringing up as the key to success (quoting somebody again, from the sounds of it. Sometimes I swear she'd be a perfect candidate for a cult).

Oh, we haven't told G. or J. about working on (close to perfecting!) "Prawn Gardens" in the R.'s basement yet. That'll be a cool surprise.

When G. said he'd been practicing on the organ at home a lot, Jay joked he'd been going at it so much his "wang" was raw and his gym socks were as stiff as 2 by 4s. G.'s face turned beet red, as if his deepest darkest secret had been announced on the nightly news. If those two knew even <u>half</u> of what we've seen up close ... ha ha ha.

卌 ||

Poof, a whole month flew by just like that. We've kept at practicing (in ones, twos, and threes, minus G., usually, b/c of deep fried chicken, etc.), but the four of us together has seemed impossible.

The good = we'll probably be able to get through our own parts.

The bad = all together we'll be like strangers, four players but no team unity. That's easy enough to fix, I hope.

卌 |||

We've all listened to "Metal" a thousand times by now, so when G. played his version on the organ for us when his dad drove Mrs. W. to Overwaitea for the weekly grocery run, we compared it to the original. Maybe that's never a great idea. Anyways, if we listened with just our ears (and didn't look at G. licking his lips and concentrating so hard he might get a nosebleed + blocked out that organ, which mixes bible thumper and cornball and tacky into one ugly machine, and the fact that we were standing in a living room with beige carpet in broad daylight), the playing sounded ... pretty good. Not 100% accuracy, b/c that's impossible without the same model of synthesizer (oh yeah, and a recording studio), but maybe 80%.

On round #2, when D. did some jingly stuff on the tambourine (and struck poses for the imaginary camera, naturally), we could almost picture the whole thing coming together and even impressing a judge or two ... We don't know for sure that there are judges. But what else could there be? Maybe the MC will measure the audience's clapping ... ?

If people are like how we used to be, they'll only know "Cars" b/c it gets played on the radio a lot. They'd compare us to Gary Numan and we'd sound like amateur hour. Hardly anyone has heard "Metal", the radio never plays it, so the audience won't know any better. It could be our own song as far as they're concerned.

D. thought of dye-ing a sheet black and sewing it to fit over the organ, like a shroud (sp?). Later, she told me she'd coach G. on not looking like such a moron when he's playing and to locate a couple of people in the audience, to make eye contact with them a few times. More wisdom from modeling school.

She's really big on making a good impression. This time, I think she made a useful point.

卌 ||||

On the weekend G. dropped off the drums that D. got for free, practically. We set them up by the back wall today. The room's getting crowded, so it was smart for the boys to drag that gross chicken beheading table into the back 'hallway'.

Then they all stared at me as if to say, "Ok, E., let's get the show on the road."

A practice run with just me alone in the room would have been my first pick, but . . . They watched me go through "Metal", "Prawn Gardens", and "Obituary Column", which were on the C-30 tapes, D.'s 'assignments' that J. made for us.

Even though I felt like I was in court and knew for sure that the jury had already found me guilty, it turned out pretty ok.

I had to stop a couple of times and begin again (the sudden changes in patterns totally tangle me up), but altogether I think I did a C+, B+, and B. We started at F--, so not bad. "It's all relative", as they say.

Déviation: Pink

Putting his money where his mouth is and flapping around a two dollar bill in the kitchen, Edmund bet that pretty much zilch bested Peter Sellers as Inspector Clouseau: "The guy's pores just ooze funny."

Sensing the easiest route to a win-win situation, no one bothered to muster a rival name.

Without any takers Edmund placed the challenge in suspended animation, tacking the prize to the cork board.

But thanks to a decade of silver screen and boob tube appearances the subject never sank far from sight. And after the performer's fatal heart attack and the news tributes that mentioned in passing a troubled life beyond the studio, his masterpiece, the Chief Inspector, sparked unpredictable outbursts of Edmund's studied bumbling. Ludicrously-accented exclamations boomed across rooms. And whenever opportunity arose: swinging karate chops to fend off an imaginary lurking Cato, which he'd swap for Sergeant Schultz and "I zee nuszink–nuszink!" if he sensed the audience growing weary.

Gordyn resented Edmund's genius hero, with occasional seething fury powerful enough to surprise him. Normally he'd connect feelings to causes right away. He considered Dee's all-purpose explanation—jealousy, for her a daily fact—but couldn't see how that fit.

Two years before, Edmund had corralled his eldest into a 7 o'clock of *The Revenge of the Pink Panther* at the twinplex. He'd been married long enough to know Delphine's policies inside out, including the line about never being in the mood for the cinema's hubbub and glare. She disliked popcorn too, whose irksome kernels lodged in her dentures. Television from the comfort of her own chesterfield, in her estimation, felt second to none: "No fuss, no muss, no problem."

Relief from August's smothering boredom and heat would have been enough for Gordo, who insisted on Gordyn shortly after. To guarantee success, though, Edmund dangled a carrot: a bribe about the two of them making a final push to prep for a learner's license, starting with that night's trip over the bridge.

Gordo had shrunk into his velvety seat when the story wound up on a country road and caught the Inspector slowing to a halt at a red light. There, a glamourous woman in an off-white fur coat paced inside a glass bus stop opposite his car. She asked for a ride. As the indecisive Inspector sputtered, she slid right in. After a minute of small talk, the brunette yanked back a wig to reveal that she was he, Claude, with a purse that housed a gun. He demanded the Inspector's clothes. And the Peugeot. Kicking out the stripped Inspector into the cold night, Claude snidely offered his dress, "an original Dior," and drove off. At a trap seconds up the road, one complete with a fake detour sign (*Déviation*, it read), the

Inspector's would-be assassins machine-gunned Claude instead. The Peugeot veered off and slammed head on into a tree. A ball of flames filled the screen.

"Good riddance to bad rubbish." Watching almost any villain dispatched, Edmund responded with that saying. He tipped the tub of popcorn at his son.

As with Inspector Clouseau's previous adventure, not to mention anything to do with sports on TV, Gordo wondered if he and his father's eyes actually took in the same scenery.

Gordyn couldn't remember the start-to-finalé plot of an earlier movie is the series. Even its name eluded him, since the lot all blended, more or less, into a giant reel of gags and outlandish Clouseau disguises.

Still, one scene remained so vivid he may as well have lived through it. He'd accompanied his father to that one too, though in the outskirts of the city. On the drive he'd listened to his father go bitterly on and on about the Olympic stadium—"The Big O," Edmund kept calling the place, as though he'd never heard that expression used in relation to sex. "When your grandchildren are stooped and grey, they'll being paying off that damned Big O," he declared, causing his son to bite his cheek to stymy giggles.

In the Pink Panther's *Return* or *Retaliation*, the trench-coated Inspector had followed a butler, his suspect, to the Queen of Hearts, a tiny dinner theatre in London with an awning and neon sign in electric pink. Inside, a gushing maitre'd greeted him. The man wore a snug orange pantsuit with a heart-shaped cut-out that advertised an exposed nipple. The stern bouncer, a towering short-haired woman, stood nearby in a black suit.

The guests, Gordo understood, were as queer as a three dollar bill, the expression courtesy of his father. Fruits.

The men propped at the bar wore silky scarves around their necks and smoked cigarettes with a nervous flamboyance. They all sipped bright cocktails, not beer. The waiters swooped and glided instead of walking—more butterfly than sasquatch. As though on stage and needing to be comprehended from seats at the extreme rear of the auditorium, the men acted with fluttery exaggerated gestures. They appeared to gossip exclusively, in hissed whispers.

The Queen of Hearts had struck Gordo as dolled up with upholstered, grandmotherly taste, with scads of flower petal lampshades and drapery for miles. Paintings overwhelmed by immense golden frames sat atop wallpaper of a busy geometric pattern.

The maitre'd informed the Inspector about a show commencing.

Gordo and his father had watched the butler, introduced as Ainsley Jarvis, wander through the crowd in a wig and a pink sequin gown. Before a fight broke out, Ainsley embarrassed the Inspector with a love song about a lonely queen in her castle.

The scene of the singer's final appearance, minutes later, lingered on his corpse. He'd been stabbed to death in a backstage room awash in pastels. Stiff on the floor, but with his pearly satin high heels and pale nylons resting on a stool near the makeup vanity, he reminded Gordo of the Wicked Witch of the West, pancaked beneath Dorothy's house.

The scene was meant as another gag; Ainsley Jarvis seemed placed there as a gross out, a lesson of some type, and a thrill to watch, like a school grounds fight.

Claude in a different costume, in other words.

Weeks past a grateful exiting of the movie theatre and pursed-lipped reception of his dad's return drive recollection about almost bumping into a pair of *them* swishing down a street in Montreal, Ainsley Jarvis had pushed into Gordo's thoughts. The gut-centred pangs felt familiar. Impending math exams and the boy's dank changing room after gym class caused the alarming wooziness too.

Gordo imagined Jarvis' life—obedient butler by day, outrageous gowns at night—as a curled strip of film inching backwards. The last frame showed death, of course; but the scene didn't depict wise old age, the performer comfortably propped up in a bed and circled by family, friends, and loving tears. Instead: murdered, in a dress and wig, and serving as the main draw at a perverted freak parade. The butt of butt jokes.

Like everyone, Gordo saw the character as ridiculous. As foolish and comical as Inspector Clouseau, Ainsley-Jarvis had no near counterpart in real life. But the Inspector appeared worldwide in movie after movie, attracting promotions, beautiful ladies, and fame. Along with the bad guys with guns, Ainsley merely died violently.

Understanding that his parents would call it a "mountain out of a molehill episode," Gordo brooded nonetheless.

If rewinding the film of Jarvis' history to Gordo's age, what would he find? A poor kid in an English village who stood out, paying attention to fabrics and style while caring in no way about sports and team names, and who felt drawn to the stage knowing all the while that meant everyone could judge him and cut him down to size? Would he graduate, or just drop out to avoid hallway jeers and threats? As he sat on the train bound for London and sighed bittersweet relief at watching his hometown shrink into a blob and, finally, scarcely a thread on the horizon, did he fit the definition of a hero or a coward? In the city he'd step on the platform and do an excited little Mary Tyler Moore pirouette. Passersby would frown. And what next? He'd audition at theatres but get hired by a department store. During one shift he'd overhear two clerks gossiping about the show at the Queen of Hearts . . .

Was each step preordained, a fate, all leading up to a gag death, a male corpse in a dress? Gordo didn't know who to approach for answers. What questions to pose perplexed him too.

In air-conditioned twinplex darkness, Gordo had felt gurgling acid indigestion and his heart sinking.

In high heels now, the Inspector called Cato an Oriental fool for converting his apartment into a brothel, and declared, "I'm not your ordinary, run-of-the-mill transvestite." Edmund guffawed with the rest of the audience and slapped his knee. Gordo smiled for his father's benefit; he knew to expect to hear that punchline a few times in the next week. He didn't get the joke.

Snowballing private experiences since the Ainsley Jarvis movie had been educational, Gordo believed, in the exact way the first month in prison must be. Messing around with other guys but barely noticing the beavers under tight jeans that clumped jocks bragged they dreamed about / drooled over / fingered in cars, and everyday torment like clockwork from popular cliques instead of just once in a while: these occurrences meant and predicted something, he'd bet, just as thinning hair meant the onset of old age. Usually, at least.

He woke with nerves and worry on school day mornings. And now his father and this damned movie. Would Edmund quiz him about available girls—"foxes," a word picked up from who could say—on the drive home? Unleash another hilarious tale about a pansy he'd run into, maybe while stationed in Germany? Would he grow serious: "If there's something you want to talk about—anything—just say the word"? Each possibility struck Gordo as uniquely awful.

Breathing deep and listening to logic, Gordo understood that realistically he'd not wind up dressed as a lady and burned to a crisp. Or satin-wrapped but on his back with rigor mortis in a dressing room.

He also understood that the men who'd written the words he and thousands of others across North America were listening to and had heard variations of just two years ago in another *Pink Panther* installment probably sat around a table and brainstormed in much the same way students did for group presentations in Geology ("The Volcano: Friend or Foe?") and Biology ("The Green Miracle Named Chlorophyll"): throw a whole bunch of inspirations into a pile and vote on what ones work best, which in this case had ended up with an exploding *tapette* car thief—how hilarious—for no other reason than the scene exposed the audience to an odd but exotic sight that incited hoots and heartfelt clapping. And, he'd admit, there was something funny about someone other than a woman in a dress—a chimp, a scarecrow, a man—even though dying for the choice felt like a severe punishment.

Despite his body's indigestion and a frown line on cruise-control, he comprehended too that the story was as made up as *Pinocchio*. It probably reflected only a writer's peculiar sense of the world, not any fact set in stone.

And yet. Gordo wondered about assigning homework to team guys at school and their girlfriends: "Describe a queer in one hundred words. Staple a drawing of this figure to the assignment before you hand it in." How near would their guesswork be to Claude and the cabaret singer? He'd bet on a close family resemblance. Limp wrist. A strappy purse dangling. Lisping voice. A girlish step. Fluttery hands. High heels. Wisecracking and innuendo. Can't throw a ball to save his life.

Gordo knew the drill.

Gordo could put two and two together, and there stood the problem. The answer, while correct, spelled certain doom.

When non-quite-ancient Miss M in Biology asked whether tribalism originated with DNA, she didn't turn from the blackboard since the answer was so obvious; and History class' certifiably ancient Mrs. P, whose fiancé had drowned at sea in WWII, clasped her gold cross necklace when she said "the situation of in groups and out groups has existed since time immemorial." At core: life's cruel; the game's rigged; everyone's equal but some matter way less than others. Get used to it. The misfortune, then, came packaged with existence itself and only turned into a misfortune for whoever got assigned to the losing team in the delivery room.

Gordo saw two main concepts of The Story of Life played out that supported this view. The hugest one by far, which he witnessed practically every day, didn't appear to have changed all that much in centuries. It began with Mom and Dad, maybe, or the Bird and the Bees: "You'll eventually meet The One, you can just tell, and before long you're shacked up and married and a kid pops out and you need a bigger place, so you move out to the 'burbs, where schools are good and there are trees and a bit of space to move around in, and then it's another round of diapers and packed lunches, and before you know it grandkids are coming over and bouncing on your knee."

Survival of the fittest meant sticking close to tried and true because—. He'd looked up at the screen, where the Inspector approached a hotel lobby in Hong Kong, and advised a blonde woman in a black wig to "think yellow." Because—that's what everyone else did, which meant a larger pool of people, which meant a greater chance of reproduction. Facts.

Gordo wondered for a moment about evolution. As if the apex of feats, species-wise, meant knocking some girl up and making sure that before you croaked half of your DNA continued on though another body! What a feat, big deal, he'd thought. Any Tom, Dick, or Harry could do that. Any rabbit. Objectively, though, the whole supposed miracle looked boring and ordinary, maybe a notch above a sneeze and a few below the invention of language, especially compared to a real accomplishment like the Great Pyramid of Giza. Or Versailles.

People treated the primary story as a priceless family heirloom, the greatest gift; practically everyone accepted it with gratitude, passed it down to their children, and so on.

Even when the thought occurred in the first place, hardly anyone dared to question the gift-giving and say, "Thanks but no thanks, that doesn't really match my décor." And not for long when they did. Eventually, all those kids in school making loud public vows to jump into the beach bum lifestyle in Malibu, or to give a permanent finger to the mill and their parents' dull routine found themselves heading down the aisle, as though made of iron filings and pulled by a magnet.

The other version, the third-rate story that called his name, and which always turned to be less popular than math homework, extra laps, and cafeteria shepherd's pie combined, appeared to offer a fairy tale's forked path. One, heavily trod thanks to sheer bad luck, led to a hell of lonely miseries: the alchy hobos wandering down by the railroad tracks; cursed girls in school known as whores and noticed only as gang bang material; veteran drinkers with pickled livers at the Legion; Chester. Through a lucky break or willpower or both, select unpopular others veered for the other fork; they left town and started over. True, these escapees might catch a bus and wind up in a worse situation in the city. And maybe not. Even Ainsley Jarvis managed to bathe in limelight before getting stabbed into oblivion.

Gordo pictured turtle hatchlings crawling to the sea and salmon swimming upstream. Since the cosmic odds favoured his failure, he'd figure out a way to beat them.

★

On a rainy afternoon of hazy projections into a dazzling future, Gordo had confided in Dee that he was bisexual.

From cop shows he recognized a false confession.

He wasn't a man protecting his wife or child, though. The person needing protection was himself. Saying "I'm a queer" out loud meant so much the sentence practically reverberated; and it came weighted with negative outcomes—he took a half-minute to think of chain-reaction awkwardness, embarrassment, and fear, a perpetual aura of shame, being condemned as unnatural, a locked-up perv in a dress who required a doctor's opinion—and no positives except for the sheer relief of speaking the truth.

Consequently, procrastinating or stalling or simply changing the topic made a world of sense. "I'm biding my time," his father always concluded when Delphine broached the topic of jogging. Gordo saw the wisdom of that approach.

And based on evidence from high school, the shadowy existence of the cornholer was, above all, worse than a pathetic waste.

He'd mapped the options, distantly, with the same reluctance as kissing a corpse.

From the town's point of view, the choices were so restricted as to not count as a choice at all: to not exist in the first place, or to be smothered in the crib, a mistake, an abnormality, on par with a baby born with flippers for arms or a walnut brain; to disappear—somehow, it didn't matter: over the bridge, into the bottle, with a suitcase in the dead of night—because the citizens of the Bend municipality permitted no room for his kind; to accept expressions of hatred and contempt as the natural and deserved punishment for the crime against God / nature / society; to wave goodbye to everything and everyone and beeline as soon as possible for the big city, like a refugee, a displaced, unloved person from an awful war, and to make ends meet in a ghetto or scrape by in the safe obscurity a few cities allowed. Supposedly. A whole adulthood of pretense held promise too.

If life's workings inevitably produced a handful of out groups, he figured his own couldn't sink much lower. Other losers—

Athena, a tubby Greek girl nicknamed Arena; Vince, a tall stick of a kid with a lazy eye whose acne overlapped with scaly eczema; a stoner, Rocky, who was stupider than a post and as mean as a bear when provoked; poor, greasy, and blindly optimistic Fiona—managed to seem so helpless, such easy targets, that not much fun could be found in attacking them in hallway after hallway.

And near to him at the very bottom, a slut at least had her uses because, guys proudly announced whenever they fixed her in their sights, anyone could show up at her house and chuck pebbles at the bedroom window, or offer her a ride home or just give an impromptu telephone call to her—these strategies, he'd overheard, came naturally to boys with blue balls—and she'd be a willing participant, grateful for the minutes of attention.

Guys suspected of being queer, though, had no usefulness except as perpetual targets, as disgusting objects to measure yourself against. As a cautionary tale: don't become this. In a roundabout way too, their value paralleled that of a basketball hoop or a hockey net: the more times you scored by hitting it, the worthier you proved yourself invaluable to the team.

A bad habit like checking the mirror for outbreaks, Gordyn now and then pictured the thick swirls of fog inside a fortune teller's crystal ball. The fog refused to lift; no picture of dates and going steady and falling in love floated up, not even partial clues amidst the haze. A career, in contrast, struck him as a cinch, just riding the elevator to the top over a few years of non-stop toil. The normal other parts too—a bachelor's pad and later a house, a beater and then a new car, friends, fun hobbies, and the rest.

Romance, though, remained a question mark.

As for the courtship story of his parents—meeting at a dancehall near Quebec City's military base, and Edmund showing up the following Saturday at Delphine's crowded family home with a bouquet of carnations for her mother and a box of chocolates for her sisters to share ("Knowing whose palms to grease never fails," Edmund joked, undercutting the saccharine taste of the courtship)—and the local updates, which involved popular girls in school wearing boys' team jackets or rings placed on necklace chains and displayed for all, holding hands, or a girl spotted getting into the passenger side of a car, etc, they looked no giant step from *Happy Days* or whatever happened in the novels from the Victorian countryside that Miss L gushed about so intensely her eyes practically crossed.

Those scenes didn't make sense for Claude or Ainsley, or for himself, for where could they participate in the necessary rituals with causing a violent fuss? A broadcast of Potsie and Richie Cunningham making out in a car might cause actual riots. And if a boy from school followed Edmund's lead and knocked at the door holding chocolates, his parents would freak—punching him, dialing the police, or sitting everyone down for *a talk* that'd stretch out for eternity.

And that would be that. He'd have better luck dating a horse.

As for him striding from English to Socials in the team jacket of Brian K, he might as well pitch himself in front of a freight train.

Secret and behind closed and locked doors, spoken about in whispers or not at all, illicit and criminal in reputation if not fact, never ever in public: these, he was learning, applied to his future sex life, which also meant his romantic life. Inseparable, the two showed flip sides of the same coin: a nervous and fumbled but polite request to dance at a sock hop could easily result, over a matter of weeks, in the passenger car door invitation, making out at the gravel pit, and going all the way. After that, the modern version of a shotgun wedding didn't seem out of the question. Just not for his side.

"Wasn't that a gas?"

The olden days saying came from barbershop weekends.

Gordo had pulled away from Edmund's playful elbowing in the parking lot, convinced at that moment his father insisted on passé expressions only to annoy him. To get under his skin. As for why, who could define anyone's motivations. Gordo thought of quipping, an evolving tendency both parents but especially his dad despised. "A real peach," he could exclaim with a skin of politeness over a furious disdain, or "Totally, the cat's pajamas," and they'd be back to the silent tug-of-war of barbershop jamborees, with Edmund urging reluctant, jaw-set Gordo to mix and mingle or at least try to impress a nice girl. "Crawl out of your shell," and the like, and Gordo thinking, "How about crawling *into* your shell for a change."

To a quip, his father would sound that deep universal parental sigh of defeat, frustration, and all-round disappointment. "Nobody appreciates that superior tone, young man," he'd respond, because that's how he always began.

Gordo could tell too that a stretch of moody silence—while at the wheel after sunset Edmund appreciated conversation—would generate delicate or gruff probes along the lines of "What's going on inside that head of yours these days?" And any honest answer would leave Gordo exposed, an open wound his father would expect to dig through and then patch up with elbow grease and a little manly know-how. With this one, though, he'd flounder: "Oh boy," maybe, or "That's a doozy," all leading up to the conversation closer, "Give it time, I'll bet it's just a phase."

"Well, I have to say that was pretty good." Gordo had watched his dad's educational show of precision driving: shoulder checks instead of mirrors alone, signal lights in the parking lot, hands at ten and two. "So which character do you think was better, the salty sea dog from the Salty Sea or the Mafia guy, Mr. You Know Who?"

Notebooks / November

OK, how about "My Clone Sleeps Alone" (<u>etc</u>.) next Friday??

As per . . . Dee = next door with a kid and the parental units will be glued to the set.

Let me know.

Can't . . . He's out with his 'special lady' and needs me to guard the palace.

Venture: ID / November

Stranded with no gleam of promise a block and a half north of Bottlesburg's main drag, Les's persisted. Behind a sporadically busy street currently growling with panicked merchants fighting a city hall-sponsored bypass they predicted as the coffin's final nail for downtown (the first: malls twenty minutes in any direction), the shop stayed open four days and two nights each week. Between a do-gooder thrift store stocked with *Hell . . . or Heaven?* pamphlets and a pawn shop with a sunken striped awning strewn with curled leaves, the shop drew men who hustled in and out at odd hours.

After a leather collar of silver bells hanging from the doorknob jangled and a sloping floor snagged the door and drove Gordyn crazy, any unsuspecting browsing shopper would meet a cavernous, dimly lit business that sold pro-wrestling, RVing, and skin magazines on a long plywood rack, used thrillers, Westerns, and Stephen Kings, and out-of-reach paraphernalia loaded inside a glass case, a portion of which Gordyn delivered.

The sandwich board outside highlighted Smokes and a stock of Authentic Hookah Pipes The latter forced Gordyn to wonder about a band of low-profit counterfeiters selling door to door from a van loaded with boxed forgeries. A display row of five with red octopus arms and dusty bulbous etched metal bases languished behind the cash register and seduced no admirers.

Whoever Les was, Gordyn never said a word to him. The proprietor evidently preferred to let an interchangeable series of skinny, marble-mouthed guys with standard brown rocker hair handle transactions. They yelled out like clockwork, reminding dawdling men about the store's enforced reading-without-buying policy.

Merv had written Les's on that list of contacts he normally supplied via Ronnie. Les ordered double the usual amount.

And on his initial drop off there, a matter of 45 seconds, Gordyn paid virtually no attention: Les's side street address and stuffed junk shop interior followed the similar formula of Frank's (in Clearbrook, magazines at the back, sunglasses instead of hookah pipes) and RG's (up the hill in Abbotsford, paperbacks in a wire rack, power tools crammed in the glass display unit, magazines opposite the till). Through his mother's eyes Gordyn noted how all the owners were strangers to vacuum cleaners and Windex bottles; even the convex spy mirrors looked felted with grime.

A fresh visit to Ronnie's Brackendale bachelor pad, unexpected, came about after Merv showed up shifty-eyed at Brownie's and muttered "hold the slaw" along with "drop by later" and "Ronnie had a relapse" as he ordered two white meat Snack Paks with a put-on casual voice. The cheapskate deposited nothing in the tip canister.

Coming up with no clever reason to refuse, Gordyn agreed before yelling the order to Fiona.

Ronnie's mysterious injuries healed slowly alongside irregular setbacks that seemed as much mental as physical. Psychosomatic, Gordyn had concluded. Swinging open the screen door Gordyn would find Ronnie under blankets and ready with half-baked, single-sentence excuses—"Been a rough one" and "Need to take 'er easy for a bit"—that explained nothing except the need for someone else to pick up the slack.

Gordyn had narrowed Ronnie's story to two possibilities: he'd scrapped with a bruiser and gotten beaten to a pulp, or had fallen hard, possibly from a height while plastered. The beaten up below the neck theory opened the way to a second round of likelihoods, ranging from probable—angry drunken fools in the parking lot of the Belle-Vue, or near the bowling alley entrance—to sensational (if a stretch): a formerly crossed cellmate or exercise yard foe, a rival of Merv's firing a warning shot at a proxy, an encounter with a thug in quest of secrets Ronnie happened to overhear.

Criminals presented underworlds and mentalities Gordyn believed as belonging to a unique category, one in symbiosis with regular, visible society like an evil Siamese twin or a submerged but handy personality of occasional Mr. Hyde savagery.

Gordyn had followed the horrific newspaper articles about The Killer Clown, and without setting about to do so he realized that a man, any man, could present a deceptive facade, or will a convincing mirage into existence—the respected, duty-bound citizen and competent owner of a painting, decorating, and maintenance business, say, who kept bodies buried right next to a back yard barbecue pit where his neighbours dropped by for grilled steaks slathered with his famous sauce with who knows what for ingredients.

But he conceded too that such absolute duality was far, far from usual, and that if two-facedness did in fact exist it usually turned out to be skin deep and understandable: at Brownie's, Fiona's happy-go-lucky Jesus Freak personality that accepted God's Plan and her lot in life equally probably came twinned with a raging girl who expected comfort and success and railed against the unfairness of poverty and greasy hair, neither of which she could disguise. And Harjinder's official nose-to-the-grindstone persona barely papered over the fact that he yearned to boss around and mistreat underlings who'd take anything so long as they kept their jobs. For Mr. Swanson, meanwhile, "living the dream" and owning a string of business successes appeared to be the man through and through, the under-self perhaps wanting a larger dream in which to live—Las Vegas weekends via Lear jets, and the rest—and a lengthy gold chain of franchises from coast to coast.

Exiting Les's for what he hoped was the last time, Gordyn stopped at the door. A poster advertised a Battle of the Bands at the Bottlesburg Inn, five minutes further west on the highway that snaked toward the city. Besides the expected proof-required age restriction, contestants had to pay an entry fee. A half inch of small print outlined additional rules.

He yanked out the staples, folded the poster, and stuffed it in his back pocket.

Notebooks / October

Looks ect

White shirts and black pants. Everything worn backwards ✓✓
Outfits made from lumberjack shirts
Tourists (Hawaiian shirts etc)

Mechanic's overalls taped tight at the waist ✓✓✓
Bleached overalls, paint words on them?
Eyeliner and everyone's hair slicked back, dye?? What about shoes???
Long skirts with blazers, belts ✓
Black tape??
Sex androids!?
~~The Siblings~~ ~~2 Plus 2~~ ~~The Pears~~ too SUCKY
The Morticians The Morticias??

NOTEBOOKS / DECEMBER

Finalists

~~Throbbing Gristle~~ ("Hot On The Heels Of Love" - too hard)
Visage ("Frequency 7" instrumental for intro)
★★ Moev ("Obituary Column")
★ Siouxsie and the Banshees ("~~Hong Kong~~ Prawn Garden")
★★Blondie ("Eat to the Beat")
B-52's ("52 Girls")
★★ Devo ("Smart Patrol/Mr. DNA")
★★ Ultravox ("Mr. X" instrumental for intro)
~~Joy Division~~ (audience will cut wrists)
★★ Gary Numan ("Metal")
The Normal (maybe)
Cabaret Voltaire (too much?)
Martha and the Muffins ("Trance And Dance" - too long??)
~~The Sex Pistols~~ (not a good match)
Flying Lizards ("Money (That's What I Want)")

ORIGIN STORY: III

Gordyn steered Dee, who cut through a hallway of milling students with a fearful decisiveness. The stride hinted at a godly prophet charging with a flaming sword.

At the second-floor stairwell outside of the Social Studies class normally presided over by bearded jogging maniac Mr. H, Jay leaned by the grey metal rails. He watched kids' heads ascend and descend. Right next to him a girl sat on the floor.

Gordyn parked his hip against the rail and looked down. "This is Dee."

Without looking up, Jay's sister lifted her arm and pointed a finger, gun-like, at her own temple. "This is Em."

"My dad is of the opinion that Em's manners leave a lot to be desired." Jay rated his sister as hot and cold, mercurial, an apple that hadn't fallen far enough from the tree. On some days, at least.

Dee felt surprised. She'd heard "Em this" and "Em that" from her brother and his new friend for weeks. She expected charisma, style. And yet there the creature sat, surliness itself. She crouched in front of Em and held out her hand with fake trembling, picturing a child's dumb inspiration to pet a chained Doberman. "Pleased to meet you."

"Same."

"I like your hair. Do you call it ash blonde?" Dee smiled. "Anyways, it's a good length for your height."

"Oh, gee, thanks. I'm glad you approve."

"We gotta take off." Gordyn made a thumbing motion toward the gym.

"Yeah. See you later." Walking backwards, Jay waved to the girls. He stopped, raised his voice. "Let's meet out back after last class, okay?"

"Yeah, sure. You know where I'll be."

"Yup. See you there."

"Men of mystery." Dee sighed, annoyed at being dumped with Miss Crabby. "I'll bet there's a story there."

"Knowing my brother, yes."

In jeans and striped rugby shirts the boys disappeared into a thicket of the same. "God, Gord practically pushed my tongue down your throat. I guess we're supposed to be instant friends. You wanna head outside for a bit?

"Sure, let's go out behind Woodworking. I need a smoke."

"Okay," Dee said, thinking *gross*.

Rehearsal: Organ / October

Along with the rectangular oil painting of swirled tropical sunset hues, the rumpled corduroy couch Dee referred to as nutmeg (and, when in a mood, *merde de chien*), and the maple dining room set with two leaves stored in the upstairs closet by the bathroom that they'd wrapped in blankets and hauled from suburban rentals, Gordo and Edmund had lugged the mahogany veneer organ from one living room corner to the next.

Of standard design, it existed to bother Delphine. "Nothing but a dust magnet," she complained.

No one sat on the bench of textured walnut leatherette, or fiddled with its parts—pedals, shrunken tiered keyboards, and panels of Lego-bright plastic switches.

Regardless of address, in the Spenser household Swing, Bossa Nova, and Samba backbeats proved as popular as dinners of fried liver.

Once Delphine decorated the top—a starched Quebecois doily behind an attached music stand of filigreed wood, her souvenir ball of glass with shells and a baby starfish suspended in the middle—the organ sat visible but undisturbed, like a museum display of an olden days parlour where families entertained themselves after Sunday's church service.

Passing by it, Dee and Gordyn fantasized about termite infestations and localized electrical fires. Malicious vandals with chain saws.

To Gordyn's suggestions about placing a classified ad, abandonment in a back alley, firewood, or donating the eyesore to needier relatives or a threadbare church, Edmund replied with "sentimental value" even though he barely looked in its direction and never played a note. Or, "your inheritance"—facetious, but considering the sad pile of money in the bank not all that funny and more or less true.

When Gordyn pulled the bench away from the organ and rested his ass on its cushiony top, he faced an undecorated eggshell wall adjacent to the dining room set. The paint contained the barest hint of gloss. From his mother, he understood that such a surface allowed for easy cleaning. Whatever the utility, the wall's creamy institutional blankness could never be an inspiration like the poster of Claude Monet's waterlilies in his room.

Staring at the flat surface and shutting out family noise (unvarying: his being completely alone for more than ten minutes a rarer event than chain lightning) parted the curtains to dim futures. They didn't seem nearly as miserable as Airstrip One and IngSoc but caused shudders of what-if? cold sweat.

He imagined the boredom and humiliation of a meagre job in a mall's lowest-rent wing, or tucked away on a loser town's side street. He'd wear the same tweed suit week after week, and supposedly make a killing from selling organs and pianos on Affordable Layaway but in fact press his nose to front window glass, waiting for customers to step inside. Instead, they'd hurriedly pass by, as though he owned a funeral parlour or the store caused leprosy. At night or on weekends he'd play "Bringing in the Sheaves" or "Here We Come A-wassailing" in a church basement. He'd force a smile at the soft cooing applause from a handful of widows who'd moments before served Orange Pekoe in floral china cups while assigning cookie recipes for the Christmas bake sale. And he'd agree to an endless singalong of "Those Were The Days" at one of a Fiona-style woman's casserole and potato chip potlucks. Thirsting deeply for much more than the one glass of rye and 7 her cheapskate husband served he'd wonder how to magic another round without appearing like an alchy.

Gordyn called the organ tacky, partly because his parents forbade the word for general use (alongside "hate," "doesn't agree with me" the preferred phrase; in a pinch, "dislike" would serve). His particular blanketing fondness for dismissing clothing, objects, hairstyles, recipes, and entire landscapes as tacky, he knew, rubbed them the wrong way.

Having learned just how unwelcome his snobby pronouncements had become at home, he seethed about the evolving list—the ketchup and crumbled crackers on meatloaf, the old-fashioned push lawnmower, the artificial Christmas tree with clip-on branches, the crisp doilies that routinely arrived layered like crepes inside family parcels from Quebec—to Jay, who returned the volley with floor-by-floor samplings from his own house.

They traded these affronts to good taste as other guys swapped hockey cards.

But until a futuristic flat black synthesizer showed up in his bedroom wrapped in a bow and ready to be plugged into the nearest socket, the organ, that inconvenient and hulking embarrassment, would have to serve. No other option presented itself. Without those foundational sounds the band was as good as kaputt.

He had to be careful to raise no questions about the sudden, hypocritical interest. Not catching his father's eye was crucial too, for that could be—would be, in a heartbeat—interpreted as renewed openness to music, which also meant stepping back into barbershop weekends and harmonizing and memorization practice sessions in the basement. "Sweet Georgia Brown" grated his nerves raw.

To his dad Gordyn mentioned a cruel school project—sprung without explanation—whose vaguely explained but sadistic complexity demanded extra home rehearsals. He plugged one set of earphones into the cassette player and another into the organ, feeling idiotic while thankful for the restraint of his parents (Dad splayed in a recliner, Mom swaddled and curled on the couch) and for Dee, who watched TV on her stomach as though accepting the unfair homework claim at face value.

He wrestled with "Metal" first. To his ear the band needed to play three distinct sets of sounds before the catchy science fiction lyrics—"We're in the building where they make us grow / And I'm frightened by the liquid engineers / Like you"—began, barked in a high, reedy voice he had no trouble imitating. Each flourish of keyboard notes and beats was one-handed and simple; the pairing, however, explained the reason why Gary Numan's band must have synthesizers piled high as lumber. Singing during all that made him hope that Jay would accept a turn at the mic and that his voice didn't cause dogs to howl.

★

The prospect of borrowing the organ loomed noose-like, a considerable impending problem with no instant fix.

If he asked politely, his father would kick up a ceremonial fuss—"You scratch it, you pay for it!" and the like—and help him lift the beast ("with your knees," naturally) as his mom navigated them through the front door. The two would bicker lightly about how she could direct so professionally but drive with turtle speed and bat blindness.

Sticking his Dad's pride and joy in a moist dusty barn in the middle of a field that probably teemed with nesting mice? For months? And using it to play music with his underage sister and her underage friend and his underage friend in a bar somewhere where having beer slopped on it appeared to be the very least worry? Gordyn guessed the sentence that would come from his dad's mouth: "Not in my lifetime, I kid you not."

Before dismissing the plan as hopelessly complicated and less achievable than a manned flight to Mars, Gordyn had mapped out a breaking-and-entering ruse. Jay and Em could sneak in through an unlocked basement window one evening after he'd convinced his parents that once again his ever-dragging, ever-elongating feet begged for a fresh pair of running shoes for gym—with a few strokes, a hand plane in Woodworking could shave rubber soles to nubs.

Once indoors, the thieves would leave cupboard doors ajar and swat a few soup cans to the floor and whip living room cushions into disarray. They'd sneak the organ outside and leave it tucked away under a tarp in the back yard, where Gordyn would later borrow Merv's van and, under cover of darkness with Dee in tow, heave the organ inside and drive up to the rehearsal coop, his parents never the wiser. Before-bed tea laced with Valium would assure the gang's victory.

Later still, he'd make an anonymous, accented call to the cop shop, and the organ would be returned undamaged.

Neighbourhood families moved in and out at irregular hours like tramps; he'd leave the organ sitting in the driveway of one of the empty places.

Already wary of these fly-by-night ne'er do wells, his mother would say "Typical" with disappointed heads shakes and pursed lips; she'd begin pressing for a move to a better address, where people hadn't yet descended to savagery.

As plans went, he realized in three seconds, walking on water had to be easier.

Déviation: ALBATROSS

Technically, the gang understood, each member embodied a unique case of virginity. Along with all other kids, they'd also registered that "technically" contained loopholes, fine print. One- and two-handed masturbation, for example, and the same with household accessories. None of that counted.

Whoever defined the monumental, life-defining word way back when—the slave of a stern bearded Mesopotamian pressing cuneiform into soft clay tablets, or a toga'd Roman bigwig judging temple priestess applicants—had proclaimed that losing virginity meant going all the way. And the rule just stuck. That meant anything in the range except sexual intercourse between a male and a female (aka coitus, aka penetration, aka doing it) counted as sexual, true, but not as the real McCoy. A sex-crazed virgin, for instance, might completely snap one day. She'd blow the entire home volleyball team (spares and coach included) and then do the same for the visiting team; although she'd be called a total hosebag mental case by everyone and shunned as well, she'd still be a virgin. Technically. And so on, right down to jacking it with whatever tools could be grabbed, wet dreams, and what the guidance councillor had been terming "heavy petting" in Sex Ed classes since the era of *Sputnik 1*, which caused multi-generational eruptions of titters and cartoon visions of dog spines buckling under the pressure of overly enthusiastic owners.

Another of the idiot tales that captivated idiots, virginity signified absolutely nothing. Alone in his room and stretched out on the bed, Gordyn had devoted ample thought to the subject.

As a rite of passage, it struck him as hollow, on par with graduating from elementary school. Or tying shoe laces. In the long run: big whoop. At the same time, it mattered deeply, though with differing reasons for boys and girls.

For guys in school especially, and to a slightly lesser degree to his father, a chasm as gaping as the Marianas Trench existed between having mastered the art of masturbation after a hundred, or a hundred thousand goes—until your tool, levitating with a will of its own in rapid up-down-up cycles, felt chafed and practically blistered from the last bout but still ready to go off again, and you'd unleashed enough spunk to repopulate entire planets, solar systems—and having poked inside a birth canal, for no time whatsoever, for the instant it takes to sneeze or to clear a throat. But voila! with the one—and only that preferred one—you no longer belonged to the immature, boyish virgin category. Once proudly revealed, the evidence trumpeted "Now he's a man" with the undoubtable authority of God in the burning bush.

Having begun masturbating at twelve by humping the mattress each and every morning and continued regularly but expanding the locations and techniques since then, the frantic, urgent events—short-lived, yes, but tied together as close knots on a length of string, they'd run from the bedroom window to the cedar tree far across the creek, *at least*—led to the unavoidable conclusion that in his own way he matched Xavier Hollander. If, as she'd written, years of experience had trained her to automatically and instantly solve the puzzle of any client's needs, Gordyn could make a similar claim for himself, his eager client never unsatisfied, nor ever out of reach.

He'd fathomed as well that while technically a virgin, he ranked as a special case.

Thirteen months after he'd begun to ejaculate in blissful solitude, he'd screwed Evan, a stoner dimwit cousin on his father's side and nearly two years older, twice in the hobby farm's wobbly barn-red chicken coop that Evan's dad hadn't gotten around to demolishing (and once—Gordyn's first carnal regret—within a maze of footpaths snaking between poplars and slumped tall grass off a river road that Evan had heard about, while being watched by a crouching but motionless grey-haired man whose barking mutt crashed through nearby bushes and chased anything with feathers).

Also: before Evan and later, he'd entered into bedroom—and basement and forest path and carport—contests with a nervous handful of shifty, pent up, and hurried boys, the goal of which began with the daring question and competitive challenge of who'd take the shortest time to shoot, and ended with various forms of improvised pretense officially related to self-improvement: secretly jerking each other (awkwardly seated side by side first, followed by standing face to face) just to practice managing the sensation, eyes squeezed shut while envisioning (they'd proclaim categorically beforehand and afterwards) how Sharon K or Miss L would handle the needy flesh (dry once, then spit-coated, then swabbed with hair conditioner, hand lotion, and Mazola snuck from the kitchen); and, a few sessions further in, they kept their eyes closed (kind of) while never-says-no mirage Sharon K or Miss L sucked them off; and as the educational projects were reaching their logical termination points, one boy thrust his way into spurted ecstasy between the clothed (then naked except underwear, then fully naked, then slicked with a gob of Crisco shortening) thighs of the other in order *to practice*—just as every MVP in every sport must—so that when the big day arrived, the gradually willing but now exhausted and newly bow-legged girl (the very mark, every guy agreed, of a well-fucked slut) would be blown away by his astonishing, Pelé-like talent and pass word on to girlfriends, which would eventually drift toward their boyfriends, and so on to the whole school, every pocket of it, in the general way all reputations were locked into place, a communal map pinned with locations and events.

Other memories he could retrieve with vivid details: in a rest stop parking lot (his family stretching their legs) he'd spent two hot July minutes watching a guy his dad's age reclined in a rust bucket El Camino as he whipped out his sausage from a navy velour sweat suit and manhandled it showily, like a cobra before a mongoose; Gordyn had jerked in time with guys in adjacent stalls at department store restrooms (while shopping with his family, by himself, and with the gang); in the same pungent locations, he'd shown off erection after erection at urinals and twice let an older guy reach over for a half minute of reckless, joyous stroking; and in a rush with a skin magazine or catalogue he'd jacked off—standing, kneeling, flat on his back—in practically every master bedroom where Dee had babysat.

If an inventor came up with a wearable device for men similar to that machine for milking cows, Gordyn believed he'd be an overnight millionaire.

As for romance—making out for hours, gazing into dreamy eyes, whispering heartfelt poetic truths—none existed before, during, or after.

A man at a trough urinal had clasped Gordyn's shoulder and squeezed while coughing out a husky-voiced thank you. Though his cousin said "We gotta get out of here" or "Let's go" seconds after he shot, the fact of ongoing invitations implied affection of a kind.

That all made sense.

Guys weren't supposed to gush or hunger for the magical day they clinked champagne glasses after the trip down an aisle strewn with flower petals.

Notebooks / December

So, do you think we should quit our job when . . .
[ ] When we've raised X amount of $
[ ] We reach a specific number
[ ] Some other reason (what?)
Return your answer today, OK?

Diary / Rehearsals

卌 卌

To be honest, this entry should be before the last one. To be honest again, I'd be BSing if I said I got too busy. I didn't feel like it, I guess. I get how grown ups are expected to go to work 5x a week for their entire lives (= over 12,000 days of slaving vs just 4800 of weekends!!!), but I don't get why they agree to that. "Sure, I'll be a slave, why not? I've got nothing better to do." God.

After a few years of a cracking whip, I'm going to show up 3 or 4 max.

Anyhow, that was two weeks ago, and I can hardly remember what I ate for lunch today. The reason doesn't really matter. I didn't write then but I'm making up for it now.

D. and I finally decided to give the guys the "Prawn Gardens" surprise.

D. knew that she (a) had to babysit and that (b) J. was hanging out in G.'s room. Excellent timing, in other words. She telephoned from the R.'s and asked her mom to call upstairs to the guys b/c she needed some help in the basement. Mrs. W. must ~~of~~ have made it seem we were in trouble or something b/c they were pounding on the front door a minute later. (Mrs. W. stayed home, thank God! When they got back G. told her that Mr. R. had offered a huge bonus if D. organized the basement and she just needed them to lift a box of encyclopedias. I think Mrs. W.'s afraid of basements or something. (It's a long list.))

D. stood on the other side of the door and yelled for them to wait exactly one minute and then come straight downstairs.

We were ready when they did.

D. pressed 'Play' when the door to the basement swung open and that gave us the 25-second instrumental part until she had to sing "Harm ful el e ments in the air air". She made pinging sounds on the glass pie plate with a fork and I counted beats with the foot petal and followed the rest of the song. I think little Damien thought it was early Christmas or a birthday party b/c he was super-excited and running around in the 'dance floor' part in front of our taped-on 'stage'.

Based on his reaction, we'll get a record contract and a Lear jet one of these days! The guys nodded too. They totally approved!

D. wore this sheer moo moo thing she'd ripped out from the back of Mrs. W.'s closet. Plus, all her bangles, which she shook along with the song. We'd worked on the jerky dance we think goes with Siouxsie's singing. D. really spazzed out while she sang, shaking and flapping her spread arms like a huge crazy bird taking off. Under a spell, without a care in the world, just attacking it. I couldn't really do much b/c I was drumming, but I rocked my head back and forth. Picture a broken robot still trying to function. That was me. Only with a swim mask, for fun.

It's all like acting, I guess. Concentrate on the role. Forget the audience. Then go for it!

They clapped and smiled and clapped some more.

G. didn't give us one word of advice, which seemed like the day's absolute miracle. It was a "thy eternal summer shall not fade" moment. A huge rush, in modern lingo. That song is definitely in our Top Four. (Now if only we can do the same thing in front of someone other than those two and a little kid in a basement. Eg., a room full of strangers . . .)

𝍸 𝍸 |

For various legit reasons everyone except me was busy today (J. was underneath the car and other two had to visit Mrs. W.'s sister's brand new house in a subdivision by Surrey). Rain poured by the bucket and I was bored and there was no way I could watch Saturday TV all afternoon = sports, beyond tedious + a total waste of time.

So . . . I'm at the end of the driveway under my new bubble umbrella with red trim when Mr. Suspicious, wiping his hands on a rag, asks me where was I going. I say to D.'s. I turn left toward the coop and he yells out "Wrong way, missy" and stands there in coveralls with his hands on his hips in that way he does when he's ready to pounce.

It felt like the cigs in my jacket pocket were super-visible and a minute later I'd be seated upstairs at the kitchen table listening to a lesson about the unhealthy stupidity of it all coming from someone who smokes and drinks and tokes and who knows what else. God! Parents and double standards = straight from hell!

But then he looked down at J., who was sitting on the carport floor wearing a toque and a scarf and looking very crabby b/c who changes the oil or whatever on a cold rainy Saturday??

Mr. Suspicious waved then and "No later than 4:30, got it?" (J. told me later that he'd said a shortcut ran right through a field across from the tree farm, and since X doesn't go anywhere except in his prized convertible, he had to believe that story as truth. As with a fairy tale giant, the secret for success is tricking him and keeping him well fed and unaware.)

In the coop it was spiders up in the corners, the drums, raindrops, and me with dry feet (gum boots = ugly but they get the job done!). I could see my breath.

I warmed up by speed-rubbing my hands and doing a few jumping jacks.

After I got over feeling idiotic about talking to myself in a deserted building I felt devoted (and, to be truthful, I gave myself a pep talk about wallowing and taking the bull by the horns. Someday I'll be a terrific parent. Or coach!). Anyways, I just sat there and went through the songs, 1, 2, 3, then 1, 1, 1, and so on in different ways and looking outside at my silent fake audience—the field and wet trees and heavy clouds that would be perfect for a really dramatic funeral. Spiders were actually watching, though, I guess, but who knows what a drummer looks like through eight teensy eyes. A spastic giant, maybe, an enormous storm? A mysterious thundering stampede? A threat, for sure.

So . . . before I practically had to count the beats out loud to stay on time. I've graduated to somewhere between competent and semi-competent now. Hope springs eternal, right?

I practiced till my arms throbbed. Who knew that drummers needed to be so fit. I should take up jogging. Maybe.

Oh, there's a problem (okay, that might not be a problem at all). Drum machines that Moev and Gary Numan use sound as synthetic as Cheez Whiz tastes. For 'old-fashioned drumming', which is what I'm doing, I don't sound like a drum machine. Maybe I have to act more robotic, so people will get it? Really, though, does that make any difference . . . ? It's not like the audience or the judges will stand up to yell and demand that the performance stop because the drumming didn't sound as artificial or mechanical as it's supposed to? Probably, I'm overreacting. I'll give the robotic thing a shot, though.

There weren't any lights on at Mr. T.'s. When I knock to do reading, about half the time he doesn't answer. I'm pretty sure his hearing is totally fine.

I don't know how he stands all that darkness.

𝍸 𝍸 ||

Full steam ahead!

ps. I'm a bit worried. As per usual J. seems the least interested in sticking with it. He gets bored in the way other people get excited. Something else by now has probably caught his eye. I really hope he doesn't just quit. That would be crummy + ruin it for the rest of us. I won't say anything to jinx it and pray for the best.

𝍸 𝍸 |||

Yay! Hallowe'en falls on a Saturday this year. That translates into a school thing on Friday and then a weekend party, a 'cameo'. As an experiment, we're going to try out two sets of costumes, boys vs girls, and see how other kids, our 'test subjects', react. We might learn something useful.

J. and G. announced their choice: "The Village of the Damned" (or "Children", maybe there are two movies??). And since the movie was in black and white, we'd try for that too. That means pale grey foundation that D. would mix, white-blonde wigs styled à la Dorothy Hamill with curled-under bangs, etc. The kids go to a private school or something, so ties, cardigans, turtlenecks, plaid skirts and dress pants. That's pretty easy.

I don't know why the guys chose that. But The Damned is an excellent band name, that's for sure. To me, dressing as four possessed kids seems dumb. If we walked on stage in those get-ups, people would start laughing. And, I'd bet, they wouldn't stop right away, either. I know I wouldn't. Girls can maybe pull off wigs, but J. and G . . . . I dunno. It's more like a joke than a look we can or should try to pull off. At school, especially.

I zipped around with D. forever, and we passed costume ideas back and forth. Every single one turned out to be junk. You'd think we'd come up with something worthwhile, with the snap of fingers. But no way. Everything seemed pointless or boring. Or cliché.

Then . . . I mentioned painter's overalls and D. brought up dip-dyeing, which she'd done in Home Ec. A marriage made in heaven, ha ha.

We decided that I'd come by her place on the Saturday before and hope that lightning strikes. I figure we can't go that wrong with black dye.

("What are you?" had to be the #1 reaction, and said like, "God, what are you doing here looking like that, I can't wait to move away from you and then point at you and whisper from the other side of the room" by girls in leotards dressed as black cats and guys going as Kiss or in miniature capes and pinching their noses while saying "Consume mass quantities!" A school dance at daytime is never a great plan. And costumes with monster makeup at 2 in the afternoon just looks sloppy. It's "e'en" for a reason!

Kids nicknamed us the village idiots, and I swear I could see J. and G.'s reputations sinking fast (eg., a sped-up movie of sunset). G.'s definitely sunk below zero now.

Freshly dyed fabric rubs off on skin, we also discovered.

At Krysta T.'s party, which wasn't in the top 2 popular parties, everyone asked us the identical "What *are* you?" question, and seemed uninterested in the answer, which wasn't very creative anyhow. We switched from "Just something we whipped up" (But why??, on listeners' faces) to "Punk rockers" (But why, part 2, on listeners' faces).

I know that big companies send out questionnaires to test new developments (eg: "On a scale of 1 to 10, how much did you enjoy Smoked Salmon Potato Chips?"), but what happens when the answers are just pencilled-in instead: "I dunno", "They're ok", "So so, I guess"? At best, that's what we got: "That's different", "Huh", "Oh, I see", "Well . . . ". Nobody gushed or said, "That totally rocks". "Confused" and "Inconclusive" had to be the basic reaction of our test subjects. Then again, groups didn't form a circle and try to stone us to death. Blessings counted, right?)

卌 卌 ||||

Okay, too many ideas is just as bad as none at all.

卌 卌 卌

Cold and blue skies. Today our drafty coop could pass as an iceberg. I guess insulation for chickens wasn't all that necessary way back when. Plus, they have feathers. Playing with gloves = a total joke. Our fingers ached, and then some!

For the next times (no chance it'll warm up this month), we have an old coil heater at our place I'll sneak down. We thought of candles, but pictured an accident and burning down the whole place. In addition to everything else, we'd be grounded for eternity. I don't know how expensive electricity is. Mr. T. won't forget to mention it, I'm sure.

To get the blood flowing, we slid-skated on the pond instead. Nobody else had been there, not even tracks from rabbits or a deer, just sandy drifts of snow. I love when that place freezes over. It gets pure. Like Antarctica.

J. told us about an opera he'd heard on the radio about a bunch of 'starving artists' who are not just looking the part. They literally have no food to eat and burn their own books for heat. He didn't go into wall-to-wall detail, but the point seemed to be that being dirt poor and an artist isn't worthwhile b/c you either die or have a broken heart (or both) <u>and</u> if you're not poor and suffering, then you can't make real art. A lose-lose situation that sort of makes you wonder "Why bother?" Maybe he skipped over a part.

Normally we just look the part but today it felt totally legit. J. was just telling a story, but we all felt a bit guilted out for just playing around on the pond b/c the weather we felt chilly. Boo f-ing hoo. We decided to follow our own trail back across the crusty snow, Suffering in the Name of Art (ha ha). Inside, after awhile we put off enough heat to get comfortable. Gloveless too.

I'll bet each one of us would have given up already if we were trying it alone. Guilt and competitiveness and having somebody relying on you seems very motivating. (Maybe I should become a coach!)

We've all listened a million times and swapped different ideas, but still can't agree to the lyrics of "Obituary Column" (b/c of the singer's style of pronounciation (sp?) and the band putting her voice in the 'background' of the song). We thought of writing to Moev (MOĒV? That's how the name is spelled on the EP), but other than the "Noetix" label and "Studio Brothers Studio" there's no information on the record, not even an address (and calling the operator at Information and getting the number and then calling the studio receptionist etc etc etc could take up days, and even if we manage to get hold of the band they might say "We didn't print lyrics for a reason, so figure them out yourselves, good bye").

We're going to fill in the blanks instead.

There's a line about "the light is slowly fading" and another that's, "Such a meagre existence / Where is your Christ now?" (we do agree about this <u>now</u>: G. tried very hard to convince us all it was "Where is your cat now?", as if!, but we told him in addition to glasses he should consider a hearing aid). Anyhow, we think the song's about being part of the herd and just going through the motions with everyone else, being living and breathing and working etc, but not really being <u>alive</u>. That makes sense. And then, eventually, your life is nearly over and you have nothing much to report, no big accomplishments, nothing except "I kept a steady job for 47 years and kept my family fed and a roof over their head." Big whoop, what an accomplishment.

We'll make the other lyrics we're adding continue on with that idea. Also, before the singing starts there's an instrumental part of 50 (!) seconds. That's too long by a mile. We've got to cut that down. For some reason all the songs start that way. And when you add them together, it means a lot of standing around and waiting for singing to start, from the audience's point of view. And ours: staring at an audience with "Get on with it" shooting from their eyes. That's bad news.

The other plan … in the works. After that, we'll be legitimate. Maybe the monkeys are getting closer to "Macbeth"!

卌 卌 卌 |

We 'broke up' today. Just like a real-life band. Actually, D. wanted to try out some new ~~manueouveres~~ moves for the stage. J. and G. thought that figuring out how to play in synch with each other and working on some eye contact was crucial.

I worked on a new song:

She's a dreamer, a pretty schemer
Wants so much more than
The world has given her.

I'd written 'He's a teamer', which gave me the giggles, as did 'lemur' and 'femur'. The idea is they're opposites, but they meet and convince themselves they're right for each other, but they're wrong. Tragedy. More later.

p.s. Untuned 'borrowed' guitars are now leaning against the purchased drums. Along with the paint job, the coop looks like a studio where some psychedelic hippies would have hung out. Or a rehearsal hall for *Godspell*. But from the outside it just looks like a dilapidated (sp?) farm building. Except for Mr. T., it's all ours!

卌 卌 卌 ||

Gulp!!

G., Mr. Experienced, marched right up to Mr. S. in the hall outside of Band today b/c he wanted to drive home a point, the point being that it's not the lead singer but the drummer who's the real backbone of the band. Even though that's what no one believes.

For some reason, Mr. S. looked at us as if we were from another planet and had asked the weirdest question of all time. He started talking about band leaders and symphony conductors, which was beside the point.

G. got into 'rabid dog' mode and said, "Well, actually, Mr. S. we're specifically asking about a rock and roll band, not an orchestra". Mr. S, who obviously just wanted to get to the Teachers' Lounge to grab a smoke, frowned. He said, "You seem to know the answer already, Mr. W. I'm not sure how I can help you. Now, if you'll excuse me . . . ". He made a slow downward karate gesture, as if to say, "Please clear the pathway, or else".

I believed G. already but had been giving him a hard time. Nobody ever appreciates 'advice' from know-it-alls (even when they're right).

The success of the band now sits on my shoulders, Miss Metronome. Yay.

卌 卌 卌 |||

The flu is going around, and G. feels like death warmed over. Looks that way too and a total complain-a-thon, D. said when she met us (rain = cats and dogs, so three gold stars to her for dedication).

The three of us practiced doing "Metal" and "Prawn Gardens" (which, we've more or less decided, are songs #1 and #2, gloomy followed by fun and "tit shaking", as D. sees it) over and over for two hours straight, no break and the cassette player turned up so high it felt like we were playing at a concert (ok, a concert playing to no one). We stopped after thirteen run-throughs b/c we were hot and dizzy and our hands throbbed. Also, at any second the tape probably would have started to stretch out or completely melted.

On a spare yesterday (it's Sat. before bed now) J. had watched the coach make two guys barely scraping by on the v-ball team set up and spike.

Coach F. just sat on the bleachers for the hour flipping through the newspaper and droning, "Again. Again. Again". He hardly even looked up at them. J. said guys were spares and normally only warmed the bench b/c "they need to learn to aim inside the bowl". The idea being that instead of over-thinking about how to do it each time, the movement and the accurate aiming become as automatic and easy as walking.

J. thought the same thing must apply to singing and playing.

"Practice makes perfect", as they say.

Plus, we can tell how idiotic we look right now, on par with those shy kids forced to give a presentation and just standing there, trembling like a chihwauwa (sp?) in a snowstorm and reading in a whisper from cue cards and barely looking up. <u>Torture</u> for everyone.

That needs to be fixed, inward   outward, so for the final four run-throughs we yelled stuff at each other like in a drill ("Look up!", "Shake your shoulders!", "Move your arms and take a sudden step forward!", "J. smile at D.!"), all the while trying not to laugh and for sure not stopping. Totally concentrating. I'd say that makes being on a team look like a cinch.

We debated about how to stitch together the spaces between songs, from nothing to saying something (eg., "Here's a little number you might not know. It's by Blondie"). Being mute will probably seem amateur and closed-off, which would be bad. Too much talking, though, and you're cheesy, like a Miss America host. We decided against deciding.

If we were the Partridge Family, all this would come naturally. But we're not and it doesn't. There's no script. But . . . compared to last month and the month before that, I'd said we've improved. By leaps and bounds, as teachers sometimes say.

𝍸 𝍸 𝍸 ||||

Selling out came up as a topic this afternoon. As in, is the point to give the audience entertainment (= Top Ten Countdown songs they already know and can hum along to), or for <u>us</u>, to show our taste (or 'vision' as G. calls it) and if the audience approves that's cool, but not the primary reason for doing it.

If we came to any conclusion, I missed what it was.

More than anything else, I'd say we're excellent at talking about stuff and not coming up with anything concrete. Maybe going into politics would be a good back-up plan if (when?) fashion designers etc in New York City belly flops.

Notebooks / January

Top 5

"Metal" - Gary Numan (3:30)

- opening song. G on stage when lights go up, plays opening bars, others come on before the lyrics start

Or: all on stage, backs turned except G. Each one turns when their part begins?

Or: frozen on stage in black coats, as G plays the opening bars the rest slowly begin to sway, nod heads, as if music is waking them. (Too Drama class??)

Or: ???

"Smart Patrol / Mr. DNA" - Devo (6:05)

"Obituary Column" - Moev (3:32)

"Eat to the Beat" - Blondie (2:42)

"Hong Kong (Prawn) Garden" - Siouxsie and the Banshees (2:54)

Subs??

Venture: Raceway / October

Drag racing fumed with heat shimmering above painted metal, vaporizing fuel splashed on baked asphalt, and the skins of fat tires burned into smoke. On overcast days cool airstreams crept over from the river and across the motocross track's tire-chewed mud, and swirled funky marshiness into the carnival atmosphere.

Management cancelled for rain. The noise-offended or engine-bored few could lift their nostrils to sniff out the oily currents of browning corn dog batter that drifted sporadically from behind the grandstand's wooden planks.

Races zipped along in a series of exhilarated heartbeats. At the green light that followed red and amber, twin needle-nosed dragsters—chamoised until glossy—streaked in close parallel to the finish line within seconds, their parachutes blossoming brightly, and all the while colossal revving engines with braggart chrome mufflers deafened thrilled spectators and spellbound track crew. As guys scrambled to set up for the next quarter-mile run, whole families marveled at the temperamental exotic vehicles and debated the techniques of the previous drivers, who'd shown up in trailer-hauling RVs from as far off as Calgary and Spokane.

By virtue of her job, Em watched all the goings-on from close up. Glad for the money, she felt *comme ci comme ça* about fast cars burning rubber. If she missed a week or three, no big deal.

The kind of man who spoke easily with strangers anywhere and at any time, Em's dad naturally rubbed shoulders with drag strip management. On blue-skied Sundays he left for the track at mid-morning and hung around well after the raceway emptied, drinking while reminiscing.

To Em's eyes his efforts there consisted of huddled exchanges between the observation tower and the start line with other men in green glass shades and short white jackets emblazoned with oval patches for motor oil companies and parts manufacturers. She couldn't say if the raceway paid him or he just volunteered to get near the action. He acted—squinting, pointing, shrugging, nodding—as if the smooth running of the entire operation had landed on his reliable shoulders.

He'd enlisted his only son, mistaking Jay's ready mask of agreeability for filial enthusiasm. Right after a day of shaking hands with the raceway bosses Jay began to conjure excuses out of thin air with a magician's ease—extra-tough school projects imposed by vindictive teachers, burgeoning and pressing if hazily described extracurricular responsibilities, résumé drop-off missions for a suddenly crucial part-time job. As always, Joey bought the excuses.

At once curious and reluctant, Em filled in.

The majority of her responsibility involved standing still, waiting, paying attention, and wearing white jeans beneath a boxy regulation green golf shirt she longed to alter. Or to set on fire. She drew the line at a baseball cap in matching green, stuffing it in a back pocket just in case.

Right after each race, officials perched high in the turquoise siding-clad observation tower—a tall upright plywood shoebox that was hollow except for stairs that led to a glassy airport-style room at the top—compared stopwatch findings. The guys wrote precise time results on a piece of paper and dropped the information down a chute in a tiny sealed envelope.

When one landed Em grabbed it and ran to a racetrack official, who read the numbers and returned the envelope. That was half the job. She called the man in the black and white striped shirt an umpire, aware that another title, a proper one, must belong to him. After pausing at the strip's asphalt heart, she'd hustle back thirty yards to the chute and place the envelope in a lock-box. At the end of the day she knew to bound up the four flights of stairs and submit the lock-box and its key; in the lookout she watched the only woman in the tower count the envelopes. Between long draws on her cigarette, this same wordless lady recorded the hours of Em's shift.

With the exception of the electric instant when the envelope thunked and Em dashed to the track with the make-or-break numbers within—all that mattered in the world at that very moment—the entire endeavour felt ceremonial and glum, like church, except way louder.

Introducing Em as his "second in command," her father then speed-walked his protégé through the fenced-off area for drivers, crew, and officials, and explained that racing was a high stakes business and that despite looking like a ghost town in the making—dumpy buildings, crumbly access roads, drooping chain link fences, thick dust coatings everywhere—the Bend's drag strip played a crucial role on the circuit. He also said the place stood on its last legs and at the end of the season the city planned to reclaim the leased land and convert it into a competitive industrial park as part of the multi-pronged improvement plan. She couldn't care less.

Em enjoyed watching the animated crowds and did squirrel away the money, the fixed hourly rate a novelty. When she'd picked strawberries and later raspberries pay depended on how quickly she filled each flat; week by week the amount increased as she learned the steady mechanical style of the veteran pickers. At the tower's base, in contrast, she might sprawl on the ground like a drunk or gaze in wonder at deep blue sky or sneak cigarettes by the dozen, and her pay would never vary.

Stupefied with boredom and fitting herself into a thin wedge of shade that moved with the sun, Em lost track of how many races had run or the number of envelopes she'd handed off and then returned. She perked up at the announcer's voice—"Okay, folks, get ready for the last blast of the season"—and tracked down the contraption studded with three floodlight bulbs and cobbled together with wires and a wooden fencepost painted white, then bolted to a pyramidal base of hammered 2x4s: at dead centre between two dragsters, the red bulb at the top currently glowed.

With rushing passersby, frantic crew, and the handicap of standing a smidgen over five feet, she heard but couldn't spot the rivals squeal away from the starting line. She counted to twenty quickly, caught the rising murmur of several hundred people saying "Oh," "Wow," and "Jeez" in unison, and exposed herself to the blaze of unseasonal sunlight to grab the envelope that would momentarily drop.

At a jog, Em wove through the mobile crowd. Grown ups glanced her way, aware of what the girl in the green shirt meant to delivery.

At the lighting rig track officials joked around with crew and other jovial men, her father included, who appeared to simply *belong*, as though guests of honour at a party or wedding reception. He rested a hand on the shoulder of a guy dressed in the tribe's white nylon jacket with patches and appeared to be congratulating him.

Em guessed that from their vantage point at the track's starting line, the men could tell whether the car on the left or right had won, her envelope, then, nothing except a mandatory formality, confirmation.

Acting impartial as an official should, the umpire-guy always stood off to the side and exchanged words with another official, who held signalling flags.

As Em sought out the flagman's striped pullover her eyes fell on a profile with a Viking-blonde shag haircut and full ruddy mustache, the latter characteristic anyone in a police lineup would mistake for her father's. The last time she'd seen him, though, he'd been honking as he drove off, having calmed down since calling Dee and her rude names and forking over cash for what they eventually joked about as their first day on the job.

She hadn't known he was so tall, and breathed relief at seeing him deeply involved in a manly racetrack conversation of gesticulations and enthusiastic nods. Like everyone else there, he talked loudly, his ears temporarily deafened by revved dragster engines.

Without setting aside a moment for thought, Em understood the importance of delivering the envelope and preventing his gaze from landing on her. She knew too that if he did manage to catch sight of her snaking through the celebratory uproar, she'd somehow need to make him see that her purpose was nothing other than the information delivery, a task for which she received payment, and that while she and the other girl who'd been in his car might look similar, the spitting image amounted to a trick of light.

She slowed her usual sprint to a targeted stride, fighting to blend in and to not reveal that her father had put in a word for her and, especially, that he smiled not fifteen feet away. Remembering the cap, she scooped up a handful of hair. He'd never recognize her now. Besides, he'd mostly been slobbering over Dee.

The two mustached men might even be acquainted, she realized—her father made a point of shaking hands with big deals—and that made severing any connection as necessary as water. "This is Em, my second in command" would be absolutely sickening. If her father called out, she'd risk riling him by pretending deafness and scurrying back to the tower, to all onlookers the exact picture of professional responsibility.

Sensing manageable hot panic but no tears, she reminded herself to carry sunglasses for future shifts and choked down titters at the idea of an *occupational hazard*. She veered briskly toward the umpire-guy, inhaling the remnants of burnt tires and sweet edible notes of frying donuts. As he read the results, wrote on his clipboard, and returned the envelope, Em turned her back to the crowd. Mustache Man couldn't catch her face from that angle; she felt as good as anonymous.

For once grateful to be small and short, and relieved at her otherwise terrible decision to allow Dee to OD on her hair with honey-blonde streaks (intermingling with Copper Sunset, which was as quickly renamed Cedar Chips and Mulch by Jay; if her dad had noticed he'd refrained from comment), she wound back to the safety of the tower's stairway.

Later, and after careful planning, she'd find a way to ask her father if he recognized the tall man. Maybe saying she'd thought but wasn't completely sure that his face had been plastered on the front page of the *Bend Observer*. Mention how the case involved embezzled money, or that the police wanted him for questioning?

Her father claimed to "know anybody who was a somebody." With luck the man fell into the nobody category, a face in the crowd just passing through and then never seen again.

Em couldn't wait to get home.

She loved to gab curled up on the wrought iron seated telephone table in the main floor vestibule papered in ivy vines. Instead of the ivory French provincial phone with gold accents, though, she'd use the scuzzy beige unit downstairs, for security purposes.

At the news, Dee's shrieked "Omigod"s and who knew what else at the other end of the line would make her double over with giggles intense enough cramp her abdomen for ever.

Venture: Equipment / November

Gordyn had begun to suspect Ronnie of faking relapses.

Maybe the little guy detected in his obligation-bound young replacement a means to compensate for a laziness normally belonging to a fairy tale bumpkin who sprawled all day long beneath the shade of an oak. Or, worse yet, Gordyn considered, Ronnie and Merv might have collaborated secretly with a scheme of unknown dimensions. It would trap him like an indentured servant, forcing him to slave away for years until, at last, Merv decided the steep cost of the IDs had at last been paid off.

Grinding the van's gears, Gordyn braced his back for driveway humps and hollows. As breezes picked up the alder stands wobbled, still weeks away from their winter performance as leafless, skeletal, and discouraging. Nothing else, as he now expected, had really changed—the greying lumber of Ronnie's cabin had bowed by imperceptible degrees perhaps and the yard featured a picnic table and a hibachi by the truck camper as well as a derelict white stove, its oven door yawning open and awaiting nesting rodents.

From what Gordyn had observed, Ronnie kept no fixed routine. Nor did he bother with piddling matters like finding and holding down a regular job or making his property look halfway decent.

Gordyn's own routine changed with a light.

While Ronnie's customary abode showed not so much as a glimmer from a lamp, his pickup camper's windows beckoned with a candle's glow. Gordyn parked and veered for the portable housing on blocks. He normally caught bars of music or laugh tracks from programs that clicked off when he approached, but at this twilight heard only gusts pass between trees. Crows cawed at a distance, camouflaged.

He climbed the camper's pull-down stairs and peered through wire screen and a skinny rectangle of door glass. "Ronnie? Hey . . . Ronnie, it's Gordyn."

Ronnie's watery eyes might see a trespasser, Gordyn guessed. He pictured a shotgun's snout taking aim. Speaking louder he rapped on the doorframe and reached inside to check the camper for a switch. He swung open the sticky aluminum door.

With the possibility that Ronnie had suffered another of his improbable setbacks Gordyn sketched the best route for an emergency drive to the hospital. He'd tell his parents about witnessing an accident and staying to help, a good samaritan as taught. Supplying the convincing answer as to why he happened to be driving a stranger's rickety van in the back forty, that he'd figure out later.

A ceiling light illuminated two facts: Ronnie had not fallen anywhere inside, and that with so many boxes stuffed there he could not have hidden if he tried. Collapsed, his body would be flung uncomfortably over the right-angle edges and sharp corners of boxes in plain sight.

In preparation for moving, Gordyn's father normally drove to a liquor store, at which point clerks brightened, looking relieved to rid the store of boxes their bosses normally told them to break down and haul out back. Half of the boxes in Ronnie's camper were wrapped in clear plastic and smaller others had been strapped together so that three could be picked up as one. Not a single one advertised Smirnoff or Canadian Club. Gordyn counted boxes of various but smallish sizes printed in black: Pioneer, Grundig, Radio Shack, Technics, Norelco. He noticed an oblong one—Yamaha CS-50—beneath a bulky Magnavox.

Possession of Stolen Property, a criminal act known from cops shows, rushed to mind alongside Harbouring a Fugitive. Technically, the criminal harboured himself. Did Knowledge of an Illegal Act count as a crime?

"Hey, G-man, you looking for me?" Ronnie spoke from the base of the steps.

Startled, Gordyn felt a grudging pleasure at the first-time appearance of an acceptable nickname. When Gordo had crept in, he'd guessed that a polite correcting would result in nothing except "Gordyyyyynnnnn" stretched out into a merciless lisp.

Ronnie held a rake, but no shotgun. "Jeez, Ronnie, you freaked me out. I didn't see a light on in your . . . place, and noticed one here. I figured you might have had an accident or something, um, so I came to find you. I wasn't snooping, I thought you were here. Ok?"

"No sweat off my nose." Ronnie took a step back. "That shit's, hmmm. A guy, um, that's right, a guy I know is, he needs a . . . a dry place to store some stuff. For a while. 'Til he gets back on his feet, I mean. Y'know?"

Gordyn smirked, stifling outright laughter. He'd sputtered a better lie in kindergarten. "Does he own a stereo shop?" He understood Ronnie's crossed arms and distance as a pleading message: *Let's head back to the pop-up right now.*

"I couldn't really say."

"Huh, and still in the original boxes. He must be a neat freak."

"Well, yeah, I guess so. Different strokes . . . "

Gordyn needed to use the situation to his advantage. He realized he'd heard the phrase about a million times from the lecture-fond mouth of Coach F, of all people. The tyrant made detecting and implementing advantage an invaluable centrepiece, the foolproof strategy of every rallying pep talk / team huddle / post-game sermon in the change room, from basketball to curling.

"Anyhow, it's getting late. I suppose we should—"

"Yeah, I was out back."

In Ronnie's wide gesture, Gordyn saw all of Brackendale, now a few distant porch lights, darkened fields, and tree clumps in silhouette. He pictured junked trailers and salvaged appliances littered along the property's rear border and Ronnie riffling through them with the gleeful fascination of a scrounging vagrant. When striding he probably leaned on the rake.

"It's a good thing narcs don't visit. I bet they'd get pretty suspicious." Gordyn directed his gaze past Ronnie's left shoulder. "If they found out, that is."

"They don't listen to reason neither. Call you a damned liar right to your face."

"Yeah, well, all the more reason to keep them off your land." Gordyn rested against the TV box, arm outstretched along its chilly top as though he'd already owned it for years. Possession is nine-tenths of the law, he thought. "Hey, Ronnie . . . Your friend . . . Do you think he'd mind if I borrowed something?"

"Jeez, hard to say."

"Or maybe he'd rent it to me. Help him get back on his feet, right?" He looked down at Ronnie, sensing the advantage of height and the thrilling inevitability of a win.

"Yeah, I guess. I could ask."

Since there was no friend, no getting back on his feet, no storage until then, and no borrowing nor renting, and no asking, Gordyn felt tangled in improv'd deceits, a talent, he'd discovered in Drama class, he'd ordinarily call stunted. "That'd be great."

He wondered about the next destination for the boxes. The route from warehouse or storeroom or truck trailer to storage at Ronnie's under darkness made sense. But after there the trajectory petered out. Wherever the stolen goods appeared, the black market merchandise must sell at pennies on the store-price dollar.

Ronnie backed up, visibly uneasy, neck craning as though cops already swarmed the property. Gordyn imagined the guy's mental gears churning at a turtle-driver's speed.

"Do you want to call the guy tonight? Since I'm already nearby, I could use the van. That way I won't have to, um, disturb your privacy on another day."

"Oh, jeez—."

In Ronnie's expression Gordyn detected the face of a man used to and comfortable with following explicit instructions and who lusted in no way after the freedom to blaze a trail of his own making, nor even to set the pace. The brown nosers in school turned into the office yes-men his father complained about and always compared to French collaborators in World War Two. Ronnie had yes-man locked into his DNA.

Body language, a faltering voice, shifty eyes: no one could miss Ronnie's weak timidity, Gordyn decided. It would draw guys—types he recognized and feared in school—who'd capitalize on it and take advantage of the weakness. Wolves and sheep, he thought: as if a third option existed.

"I'll load a box, just one, okay, in the van tonight. That'll save both of us time. If he, your friend I mean, says it's a bad idea, I'll return it right away. He can just call Merv. Okay? I won't even open the box until I hear from you. You can check with Merv. I see him all the time." Gordyn watched Ronnie, gauging his posture for signs of a panicked attack. Would the little man dial his crime ring boss minutes later as hungry crows on power lines kept kept watch for the foolish movement of hungry mice? No. Ronnie's nervousness and downcast expression communicated defeat.

"Okay, okay, it's a deal. Just between the two of us, okay?"

"Okay, for sure." The thieves wouldn't miss one box, Gordyn guessed. Stock-counting with Mr. Swanson's degree of paranoia struck him as unlikely. No criminal could be that anal. They probably boosted merchandise and unloaded it in bulk, ripped off whole delivery trucks or warehouses of goods. That's what he'd do. And faster than Ronnie's contacts too.

Gordyn wondered whether a criminal mastermind was made or born. If he set his mind to the goal could he surpass Merv, rise up in the ranks, sit at the head of the godfather's table, give commands, order executions, wage war over territory? Maybe.

As for Ronnie, he might be allowed to polish his shoes. If he behaved, that is.

Venture: Shoot I / October

The Cage couldn't hope to hold a bear or tiger, but roving team guys never sighted without a uniform of white-striped green trunks under grey sweats claimed it as a hangout zone, a creaky and clanking annex to their official playground of hoops, nets, and painted lines on hardwood. Hollow chromed metal tubes welded into a cube and decked out with iron plates, cables, and padded benches in maroon vinyl for chest and shoulder presses, its enormity commandeered a too-dinky concrete-floored room that might have once stored equipment for classes or the janitor. In keeping with the afterthought feel, above the perimeter of knee-height scuff marks the walls gleamed dully in yellowing eggshell. A triangle of long fixtures had been screwed into the ceiling; each track held a pair of humming fluorescents.

Everyone but jocks avoided the unventilated clubhouse like the plague. When its swampy air didn't remind student of the importance of clean feet, BO stick, and laundered gym shorts, three cinderblock walls guaranteed morgue temperatures every morning and visible breath on cold snaps.

Emptied of the targeting mouthiness of Brent S and Brian K that formed around the same handful of root words—fem, fag, frog, mo, stick—when turned on him, the severe lighting and chilly metallic gleam inspired Gordyn. Trying out black and white film in his dad's Pentax, he projected fiddling with settings and adjusting the timer to get really harsh and angular shots of the band. Moody too, with eerie cast shadows. Dee and Em could stand within the Cage, maybe, and grip the frame, staring out with the dead eyes of decommissioned androids. They'd never go for stripped bare, but that would also look cool. Or: he and Jay as pallid machine-man cogs in torn undershirts monitored by sadistic futuristic lady overseers, all rouged cheekbones and slicked-back hair. Very *Nineteen Eighty-Four.*

Still, a brain overflowing with inspiration wouldn't add up to much if circumstances blocked the gang from spending an hour or so in the room without interference.

Alongside money and band equipment and practice, now the Cage. Another gargantuan hurdle. Gordyn had begun to think of their whole project as cursed, reigned over by a strange conflicted god pulling strings from high above. Siamese twin in form and joined at the hip, the two-headed entity possessed no single mind to make up. As a result it couldn't be called indecisive so much as eternally self-divided and sibling-argumentative. And the schizoid biddings from the creature's mouths felt akin to a cat's paws from a mouse's point of view: boom ("A waste of time, don't bother, nothing's worth it, give up") and bam ("Go for it! Give it a shot! It never hurts to try!") back and forth, over and again, helping in no way.

Gordyn fretted. Requesting permission from the coach (cat with mice situation, part two), or showing up in broad daylight, camera in hand, wearing radical shoot makeup and outfits would offer nothing except an invitation to a gang bang of eternal ridicule, never less than joyfully spat out. Given the choice, who'd ever choose actual masochism?

There's always a ready-made blank wall in someone's bedroom where the four of them could stand, Gordyn supposed. Smile, click, click, and they'd be done, a routine family portrait. Why make anything difficult when the standard approach serves perfectly well?

Gordyn steered Jay quickly along the gym's edge, and made sure his collaborator got an eyeful before they scurried to unmonitored safety outside.

Ambling counterclockwise on the empty oval track they avoided the grass filler—an inviting dewy emerald carpet at a glance, but in reality a wet sponge and hell on suede. Directly overhead, low slate clouds threatened another bout of rain.

"So, what do you think?"

"I see what you mean. Excellent."

"Now what?"

"Well . . . we could tell Coach that it's an assignment for Art. Or maybe I should. He'd never check with Mr. B all the way upstairs in the art class. I bet he'd lose interest right away. But we'd definitely cause a scene. Maybe—"

"Okay, I know where this is going. Let's hear it."

"We could jimmy the doors, you know, make them seem totally closed and locked but that's just a trick."

"And sneak in after, right. The school's a dead zone at night."

"Yup."

"Boy, the parental units really ought to be wondering about our 'school projects' by now. It's like we're in Harvard or something."

"I know. Maybe this time we should say a fund drive. Or a white elephant sale. Something new."

"I guess. Anyhow, let's check out those locks first."

Careful not to hang out too long at the gym's northwest exit to the track field, Jay and Gordyn checked the mechanisms. Nothing complicated. Silver furnace tape from home slyly peeled over two sets of door locks in the late afternoon. What could go wrong?

They agreed to the necessity of surveillance, on the off-chance that Coach or one of his minions noticed the handiwork.

Not nearly the easy target that Gordyn embodied, Jay could hang around the bleachers after school, blend in with a grey kangaroo jacket, fake doing homework, and kick back balls that landed nearby. He'd hear about any discovery.

Right away, Team Einstein would suspect cigarette-addicted losers from Auto Shop. Ever since their first oil change those guys had been saddled with a reputation for vandalism of legendary proportions.

Notebooks / December

Dear Sir,
I am writing in response to 'Start your Profession Today!', your newspaper ad about how to get songs published.
I would like to know about the benefits of getting my own songs published and the costs involved, so please send me a brochure or pamphlet.
I look forward to your reply.
Yours sincerely,

Notebooks / October

Venture: The Camp Job 1 / November

Over the first few weeks of Grade 8 Dee picked up on the definite change in atmosphere. A growth spurt had left her sporadically achy and a full head taller than posturing boy-sized guys, who hurled cracks about tits and rattled zippers from the safety of mouthy groups. Or, rushing by, their gazes settled on her upper body tentatively as though unclear about its true nature—a shady oasis of refreshing water or a tricky annoying mirage? But while the sheer volume of chattering students thundering down wide junior high school hallways naturally promoted a mushrooming assortment of girl cliques and boy hangout locations—some choice, others a punishment; the further from the gym's double-door entrance the scuzzier—the essence didn't feel that different from the rooms, mowed patches, and parking lot she'd left behind the previous June.

As she kneeled on a chair steam-pressing an apron—red and white gingham with fruit appliques, a B+ project for sure, and soon to be wrapped up as an A+ gift for her mom—and struggled at the communal construction table with arm hole darts (a project requirement) on a denim vest with mandated contrasting pocket flaps (she chose acid green satin, foreseeing the C-- abomination's future home in a roadside ditch), though, Dee listened to outpouring declarations about a common topic. The girls, all of them, *obsessed*—a newfound word with infinite applications, along with *paranoid* and *neurotic*—about buying and starting a hope chest. Or, they described packing and repacking a specimen they'd already obtained: to the brim, with bath towels and grandmother-embroidered pillow cases. Without that hope chest, a girl might as well sign up for a nun's life.

Overlooking the purchase of a crystal brandy decanter, Dee learned, proved deadly. Certain objects could make or break a marriage.

The two regret-faced guys of the class shared a rear table. Miserable and ashamed, they barely lifted their chins to speak to each other, evidently dreading the teasing—"Hey, Robbie, have you finished sewing your bra yet?" and the like—that pricked at them each time they joined the boisterous top floor's log jam of bodies flowing toward stairs.

Inside the Home Ec room, girls defining themselves frequently and out loud as "naturally more mature than boys" stomped to the back of the room immediately whenever Mrs. H announced a pressing need to step out for a moment. ("A nic fit" and "a bladder the size of a pea" the rumoured culprits since the woman appeared far too ancient for sanitary napkins). In clusters of two or three the girls demanded answers, the masculine point of view on the necessary goods for a happy household, though not before ritual sarcasm about the boys' puny frames and Neanderthal sewing skills.

At "Truck keys," and "A paper bag" Dee snickered, aligning with the hairier sex's total immunity to marriage fever. Why shouldn't the boys torment their pushy counterparts? They'd just heard "I could snap you like a twig."

Along with the boys, Dee had never heard of a hope chest (was the hope that it would not remain empty, or that a groom would propose before the bride-to-be sagged or dried up?), though a dowry, the word some of the girls spoke instead, sounded familiar from her mother's era. Piled atop poodle skirts and bouffants. She thought the idea belonged in a marooned past whose dumb hourly discomforts had nothing to do with modern living in designer jeans.

A newbie in the suburban district but outgoing, she soon found herself answering Home Ec's burning question with lies. "A velvet-lined silverware set from my French mother's side of the family," she exclaimed. "A pewter ice bucket engraved with 'Eternal Love.'" Dee reminded herself about the details. If and when one of these nesting birds invited herself over, she'd better have a plausible excuse ready. With "Let's see it!" seeming unavoidable, "Stored for now with my grandparents in Montreal" sounded vague but legit enough to keep them satisfied.

Dee had thought her own sincere but smart ass answers like "Rat poison" and "A one-way ticket to Paris" sounded a bit much for these girls, who strategized like generals. Especially because they'd already decided that for a life stretching out along seven decades, a ten-yard promenade down the aisle in white lacy froth and pearly satin pumps would be as grand as it got. She kept the bad attitude to herself. Since she'd learned the phrase three schools before, "When in Rome . . . " had never let her down.

Indulging her only daughter's premature mania—which, Delphine supposed, went hand in hand with a training bra purchase years earlier than her own—required an ice cream pail of warm sudsy water in the basement.

Delphine swabbed an engraved cedar chest, bringing the gift, she witnessed after no little effort, back to gleaming life.

From its jumble of discardable leftovers from three-quarters of a continent away, she kept a recipe book filled with stewing hen and brisket ideas as well as clippings from newspapers and family cake and bar favourites printed on cards that she'd long regarded as fitting into an bygone era where making biscuits and soups from scratch was less a time-consuming luxury than a rule and the undoubted sign of womanhood achieved.

Thank God that had ended. The art of silky gravy had permanently eluded her.

Delphine replaced spittle-stained bibs and ratty swaddling cloths with a satin-trimmed white baby blanket. On a whim she splurged on a discounted starter set, five Corelle dinner plates and soup bowls in Old Town Blue.

Before evolving interests left the chest a clunky eyesore Dee couldn't just re-abandon with other basement junk, she bought slate green ceramic candle holders and nested mixing bowls in autumn leaf hues. Dee envisioned a fancy anniversary dinner served in three courses to her husband, a suited businessman in the city with gorgeous Lee Majors hair. As for how to fill time between waving goodbye at 7:30 and serving filet mignon eleven hours later, she saw herself switched off and sunken in a buckling chair while conserving the battery, a fembot awaiting further instructions.

As something to do, wedding day and wedded life planning struck her as boring. Futile. She'd rather flip through textbooks while waiting at a bus stop. Or try out new blonde streaks. Scouring the 10 x 12 bedroom for the most out-of-the-way spot, she eventually slid the chest beneath the wicker dirty clothes hamper in the closet next to her bed.

The summer before that first of three Home Ec classes (from baking powder biscuits to roast beef with au jus), Dee became curious about God's Love. Signs and billboards had sprouted everywhere and emphasized those words above drawings of hands clasped in prayer, bright enticing rainbows, and doves in flight holding what Delphine explained was not food for its chicks but an olive branch.

With such prominent guarantees of goodness the ads brought her back to the harpsichord notes and heartfelt "Let's keep on lookin' for the light" of "The Morning After," which she and

Gordy had loved and performed in countless four-minute blocks in their rooms as a choreographed duet. They'd have skated it if they could. Unlike suspicious American TV ministers with their smiling threats and tacky hairspray addiction, the godly business of the signs belonged with the unflagging hopefulness of those grimy passengers climbing through the dangerous topsy-turvy passageways of the *S.S. Poseidon.* Right toward salvation.

Dee checked shoeboxy modern churches on close-by streets—picturesque ones of heavy stone or pristine white siding and an elegant steeple nowhere in view—and decided against each based on minuscule clues and trustworthy gut feelings: size mattered (towering crosses evoked sin and punishment and an eternity of feeling guilty; weeds and rinky-dink parking lots pointed out a lack of popularity that must stem from something), as did style (few to no windows brought to mind a bunker and a deranged minister finishing a sermon of poisonous words for the entire brainwashed congregation, while wide panels of stained glass hinted at a civilized appreciation for beauty, which she shared with them).

Impatient, she nevertheless held out for the perfect fit.

Settling in the Bend, Dee spotted a single painted board for Miracle Valley nailed on a fir tree lopped off at the thirty foot mark. She pictured a secluded colony of hard-working farmers there tilling peacefully as their wives baked crusty loaves. During another exploratory family drive a newly erected sign for Camp Luther in dazzling white, the size of four plywood sheets and planted in a corn field off the highway, drew her eyes. The billboard spelled out the camp's twin mission of Compassionate Love and Salvation in a setting that promised recreation in the form of a trampoline and a dock stretching far into a lake.

Waiting a few weeks, she asked Delphine and outlined the numerous parental benefits as well as what a grandmother-voiced secretary she'd called had mentioned: "...special considerations for less well off families. Charity begins at home, dear, and generosity to the poor is God's way and our own."

Without any prompting, the lady threw in, "The heart is deceitful above all things and beyond cure. Who can understand it?" Dee kept that creepy part out of the conversation.

Delphine blew a fuse about being lumped in with welfare bums but agreed that her own religious instruction had caused "no lasting damage." She intervened on Dee's behalf when Gordy and Edmund began calling her Mother Superior, St. Deanna of BC, and The Grand Inquisitor.

The camp emphasized "traditional fun," which made Dee wonder about what threat "untraditional fun" might pose. Camp Luther promised outdoors adventure on an island equally attractive and conveniently located.

Dee conjured scenes of sing-alongs, horse trails, and skit nights, and eventually witnessed campfires, badminton, and an hourly obsession with crafts, which all somehow tied to Jesus and carpentry and additional chanting songs.

She lugged home a macramé owl and God's eyes in bark-toned yarns, but abandoned painted rocks on camp window ledges and deposited tropical sunsets dabbed onto artist's conk amongst the cattails of the island's fertile ditches. The camp taught candle- and yule log-making too, which like crafts seemed meant to tether children to vaguely biblical values. Pondering the habit, she supposed, minds and hands busy with wax, hammers, and wool couldn't light cigarettes, or reach beneath bras and panties.

Grit-nailed, Dee made "conversation pieces"—coffee table candles made from melted paraffin poured into a bowl- or bottle-shaped indentation in sand. Another started as a milk carton filled with ice cubes interspersed with plastic flower petals, holly leaves, and glitter; the poured paraffin hardened as it melted the ice, with the resulting cubic candle standing upright with mysterious holes and coloured bits trapped inside.

Camp leaders and elders mentioned wholesome fun often, she noticed, but only as a way toward necessary godly values.

To them fun for its own sake defied logic: just as candle-pouring opened the door to a story about lamp oil, wisdom, and spiritual readiness, hotdog roasts and inner tubes races signaled God's infinite love or illustrated the shiny kind of existence people could attain once they'd expelled dark sinful impulses from their ever-susceptible hearts. Smacking badminton birdies back and forth over a net had to be *educational*. Otherwise, why bother?

Any moment offered an occasion for Instruction, apparently; "the only necessary equipment is God-coloured glasses," she heard, and guessed that a manual similar to the one Gordy had brought home from Brownie's circulated with that very phase recommended as an all-purpose philosophical outlook.

Unlike lippiness or the gift of gab, apparently, a saintly disposition required constant training and reinforcement.

Shaped like a slug elongated in movement, the island a few minutes east of the Bend teemed with weekenders during hit and miss summer weather and looked more or less abandoned between October and May. That slug's torso had been chopped up into hobby farms of private property that looked identical from the road: a fringe of willows and hazelnuts or electric wire fencing at the front, flattish grazed pasture sided by an unpaved access road extending to a semi-visible house or cabin built on a slope to overlook the dark muddy lake. At dead centre, a handful of owners (or, likelier, their children) had dug septic tanks and slotted in short rows of trailer homes for revenue.

Technically, Dee's father told her, the place was an oxbow island. Also, a billabong, which set up "G'day mate" if they stopped at the place's only corner store for pop. Arms crossed, Gordy defined it as a cesspool, his gaze sweeping from reedy lake water to doublewides, cluttered yards, and locals he christened "Inbreds."

However empty the majority of the land appeared, traffic ran from the beginning to the turnabout five minutes opposite because boats launched at the sloping point. And at the very base, immediately after the blip of a white wooden bridge over cattails, salmonberry bushes, lily pads, and lazy currents that flowed from the adjacent river, sprawled a blight of local renown, The Everglades. The spot obviously referred to Florida, though not to sunsets through crossed cocoanut palms and a turquoise sea, nor even to Disney World or the swampy bayous of swerving hovercrafts and dangerous submerged reptiles. Other than the borrowed name, curves of imported sand, proximity to water, and families that might make an otherwise leaden winter day exciting by watching the Daytona 500 on TV, the flat place registered as anything but tropical.

In keeping with other valley slough habitats upriver, the Evergladers stuffed their fenced island plot with RVs, trailer homes, pop-up campers, and postage-stamp yards strewn with antennas, painted rock turtles, sunflower whirligigs, and plastic wildlife (fawns, owls, flamingoes). In summer Evergladers in aluminum frame lawn chairs admired or laughed at water skiers of varying skills while complaining about speedboat noise. Beer-filled red and white coolers, Dee noticed, were a popular accessory. Illustrated beach towels hung from improvised laundry lines.

The Everglades, she decided, had been named hopefully; along the lines of a retarded child, though, it hadn't developed quite right.

A two-lane road with a single elbow turn ran up the island's spine; nearly at the end, and the same as—Dee later heard—the halo on an angel with muddy feet, stretched neat rows of mahogany-stained plywood cabins and the well-tended lawns of Camp Luther.

Dee tossed lawn darts and played (then ref'd) volleyball and joined campfire songs that never failed to circle back to one inspirational Bible passage or another—a momentous one, outlined at morning Thought of the Day huddles in a way that caused little confusion and incited no troublesome questions.

These stories from the Good Book, vitamins for the soul, featured the Good Samaritan (Be Nice), the Daughter of Jairus (Faith Saves, Even in Situations That Look Hopeless), and Adam and Eve (Obey God's Law, or Watch Out). Other lessons, whose contradictions the elders seemed happy enough to smooth over, implied a need for elaboration: Cain and Abel (Envy is a Canker that Will Consume and Curse You and Your Offspring and Their Offspring Forever), John the Baptist (You Might Open People's Hearts to the Ways of the Lord and Thereby Do God's Bidding, But You Might Also Get Decapitated and as a Result End Up in Heaven), and Abraham's burnt offering (something close to God Will Put Your Faith to a Test and That Test Can Only Be Passed

With Faith in God), the last a surprise to Dee since she'd expected a tie-in to *Burnt Offering*'s delectable nightmare story—and her dad's movie treat for three—of horror beyond imagination, a creepy chauffeur, and a shrouded old hag in a rocking chair.

Within a few days Dee found her place organizing the little kids—babysitting in a new guise—and checking with the older teens and ladies in the main office about the schedule of events.

Dee said thanks and mentioned feeling uncomfortable in front of a crowd when offered the chance to regale fire pit listeners with action stories set at Red Sea shores and in downtown Sodom. Ditto for leading a prayer at long, paper-covered plywood tables before breakfast or lunch. The camp reserved dinner sermons for elders, whose grandparent-style yarns about their youthful adventures and indiscretions always ended with them lifting a bible—a personal copy, black or white, never far from reach—swaying it like a hypnotist, and cracking the pages open to an instantly-located passage that connected ancient words to their own autobiographies of sinful temptations and glorious redemption.

To Dee, corralling kids in single-file lines and explaining the intricacies of games came naturally. Bible instruction did not, if only because—and in contrast to Abraham—she doubted that any robed god floating nearby, always ready to fill her mind with perfect wisdom and enviable clarity.

At camp she'd once been handed a keyring by Rose, a flaky, sandy-tressed older girl possessed of questionable taste in baggy but thin home-sewn farmer's wife cotton print shifts that didn't hide much, and organizational skills bad enough to count as sinful.

Rose appeared to grow flustered when asked any question as she walked; she'd say, "Hold on!" and stop to visibly focus as if reading lips, at which point the question needed to be launched again.

Retrieving hot dog packages from a locked cooler in the kitchen—an uncharitable padlock, Dee noted—Dee kept the keys for no reason other than she'd stuffed them in her purse; and when Rose neglected to request their return (and later failed to appear altogether, having called her parents to pick her up, only to receive words of judgment, harsh ones from younger camp councillors and a gently intoned one from an elder: "Not every soul is meant to carry out God's business"), they rolled around unnoticed.

Watching Rose, Dee guessed she'd thought that Christian ways would involve twirling in a field wearing a headband of garlanded dandelions and plenty of spirited chanting about world harmony, a notion that might have made sense a decade earlier. Considering Rose's dreamy disposition and sieve's retention, Dee felt blessed that a nuclear power plant hadn't hired them as technicians. A panicked kaboom situation would freeze Rose.

Once she began searching out locks, Dee discovered the camp was lousy with security. Combination and padlocks everywhere, from the front gate and chained boat launch to cabinets, storage rooms, drawers, and cupboards.

The elders kept grubby inquisitive hands away from containers stenciled with "Property of Camp Luther," "Forewarned is forearmed" seemingly applicable in the case of several campers whose desperado parents hoped that a three-week getaway in summer would nudge juvenile souls toward the path of righteousness. That failing, they'd delve into the other scare tactic options to straighten out smart aleck sulkers, confirmed cigarette smokers, and supposed criminals-in-the-making: distant stints as cadets and at Katimavik; or, the ever-popular School for Wayward Youth, scary because nobody had ever seen or visited an actual one, and so they filled in the blanks with straitjacketed padded asylum confinement, ill-lit passageways of dripping pipes and peeling paint, and intimidating glimpses of savage warden versus helpless prisoner tussles remembered from movies.

VENTURE: FENCE / DECEMBER

Jay dropped by Belle's on Saturdays seldom enough, he calculated, so as to draw no unwanted attention.

Lifting teapot lids and studying porcelain vases with "Czech" and "Made in Japan" tags, he replied with "Just browsing, thanks" when asked, the prepared excuse about looking for an anniversary present safe for later use.

By listening to Belle (and to Belle's sister less, since she quietly indicated that her confident transacting partner downstairs took charge), Jay figured he'd learn the basics of pawn shop negotiations. And the missteps.

Belle demanded proof of purchase or a receipt if an impatient, pushy guy came in with stereo equipment but no boxes or a kit of work tools scratched with names that didn't belong to the seller. "Yeah, that's my cousin" got them nowhere.

Jay believed that she'd get her business license revoked—or worse—if cops found out. Trafficking in Stolen Property, on prime time cop shows at least, amounted to a felony crime when the person in Belle's position knowingly acquired goods with iffy origins. "I'm the victim here, your Honour" wouldn't amount to much if her history or face hinted at the contrary. Brushes with the law were fatal.

Years of hearing bald-faced lies and mumbled half-truths had evidently honed Belle ears and eyes. If younger and not permanently perched on a stool, she'd be a first class store detective.

Worryingly, Belle announced herself as no-nonsense and used crusty sayings from Jay's father's supply, including "Don't piss on my back . . . ," in her case "on my leg," and, after a would-be cheat left in a huff, "I didn't trust him any farther than I could throw him."

As overheard, the tug-of-war routine of trading household goods for cash could be memorized by a chimp—

"Okay, whatdyasay Belle?"

Before the answer, "(x)," Belle made the man wait. Her nodding, chess-style pause signified careful mental tabulation.

"Sheesh, lady, cut me some slack! Howbout (x + 25%)?"

"C'mon, you can't expect me to pay that and stay in business too!" She'd fish her hand around in the box of goods or stand back, arms crossed, as though reevaluating every nook and cranny of the seller's offer. "(x + 5%). That number's final."

"Geez. Okay. Deal."

From mall department stores, he'd begun with lifting mechanical pencils and fountain pens in velvet cases. Jay added porcelain, ceramic, and crystal living room trinkets, which were easy to snatch and hide. A magnifying glass, two rings, a watch, expensive playing cards and poker chips, a tiny framed drawing, leather billfolds and change purses, a brass bell, and condiment pots from France all fell within the *open window of opportunity* category.

For safe keeping, Jay chose a black garbage bag, settling on the jumbled tool and miscellaneous storage room in the carport, Joey's clubhouse, as the least likely area his dad would squint at with suspicion. Em and Jay's bedrooms? The worst choice.

To the anticipated question about place of origin Jay decided on collector grandparents, whose overstuffed household had become his family's responsibility after they'd died mere months apart. The grey-haired love story, he imagined, would short circuit Belle's wariness. The loss of dear family members couldn't hurt either.

If she demanded greater detail—as in, "Why are you selling your grandparents' stuff in the first place?"—he planned on admitting to one of two motives: he needed the money for hockey camp or for a beater so that he could drive to work once graduated.

She'd call BS on anything else, he bet. He'd choose the best story at the right moment. Outfoxing Belle at her own game would be way better than getting away with the mall scams. And if she saw through his pretense, he'd say "Okay, your loss," and never return.

He grabbed items that matched the story he planned to tell, and drew a line at the temptation of those countless boxes in the coop. True, Old Man Thesen probably wouldn't miss all of them, never mind a handful, but he'd also been super-nice and generous. Stores already paid insurance for loss of merchandise, he'd heard, and compensated for it too by jacked-up prices.

They could afford a missing pen. Or a dozen.

He left Belle's feeling like the hero in "Jack and the Beanstalk"—almost defeated at one point and victorious the next, though Belle seemed more like a hoarding dragon than a hungry giant, and his gore-free experience really a baby step toward future negotiations with landlords, banks, and clients.

Without a hitch or a hiccup, he'd traded a full and neatly arranged cardboard box of stolen goods for money. And, "used exactly once, I swear on my sweet mother's grave," a bass guitar.

He'd keep the guitar hidden in the coop until the gang's next meeting. The surprise would be at least as excellent as Gordyn's with ID cards.

Venture: The Camp Job ii / November

Cross-legged and hunched on her bedroom carpet in half-year cycles, Dee sorted through the annoying miracle of ever-mounting purse junk. She found class notes, pennies, linty lip gloss tubes, corners of granola bar, and sheets of homework that had been assigned, folded into oblivion, and forgotten.

During one cleaning day she retrieved the keys, twirling the cool metal ring on her finger. She pictured flighty Rose and her homemade cotton shifts. Already married by now, Dee predicted, and seeking part-time fulfillment as a Lady's Hospital Auxiliary shop volunteer, or a candy striper in the old folks ward. Possibly, she resided at home, a half-adult with a muddled head who'd retreated inside a girlish fantasy world of whispering dolls, tea parties, and dress up.

The keys wound up in the closet for no other reason than the cedar chest attracted Dee's gaze. She'd hold off on pitching them in the garbage. On a Sunday drive sometime, she'd direct her father to the camp and hurl the set at the Main Office porch, a haloed example of a modern day Ruth.

Dee remembered too that camp management used the largest storage room, behind the open-air kitchen, as a free-for-all zone, chaos piled to the rafters with flippers, masks, inner tubes, racquets, and slumped air mattresses. Adding shin-gouging obstacles to the already cluttered heap: portable chairs necessary at impromptu guitar-led concerts for weekending parents that favoured joyous sing-a-longs (upbeat "Put Your Hand in the Hand" over morose "Rock of Ages") and boxes of donated books deemed too racy or not Instructive enough for ever-susceptible Camp Luther guests. Cardboard Lost & Found boxes sat out until the season's final day; the senior youth guide wedged them in last, the whole mess a bulky teetering surprise for his replacement on the following May long weekend.

Dee had volunteered to drag out the entire inventory at the end of her one paid summer. She spray painted the interior with fluorescent location slots for use by future counselors. Naturally, she carved out room to spare.

Over autumn Dee scoured the basements of babysitting gigs while the rest of the gang agreed to keep their eyes peeled for classified ads and stapled For Sale sheets on telephone poles. A gloomy Prawn Gardens meeting revealed distant possibilities: while kitten litters and garage sale toys surfaced at dime a dozen rates, guitars came at a premium.

The leftover options felt no better than deciding between fried liver with onions or steak and kidney pie for dinner: borrowing or stealing from the Band room, saving up for the pair of instruments sitting in the upstairs window of Belle's, revealing the band to the parental units in order to butter them up for a huge favour—a downpayment on two guitars from the mall—that had to arrive with pleading and promises of eternal gratitude and good behaviour, etc, etc.

The lack of promise felt either completely unappealing or, in the case of breaking into school, discouragingly complicated and riddled with a line of predictable repercussions from the administration in the form of Gestapo assemblies with the torture of repeated droned words—"culprit," "disappointed," "it's a sad day when," "delinquency such as this hurts everyone."

With depressed spirits looming, Dee fished out the ace-card she'd been saving. She waved the keyring with a flourish: "Ta da!"

Seeing blank, quizzical, and frowning faces in triplicate she continued, whirling them on on a raised index finger. "Keep your eyes on the ring. You're feeling relaxed. You're opening your mind . . ."

Dee and Gordyn asked to borrow the car for a movie in the twin cinemas across from the mall in Abbotsford. They mentioned *The Fog*, aware that Delphine hated blood and creepy crawlies even more than cineplex lights, line ups, and pushy so and sos. She'd never go. Edmund, acting chivalrous for reasons of his own, vowed against tagging along unless his better half agreed.

If quizzed afterward, they could say it had been a total gross out and offer to tour her through a gallery of nauseating but made up details. "Spare me," Delphine would sigh in a matter of seconds, "I'm not kidding you."

At Cedar Hill and 7th Gordyn pulled over to let in Em and Jay, dressed in jeans and layered T-shirts but complaining about the cold snap.

In the stealthy manner of bank heists they'd caught on prime time, the plan's A to D simplicity—drive to the island in the dead of the season, sneak into the camp under cover of darkness, break into the storage hut, abduct two guitars and an amp—relied on the accuracy of Dee's information. If some keen Bible Thumper had rearranged the equipment the plan was screwed.

With "I should know, God," Dee had assured (and reassured) them: the camp closed for the season right after the Labour Day weekend. She remained confident that while a handful of elders occasionally drove in for future event-planning purposes on intermittent Saturdays, they met during daylight hours. After all, they weren't satanists. Yes, a caretaker couple resided there year round. But the stooped and ancient geriatrics hardly mattered. They watched TV constantly, and at a volume that would allow a herd of elephants to rumble by without attracting notice. She'd fire their retired old asses in a heartbeat.

Stealing from a church looked on par with purse snatching at an old folks home, they believed, but borrowing without permission—the true goal, the gang had agreed—kept them on semi-solid moral ground.

Dee mentioned that she could sweet-talk one of her former bosses for permission, no problem. But tracking down an elder—who might be wintering in Arizona or Mexico, or further afield with missionary work—presented a surmountable problem that would require chunks of time and effort and diplomacy, not to mention revelation. Temporary use, then, just meant ease and crucial expedience. And, anyhow, they'd care for the instruments and replace them well before next season's opening weekend; it would be as if nothing had gone missing, not really, and no so-called crime had taken place.

Dee told the gang that counselors borrowed items all the time—a clipboard in the main office held page after page of staff signing out flippers or inner tubes for after hours excursions and the dates they'd returned them. At heart camp rules meant Guidance, a popular word there, not edicts from Stalin. Besides, during off-season the stuff just sat there growing mildew and buckling from constant moisture. In a way they'd be rescuing the instruments from a sad fate of neglect and slow-growing rot.

The details: Em ready and waiting at the car while Dee led the blitzkrieg to the shed. For added expertise Jay brought walkie-talkies with fresh 9-volts.

Eastward along the quiet residential streets of the Bend and the moonless highway, they bantered about what if scenarios. A car approached and slowed, or a curious dog owner came into view? Em volunteered to say she'd "flooded the engine, or something," aiming to sound like a dumb girl who could barely manage to change gears. She rolled her eyes for her brother when Dee—an expert at everything—recommended a gooey coating of lip gloss to complete the effect.

If worse came to worst, they settled, she should huff with visible impatience, declare she'd waited long enough, and turn the engine. When spark plugs miraculously fired she'd smile, mime wiping sweat from her forehead, and wave goodbye. Winding around the cul-de-sac, she'd whisper at the walkie-talkie, and pretend to head back to the highway. Once the helpful interloper faded from view, she'd pull into the oasis of a darkened driveway.

With borrowed goods in hand, the gang would know to hang back until further squawks from her walkie-talkie.

Other possibilities raised involved a lurking hook-handed maniac and a swaggering patrol cop drunk with power, facts so unlikely they elicited only guffaws and "Right, as if."

Anticipating a changed lock, Gordyn packed a screwdriver with interchangeable bits, his dad's favourite.

"You'd better kill the lights." Jay felt the thrill of pulling a phrase from a crime show for a speaking role in real life.

Gordyn pulled over close to the ditch's lip, fretting about the deep well of watercress and brambles Dee had warned him about. Wandering in the dark and seeking a telephone to call a tow truck? Disastrous.

Streetlights installed in chintzy numbers by the municipality cut their worry in half as they flung open car doors and took in an evening of perfectly calm emptiness. Still, since the highway turnoff they hadn't seen so much as a taillight, and that rendered the plan of hiding in plain sight an impossibility. Strangers up to no good: any random passerby would decide that instantly.

"Fingers crossed," Em whispered.

Tiptoeing for comic effect in a familiar setting turned crime scene and bubbling over with escalating hilarity, Dee waved to Em before veering off into a grassy ditch cut with the semblance of a packed mud trail. A gap between the green chain link fence and the solid wooden one that ran the length of the property to the lake gave them access.

The camp's front portion contained administration offices, check-in, and the caretakers' unit, Sphinx-mute at the moment except for a buzzy yellow porch light.

Between the row of four cabins behind the front office check-in stood a windowless shed stained an ordinary chocolate. Dee pointed to it, smiling widely and chewing her lip to staunch giddy urges toward laughter. Gordyn and Jay waited by the salmonberry bushes as Dee dashed across an open square of dew-soaked grass. Moments later a rubbery octopus arm reached out from within the room's darkness: success.

In a low elated voice Gordyn sang, "There was blood and a single gun shot, but just who shot who?" He pushed Jay, who stumbled a step before resuming a crouched skulking along the border of bushes. Hugged close to the office and cabin walls, Jay slipped inside the storage room.

Watching his friend disappear, Gordyn followed the same reversed L route.

"Inside." Jay lowered the walkie-talkie volume to nil.

"This is totally a mess." Dee snapped her fingers. "Just like that, I'd can whoever was responsible for this garbage pile." She jabbed light into four corners.

"God, Dee, keep it down. It's not like a mess matters."

"I told you, Gord-un, we could rehearse here right now and they'd hear zilch."

With no guitars ready to snatch, just chairs and inner tubes leaning against canvas-draped boxes, the plan faltered. Dee grabbed a leftover Tony the Tiger beach towel and kneeled to stuff the door gap. She flicked a switch. "That's better. God, what a disaster area."

"What if they moved the guitars and stuff into the office?" Gordyn began lifting and dropping canvas sheets.

"Not a chance."

They'd decided that speed was essential, even though Dee had reassured them they could stay all winter without being noticed. The pious caretakers dreamed of one kind of thief in the night, not an ex-employee dipping into equipment storage at the dead of autumn. As for trouble, they'd maybe peek outside for burst water pipes or roof asphalt ravaged by off-season storms.

"Instead of asking dumb questions, slightly older brother, how about you dig around in that corner. We can get through all this in a jiff." Tearing at a canvas next to the door rewarded her with the thudding fall of a box of paperbacks and a tambourine that crashed to the concrete in a deafening jingle chorus.

The guys froze.

Listening for movement and hearing nothing, Gordyn opened the door a crack.

Dee continued peeling back canvas sheets. "God, I told you they're . . . well, they say 'a tad hard of hearing.'" She moved right, lifting and lowering canvas blanketing systematically. "No. No. Not yet. Voilà!" She aimed the flashlight inside the pair of cardboard boxes and spotted a hodgepodge of plastic recorders at the bottom, a pair of bongo drums the wife of a camp elder had picked up in Cuba, and an offensive squawking cornet her fantasies had packed with sand. "I love it when the Bible keeps its promises: 'Keep on asking, and you will receive what you ask for. Keep on seeking, and you will find. Keep on knocking, and the door will be opened to you.' Our door has been opened, thank you Heavenly Father. Now let's, um, vamoose."

Fidgeting with nervous excitement, window open to the damp night air, craving a smoke, gripping the wheel, tilting her eyes upward to the rear view mirror every twenty seconds, and feeling ridiculous at thoughts of *Halloween*, the Manson Family, or a patrol car rolling up, Em turned the ignition key for the distraction of radio. Either too loud or low, the noise aggravated her further.

She snapped on the interior light and reached for her purse in the back seat. The song's lack of progress astounded her; at a dozen or so lines, any real poet could have written it in an afternoon or during commercial breaks. She gazed at the chicken scratch—

The girl falls, cracked mirror,
They stand outside, ~~they~~ no one can~~not~~ hear.
~~In the room~~, eyes ~~fading~~,
Locked room, ~~eyes dimming~~.
~~a blank~~ stare.
an empty

Knuckles rap: "Are you alright in there?"

Em hummed the meter, understanding herself to be idling, poised for the inspiration of the chorus to find its way to her mind. Inspiration is fertilizer, she saw, and in that case whole cups of it could settle in her seedless cranium without effect. She needed a starting point for the chorus: what did she want to say?

After checking the rear view and the walkie-talkie's volume she closed her eyes, picturing a happy-looking but worried vacationing girl alone in a public bathroom. Outside the family smiles, excited to continue the afternoon at Disney World upon her return. The girl lurches, dizzy and shocked and confused by the catastrophe she senses building inside her chest. She falters, clutches at her blouse, stumbles head-first toward the mirror above the sink. Em believed in the song's settings being divided by a door, the situation riveting. But what was the point, what did the story illustrate?

Em pictured a god's eye view of the collapsed girl and her unsuspecting family, just four bodies in an ant-like crowd of assorted thousands that represented a tiniest fraction of creation.

In thirty seconds she'd printed four lines—

Round and round the old world goes.
How it stops nobody knows.
On and on the clock ticks and ticks.
'Til one day it can't be fixed.

Re-reading the words, Em considered them either profound or beyond stupid.

The walkie-talkie squawked, Jay's voice. "One Adam Twelve. The Eagle has landed." Luck had smiled on them.

Saved by the bell, Em thought, cramming the notebook away.

Venture: L.A. / November

Arriving home after shifts Gordyn usually telegraphed a monotone "Fine" or "Nothing major" at couch occupants in answer to Delphine's question as he peeled off the leather work shoes—black lace-ups, cast-offs from his dad—mandated by Brownie's regulations binder. With a showy thud he'd exile the rancid items to the front porch, per parental edict.

The living room offered TV noise but no consolation. He'd hear "Yeah, just wait till it's full time" and similar from Edmund for the nth time when, he believed, just an ounce of sympathy could work wonders. And his mom's faith that Brownie's might "lead somewhere" only curdled his mood. While "Life's the pits and then you die" might be true, just droning it out as though no other options existed could lead practically anyone to slit wrists or fatal plunges of defeat off rooftops.

Upstairs with Dee later, Gordyn normally launched furious complaints. He flipped through a catalogue of grossness: gritty dredging mixture, cold glistening chicken parts, rubbery blobs of yellow fat, already oily skin made OPEC-worthy by deep fryers. And episodes of stupidity: corny punchlines from Boss Swanson's Gatling gun mouth, Harj's escalating assholery and griping attitude, Fiona's perpetually misguided belief in the certainty of her dawning popularity when kids in fact called her Greasola if they noticed her at all.

Fidgeting as she listened, Dee longed to impress Gordyn with tens and twenties, or add to the habitual complain-athon and blurt out "Jeez, that's nothing" and "You should see what I get on my hands!"

But even if she piped up and countered with "Have I got something to show you!" her business partner up the hill kept the bills ordered, bundled, and secure inside a KerPlunk box in the outgrown games and clothes zone of her bedroom's walk-in closet.

Safe-keeping made better sense in a house with five bedrooms, three full-time inhabitants, and no stay-home mom. Em had said that following the flushed hot face of the Mrs. Kim shoplifting incident she couldn't stand even *the thought* of getting caught again.

If the money did sit within reach, Dee also believed she'd resist the urge to tell because of the pact with Em and its total wisdom. They'd decided to let no one pry that deadly secret from their grasp.

The current plan for the dramatic reveal came from the book of magical explanations for shoplifted goods, used with curious parents: you won't believe what I found while wandering around outside! Wow, what luck! The boys might recognize the handy line (exclaimed previously for Jay's futuristic wristwatch, Em's miniature bust of Nefertiti, and so on) and doubt the one-in-a-million turn of fortune, but Em promised that if they stuck with an identical story word-for-word, all the gut suspicions in the universe wouldn't matter.

As for specifics, they remained undecided. Dee favoured a wallet choked with cash, stranded curbside as if recently dropped.

Rightly concerned about the boys' details-oriented questions needling them about material evidence (ID, a credit card, the wallet itself), Em proposed the fluke discovery of a mysterious plastic bag tightly folded and taped and then jammed into the crotch of a tree as reasonably likely, or registering as less far-fetched anyhow. She'd show Jay and Gordyn the find (having already found a red bag by the art class kiln and a perfect alder with a Y-shaped trunk near the electrical substation a block from school) and that would be that.

From there they could all spin satisfying tales of finders-keepers, maybe wondering aloud now and then about what kind of criminal transaction the girls had interrupted and who'd eventually paid what price. Stoners routinely handed over bills for aluminum foil-wrapped pot and mushrooms in school hallways, at the smoke pit and bowling alley, and probably even inside bathrooms at the Dairy Queen. It made sense that when those dealers bought in bulk, they'd outsmart cops by arranging exchanges at unremarkable spots where each party showed up at different times. Trees, for instance, would be perfect, as would the dry ground beneath innocent-looking juniper shrubs.

Em understood that though the secret, way-out-there part-time job she and Em had invented—dabbling only, definitely not a legit career they'd talk over with sharpened pencil notes, earnest nods, and what if charts with the Guidance Counsellor—took the prize as omigod-worthy, when anyone sat down and calmly thought over the basics, it wasn't *that* outrageous. The minuses stood somewhere between what she'd heard non-stop about Dee's Aunt Florence's shifts—manhandling gross body parts, basically—and unlike with that pair, no clean up, stink, or death for six plus hours wafted their way. No exhausting overtime, either, and no bosses or complaints to speak of.

And as with any occupation, the efficient exchange of A for B mattered. For X amount of time the arrangement demanded that worker bees accomplish this, that, and that with a certain level of skill, speed, and professionalism. And willingness. If they didn't measure up they'd hear about it and get written up, or else turfed and begin pounding the pavement, résumé in hand.

Boring and repetitive (cashiers and burger flippers everywhere, handing out rental shoes at the bowling alley, pumping gas) paid peanuts for long shifts, and dangerous or super-skilled meant cheques to brag about. Clearly, theirs somehow fell into the bodily harm category because negotiating with a driver and getting the job done—as Em had come to call it—took hardly any time and could be as mechanically simple as tossing newspapers on front porches, when you didn't dwell on it too much.

As for the exposure, despite reputation the actions still didn't feel on par with the poisonous core of a nuclear power plant, one touch and your flesh begins to rot and fall off in lifeless, contaminated chunks. Visible or otherwise, prostitution's cursed marks of corruption were, they'd discovered, something of an old wife's tale.

Besides, just a single pay period at the cedar mill—home to finger-hungry blades, precarious log piles, massive trucks, and air heavy with sawdust and smoke—sounded way more damaging to body and soul than sitting close to a grateful stranger and yanking on his wiener for a few minutes while he slobbered over your bra.

The first guy had been a novelty, for good and bad they'd concluded later, and educational. The episode landed between the exhilarating/scary/practically adult first time behind the wheel and the never not inconvenient arrival of every girl's first period (and in their cases, bright and early on a junior high morning).

What had surprised them eventually was the striking difference between what they'd expected as factual and what actually transpired over those short minutes inside cars, with the heat blasting on side roads by pastures, a logging route, and in amongst gloomy needled trees by the dam.

They'd felt foolish afterwards, like hicks in a huge city or those JWs packing luggage for a glorious doomsday trip to heaven that never transpires. Concluding that they ought to have known better, they blamed TV and what passed for communal knowledge, as well as their own sort of forgivable gullibility.

For the sake of cliffhanging drama and advertiser dollars, and worthy Nielsen ratings too, CBS and the rest needed to amplify and distort. Suck in as many people as possible. After all, what use would *CHiPs* have if nothing much happened each episode except sitting at cop shop desks? Or where, as with the Bend, patrolling in cars and parking behind billboards in wait for speeding drivers and writing a ticket now and then turned out to be as exciting as the episode got? Who'd bother watching that *reality*?

Confusing as well, and for the sake of standards or fines maybe, TV allowed nothing X-Rated or even Restricted. It added up to showing a lot of nail-biting chase scenes and Mexican standoffs and nothing whatsoever of behind-closed-doors others.

If a lazy-but-cool Socials or History teacher lugged in a projector to show *Dawn: Portrait of a Teenage Runaway* as a sobering lesson about the Evil Dangers of Prostitution, the class would learn the movie facts everyone already assumed about the subject. Within a few shy steps of the dusty bus that had driven in from a winding string of Nowheres, USA to the hectic littered sidewalks of Los Angeles, the doe-eyed young woman would be spotted by a pimp—who paced around the depot all eagle eyes and wolfish smiles, or idled across the street in a tan Lincoln Continental. She'd be seduced and worn down in no time, soon coerced into strutting around wearing a tight scarlet jumpsuit under an unzipped rabbit fur bomber jacket. Sweet talking, or "You owe me now, don't you missy, nobody gets something for nothing," or a few startling face slaps in a brick alleyway kept her in line.

Once broken and enslaved, it'd be go, go, go: sinking into cars that slowed to a crawl at regular intervals, smacked around for letting a loser get away without coughing up payment, threatened by a quick-fisted creep in a truck with a hidden switchblade, and hassled by dirty but also holier-than-thou cops; tearing at the wigs of veteran streetwalkers (who defended plum corner territories with animal clawing); befriending doomed frail girls lacking the grit for street living; and struggling without success to escape because—as the months had schooled her—she didn't really want fame and stardom as she'd previously and feverishly dreamed. Gradually she'd realize that she actually hoped to meet a nice normal guy, a provider who'd love her, and to settle down to raise a family better than her mother could ever manage. And making that happen would be possible only after the pimp got off her back.

Every parent and child had absorbed that fearsome bedtime story from the airwaves as dictionary truth. Neat and benign, though, the girls' own non-televised side road transactions passed a useful alternative into their hands, a surprise perspective from an unexpected angle.

After the married super-fake-friendly-then-rude guy in the polished two-tone car and "Let's give it a shot," they'd stepped forward with care. Locked door and empty classroom talks had led them to expect most of the danger and criminal lows, highs, and middles of the World of Hookers (if not all: the stylish pimp in a full-length fur and medallions who strutted around and could turn on his girls in a rabid dog frenzy really only made sense for Los Angeles or New York). That terminal place was several steps further down an iffy, shadow-strewn path from the World of Shoplifting, and an impossible distance from the familiar, room temperature World of Babysitting, each girl's first career step.

The girls planned with caution, jotting down ideas camouflaged within class notes. Coded pre-class meetings gave them chances to figure out which ones to act on.

While coming up with neat lines of dialogue that contained tart, lemony bits of warning for the customer, they decided first off that gut instinct and the aura the car gave off had to be crucial look-before-you-leap factors.

Dee suggested developing sassy but street-wise characters to assume—Em's secretarial, cautious, and loyal basically, and her own that of the expert negotiator who knows what she knows and takes no guff.

Em thought up penciling the car's license number in her notebook and in plain view of the driver.

And Dee added that once inside the car she could allude to illegality; it would work wonders, just as it couldn't hurt to breezily mention how any jury's angry, condemning stares would fall on a pathetic middle-aged man who ought to possess better scruples: *taking advantage*, how dare he!

In every front seat, they'd outline an unbreakable rule: "We operate as a pair, no exceptions."

Giddy, they tested out situations in Dee's room and when thundering along school hallways on afternoons if their brothers had already taken off.

Dee worked out the tone of a line—"I started babysitting at quite a young age, and my parents taught me to be careful"—and positioned Em as the intended audience, a guy who figured he could get something for nothing, or coax the young women sitting in his front seat to go further than they'd bargained.

With mutual tittering, Em's Velvet reached out to shake the hand of Dee's Crystal: "Pleased to meet you, partner."

But what they experienced turned out differently.

A man would stop to ask how far they were heading. There'd be glances and smiles and chitchat and flirting and fake-coy answers to fake-everyday questions related to the weather, the river's levels, traffic, and their shopping destination. Small talk skipped forward at varying rates but with a steady, natural momentum to the topic of school, boys, dating, appetites, and what one man called "carnal knowledge." Usually, at that moment, the offer materialized in the form of a harmless mild suggestion ("How'd you girls like to try something with me?") or generous kindness ("Between you, me, and the fencepost, I could offer a little incentive"), as though the guys were mayor-praised citizens helping Girl Guides with boxed cookie purchases.

For Dee and Em, the idea was in-and-out, nearly the same as what the Angels would do. Delicate undercover mission accomplished, they'd retire and rest on their laurels, despite the fact that both Delphine and Ms. M., the girls coach, advised against that kind of self-satisfaction. "Always ready yourself for another mountain to climb," these authorities chimed in eerie unison, implying that any wise woman ought to expect constant obstacles of vertical rock, an unchanging fact.

With ATFs ("No rest for the wicked" and "veil of tears"—whatever that meant) that coiled ghost-grey through her sentences and hinted at a philosophy of ongoing near-defeat, Delphine would summon VD at a minimum, with a shallow roadside grave as the likelier destination before flaming Hell itself. After she totally freaked out, of course, and blew a gasket in her head. Keeping her and the rest completely in the dark, then, struck the girls as necessary wisdom.

With their knowledge and caution, a summit in Dee's bedroom concluded, nothing would touch them, and vice versa. They'd be cats with mice, yes, but also cats protected by an impossibly thin and perfectly bulletproof clear film. To the outside world, their hands would be getting dirty, smeared and stained vividly with sin and who knows what else. They'd see the truth, though, of course.

Since they couldn't exactly drop by the Guidance Counsellor's office, or talk to girls rumoured to do it at a discount (or for nothing at all), they guessed they'd run into sheer luck.

Or else, they were tempting Fate, as parents everywhere liked to say in warning tones, apparently chock full of faith that such a creature floated high above and, after being taunted and teased one time too many, finally acted with a cruel retribution worthy of its godly stature.

They eyed looming retirement with peals of laughter. A profitable career nobody but them would scarcely guess even existed that had the lifespan of a moth: perfect.

Eventually reined in by husbands and kids, pages of responsibilities, and Playtex girdles, they could summon the memory of daring and freedom like a grizzled prisoner recollecting the glorious spree before he got caught.

In their armpit bend of the sodden Valley, they'd encountered no sign of any sleazeball expecting to become a slave-driver boss who'd use them up while ruling with an iron fist. No creepy man with a switchblade and malicious intentions had appeared and tried to cram them in the car's trunk. Not a single full time prostitute patrolled her territory or screamed and pushed them off the corner. A deep V-neck jumpsuit with bell bottoms and a shiny spandex tube-top and tights ensemble would draw unwanted attention; and such a get-up struck them as overkill. So long as the guy could make out a reasonably shapely female form, wearing a zippered parka with gumboots could work fine.

Men on the prowl, they'd learned, seemed no more difficult to attract than glances with a scoop neck top.

Their work filled a gap.

With the basics mastered almost as easily as hopscotch, only unexpected interest caused them pangs of worry.

They choked with laughter at the thought of a sober explanation of the job's advantages point by point, absolutely sure that no one (brothers included) would even bother trying to understand.

Within minutes, threats would be uttered from strained parental throats—grounded forever, a padlocked bedroom, every second and step outside the house accounted for, swift exile to a nunnery, reform school, or devout elderly relatives at a country farm, shame that would last the family for an eternity. Head doctor emergency appointments too.

Honesty, then, and Vulcan appeals to logic appeared as useless as spike heels on a cat.

Instead, they'd just let others take their innocence for granted. The key? Looking the part—acting as though every Saturday tick-tick-ticked by with the normalcy of routine (especially for Delphine's benefit: when sniffing out a brewing conspiracy, she grew warden-like and paranoid, checking up on the house inmates in their warm carpeted cells—"Can I get you a snack?"—or quizzing them about a trip to the corner store that had taken twenty minutes instead of the usual quarter-hour).

But if a sudden disappearance for a few hours raised no alarms because the parental units had painted a wholesome imaginary picture of two carefree girls hanging out, flipping through glossy fashion magazines pages, and trying out different hairstyles while whispering about cute boys, then why correct them? They perpetuated no lie, not really; they'd just allowed for assumptions to harden into truth without bothering to intervene.

Dee fended off Gordyn's monitoring (snarky: "What's with that, um, get-up?") and offered a perky nod at sentiments from Delphine (motherly: "It's nice to see you finally making friends here") and, once, grumbling from Edmund about the car belonging to him and for family business and not for joyrides, giving any reply the shape necessary to stave off suspicion. She made fun of her style choices for Gordyn's benefit, smiled fully so that Delphine felt no further guilt about the latest move to the latest neighbourhood, and bowed to Edmund's occasional need for head of the household laws and putting his foot down.

Based on her answers, Em's dad didn't exactly have bloodhound instincts; he'd never think to look for signs, just as any parent would never ask the child "Are you a cat burglar?" or "Have you been to the moon?" Why would they?

Dee suspected that Jay might have clued into their secret, or at least part of it. He didn't say a word, though, and that meant the same as knowing nothing at all.

In planning sessions while secure in Dee's bedroom, they'd thought to anticipate potential disasters, escape plans, and do and don't moves.

They concluded that acting like newbies who'd fallen into the situation by accident would work better than used up, seen-it-all veterans.

If a guy with a face young enough to easily remember high school picked them up, he'd get crossed off the list as too close for comfort. Accepting the ride was fine, but that was all.
They drew the line—standards!—with too old, and bantered about a lady pulling over and wanting them to try something. "Yeah right, as if" they chimed, but Dee promised she'd give it a shot for extra money. The location presented challenges too. Except for getting murdered, the very last outcome they'd want would be an eyewitness who couldn't wait to get on the phone with the juiciest of news. (That parents and neighbours would find out passed breezily through their thoughts: based on the likelihood, lighting strikes merited greater worry.)

Faced with so much potential for explosive disaster, they half-joked about an old man who'd be so flabbergasted by their attention that he'd pay with gold or offer a wheelbarrow of cash.

That their dads spoke with such hopeful melancholy about finally retiring now made perfect sense to them.

The men, who freely offered authentic-sounding names like Bill and Ed and asked for theirs, gave their passenger-guests (Jacklyn and Christy alternating with Velvet and Crystal) reason to ponder layers, complexities.

Beyond what they—and everybody else—could tell about the surface (that, design-wise, guys needed touch like this more than girls, or at least openly bragged about the burden of their sex drive; that they could be driven to extremes to satisfy the pint-sized Napoleon stuck inside their jeans but still tyrannical), Dee and Em saw the guys as helpless, in a way, as when a baby wets his diaper and wails and squirms and struggles until in a matter of seconds the babysitter—so indispensable!—whips off the soaked fabric, wipes and powders, and pins on dry warm cotton. The creature coos with pleasure, instantly forgetful of the hideous discomfort of seconds before. A few hours later, naturally, the same story unfolds.

On TV a guy might mention a motel he'd heard of, or suggest a drive to an empty shady setting. Eventually, he'd make a move—begin to unzip his jacket or reach for the front tab of his trousers. After that was anyone's guess, because the scene faded away, returning only after the fact, when Dawn or one her defeated TV sisters sobbed quietly, looked morosely into the mirror's harsh light, or braced herself for an encounter with Swan or his TV brothers, a boss, a protector, and, as often as not, a sadistic punisher.

In the girls' case no hotel rooms and no hint of punishment thundered ominously into the their secretive temporary reality. No threats or blackmail either, and no guy trying to weasel out of paying for *services rendered* (the phrase they adopted after hearing it muttered by their second customer, a real estate agent, supposedly, who'd paid readily—first joking about writing a cheque—even though the entire detour from the highway and back had taken no more than fifteen minutes, and who basically finished at the instant he began).

Within seconds of a throaty groan or chanted "Yeah, yeah, yeah" the man always returned to being a stranger. The well of shop talk evaporated; formerly intent eyes with a pleading expression skittered past the dashboard and toward the horizon. He'd adjust knobs, turn down the suddenly unbearable heat.

After the driver forked over bills, the car air thickened with change, as though molecules of awkwardness, tension, and embarrassment hissed from the pores of three bodies and filled the space much as breath steamed up a windshield.

When he said, "Well now . . . ," or "I needed that," or "My wife won't—," or "That felt just right," or "I guess we should—" and rubbed his hands together in a worried-looking way, the correct hostess response, their role now, eluded them.

The quiet setting—intimate and formal and not quite either—struck them as uncomfortable, akin to the close hug from an ancient, teetering relative who was never without a disconcerting (clammy, feverish) temperature. Before and during felt dreamlike and lighting quick, but the afterward moments lingered with the persistence of a thick cloud over the sun.

What the men saw in the willing girls pressed next to them on the passenger seat amounted to a mirage, they intuited, and clearly not what they recognized as true in themselves.

Daring but nurse-like, their involvement, with its puny lifespan, summoned few emotions other than giddy excitement and mild distaste. And the secrecy—shared—made them think of a possession treasured especially because no one else had any awareness of it.

Glimpsing or imagining the man's point of view creeped them out: did he long for a friend of his own daughter or the daughter herself, the girl next door, or his wife from when she was younger and out of reach? If so, they were receptacles for his fantasy. Who could say.

And pondering these unanswerables? Completely pointless. When the passenger door swung shut, everyone concerned couldn't wait to leave and speed back to official reality. As though nothing except courtesy and hitchhiking had occurred. Whatever the job's wage, there were limits to how much you'd do for the money. They could say that for sure.

Venture: Shoot 11 / November

On her first walking tour of the family's brand new, government subsidized, and capital D-shaped neighbourhood, which also turned out to be the last, Delphine had whispered about, or pointed accusingly at, a landscape of eyesores—littered squares of unkempt lawn belonging to Neanderthals too lazy to haul junk (recliners, car motors, and warped particleboard scraps) to the municipal dump or to pick up after the scruffy mutt; long-parched junipers that sat russet and dismal in plastic buckets on concrete stairways; a painted Santa and sleigh of plywood sprawled and gathering moss on an asphalt shingle roof; an unhinged railing; a peeling curbside baseball. "A 'planned community,'" she'd quipped. "As opposed to what?"

The gist of her overall findings, a report card, came in a muttered line at a fence post capped with a doll's head: "D for dump." Edmund didn't bother rustling together a jokey retort.

At the close of the circuit she'd grimaced at a bent aluminum TV antenna heaved into the streamlet that ran behind the back fence. "What is with these people?" Back and forth she rubbed a fretful thumb along the opposite palm.

Trashy neighbours lacking the bare minimum of pride made her blood boil, she'd announced in three provinces, and they alone gave her ample reason to keep busy indoors. The dumbfounding fact of an entire subdivision built on a slope and the position of their house at its base irked her too, as though slob outlooks, wall-to-wall indifference, and plastic doll parts would creep downward and pool around their meantime home, offensive as sewage.

Almost hidden by damp overhanging salmonberry branches, the antenna demanded a few hard tugs. Gordyn balanced it above his head and lurched up the slippery mud embankment. Feeling idiotic and feeble, he kept a look-out for prying eyes. He dragged the relic along a chip trail after that. Lugging the unwieldy shape to the hilly field of tall grass above McRae Avenue could wait till after dark.

As for the discarded TV console whose bulbous cathode ray tube had been staring outward from the side of the McPherson place for ever, he'd need Jay's help for a night raid. The McPhersons wouldn't detect a dozen pieces stolen from their public junkyard, never mind one. And Delphine might thank the unknown culprit for helping make the place, now with a "White Harlem" label slapped on, a tad more presentable.

For the band's official debut he had in mind a nightmarish style of story, different than the straightforward movies he'd already made starring Dee. It would capture 1980 to the letter.

The gist of this one wouldn't involve any scenario with a clear plot. He thought *demented* and *surreal* captured the mood.

Instead of A to B, there'd be cut up, kaleidoscopic images, a jumbled order that needed to be puzzled over and pieced together—Em and Dee smashing the TV screen with a sledge hammer, Em striding though the field with antenna parts affixed to her back, Dee and Em traipsing down the street at night and shielding their eyes, vampire-esque, from the glare of streetlights, Jay wearing black gloves and shoving his fist through a mirror, and himself in a field of tall brown grass playing what would look like a synthesizer set atop an ironing board. Somewhere in the mix: the hands of a clock nearing twelve, maple leaves trapped in chain-link fencing, a cat scurrying, and whatever else caught his eye. Lunacy. Garbage. Shadows. *Méchanceté.* Threats of violence looming. The end is nigh. He'd turn the video camera to Tammy Faye Baker bawling on *The PTL Show* and, if possible, splice it in at random intervals. All in black and white; he could figure that out.

Dee and Em could dress in Edmund's military coats and then . . . a few details could be a collaboration, he decided.

As for why, his parents would ask out of habit and assume a follow-up movie night in the near future, a late flowering of creativity before their eldest grew practical and settled down. His dad's main interest, as usual, would be the care and timely return of the video camera. The A/V Department monitored loaned equipment with warden eyes.

★

Gordyn had settled on a wild undulating field of criss-crossed trails for his first movie, the most memorable part of which turned out to be a last minute inspiration: ray-gun beams etched by pin frame by frame on an 8mm celluloid strip under a magnifying glass. For the next one, using a video camera and tripod combo his father had borrowed from work, he'd captured Dee in tousled Nancy Wilson hair. Ironing clothes as though exhausted, she pounded fists against the wall (twice: the first time she collapsed; in the follow up, she barreled—now defiant and victorious—toward the camera), let dice drop on the dining room table, and played solitary poker. She placed poker cards thoughtfully and, later, threw them down angrily and backed away from the cursed game. For the world premiere broadcast he'd played "Straight On" on the stereo to accompany a film whose only sounds came from mechanical clicks deep within the likewise loaned video tape machine.

In a perfect world he'd have an abundance of time. An assistant too. With a director's decisive orders he'd set up the show well in advance; the helper would run the tape machine while he and the gang performed, the audience quite agog despite ritual eye rolls at any step out of the ordinary. The band battle ran on a tight schedule, he knew, and as with changing scenery and costumes between acts on stage, speed and efficiency mattered. His show, then, had to cut corners, achieving something—since everything stood out of reach.

He thought of slides magnified and slid overtop clear spotlight gels: photographs instead of moving images. Lame. Still, onstage they'd look freaky and alien, especially compared to other bands climbing the platform before and after the gang's turn.

Envisioning the gang jerkily dancing in position with the images flickering over them like flags in the wind, he smiled at the coolness of a photograph of him in the field at night playing a fake instrument that would be projected on him in actuality. That rippling doubled effect would be worth the price of admission. As for the fully choreographed movie version, they could set that up in the basement at a later date. The encore performance for the masses.

But the set-up time demanded military precision. Failing that, stills would cast undecipherable shadows on the band. With them they'd capture attention and, better yet, cover up any blunders the gang might—certainly had to—make. Better still, projected warped images could mask their surplus of nerves with far greater coverage than any amount of makeup.

Venture: Inn / December

Jay repeated two words of encouragement—"Won't happen"—as Gordyn ran through what-if scenarios before the pub meeting.

Gordyn anticipated a watchful tough guy, a scarred veteran of fights over territory and lost bets and whatever else caused men to start swinging fists and pool cues once they'd downed a few. This bartender, who'd seen it all and witnessed every form of deceit just like St. Peter at the pearly gates, would expect nothing but the same from solitary and spot-lit Gordyn.

The fewer to show up meant the fewer mistakes, the gang had decided, and Gordyn definitely looked the oldest. Jay would keep watch in the van.

After wiping the bar counter and tossing the rag out of sight, the man would be sure to demand something or other—a birth certificate on top of a driver's license, say—or rattle off a barrage of age-related questions calculated to trip up unskilled liars. And just like that the gang's adventure would end before it had begun.

Though old, the highway-side pub possessed the appeal of a slumped and faded cardboard box used for packing. Budget renos over the years had stripped away details, including windows (into whose frames plywood had been nailed), and even opted against an eye-catching colour scheme: painters had coated each stucco wall and all the trim in an unappetizing shade that matched soupy porridge.

"God, this is it? What a find."

"Maybe it's better on the inside. I'll give you a full report in ten." Gordyn returned Jay's thumbs up gesture even though that passenger's sarcasm gave his feet further reason to drag.

Near the foundation Gordyn noticed mould colonies and a rim of grime from where rain had splashed. He supposed that management didn't give a shit. Either that, or they had a strategy: with almost no upkeep prices fell—low overhead, as Mr. Swanson taught. Also, bargains never failed to buy people's loyalty.

Roaring off the highway—the van's muffler speckled with holes that Merv meant to fix—Gordyn had parked in a lot empty save for three pickups and a Trans Am. He'd thought that was a good sign. A huge rowdy crew of drinking buddies would make facing the man that much worse.

Windowless fire doors opened to a cavern featuring ratty stools, Tiffany lampshades, and yards of flattened indoor-outdoor that had seen better days. The room felt dimensionless thanks to someone's heavy hand with black paint.

Compared to neon-lit taverns he'd noticed on TV, Gordyn found the beer parlour sad and unloved, as though someone had begun moving out and then stopped. Maybe cheery decoration became unnecessary when loud voices coming from mobile bodies poured into the place.

As a glimpse into adulthood the place offered him no reasons for a breathless countdown to nineteen.

A regulation middle-aged man with a moustache dragged a wet cloth along the varnished wood bar, as though lifted from prime time. A line of liqueur bottles sat on a narrow glass shelf behind him. The man looked up, raised his brows into a question.

Gordyn realized the guy expected a drink order. "Oh. Hi, can you . . . where does one sign up for The Battle of the Bands?" Two guys in jean jackets swung around to size him up; uninterested, they returned to lifting beer mugs.

Where does one, he thought, way to blend in. God.

"Form's right there by the coat check. Fill 'er out, drop 'er off at the motel's main office outside, pay the lady there. Cash only. Too many bounced cheques, now they're sticklers."

"Okay, I see it. Thanks." He sent the man the briefest of nods.

The sheet required less information than job application forms he'd filled out in the summer. No space for even one Social Insurance Number. The form asked nothing about the players, demanded no proof of their age. He wrote "River Bend City" opposite the "From:" line and "TBA" at "Name of Band:." He'd swap out TBA later.

Gordyn could think of nothing else to say. Pushing the door, his eyes winced at exposure to late afternoon's stony winter light. Jay smiled at his enthused thumbs, both held high.

A woman stapled papers in an office behind the front desk and didn't notice Gordyn until he clanged the bell.

"Just a minute. At my age, if I don't write something down it's gone in a flash." Gordyn smelled the delectable staleness of cigarettes butted in an ashtray. With her approach he inhaled smoke, coffee, and perfume. The woman, older than his mother, had a permed shag in tabby cat orange that suited her kindly face. "You looking for ice?"

Gordyn reached over the counter and handed her the form. "The guy said to pay you."

"You need a receipt?"

"Sure." They'd have memories, but a scrapbook souvenir would be fun too. "Thanks. Tax purposes."

"Sure thing." She winked and turned for the office desk. "Good luck. Oh, Christ on a cross! I damn near forgot. I'm supposed to check ID."

"Oh sure. Just a sec." The test, of Merv's skill and the gang's scheme, had arrived. He retrieved the card and passed it to her.

The lady barely had time to locate his birthdate. No holding the card up to a lightbulb, no tilting or running a thumb across the surface, no checking edges. "Not bad for a driver's license." With a second wink she returned the card, further questions unasked.

"Just good luck, I guess." He'd thought to say, "Really, it's all a matter of lighting," but figured she'd expect a different answer coming from a guy's mouth.

"Okay, it's official. TBA's good to go. Good luck!"

Gordyn smiled at her joke and motioned, a wave that turned into a salute.

Before rumbling out of the lot Gordyn forced himself to revisit the pub's dark interior. He ran across to tell Jay that a scouting mission had to be a wise manoeuvre.

He nodded at the bartender, motioned at the stage with a thumb, and crossed the parquet dance floor.

Far within the neon-lit darkness before bodies filled the place and additional lights flicked on, the stage practically merged with the side wall. The whole area might as well be a black hole.

Gordyn picked out details as his eye adjusted. A few black spotlights hanging from the black ceiling. Two panels of ruddy curtains—velvet?—on both sides. In the back a change room maybe, or storage? A slightly raised platform for the drummer. Large boxy speakers. The pint-sized stage floor at hip level. A mic stand. There'd be a bit of room to move around but—phew!—no huge empty floor they'd have to fill with their showman expertise. He climbed five stairs and strode across the plywood. It didn't bow but sounded hollow. Gordyn spread his arms wide, trying to capture the dimensions. In the coop they could chalk the floor and practice not overstepping the boundaries.

He foresaw them on the stage and looking down at a crowd of upturned faces. Was it battling musical gladiators they'd be, hoping to entertain a jostling crowd of plebs? Or heaven-bound Christians waiting for the emperor's right hand man to yell "Release the dogs"?

Gordyn didn't wave goodbye when he left. The bartender would expect that. He let the door slam shut.

DIARY / REHEARSALS

卌 卌 卌 卌

It's a miracle but Mr. X., G.'s 'connection' from downtown, came through with fake ID. We thought we'd try out the cards as a test and also to check out the competition. Plus, it's a good idea to not act like 'virgins' when it comes to talking, ordering, paying, etc etc.

A bar!!

Getting booted out before we even stepped inside = a disaster, so we decided our only option was to try to look as grown up as possible. D. piped up that she knew some makeup tips (<u>of course</u>) that would help out. In normal makeup I look about 15, so unless she's got a grey wig and a wrinkle-making kit . . . We'll see, but I'm not holding my breath. We joked about over-stuffing my bra so the bouncer would gawk at my toilet paper rack instead.

On Friday night we said Hi to Mrs. W. in the living room and zoomed upstairs. In her room D. got the guys to smudge a patch of eyeliner on their jaws and rub it in, just to see. It was supposed to pass as 5 o'clock shadow in dim bar light. More like bruises maybe.

For us? "Total hookers", she cracked, and then we debated about what style of hooker. We settled on classy.

We'd all finish putting on the stuff in the car since officially we were going to a late movie across the bridge. D. crammed her purse full.

You know how really bad shoplifters look super-guilty the very moment they cross into the store? Before they've even touched a thing. They slide their eyes around all nervously and move in a way that makes anyone else believe they're hiding something. Their expressions are shifty, guilty as sin. Well, that was us closing in on the front door, all thinking to ourselves, "Act like you own the place", which we'd landed on as important + just as necessary as dressing the part.

The boys seemed like they were in Halloween costumes and from the neck up going as hobos or coal miners. (G. had wanted to do eyeliner but D. nixed that, thank God. For someone with his reputation, he never fails to come up with the <u>very worst</u> ideas). J. had borrowed one of dad's green lumberjack shirts for the "mill worker look" and a gross T-shirt under it that said "Makin' Bacon" that showed two pigs doing it. G. in his dad's wool coat was kind of like an army officer or something, but a deserter.

D. called them the missing Village People. I had to agree.

She'd also thought (deciding for the both of us, as per usual, and especially b/c I wasn't overflowing with ideas) we should go for "Valley scrags" instead of the first plan. Those tough drop-out chicks who still like to party hearty when they can afford the babysitter = more likely at a bar in Bottlesburg (which is more or less the exact same thing as the Bend, only a few miles downriver) than expensive L.A.-style call girls that no one could afford. If we matched that we'd probably fit in way better. Fitting in was the main idea.

The outfits? Jean skirts and black scoop-neck T-shirts, tights, hoops, a bunch of gold chains, eyeliner like tar, paved-on rouge, pink lip gloss. We practically died in the car from hairspray fumes to keep the backcombing in place. The boys thought we looked like total cock teasing bitches (in a good way).

Oh yeah, in case anyone asked we were double dating. Eww.

I wasn't sure if I was supposed to be on a date with J. or G., but I guess it didn't matter. We didn't hold hands or fake make out or anything like that.

The double-dating idea came from *Happy Days*, G. said. None of us knew if anyone had done that since the 1950s. Nobody mentioned it, but I knew we all hoped everyone would just leave us alone. Completely. If a guy came on to me or D., or asked us to dance, J. and G. wouldn't have a hope in hell. And, besides, their makeup would come off!

From the car to the bar's front doors we were dead silent but arm in arm, D. and J. a few steps ahead. You know in movies when there's a dangerous border that has to be crossed, and the check point guards are super-suspicious b/c they've been warned to look out for the hero? The hero is stuck sweating in a hidden compartment in the back of a truck or beneath hay in a wagon or something like that. That was us.

As we got closer D. turned and said "Smiles everyone, smiles", like Mr. Roarke after the plane lands. We did smile, but couldn't think of anything else to say. What are you supposed to say at the front door?? The guys pretending to talk about mill shifts or something would have made us all cry from laughing. Just thinking of it now makes me giggle.

Anyhow, we'd prepped lots of explanations and excuses and memorized dates . . . so getting in without the bouncer's second glance felt a bit disappointing. He looked at our IDs for half a second and waved us through. He didn't say one word, just kinda grunted. Maybe he gets told when the cops are going to show up, and only then enforces the rules in a big way.

More on this later.

卌 卌 卌 卌 |

- We'd already decided that complicated drinks like a Grasshopper = drawing attention. G. ordered two pints of 'draft' and two glasses "for the ladies" from the waitress. He thought that was hil-ar-ious until D. and I grabbed the pints. The waitress said "Wanna run a tab?" and was halfway gone when I yelled out, "We're fine, thanks". God, it wasn't a difficult question and we practically froze.

- If anyone noticed us come in or paid attention after we grabbed a table, I didn't see. Phew! If a guy had come up and asked me to dance . . . It's easier to picture D. saying "She's with me. Back off, creep-o" than G. doing whatever it is that guys are supposed to do to protect their territory.

- Everything was wood or painted black and looked run down and cheap to begin with. It wasn't busy yet, but the air reeked of beer and cigarettes, perfume (lousy, from hairspray cans) and a gym change room smell and wet boots. It was gross, but being undercover felt so fun. (The Ladies room was <u>disgusting</u>. I wish I'd had a tape recorder b/c the women meet there to talk about guys and other girls who are snobs or bitches or boyfriend stealers or "a total scritch who's gonna pay the piper tonight", etc etc. Mix school with jail and that'd be it. I felt like one of those staring blonde children with bangs from "Village of the Damned", only I tried to blend in more, touching up my lip gloss with D., blowing smoke rings in her face, and muttering about G. and J. in a way that sounding like complaining, with lots of "God" and "Christ". We were giddy, practically on a different planet. Mostly, I wanted to be a fly on the wall. D. asked a girl for a spritz of Eau De Love with "I totally love that shit", which I thought was super-brave. When she lent the chick concealer, she didn't offer any tips, even though raccoon eyes needed a few. That chick should lay off the chocolate.)

- G. and J. carried all of our coats etc to the car. The less smoke smell, the better. It's not like we'd have time to stop at a Laundromat on the way home.

- The bands = all guys. Black Out. The Squirrels. The Cavemen. Johnny and the Skids. The best was 'Johnny' b/c he'd obviously done it before and 'connected' with the audience. No one was our age, but Black Out was pimply, on the younger side, and barely looked up, which, we all saw, is a bad move. Good to know for sure. The Cavemen were already drunk, slurring. They were way worse than we are now. <u>But</u> they were having fun and joked around and said "Pardon us as we start from the top" midway through "Witchy Woman", all of which made them popular.

- <u>Nobody anything like us</u>. <u>This is probably a bad sign</u>. (Try to find another contest?!?)

- Guitar solo or drum solo, or both. (= boring, but guys in the audience really like it.)

- One ballad, sung to the girlfriend at the front. Followed by a heavy rocker, the big finalé.

- Everyone watches the first band intensely, but no one dances, so going first is bad luck.

- One guy had a raccoon tail tied to his guitar, but no other 'effects'. No choreography, just the lead singer trying to act like Mick Jagger at the mic and the two guys on guitars "jacking off" while facing each other (G. said, and he's the expert).

- Boston, Supertramp, Led Zep, AC/DC, The Eagles, Kiss, Styx, Prism. "Radar Love", two versions of "The Dream Police", and one of "The Devil Went Down to Georgia" (The Cavemen, definitely hammered) that a few guys (maybe their friends?) in the back booed and then bellowed out "Order those tools another round!".

- D. and I matched pretty close. Jean jackets with the collar flipped up is the most popular look, along with silver hoops and sprayed perms (like school, only <u>way more volume</u>).

- There were judges, three of them. Peter something (the announcer introduced him as a "real estate mogul in his own mind"), Mike, the day manager of the bar (who stood and bowed in a funny way, like a curtsy), and a guy from the city who was described as being "in the biz and on the look out for bright new talent". Those three sat at a table off to one side (I guess so that the band plays to the audience in the front and not turned toward the judges). They scribbled notes.

- The Squirrels ended with a really good version of "Rock and Roll". Lots of couples shaking (as with school dances too, people dance after they get a bit hosed first). The drummer was wicked. They won. The announcer joked that the runner-up would wear the crown if the winners couldn't fulfill their duties. And the lead singer of The Cavemen waved, pretended to cry and air-kissed the crowd. Third and last place = not announced. That's got to hurt.

- After that, a regular band was setting up. They'd play until who knows what time. We didn't stay for long. Mr. or Mrs. W. would freak out and imagine the worst if we were ultra-late.

卌 卌 卌 |||| ||

Huge news!! Gordyn found a solution to the organ problem. That saves us the embarrassment of its 100% tackiness. And, anyhow, we hadn't come close to figuring out how to pull the wool over Mr. W.'s eyes about how we wanted to lug his prized possession to a secret semi-outdoors location for a secret project that had requires fake ID (and other things I won't bring up here).

Some lies are way too complicated to try out (and make convincing) unless you're a con artist with practical experience.

G. said, "The less you guys know the better", which I think we all heard as "I've got a juicy secret but I'm not going to share it".

D. looked at me as if to say, "Maybe we should tell them", and I said to G. (but also to D.), "Okay, no worries, we totally understand".

Then G. said a friend had loaned the machine to him, like he has this big collection of secret cool friends with synthesizers that we don't know about. Yeah, right. We're all stuffed packages of secrecy.

𝍸 𝍸 𝍸 𝍸 ||| - 𝍸 𝍸 𝍸 𝍸 𝍸 ||

Ever since our 'educational' night out, we've been going back and forth about if we should 'fix' our song choices, etc etc, and if so how much (or in what ways). We're practicing still, but sure as can be whenever we take a break the topic comes up over and over. Jeez!

We can't decide on anything b/c each one of us can't make up our mind.

J. joked that we can just play "Smoke of the Water" four times in a row if pleasing the crowd is all that matters. We could do each in a different style, for variety.

No one wants to do that, natch.

But is putting on the show we've more than half-planned just a waste of time and money, a slow lead-up to a death-by-embarrassment, as bad as those "Gong Show" contestants booed by a live audience? And then they're puzzled and shocked b/c they thought they were actually quite talented? What's the point of all this anyway? I'm not very sure at all.

On one side, playing for the masses . . . It's totally selling out by giving the audience nothing but what it wants or expects. With that, there's nothing new, no moving into the future like what we've seen and heard in that record shop in the city. Nope, just the same old, same old. We might as well be our parents and living in a world where The Slits or Joy Division never happened, only Waylon Jennings, Donnie and Marie, and Glen Campbell, and now - poof! - 1981 right on the horizon.

But, that worked for The Squirrels, obviously, b/c they won (even though the judge from the city was searching for fresh talent, supposedly).

The other side . . . making them hate us by not giving a shit about them or about entertaining them and instead basically saying 'screw you' to them and doing exactly what we want. (Like

G.'s 'a night at the Blitz' idea and my own plan of having us pretend to be from Moscow or Berlin and have D. be our 'manager' and the only one of us who can speak English.) I have to admit that while my idea (and G.'s too, I'd bet) is about doing what I think is a totally wicked idea, there's another part that's about giving the finger to what everybody else already says is a really neat idea (eg, Boston and "Radar Love"). An 'Up yours, losers' reaction.

D. thinks Blondie is our mid-way answer b/c (1) it's sexy, and sex sells, and (2) it's popular but on an edge and not Deep Purple or old junk our parents play.

My dad calls compromise a "four-letter word" (mostly when he's mixing behind the bar and getting philosophical about marriage). I think he has a point.

But there's also that saying about "When in Rome . . . ".

For this situation, both apply.

卌 卌 卌 卌 卌 ||| - 卌 卌 卌 卌 卌 ||||

We're also still 'talking about' (arguing over) the final song.

For some reason, it's becoming an issue in the way the others weren't. G. thinks Devo and "Smart Patrol/Mr. DNA" is best, b/c it fits into his "master plan". Being super-complicated, that one's less about showing off our style than our know-how, like the technical rounds in figure skating.

I don't know who said it first, so let's just say everyone came up with the idea of taking a well-known song and mangling it, so that it's recognizable but distorted. Looking back, it seems an obvious way to do what we want and to give the audience something IDable to grab on to.

We did "Iron Man" in a Numan style ("War Pigs" and "Paranoid" are in the running too) and tried Kiss, which wasn't that great.

Then we thought about "This Land is Your Land", "The Tommy Hunter Show Theme Song", and "Snow Bird". And for fun, favourites of the parental units. "Wichita Lineman", "Mr. Sandman", "Luckenbach, Texas", "Do You Know the Way to San

Jose?" but as done to show our personal style. It'll be weird and funny but kind of cool, that's the hope. D. sang "San Jose" in her jerky Siouxsie style and the effect was . . . quite memorable.

As for my own song . . . I'm not sure. No one's totally against it, but nobody's (me included) super-gung ho either. I can see why. It shows off our originality, yes. At the same time nobody except us knows it at all. With "Do You Know the Way to San Jose?" the audience would at least recognize the original tune. I guess this is a honey/vinegar situation. The question is, which should we go for?

Maybe eventually we're probably going to have to flip a coin about this and see which gets chosen.

卌 卌 卌 卌 卌 卌

<u>The Iron Curtains</u>!!!

I think that = an excellent name for us.

The real miracle is, everybody else does too. (Ultrabronz, the other one I came up with, got nothing but 'No way, Jose'. It sounds too much like makeup. So judged J.)

卌 卌 卌 卌 卌 卌 |

God! Mrs. W. picked up from her bedroom and listened in when a guy from Bottlesburg called for G.

To "So, young man, who and what was that all about?" (etc etc) G. explained that for fun he'd volunteered to be a Manager for some kids at school, like Reuben Kincaid on "The Partridge Family". She was glad he'd found his niche and was fitting in.

(G. called J. as soon as possible, all bullistic (sp?) and PO'd b/c what she'd actually said was "finally fitting in", like he just hadn't been trying hard enough before or something. I don't know what kind of school she went to, but it sure wasn't BSS. I wonder how she'd react if he told the truth: "Mom, except for D.F., the school's #1 picked on queer, I'm for sure the most unpopular guy for the exact same reason." I know that if I stood in her shoes, I'd promise to burn down the school. Ha ha. I'm pretty sure I wouldn't do it, but an offer in that vein that would make him feel way better.)

Oh right, the guy calling had picked names from a hat. We're going on stage . . . 2nd! Not bad. 1st or last = you might as well give up before you start.

Now all we have to do is rehearse for another million years, get there without any major f-ups, and play for judges and an audience without passing out, barfing, or tripping right off the stage. Oh, and it's on a Friday the 13th. Gee, I wonder what could go wrong? (We'll see soon.)

𝍸 𝍸 𝍸 𝍸 𝍸 𝍸 ||

The big day!

In all honesty, just getting to that cruddy dressing room felt as good as a miracle. Actually, it was two rooms. Next to the stage there's a curtained-off place that one of the burly organizer guys called "the holding cell". It's for storage and where the band that's about to go onstage stands around. Then a door and a bigger room where the other bands hang out. Posters, ashtrays, bottles, and cans were everywhere. The coffee table couldn't hold any more junk, and some previous band had made a pyramid of beer and pop cans right in the middle. The smell matched the décor (= 100% gross). A pig sty, guy-style.

The head a-hole in Saxxon (who, we found out later, had named the band after himself and added an x!) was stretched out on a ratty old recliner when we went in. He kept pulling up his guitar's strings one by one and checking the note it made or something and letting the string snap back. Then he looked up as though just noticing us standing there. "You don't look old enough for shit", he announced, stubbed out his smoke, and showed off with a little guitar solo. Right off he nicknamed us The Diapers, as in "The Diapers are going to crap their pants* out there" and "Pew-ew, someone needs changing. Better cry for Mommy, Diapers".

What a loser! He was trying to psych us out, obviously. I guess he thought that if his band took this contest, it was only a matter of time before Saxxon was at the Coliseum and looking at a sea of flickering cigarette lighters and rocker chicks throwing bras and stuff. As if. That's like believing that one A on a math test means you're going to win a Nobel Prize. Yeah, right. Saxxon had a ponytail that was wispy and thin b/c he'd probably dropped out of high school back in the hippy era. Good luck, Jerkenstein.

As per usual D. couldn't resist. She grabbed her top at tit level and shook it. "I can think of at least four reasons that we're going to mop the floor with you". I have <u>no idea</u> where that came from. It was like she got possessed by Coach F. She looked at me like I was supposed to follow her lead. I didn't. Sometimes it's really easy to picture her letting loose screams and attacking foes on a roller derby track. Saxxon squinted and lit a new smoke, but didn't say anything, thank God.

J. and G. just stood there (and G. later sarcastically thanked D. for 'defending our honour'). We're bundles of nerves with eye bags.

We'd parked the Merv van right next to a side exit door and we went there instead of fighting with that creepy guy and his gang or letting them see us and un-nerve us before we even managed to climb onstage. There was nothing to do in that room except jab at each other anyways. And I'm pretty sure cigarette smoke in a fog wouldn't help our voices either.

The other band there was Paradox (one x), only three long hair guys in a corner wearing black jeans and T-shirts. They kept to themselves and <u>crammed</u> using their notes—they'd actually written down a script** of their moves and what the lead singer and guitarist would say to the audience and each other. I kind of liked them b/c they seemed as nervous and amateur as we are, but a bit older. Also, they kept getting hung up on who'd do what and when. The lead singer got all strangled-voiced and frustrated and barked out, "No man, first I go 'We're Paradox', right, then Mike slams the skins, okay, and then you go 'We're here to rock you out, so get ready', got it?? Jeez Louise, it's not fucking brain surgery".

D. and I looked at each other and our eyes were smiling. Unless the missing fourth band turned out to be godawful too, we predicted third place at minimum. Woo-hoo!

*At that point we actually had on regular jeans and jackets. We kept The Iron Curtains' look hanging up in the van.

We'd tried out a bunch of different ideas and outfits (and all of them got voted down as too complicated or for making us feel like lame idiots) before we went for uniforms that didn't match exactly but belonged to the same general family.

Just like the Osmonds, ha ha.

We 'doctored' painter's coveralls we'd bought at Field's. For the girls: we wore 'pill box' hats (from the Women's Aux and bobby pinned in place) that had veils and made the outlines of bras and bikini panties in black electrician's tape right on top of the coveralls. We thought we'd look dramatic, like futuristic workers, but sexy and upbeat instead of being super-depressing, all grey and sad and miserable because all we did was work in factories and then go home exhausted. While officially 'playing cards' in the S.'s basement we'd dyed ours cherry red in the laundry sink.

We mixed black and red dye for the guys, which turned out a muddy brick colour. Rust. That wasn't what we'd hoped for. Oh well. They used the same tape too, but obviously no bra and panty outlines. We'd thought that would be funny, but also worse than useless if winning or even doing okay was part of our plan. They roughly wrapped about five inches of tape around the waist of the coveralls and then ran tape strands across their chests in a shiny X, like those Mexican bandits with ammunition belts. It looked cool, actually.

When trying them on we decided that instead of the button-up fronts we'd fasten the uniforms with brass kilt pins. D. and I wore bras underneath, so that anyone could see bits of them. The guys were supposed to go naked underneath but chickened out and brought white T-shirts. "Just in case", G. said, but D. and I totally predicted they'd never do it. I don't know what the big deal is.

D. said we should do makeup with a heavy hand b/c the audience was far away, and so on. We were plastered with rouge and eyeliner and black eyeshadow. She'd experimented for a few hours. I went along for the ride. For the guys, we went for foundation to even out the complexion. And eyeliner (G. insisted). Our lipstick shade was Midnight Plum. We snipped the sleeves off halfway down the forearm and all wore thick black tape wrist bands. (We vetoed D.'s 'statement' bangles: tacky.) The guys gave her permission to go wild with their hair-dos. She slicked gobs of gel on and then combed it forward and parted it so their faces were exposed. Flat, creepy and weird, in a good way. Noticeable, yes, but not very comfortable.

**We memorized ours. That was smart, it turns out, b/c practice there was bad enough! On the day of, when the organizers gave us a free hour around lunch before the bar opened (to "get your shit together" is what the cranky bartender guy said), so we thought that we'd be alone. But no way! I guess it was handy in a way b/c later that same day we had to do the whole thing in front of actual people. At least it was dark inside. (Mentioning a field trip, we'd skipped school. And if anyone at the Arms asked, we were prepped for "We got the day off work". Nobody asked anything. I guess it was just business as usual for them.)

Compared to the coop, the dinky stage, hollow and raised about four feet and looking at a dance floor made of wood tile squares, a bunch of stools and booths, and the bar itself, felt very exposed. Looking at the room sardined with people was going to make my stomach churn, I just knew it. Only a few guys were there at noon, but I got woozy with vertigo.

D. and I stood so that our toes could curl over the front edge. Looking down made us both think of fainting, I could tell, and how embarrassing that would be (on top of losing the Battle, we'd also wake up sore and looking at an entire roomful of people wondering if we were okay and what idiots we were). D. told me to pretend that I was nearsighted, that the only things in focus were on the stage and after that, just vague blurriness, along the lines of opening your eyes under water. She pointed at three spots in the room: centre, left, and right. "Whoever's standing there, that's who I'm going to fixate on. Unless they're gross, then it'll be in the general neighbourhood". Right away, I breathed easier.

Also, the bartender guy reminded us that we we allowed ten minute to set up, which sounds like a lot of time. It's not. At the coop we'd practiced that too, like an evacuation drill for a fire. The biggest problem was carrying all the stuff from A to B. J. and G. did the synthesizer and D. helped me with the drums. With all the rest, it took us 8 minutes (fastest) and 11 (the worst of the best).

What would be really ideal is a circular stage that rotates, like a Lazy Susan. As soon as one band finished, some guy behind the stage could spin them out of sight. As one band slipped behind a curtain the other, already set up, would be the appearing . . . I guess it would be nice to have wings and fly around, but that isn't going to happen either.

𝍸 𝍸 𝍸 𝍸 𝍸 𝍸 |||

Before changing (etc etc) we lugged the stuff to the curtained area. A guy had let G. could know he could set up the synth in advance, thank God.

Waiting his turn with D., J. paced around outside. Probably to escape the poisonous hair spray smell. He came back all excited and said that the 8 x 10 of us in the Cage was tacked up by the entrance. We all piled outside to look. Management had pinned up the one where D. and I face each other and have one foot resting on a bench and the guys are inside and looking out like defeated prisoners. Very cool. G. ran back to the van to get the Pentax. It'll look like a million years ago, when we're settled in NYC: first time, The Iron Curtains' one and only gig, ourselves posing in front of our own portrait!!!

We also found out the name of the 4th band: The Crates. The four guys in the picture had the same pose as the three guys in Paradox: just standing there. We're the only ones into style, from the looks of it. We slammed the van doors shut and got ready in the semi-dark. Laughing and gagging from nerves, but warm inside.

D. banned smoking (re: Total Hairspray Inferno (not a bad band name!))

𝍸 𝍸 𝍸 𝍸 𝍸 𝍸 ||||

Saxxon (the guy) snorted when he saw us full-on as The Irons Curtains. He didn't even bother trying to psych us out again, as though he didn't need to lift a finger b/c who's going to bother voting for such giant losers.

In that cramped little area next to the stage, we stood behind The Crates. Talking with us wasn't on their minds. You could smell their nerves, which was BO and Brut underneath nicotine.

"Ladies and gentlemen, coming all the way from their half of a two-car garage on Dewdney Trunk Road, it's . . . The Crates. C'mon, let them hear your love with a round of applause". The MC (billowy yellow shirt, rayon) read from a cue card. He sounded like a comedian with punchlines just waiting to burst out, but also super-sarcastic. We could practically feel his eyes rolling, as if he was a big shot and stooping so low by even showing up at some lame event in lame Bottlesburg. What a jackass!

The Crates made a few mistakes. Major ones, we all thought.

1. When they climbed the stairs (in the same black jean and T-shirt look as Paradox and Saxxon, how creative!) and took their places on stage, they dragged their asses. Deadly. The message: the very last thing we want is to be here right now and to entertain you.

2. They started with "Okay, one, two, and three", but before that they didn't even say a Hello or look at the audience for longer than an eye-blink.

3. Then they opened with a song I didn't recognize (b/c they'd written it??), but it rhymed "girl" with "pearl" and "Let's give this a whirl, girl" and "baby" with "don't say maybe" and what sounded like "the rest is gravy, baby". God: the worst lyrics ever. I think they were aiming for a slow-dance kind of emotional song. A "Beth" by Kiss or "Babe" by Styx. They missed by the Grand Canyon's width!!! I peeked around the corner halfway through.

Lots of people were talking to each other instead of watching. The rest faced them but took breaks every few seconds to whisper stuff to their friends. Watching that, The Crates had to be feeling worse than losers.

4. They improved a lot with "Lovin' Touchin' Squeezin'", but right after, already into "Heartache Tonight", the lead singer just stopped dead b/c singer, drummer and guitarist had absolutely fallen out of synch. "Yeah, sorry, we're gonna start that one again. Sorry", the guy mumbled. That pretty much wrecked the momentum. Saying a hundred apologies is 100% the kiss of death.

5. They finished with "It's a Heartache". They did a pretty good job on it. BUT . . . As a 'set', it sounded like a downer. I could picture them all getting dumped earlier in the day and so the mood they projected = mopey self-pity. I guess the lead singer was inviting the audience to share in his sadness, or something. I'm definitely sure that was not the world's greatest tactic.

6. They barely moved, the whole set.

D. and I went to the 'staff' bathroom during the last song. We checked our hair (D. = straight blonde with tips dyed red + me = "I'm going for Cruella de Vil meets Deborah Harry", according to Miss Vidal Sassoon). D. touched up our makeup and joked that "The Diapers are going to do just fine". She gave us last-minute beauty marks.

The Crates finished and the leader mumbled out "Thanks for listening", which sounded like one final apology. The spotlights went out and the MC guy jumped on stage to tell the audience that now was a good time to order some drinks and that he never said no if a pretty lady offered to buy him one. What a lech!

When the ten-minute countdown began, G. and I bounded to the stage after a gulp each (for "good luck") from a pint jar of swamp-mix liquor J. 'borrowed' from a certain address. Back turned, I made sure that I didn't pay any attention to the audience. Another reason to worry was the very last thing I needed.

For us, the cue card MC guy said, "Alrighty folks, up next, from wayyy up river . . . and blessing little ol' us . . . with a very special appearance . . . one . . . night . . . only . . . it's . . . ". He held the cheat sheet out at arm's length. "... T ... B ... A ... TBA! Let's give these weary travellers a hearty Bottlesburg welcome!!"

(15 minutes later: "God, G.!!!" Dee and I screeched at the exact same instant while listening to clapping and scrambling off the stage. "What happened to The Iron Curtains?" My knees were jelly and beneath the foundation I caught the flush on D.'s face. J. couldn't stop grinning.

G.'s gel had mixed with sweat and dripped from his nose. "Don't blame me. Not totally anyhow. When I drove here before and I filled out form and I paid the lady at the front desk, we hadn't decided on a name yet, okay? And I told the lady later, but, well, obviously somebody didn't get the message".

"What should we do?" D. was slick with sweat too. Her makeup was not 24 hr, as promised.

J. said, "Look, it doesn't matter now".

"Yeah, I guess so". D. fanned her face to stop the makeup rivulets. "Where were the judges, anyhow? I tried but couldn't see them at all".)

On the stage we (suddenly TBA now and not The Iron Curtains) sat in the dark for maybe one minute. I could smell beer and smoke. The Crates' BO lingered like perfume's evil twin.

3, 2, 1 ... The lights snapped on and we were bathed on the right from some pink glare and, from the other side, G.'s slide films from our night of videotaping. I could feel the heat instantly. As per The Plan, I was already seated behind the drums, an upright and stiff android with no battery pack. My Shields and Yarnell moment. I could hear murmurs: our live audience, plus they're kind of curious!

In front of me and to the left G. stood at the keyboard, intentionally frozen and angled so that his cold mannequin face was in profile. Our eyes were set at an empty stare. The styled coveralls looked really cool. (D. had spazzed out in the van ... "Get over yourselves. You won't look like skeletons" ... the guys didn't wear T-shirts. Totally bony.)

Freaked out, and heart somewhere between stopping totally and buzzing like an alarm clock, I went first. I had 7 seconds of solo drumming before G. joined in with synth chords. That went okay. The super-tricky part was our (judge-impressing??) first switch. In two beats G. had to swap from Ultravox's "Mr. X" to "Metal" and I had stop completely b/c for 13 beats the drumming in the second song begins 29 seconds after the synth, which we'd cut down to 20. During that set up, J. appeared cat-like and positioned himself opposite G. and slightly behind so that D. wouldn't crash into him or trip over his cord when she rushed to the mic stand. There wasn't any need for a guitar at that point, but we decided it made sense. He was fake playing, more or less. The simple 'bass line' matched G.'s chords.

You know that comedy routine where an olden days telephone operator gets a bunch of calls all at once and has to connect callers to a switchboard that has hundreds of holes in it? That's what I felt like. Or juggling marbles. Screwing up seemed an easy bet, just a matter of time. And which of us would turn perfectly arranged bowling pins into a scattered mess . . . (I know, I know, mixing metaphors = a no no.)

G. had given the guy in charge of spotlights his printed clear sheets, one for each song. From our end the spotlights looked like swirls of really glaring light and less glaring light. I thought of those tests that shrinks give to patients and their answers mean something, like if the blob looks like a gun or your mother, it means you'll probably do X or Y. Or have issues. Anyways, whatever the audience was seeing was not what we saw. Definitely. G.'s art project could have been really neat, but we'll never know.

Playing = totally wicked. The first switch worked perfectly. I felt sure of that. I didn't even look at the audience, so who knows what they were thinking.

When D bounded on stage, she was supposed to strut, grab the mic, and begin singing, all really quickly, like a shock + super-grabbing attention. The pounding instrumental part was meant to whet the audience's appetite and then make them follow the build-up that was like a volcano erupting.

We'd decided that the suddenness of D.'s movement, from appearing on stage for the first time and rushing, almost in a fury (as a furious android, not a fearful one), toward the mic, and then grabbing it, staring back at the audience, and snarl-singing the opening lyrics "We're in the building where they make us grow" and then joining G. in at the second line would be so memorable.

And it was.

D. charged across, staring directly at G. and ignoring everyone else. At the mic stand, she turned (sort of bent at the waist, feet apart, and swinging her shoulders around: okay, modelling classes did pay off) and in a growling/throaty style of voice she barked out that line. G. kept one hand playing and joined in. Their voices blended together as if they were twins. I wished we'd had the Pentax for that!

As we'd practiced, Dee shook and swung her head spastically. We all acted totally robotic to match the song. She looked at J., who stepped closer to her, and back to me. It's not like there's any time to jump outside of yourself and check out how the audience is reacting, but as far as I could tell (as we could tell: whenever I caught any of the gang's eyes, the message I got was "A-OK, omigod!!!"), The Iron Curtains/TBA made a statement people paid attention to.

(Oh, yeah, we couldn't really figure out shoes, so went for bare feet that we'd partially wrapped in shiny black tape at the ankle and around the arches. The effect looked a bit like futuristic sandals.)

Unlike with The Crates, the audience whooped and clapped for our first song!

When "Metal" had barely finished G. began the chopsticks sounds for our revamped Siouxsie Sioux. D. picked up the toy xylophone and held it like a violin. She banged out the "Prawn Gardens" opening notes (for effect: mostly, the synth gave us the actual pinging noises). I had to sing back-up for that one and J. did too, sharing the main mic with D. Before I knew it, the whole song had ended. I was drenched in sweat and barely had a second to think. Real bands must operate on automatic pilot. I could only guess what D. was feeling. G. kept his eyes fixed on the horizon while playing. That added to the chilly mechanical feel. J. kept his feet planted and pivoted up and down from the waist.

Even though we'd practiced "Obituary Column" so much that we'd all begun to hate it, in the end we found it super-difficult. Still. Our educated guess took it as a fact that what musicians can do on stage and what they're able to whip up in a studio = very different. We'd changed some of the parts so that we wouldn't mess up. Also, between the first line ("The mind is slowly fading") several lines came that we couldn't figure out until "Such a meagre existence/Where is your Christ now?). We made up those lyrics instead. There was no way anyone in the audience would know the song. Moev could beg every radio station in the Valley to play their song and no one ever would. As long as it sounded real, though, changing a few words made no difference.

On top of the total miracle of everything going as planned, we made people react. No one had danced when The Crates played. Not a soul. The audience stayed stone-faced. Maybe no one had had enough to drink. Anyways, I looked out during "Prawn Garden" and saw three girls and a guy dancing. 100% wow!

During practice and at Prawn Gardens meetings, we'd decided on Plan B, Plan C, or Plan D as emergency solutions. If things were running smooth and the audience looked okay (= not chucking stuff or yelling "Boo" or obviously staring huge daggers at us), then we'd stick with Plan A, Devo's "Smart Patrol/Mr. DNA". We were ready with it.

But if the situation looked terrible or close to it, then we had 'toe-tapper' back-up songs that anyone with a radio would recognize . . . even though we mangled them on purpose and made them 'ours', with the mood becoming darker, closer to Phantasmagoria than weekly Top Ten.

There were 1000s of tacky song possibilities but for fun we'd narrowed them down to "Dark Lady" (D. mixing Cher with The Normal), that Tommy Hunter Show song with "let me wander" in it, and "Knock Three Times", but more Transylvania at midnight and less bright yellow Tony Orlando and Dawn.

As the person literally closest to the audience, D. had to make the call, turn around on the sly, and signal me the choice with sign language (I'd taught her those)—

That's enough writing. My hand is cramping. More later.

𝍸 𝍸 𝍸 𝍸 𝍸 𝍸 𝍸

As G. did the instrumental bit that ended "Obituary Column", D. did a 180, with her hand held up for my eyes only. Then she showed the guys the signal:

Before "The fortune queen of New Orleans", I could hear recognition. It moved mouth-to-ear, wave-like through the audience. D. shook the tambourine all severe, like a gypsy in a duel, and put on her Siouxsie voice.

It was over almost as soon as it began. It felt . . .

Eternity in the blink of an eye. That's a paradox.

J. said "Break a leg" to the Paradox guys when we left the stage. We had to get out of the way then b/c God's gift to rock and roll Saxxon and his dumb sidekicks had started shoving their stuff into place. He didn't comment on us, not a single word. He shoulder-checked J., though.

God, you'd think that macho stuff would end on the morning a guy noticed receding hair in the mirror.

Onstage, the lead singer said "We're", then came an awful screech of feedback. He started over: "Um, Hi, we're Paradox", which was the line we'd overhead. Following the script he turned to the drummer, who looked at him as if to say "What do you want, man?" The guitarist strode to the leader singer's mic and spoke. "And . . . ," he looked at the audience and lost his train of thought. ". . . so get ready to rock out. Okay?"

I couldn't see the audience from where I stood at the dressing room door. I know I heard zilch. Anyone who's ever given a class presentation knows better than to ask a question to the audience. They're not there to help you out. No way.

If I'd been a judge I'd have said it was a tie for last place. The Crates (aka The Wet Newspapers) lacked spark. But after a minute of "Blinded by the Light", Paradox looked murderous. The lead singer shot an evil eye at the guitarist first and the drummer next, and the guitarist turned around to let the drummer know he was screwing up the pacing, or something. There's that ancient skit that has "Who's on first?" in it . . . this was the Battle of the Bands version. The lead singer missed his cue at the start of "My Sharona", which threw off the guitarist's harmony vocals, etc etc. More or less how we sounded last year. They made barely any effort to connect to the people who were five feet away. A disaster area!

D. whispered, "Last place. Totally". I nodded back a 'for sure'.

"They should call themselves Self-Destruct", J. leaned in to add.

Okay, so nobody would ever give Saxxon a World's #1 Nice Guy mug. But to be honest, he knew what he was doing. And his band had a fog machine. (We never even thought of that.) He put on the friendly face, met eyes in the audience, and muttered a couple of funny things when the band screwed up a bit. His voice sounded pretty strong. Saxxon (the band) played Fleetwood Mac, Peter Frampton, "Bad Company" and ended with "Barracuda". From the sound of it, that was a smart idea. "Give the people what they want, and they'll buy it", right?

They sounded like they'd been playing for decades . . . that's probably true.

For me, the question of who should win came down to technical skills vs artistic merit. We'd win for artistry, I'd vote. Saxxon b/c of skill (a tie, maybe) and pleasing the audience (definitely).

The Battle organizers hadn't exactly handed out giant clues about what they were looking for. All we knew to expect was that the jokester MC would announce the judge's winner before long.

卌 卌 卌 卌 卌 卌 卌 |

Chased by a spotlight, Don Rickles of the Fraser Valley jumped on the stage and told the audience that the bands would be secured in a soundproof room while the judges carefully deliberated. The words sounded deadly serious, but he said it all with a nudge nudge, wink wink voice that meant *none of this matters in the least*. He finished with that part from a beauty pageant when the guy who sings "There she is, Miss America" sets aside a minute to talk (aka, fib) about the crucial importance of the first runner up in case the winner can't fulfill her duties.

I'm not sure what his problem was. Maybe he got blackmailed into taking the job.

We stood in the room and heard the whole speech. None of the bands said a thing to each other, not even "Good luck". (Miss America contestants we were not!)

After about five minutes stood at the mic. "Alrighty, folks," he said. "There are only two names in this envelope. I'll read them in random order . . . Okay, will . . . Saxxon . . . and . . . TBA come to the stage, please?"

D. and I lost our cool. We *squealed and grabbed each other*. Just like Miss Texas and Miss Hawaii, or something. God, how old are we? Saxxon pushed ahead (surprise, surprise). The nine of us barely fit on the stage. The MC guy said (to us and the audience), "The judges told me they had to deliberate longer than usual. In the end, the third judge had to break the tie".

"Okay, folks, okay, it's the moment you've all been waiting for, but as you can see there's really only room enough for one band on this stage".

He drummed on the mic with his index finger. "And the first runner up of the Bottlesburg Arms' fourth Battle of the Bands contest is . . . TBA!! Let's give them a hand, folks! Saxxon takes the prize, spend it wisely guys!" The audience clapped, but I detected a few boos.

I'd bet that anyone in a contest throughout all of history has the same experience. You train yourself to believe that you'll probably not win, that not winning is no big deal anyhow, and that the experience alone makes it all worth the effort . . . but, secretly, you want to win so badly you'd sell your soul for a trophy and the piddly cash prize. And then when you don't win, you crash, feeling so let down and so foolish for having tried in the first place. And you tell yourself that second isn't too bad, even though you don't feel that way at all.

Suddenly idiotic, we stood there in our costumes and hairdos. And we smiled at the audience as the guys shook hands with the Don Rickles MC. He hugged us. With his back turned to the audience he muzzled us and then asked us to drop by his table later, "just the two of you gals", b/c he had major connections in the city and thought he could really take us major places (yeah, two "major"s!!). Right to the top. Yeah, right. God, does that stuff work on other girls? I guess it must. There's always a Dawn Wetherby dreaming of the Big Time who'll swallow a second helping of that bull.

We shuffled off the stage and headed straight to the van. If we had tails, they'd have been between our legs. We finished our jar of swamp water in no time.

p.s. 45.5 hours later, I'm not (quite) so . . . whatever I was that night. Low? Depressed? Discouraged, that's it. I'm pretty sure there's no After-School Special Life Lesson to take away that'll guide me toward an awesome future. I'm super-glad we went through with the whole thing, though. And that I did. Totally. Making something from nothing turns out to be way harder than you'd think . . . and 100% worth it. (God, that sounds suspiciously similar to a Life Lesson!)

Snow's falling and two tests first thing in the morning. Wish me luck!

VENTURE: HOMEWARD / FEBRUARY

With the last of the equipment packed and The Iron Curtains ensembles folded (Dee) and stuffed into plastic bags (Jay), the gang flipped for shotgun.

Just past the crammed parking lot night traffic hummed and glowed.

As listless as animation the gang lingered, complaining about the cold snap while joking, jabbing, and kicking pebbles. They replayed scenes, mimicked Saxxon, the MC, Paradox, and each other (Dee's frenzied delivery, Jay's swoops and twists, Em's metallic pounding, Gordyn's icy aloofness), wiped the oily sheen from tingling faces, and maimed Dee's sticky heat-trapping hairdos with agitated fingers. Sprinting a four-minute mile did not feel out of the question.

Listening for new squeaks and hating the wobbly rattling van and its stubborn rightward pull, Gordyn drove ten and two and wondered about further delivery runs for Merv. Come September, the money would come in handy. And beneath the gruff facade Merv did act generously.

Feet resting on the dashboard next to the sideways piddly trophy, Dee began peeling off tape by the strand, left foot first. "I think all that sweat just melted the tape's glue or something. These bands practically slide off."

Facing one another and seated with reluctant backs pressed against the van's frigid metal walls, Em and Jay batted ideas back and forth, one-upping the other.

"Okay, drive it into the middle of a field and just leave it there. Cops will treat it like a mysterious crime scene."

"Nuh-uh, Em, fingerprints everywhere. I say go halfway across the bridge and then put a rock on the gas petal. Vroom, right into the river. No evidence, no witnesses, a deep watery grave!"

"We'd have to walk home. And Merv would hunt me down, and then you guys next!"

"Yeah, good point. Maybe we should sell all the stuff at Belle's. Or some place back in Bottlesburg."

"No way, bonfire it."

"Bonfire it, including the van. Kamikaze, a blaze of glory! My dear brother here can whip up a good excuse for Merv, no problem-o. Rival waterbed dealers, maybe?"

"Speaking of which . . . Gordyn! Can you blast the heat? We're freezing back here!"

"No can do. I don't trust it. I'm pretty sure the vents spew carbon monoxide or something." Gordyn always drove with the passenger window opened a crack. "I can see the headline now: 'Fiery Finalé for First Runner Up Teens.'"

"That's pretty good. How about 'It's Curtains for The Iron Curtains'?"

"Yeah, except no one knew our actual name. 'Weekend Tragedy: TBA are DOA' would be good. They could use one of those shots from the Cage. We'd be front page news!" Much taken with 'Rage, rage against the dying of the light," Em pictured newsworthiness as a passable substitute.

"I vote for 'Suicide Suspected for Second Place Teens.' Or . . . ," Jay drummed the van's ribbed sheet metal floor. "'Battle Band Burns Brightly'?"

"Gross. You guys are so morbid, God. Next, I think we should turn that Crates song into a Top Ten hit. It'd be perfect for grad. 'You're my gurrrr-el, pretty as a purrrr-el,'" Dee crooned, her neck at a moon-howl tilt. "Let's give this a whirrrr-el, girrrr-el"

"C'mon, bayyyy-by, don't say mayyyy-be."

"After this, the rest is gravvvv-y, oh babbbb-y." The siblings reached an easy harmony.

"What does that even mean?" Em grabbed for a bagged costume. She could feel a dull ache building in her tailbone that padded seating would fix. "As in, sincerely, what the bloody hell?"

III

End Matters

I don't want to go with no egg on my face.
I just wanna go the best way that I know of.
Eww, ohh, I want to be vaporized.

—X-15, "Vaporized" (1980)

Appendix 1: 2015

> Get wise. Get wine, and one good filter for it.
> Cut that high hope down to size, and pour it
> into something fit for men. Think less
> of more tomorrows, more of this
>
> one second, endlessly unique: it's
> jealous, even as we speak, and it's
> about to split again . . .
>
> —Horace, *Ode* I. 11 (trans. Heather McHugh)

You're curious by nature, perhaps. Or as emotionally invested as a reasonable person can hope to be with nothing but black letters, numbers, and punctuation marks imprinted (ink, pixels) on white page forms.

Or else you are, along with most everyone else, neurologically predisposed to hanker after unequivocal answers to vexing questions—What ultimately happens, where does the trail finally lead?—and old enough as well to have learned with near godly certainty that individuals not yet at the end of their second decade of existence—still growing, unworldly, just kids!—have only begun to experience the _______ (insert your preferred life metaphor: banquet, carnival, journey, quest, race, battle, dream, highway, party, zoo, bicycle ride, roller coaster, twisted path, train wreck, upward climb, mortal coil, three-ring circus, vale of tears, and so on).

In whatever case your grey, cloud-like mood drifts toward disgruntlement and you mutter, "Huh," "Damn, that's it??" or maybe, "Gee, well, I guess that's that."

Still, you're left with a tugging moue and the weight of slight dissatisfaction attached to the low-volume sentence released in your midst (and by you: poolside, in bed, at a beach, on a sofa or bus, or slumped at Gate 7C while awaiting a domestic flight that's delayed "due to mechanical issues," the garbled voice on the PA system has already announced twice): "I wonder what'd happen to them next?"

Since these striving teenagers are not situated in another genre—a work of utopian sci-fi, say, in which the consciousnesses of ailing and elderly citizens are copied to the last engram and transferred via a miracle of dazzling post-Space Age technology into the vitreous Communal Nexus, a repository and permanent archive of being whose collective, never depleted wisdom assists in the fair governance and upward evolution of this gleaming, fantastically enlightened place—you can be assured of their eventual deaths.

That's momentous, of course. But, really, practically anyone would have seen that fate coming.

Before shuffling off, which occurs ordinarily enough—almost—as a result of geriatric disease or simply the cumulative fatigue of old age, they disperse. (Unconsciously over time, they re-shape the painful, troubling awareness of their parents' deaths by heart disease, cancers, and aneurysm into doors, merely three of several and therefore not the gruesome options for their own exit.)

On the lengthy soundtrack of their dispersals, rounds one and two: Visage, Young Marble Giants, Romeo Void, Cabaret Voltaire, Skinny Puppy, the bands of 4AD (etc); REM, Swans, The Smiths, Pylon, 10,000 Maniacs, The Pixies, Throwing Muses, scruffy plaid-shirted Sub Pop acts (etc).

They leave River Bend City, all of them. Two never return.

If asked, Gordyn (who legally binds his homegrown name change) quips "Good riddance to bad rubbish," comfortable with the irony of applying one of Edmund's shopworn and formerly loathed signatures. An islander and homebody with a perennially tight budget, Dee's never comprehended the appeal of backward-glancing road trips.

The other two, whose mother's flat polished granite rectangle of a grave marker they occasionally sweep clean with sleeves or hands, show up every few years, separately but compulsively, even though they tell themselves that visiting is convenient because they're passing by anyhow and seeing how the old homestead has shrunken or decayed will prove satisfying.

Or: "Just because."

Or: "There's a cute little antique store."

Eyes alert for the decrepitude of former schoolmates, each is accompanied on each drive-through by a boyfriend and, later, a partner. And, at last, an adored child for Em. Having witnesses along feels crucial; understanding why does not. Enthused (more or less), they point out the fireweed in the gaping main street lot (empty still in 1990, remarkably, and in 2014, which boggles their minds) across from Prawn Gardens (new owners and wallpaper, same lunch combos), and to kindly indulgent listeners describe the former Christmas tree farm opposite of Old Man Thesen's shack (former shack, in fact: spreading over stages, a housing development of stately neutral hues, trimmed greenery, and family SUVs).

After the predicted anticlimax of graduation the eldest siblings move two hours west first—to a nearby mid-sized coastal city, with the keenness of bloodhounds on a fresh scent.

Happy and relaxed, if broke, at university (history, English, philosophy, environmental ethics, student journalism), the guys encourage their sisters—per usual: craftily, reasonably, pushily—to give the pretty governmental and neo-hippy hub a shot, reassuring them that "Newlyweds and nearly deads," the tourist-courting destination's unofficial and unwelcome motto, contains just a smidgen of the whole wide truth.

Visits to basement suites over a handful of weekends confirm their brothers' cheerleader enthusiasm about the city. Spun wheels at home—boring go-nowhere jobs and Friday night dates at bars they shortly begin to label "tours of duty" whenever meeting for catch-up lunches—goad them on too. Suitcases packed and bank accounts closed, the sisters migrate.

They remain island-bound long after their brothers leave for taxing, long-winded, and intermittently pointless-feeling graduate degrees, promising-then-ailing / purely catastrophic / promising-then-thriving romances, hamstringing student loan repayments, and public sector careers in different large metropolises with a history of east versus west rivalry. One brother eventually takes to after-work writing while yearning for a better income from an indifferent employer; office-bound and responsible for corporate paperlessness initiatives, the other envisions a next-chapter life grounded in rolling green vistas, salt air, and crops, and begins to count the weeks until early retirement.

And the frenetic group career pinned to gauzy images of cultural capitals, nicotine-reliant models, flashy catwalk shows, fabric sourcing expeditions, contact sheets, stilettos, and regular doses of perfumed glamour? A phase, later deemed impractical. Then trivial, banal, and facile, a silly adolescent mirage.

The girls never step foot in Manhattan, although Em, at age 26 and down to her last coins after a cut-short trip with Gordyn to a handful of scorched Indian cities that reminds her for the nth time about her entrenched and puzzling lack of financial acumen, calls her brother (collect)—from a windowless room in a behind-the-scenes zone of JFK whose dull paint and cubicle rooms are seen only by detainees, custodians, and security personnel. With a tight, artificial laugh, she tells him that being held for questioning also means she'll miss her flight home. (Her would-be crime? Ganja from a laughably shady hustler in Goa, of an absurdly minuscule portion, the quality "piss-poor," she admits, mock-quoting their father, a distant stranger who is subject only to their ongoing derision, wrath, and disappointment. And to their mock-quotes: compulsive acts of simultaneous verbal memorial-building and verbal graffiti). Watching the stern guard-agent with the unexpected Russian accent tap tap tap her watch crystal, Em quips "Don't blame me, blame Nancy Reagan!"

For compelling reasons of their own, the kids' parents (and final stepmother) find themselves (1) semi-retiring to a quiet island with a golf course and (2) crossing the border and spending summers in view of Oregon orchards and winters in an affordable desert state with a reputation for RV park sprawl, chain-gang prisoners, and widespread frontier justice. The two sets of parents never meet one another.

And just as the fantastical career visions of any children (princess, cowboy, ballerina, race car driver) must make way for the practicality of unceasing bills and a miserly job market (merchandising admin, heavy equipment operator, audience services manager, executive flight centre IT support specialist: afternoon/evening position), the no-longer-kids apply for and gratefully accept assorted jobs, confident that shifts of hourly-wage work will gradually transform—through willpower and talent and luck—into meaningful occupations with ample renumeration and benefits, if not prestige.

"Ha, right, easier said than done," three of them grumble now and again, for years, worried about the bitterness that creeps into their voices so steadily.

Although Dee never steps foot on the Eastern Seaboard, she's thrilled and envious when receiving stamped postcards—how retro!—from her brother. California (Mono Lake). Fire Island (dunes). Point Pelee (boardwalk). Granada (Carmen de los Martires).

Less a far-off dream than a TV and, later, internet broadcast, Manhattan—a kaleidoscope of streets (rich, poor), buildings (ditto), taxis and stretch limos, and alleyways (crime scenes littered with battered victims or discarded corpses), and peopled by the cops (above board, crooked), criminals, and prey featured in the procedurals she's contentedly hooked on—lingers as a destination she proclaims she'd love to visit before getting too old for her knees and hips to take that endless hoofing from one can't-miss landmark to the next.

Modelling, likewise unattained at an international, national, or municipal scale, withers to a distant memory whose meaning drifts with the constancy of snow in the wind: *Remember when? I was so green / so naive / so hopeful / so deluded / so thin / so ridiculous / so ambitious / so confident / such a different person then.*

And when the father of her two children (adults now with unique sets of what they insist on calling "issues") playfully jabs

Dee on the side—whose soft abundance she sets aside a special moment or two to dislike each and every day—or he mimes the gazelle punches of the boxing ring he's only ever seen on TV and says, "I couldda been a contender" for what must be the thousandth round since their first date, the decades-old memory of earnest *Vogue* cover poses before the full-length bedroom mirror, retrieved by some censorious and punitive brain segment, seems intent on reminding her that she too could have been a contender *if only, if only*.

Carrying excess weight. After the exhaustion of troubled children. The bleeding then DOA surefire businesses. The marital down-and-outs. The moves from house to house. The pooling sense of dissatisfaction that makes Peggy Lee's morose rendition of "Is That All There Is?"—played from time to time on a radio station featuring the same melodic tunes, now called Soft Classics, that her mother reached for—burrow into her ears with the perfection of a melancholic personal theme song. Paused between a day of work and the nightly dinner, Dee's outraged, flummoxed.

Depending on her body's mix of organic chemistry and prescribed dosage of pharmacological bounty, there's an accusing finger pointing at the sadistic machinations of the universe. Or, the arm and wrist crooked awkwardly so that she's the object of her own accusation. That finger reminds her that a True Love of tortilla chips topped with black olives and shredded jack and slammed under the broiler late into insomniac nights simply replaced what she'd assumed was a True Love and a Special Calling. Just like that.

Dee chats to screens and into receivers from time to time with her brother, who has resided in North America's fourth largest city for ages, owns two homes (old brick fixer-uppers he paid trades to modernize) that he bought with his husband (named Gordon, a rich if tiresome source of jokes for awhile) before the real estate boom. He's built a god-I'm-*so*-busy career that necessitates flying often and discussing "synergistic initiatives" as a sizable government pension accrues. At home he makes sure that a plotted graph timeline for early retirement, westward migration to an island and a hobby acreage, and exotic crop farming stays on track exactly.

When the opportunity arises, Dee encourages Gordyn to talk about himself because whenever he coolly surveys her trajectory, he's unable to resist offering useful suggestions and practical advice and beneficial plans and future-eying strategies, or to pose the question that sounds simple—"How are you?"—but in fact means, "How are you, I mean *really*, *truly* and *way down* (the implication unmissable: that intractable problems and deep-seated psychological knots are there to find if she probes thoroughly enough, as his keen mind has, the probe as cold and invasive and unpleasant as the ones reputedly wielded by those silver-green aliens).

One blustery month before Em added her life's last statistic, she called Dee: "I know, I know, out of the blue, right," and laughed. "Happy New Year!"

She wondered if Dee might be willing to give her daughter makeup tips. If Dee's schedule didn't look too full.

Em could have done so herself, of course.

Makeup, they both understood, served as a pretext. Mending fences and touching base occupied Em's wintry thoughts, and while a certain fence wouldn't ever get mended because her father consisted of ashes scattered in two mutually exclusive locations—thanks to ongoing and irresolvable acrimony—Em had never known Dee to hang on to grudges.

Operating her latest one-woman business from home, Dee offered a kitchen table tutorial. "Sure, any time's good for me."

(That final stat, you ask? According to "Table 5: Fatal Victims by Role and Gender" in *Motor Vehicle Fatalities in British Columbia*, published by the Research and Data Unit of the Superintendent of Motor Vehicles at the Ministry of Justice's Office, 25 female pedestrians are killed on average annually by motor vehicles; as with 75% of these fatalities, the police report listed Em's as a "non-intersection incident." As things go, evidently, summer is the fatal season.

Before dwelling on the latest good reason to rage against his father, the wellspring of his children's every bad decision, Jay—heartsick, guilt-ridden, grief-stricken, leaden with helplessness, damned all-purpose Shakespeare's "Irreparable is the loss" cycloning through his brain with the chirpy insistence of a pop song—comes to imagine "Just my bloody luck" as the final thought generated by Em's extinguishing consciousness on a crisply cold but, the police report notes, dangerously glaring February morning.

Jay scours the web, seeking clarity, or else chilly comfort, from further stats: nationally, 4.4% of all 242,000 annual fatalities result from "Accidents (unintentional injuries)"; his sister was part of the 55.7% of women who give birth to a child after turning 30; she belonged to the 20% of common-law parents, and, short months after, to the 8.7% of common-law broken unions with shared physical custody; she stood proudly amongst the 15% of the national population with a university degree (the first female of her family, too) and within the 20% of university graduates classified as mature students; she also fell into the 18% of that university-educated populace that met the criteria for the "bottom 90%" of total income. Along with Dee, she regretted, as the lesser of two evils, her membership in the 23% of North American women aged 40-59 prescribed antidepressants.

As you might have guessed, he gradually learned that any consolation this information offers is both weak and fleeting.)

After words about children, work, hair colouring—plum auburn (Dee), espresso (Em)—and their brothers (and skipping right by marriage, romance, and active yearnings altogether, though Dee couldn't help but notice the black band tattooed on Em's wedding finger, a tale of love and loss, she imagined, and one she'd ask about later), they reminisced, reaching back, at last, to what Dee, careful of revelations in front of the pre-teen on whose eyelids she drew fine black lines, settled on naming "our first job together."

"God, I hadn't given *that* a thought for years. How utterly stupid! Unbelievable! We were so lucky we didn't—. But in those days, well, I could have justified anything, right? I thought blowing smoke rings meant I was destined to be the next Vivienne Westwood. Like that's all it takes. God, as if! It's a good thing we didn't"—she shaped her free hand into a gun—"We would have been Bonnie and Clyde but minus the . . . gore."

"I know. God, we thought we were such rebel badasses. Is that okay?"

"Yup. We did a swear jar for about a week but then I thought, 'All I'm missing is a bloody mini-van' and that was the end of that. She's bound to overhear them all anyway, so I try to keep the major ones out of my regular rotation."

"Who knew it'd be all the little things." Dee's not sure what's she trying to explain away. "A splash more?"

"I'll say." Em slid her glass across the table.

They made plans to get together, "next month, if not sooner." Neither knew the future, of course. Not a five-minute step, not a thirty-day leap.

Em left, waving and smiling with genuine fondness. Blasting heat in the truck, she typed "Makeup lesson #2" and "(Bring better wine!!)" on her phone's Reminders app while her daughter stretched upward to admire made-up eyelids in the visor mirror.

Three weeks later, Dee stood for the first time in Em's lake house bedroom (now soulless, she thought, a stage set). In other rooms stunned family, neighbours, and friends reminisced and sobbed while sorting through full-to-bursting cupboards, drawers, and cabinets.

As Dee drew open the drapes she smiled at the vintage fabric print of philodendron leaves and hibiscus flowers. So typical. While the crypt-coldness of the rental home made perfect sense, dancing silvery light reflecting off the lake felt worse than an affront: how dare the world continue!

The unwanted and inadequate intimacy of sliding dresses and blouses off hangers and resting them, tenderly folded, in boxes marked Donate, Garage Sale, and Friends/Family froze her hands, distressed her belly.

Whistling in a graveyard and snubbing decorum, Dee unreeled bright stories—of the previous month's reunion and makeup session, the scandalous part-time, limited-run job on the highway outside of River Bend City, and the exhilarating fifteen-minute brush with fame inside a scuzzy pub at the Bottlesburg Inn—to whatever ashen, glassy-eyed, and thankful mourner passed by.

Appendix II: [Database Search Result]

ti: Rocking Band Battle Showcases Valley Talents
au: Greg Dawson
pu: *Bottlesburg Weekly Gazette* 14 Feb 1981

On the eve of Valentine's Day, a few hearts were visibly broken on stage at the Bottlesburg Inn's "Battle of the Bands." In the end, judges handed a valentine to just one happy victor. Saxxon will return for the Grand Finalé in December.

Saxxon's victory wasn't unanimous, MC and local radio host Perry Robertson revealed.

A weary Robertson said last night, "I'm glad the judges supported a classic outfit, but it was absurd to choose a winner between any of them. Two at least could have shared first place."

"It was an apples and oranges kind of deal," he explained. "The bands had absolutely nothing in common." The three judges, including a freelance rock reviewer and a music executive based in Vancouver, were unavailable for comment.

By the time the smoke cleared and forehead sweat had dried, there were two standouts neck and neck for the win: Saxxon, hailing from Pitt Meadows, and TBA of River Bend City. Rounding out the performer lineup, The Crates, a four-piece, and trio Paradox did deserve third and fourth places but showed great promise.

The wildly disparate but completely valid styles of all four were evidence enough of local rock's solid future.

Marty Saxon, the winning band's lead vocalist, explained, "It was close, I guess, but there's a good reason that classic's called classic." His band Saxxon's set featured accomplished renditions of arena anthem-makers, including Heart and Bad Company. The band's tried-and-true choices may have caused the judge's split decision. While they offered nothing the audience hadn't already heard, they acted like they were born to it. Supported by precise guitar and a tight groove resulting from years of practice, Saxxon looked poised for larger venues.

In contrast, TBA's unusual and blatantly theatrical set included edgier and largely unfamiliar songs by Brits Gary Numan and Siouxsie and the Banshees as well as a tongue-in-cheek cover of a vampy chestnut by current Black Rose vocalist, Cher. The charismatic lead singer split her duties with a dramatically-posed synthesizer player. Strong drumming, by another girl, and so-so guitar work finished the picture. With TBA the real story hinged on the look, which suggested Devo by way of a donation bin. For better or worse, the band made radical style an important statement.

For The Crates and Paradox practice might one day make perfect. That decision is theirs.

With its bounty, Saxxon hopes to capitalize on the exposure. "Getting noticed by rock stations and VIPs can make or break a band wanting to make it in the cutthroat music industry," Saxon said. The band also intends to use the $100 prize money for "equipment or van repairs."

The next heat of the battling bands is scheduled for Friday, April 24.

Appendix III: Correspondence (unreturned)

Dear Sir/Madam:

I saw your ad about publishing songs in a music magazine. The ad mentioned how important registering songs is and that registration also lets recording artists find and maybe use the song on an album.

Enclosed are copies of two of my songs and money to cover the price of registering them.

I look forward to your reply.

Yours sincerely,

The Bridge

(E. Gee / D. Wallace)

You've got to cross the bridge,
To reach the other side.
What's the world you'll see,
When you hitch a ride?

Good things come to those who wait.
Do good things come to those who wait?
If there was a will, there'd be a way.
If there was a will, there'd be a way.

Many will stay,
and a few will go.
But does home mean safety
Or it really a foe?

Good things come to those who wait.
Do good things come to those who wait?
If there was a will, there'd be a way.
If there was a will, there'd be a way.

Scatter as a seed,
But find what you need.
Say goodbye, say goodbye,
Once across, your tears can dry.

Roll the dice, just roll the dice.
Roll the dice, just roll the dice . . .

Citizen's Day

(E. Gee)

A Main Street legend, he's the talk of the town.
Townies paint him a freak, a fool, and a clown.
Chester hears their laughter, sees the fear.
Here's home, he thinks, with lonesome tears.

Belong, be strong, he knows,
Be brave, he's heard, take the punishing blows.

Tess shuffles down halls, and casts down red eyes.
Girls point and whisper, while boys rub at their thighs.
What's the point, she wonders, why even try,
If your daily life only makes you cry?

Be strong, she knows, be brave.
There hope, she's heard, or else the grave.

Every man is an island,
We're all born alone.
But we can come together,
Build ourselves a home.

Sometimes, at least sometimes.
Maybe, at least sometimes

Acknowledgements

Thank you, thank you—

Readers volunteering precious hours of free time and sharing their stellar insights: Carellin 'Write Fewer Complicated, Self-Indulgent Sentences' Brooks, Dan 'Push Out the Steroidal Postmodernist Who is Hijacking Your Prose' Gawthrop, and Mark 'Cliches and Other Misdemeanors' Sampson.

British Columbia Arts Council: project funding exactly when it was most beneficial, how perfect!

Alice Munro: read over and again, "Epilogue: The Photographer" in *Lives of Girls and Women* gave me invaluable guidance and perspective about home town—and past self—portraiture.

Heather McHugh: for the ideally contemporary translation of Horace (and Princeton University Press for granting me permission for its use).

Bryan and Finn: for fraternity; plus, real and fake archival specimens (Bryan) and an enviable eye for design composition (Finn).

NON's Chris: unwavering support isn't a commonplace but, wow, it's so appreciated.

Hatzic Island and Mission, BC: without the, er, vicissitudes of my formative history with you, who knows where I'd have landed, or as what. Once upon a time, I dreamed of setting up a dental practice . . .

A lecturer of English literature residing in Vancouver, Brett Josef Grubisic is the author of the novels *The Age of Cities* and *This Location of Unknown Possibilities.* Previous publications include *Understanding Beryl Bainbridge, Contra/diction, Carnal Nation* (co-edited with Carellin Brooks), *American Hunks* (co-authored with David L. Chapman), *National Plots* (co-edited with Andrea Cabajsky), and *Blast, Corrupt, Dismantle, Erase* (co-edited with Giséle M. Baxter and Tara Lee).

Jacket design: HonkHonk Graphic Arts
Cover photo and in-text illustrations: Bryan Young
Author photo: Alexander Crouse